Memoirs of a Slave

Darrow Fowler

ISBN PRINT 978-1-09837-081-7 | ISBN eBOOK 978-1-09837-082-4

Introduction

Mary Lou

Last night, I dreamed that I had died. I was buried in an above-ground tomb, lying next to my husband. We were both dead and in tombs, lying in separate coffins next to each other. Our three children were lying in coffins next to ours. There was light coming in from the windows; the coffins were placed in concrete vaults. Then something happened. I awoke from the dead, but my husband and children did not wake. I was dressed in a white dress. I somehow got out of the coffin. I checked on my husband and children. They were still there. I was confused. I did not understand what had happened. Death was like sleeping, only without any dreams.

I escaped the tomb and walked around. I was in a graveyard. There were tombstones all around the graveyard, but I did not see anyone else. I was afraid. I felt something was wrong. The grass was green and nicely cut. The grave sites were nicely decorated with flowers, or at least some of them were.

Then I saw angels—angels with full-length gowns on. The angels were looking around. They were looking for me. I was afraid of the angels. They were beautiful. The angels were surrounded by light. The angels were flying and walking around. I did not count how many there were, but I would guess there had been about six to eight angels. Then one of the angels saw me. He began to run after me. I was afraid. I did not know what he wanted, so I ran. I ran fast. I tried to avoid the angels. The ones who were flying did not come directly after me. They seemed to point out to the other angels where I was.

Finally, I was caught.

Two or three angels led me to a huge wooden cross in the graveyard. The cross reminded me of Jesus. As I looked at the cross, I saw a large bright light behind it, and there were many angels in the light.

The angels took me and placed me on the cross. I was lifted above the ground, and nails were beaten into my hands and feet. As I hung on the cross, I looked down and saw people I knew who were dead. But they were alive. The angels brought them to me. These were people whom I loved . . . They came up to me on the cross, and their bodies elevated off the ground. The people went through me. As I hung on the cross, I felt their pain and their struggles. It was painful—their life experiences. I felt everything. Their hopes. Their dreams. Their joy. Their sorrows. It was like I became them for a moment in time. I did not say a word or make a sound. I turned my head and noticed the people going through me were then going into the bright light. They had changed into light. They were balls of light. The angels were guiding or helping them into the bright light. As I hung on the cross, many people went through me and then into heaven. The big bright light that the people were going into was one thousand times brighter than the sun. The angels were singing a song that I had never heard before. It was more beautiful than I could have ever imagined. I stayed on the cross until all the people that I affected for God's grace had gone through me. Finally, I saw my husband and three children pass through me. Each time a soul passed through me, it was painful. The pain turned into joy. After the last soul had gone through me, I was finally taken into heaven.

Chapter One

The Beginning

I was born in the year 1836 as a slave in what is called the Black Belt somewhere in Georgia. I was always told that I was blessed to know both parents. My parents were called Bertha and Alonzo Dye. I was the second-eldest girl in the family. My brothers were named Jimmy and Joe, and my eldest sister was called Mattie. The baby was named Dorothy. We called her Dot. My name is Mary Lou, and I was called Babe. I was fat. I was always big.

The man who owned us was Mr. Dye. He was called Mr. Dye by all the slaves. He was considered a good slave master because he kept the families of slaves together and allowed us slaves to jump the broom—that is, get married.

We lived in a one-room shack with a dirt floor. Most of the young ones went around naked. They didn't get clothes until they were old enough to pick cotton. The shack we lived in had a hole in the floor that Momma and Daddy used to keep food in. The hole was covered with a wooden board. Our little one-room dirt-floor shack was always crowded with Momma, Daddy, and all of us young ones.

Mr. Dye owned about one hundred slaves. My daddy and all the slaves old enough to pick cotton were in the field at daybreak. Picking cotton was backbreaking work. Everyone old enough to work worked from sunup till sundown. Every day we worked, except Sundays. Sunday was my favorite day. On Sunday, Momma cooked. Momma cooked corn bread and greens, sweet potatoes, and fried chicken. We got up late on Sundays. Usually it's dark when we get up. But on Sundays, the sun is bright and shiny when we get out of bed. Then I'll wash up real good and put on my Sunday best. Everybody went to church on Sunday, including the slaves. We slaves went to church in the woods. We built a big shack to pray in them there woods. Sometimes, we prayed so hard, I could feel the spirit moving in my bones. I would shake and carry on. Momma and Daddy would just wonder and hold on to me. Everybody said that was a good thing to feel God's presence so strong. We prayed for everything in that little church. We prayed to stop slaving. Well, that's what people got so emotional about. We prayed for it to rain. We prayed for it to not rain. We prayed for folks who were sick. We prayed that everybody had enough food for the winter. We prayed when folks died. We prayed when babies were born.

One Sunday morning after church, it started to rain, and when it rained, it poured. It was thundering and lightning something terrible. After church, some of the kids just couldn't wait in the church until the rain lightened up, so they broke out running. It was fun and scary. It was a joy running in the rain. But every time it thundered and there was lightning, it was scary. I ran fast, as fast as I could. I got out of the woods, and then there was the clearing. It was a big field. Nothing was planted there except a big old pecan tree. I was the last one. The other kids had run off ahead of me. . .

I was too fat to keep up. As I ran through that clearing, it started to thunder and lightning more and more. Lightning struck close to the pecan tree. I was scared to death. I just started to scream and run faster. Lightning struck close to the pecan tree again. It seemed like that old tree was drawing lightning to it. I was already scared out of my wits, but I couldn't stop running and screaming. The lightning struck again, but this time, the lightning struck me. It felt like I was hit in the head with a giant slug hammer.

After I was struck, I didn't feel anything. From what folks say, the lightning hit me in the top of my head and passed through my body and came out of my right foot. When the lightning came out of my foot, it dug a deep hole in the ground about four feet deep and six feet around. I was thrown way in the air and halfway back into the clearing we were running through. It kept raining. In fact, folks say that it rained harder after I was struck by lightning. I didn't know it at the time, but my daddy was running behind me. He must have come running after me when the church folk told him that I had taken off running in the rain for home. Daddy was the one who found me. Daddy picked me up and carried me home. Daddy walked the whole way to our house in the rain by himself. When he got home, Momma was there cooking. Usually, Momma was always at church, but that Sunday, she decided to stay home and cook. Well, I was out cold. Daddy thought I was dead. But I wasn't.

I didn't have a mark on me. I was soaking wet. My mouth was wide open like a trout. Daddy kicked the door in and took me to Momma. She let out a loud scream. "Oh, Lord, my dear God, what happened?" Daddy told her that I was hit by lightning. She looked me all over, pulling my arms and legs, rubbing and feeling me all over to find out where I was hit. Then she saw. It was my head. She couldn't see any marks on me, but she saw that a patch of my hair was white. It was a real small patch, just a little circle of hair, but it was bright white, not gray hair like old folks get. This was different.

By the time Momma had finished looking me over, the whole house was full of folks from church. Some were standing in the rain. Some were standing around soaking wet, dripping water all over. Daddy took me and laid me in my bed. Momma followed behind Daddy. Momma took all my clothes off until I was in my underwear. Daddy went and got towels, and Dot, Sister, and Momma dried me off. I must have fallen in some dirt because my clothes were dirty. I was covered in mud. I was told that everybody helped clean me up. I was still out cold. I stayed like that for weeks. Mr. Dye was real nice. He let Momma, Sister, and Dot stay home from the fields and take turns taking care of me. I wasn't any trouble since I was still unconscious. Momma's friends came by to pray for me every day. Momma, Daddy, and friends would hold my hand and stand around the bed and pray. The preacher was there too. Also, my sisters and brothers were there. Sometimes Momma, Daddy, and my brothers and sisters would just pray by themselves.

I was told that someone was always praying for me while I was unconscious. That seems farfetched since there are twenty-four hours in a day. Daddy and some men from the slave quarters went out one night when Master Dye and the slave foremen were asleep. They went out to the spot where I was hit by lightning. Daddy never said why he went out there, but he must've had good reason. I never saw the hole in the ground from where I was hit by lightning. Somebody must have covered it up or something.

Later on, I found out that Momma had some of the slaves who believed that Jesus was going to make me well pray for me all the time. What they did was they chose a time to pray. They hung a piece of cloth on a stick and stuck the stick in the ground in front of the shack that was praying for me. Well, almost every shack had a stick with a cloth. But what usually happened was that someone would put their stick out. That let the others know they were praying for me. Then when they pulled their stick in, somebody else would put their stick out with a cloth on it. Momma said that there was always a stick with a piece of cloth on it in front of somebody's shack.

I was unconscious for about ninety days. The day I woke up, I was being watched by my sister Dot. It was in the morning, and the slaves were in the fields. Dot said I just opened my eyes. I didn't remember anything. I thought I just woke up. Dot started to tell me what had happened and that I had been sleeping all these days. I was really hungry and thirsty, so Dot fixed me something to eat. Then she just started to talk. She talked so much, I could barely understand what all she was saying. She was also talking real fast. Dot talked about everything. She talked about the lightning storm. She talked about how I was struck in the head. She also said that part of my hair was white. Then she got a mirror and showed me. She kept right on talking though. When I looked in the mirror, I couldn't believe what I saw. On the left side of my head, there was long white hair from the front to the middle of my head. I don't think I had said anything until I saw my hair. I yelled. But Dot said I didn't look bad.

Then a thought came into my head. The thought was this: Dot is like Barnabas, the son of consolation. Then I thought, how do I know about Barnabas? Then I remembered, Barnabas traveled with the apostle Paul to Jerusalem. Barnabas was also called the encourager. Barnabas was such an eloquent speaker and preached with passion and love. He was chosen as speaker over the apostle Paul on their missionary journey. I remember Simeon, who was so black that he was called nigger. But how did I know about this Barnabas man and Simeon? No one never had ever told me about them. Why was I thinking like this? I couldn't read or write. So I just thought he must be someone I had made up and dreamed about. Also, I knew that Barnabas admitted Saul to the church, and his name was changed to Paul. I remembered how Barnabas always spoke with such love for Jesus that men's hearts would burn with the fire of the Gospel. I remembered I was a Yisraelite from the tribe of Judah. That all of us slaves here were Yisraelites. We are God's jewels. But I didn't tell Dot what I thought when she told me my hair didn't look bad. I just looked and smiled.

I looked at myself. I was wearing one of Mrs. Dye's daughter's sleeper things. I later found out they were called nightgowns. Dot said Mrs. Dye had sent it over along with medicine and some extra food. Also, I was wearing a diaper. I felt so ashamed. It was like I was a baby. I noticed the diaper because I had to go—that is, go pee pee. When I tried to get out of bed, I almost fell flat on my face.

Dot was over by the fire fixing another bowl of neck bone soup. When she saw me stumble, she dropped the neck bone soup and lunged to catch me. I could barely move. My feet were turned in. We called it pigeon toed. Dot helped me up. I stood up, but my back was bent forward. I must have looked a mess. Dot walked me over to the door. The outhouse was down a ways from slave row. All the slave shacks were on one side facing the big house. We couldn't see the big house from slave row, and Master couldn't see slave row from the big house. There's a forest between the two. It was a nice walk to the big house.

5

When I came out the shack, Lil George was tending the garden. There was a small garden down from slave row. Lil George is a real old man. Lil George is so old, nobody can say how long he had been there. He'd been there longer than any of the other slaves. He was Mr. Dye's daddy's first slave bought. Well, when he saw me, he yelled so loud that all the young ones too young to work the fields came running outside. Then Lil George's missus came running out. She must have thought something must have happened to Lil George. Lil George's missus was named Miss Bell. She was real nice. Miss Bell was always praying. When Miss Bell saw me, she fell on her knees and started to cry something awful. She kept yelling, "Thank you, Jesus! Thank you, Jesus! Thank you, Jesus!" Meanwhile, Dot kept on pulling me to the outhouse. I guess she was tired of changing that diaper I was wearing. Lil George was hoeing in the garden. He dropped the hoe and ran over and helped Dot with me. I stayed in there awhile.

Lil George must have gone out to the fields, because when I came out of the outhouse, all the slaves from slave row were standing there. Lil George must have told everybody that I had woken up. Momma, Daddy, Jimmy, Joe, and Sister ran over and hugged me. Dot just stood back and smiled. They almost knocked me over with all their hugs and kisses.

Momma squeezed so hard that I couldn't breathe. Then Daddy picked me up and took me back to the shack. Daddy set me back in bed.

"How do you feel?" he asked.

"I feel fine. I just hungry," I said.

"Dot, get your sister something more to eat!" he yelled.

Dot yelled back, "She done eat two bowls of neck bone soup!"

"Just get her some more," Daddy said.

Momma sat on the bed next to me. Momma put her hands on my head and slowly stroked my head back and forth while she said, "Baby, we thought you was never goin' to wake up. Thank God, thank God you are all right. Is anything bothering you? Do you feel all right? Momma gonna take real good care of you." Then Momma started crying. I had never seen Momma cry before. I couldn't say nothing. I hugged Momma and cried too. Sister came with the neck bone soup and set it down on the table. Sister sat down and cried too. Then Dot came over and got on her knees and hugged us all. Dot began crying too.

Jimmy and Joe came over and knelt down and hugged us. They began crying too. Daddy was also crying. There wasn't a dry eye in the shack. Soon, some of Momma's friends came in. They saw all of us crying. I don't know what happened to them, but they didn't stay long. I don't even think anybody but me noticed them come in. They put their hands together like they were praying. Then I heard them yell, "Thank you, Jesus! Thank you, Jesus! Dear Lord, thank you, Jesus!" That's all they said. Then they left. Momma, Daddy, and everybody else were too busy crying and carrying on to notice anything. Momma finally stopped crying. She grabbed the bowl of neck bone soup and started to feed me like I was a little baby. Daddy went to the door and told everybody I was fine and that I was hungry. Everybody started to smile and laugh. Then Daddy left. Everybody went back to picking cotton in the fields. Everybody but Mamma. She stayed with me and fed me.

Mr. Dye came into the little old shack. News sure spreads fast. It wasn't long since I had woken up. Lil George must have sent somebody to the big house to tell Mr. Dye.

Mr. Dye walked in and said, "Good morning. I'm pleased to see you up and about. You certainly are a miracle if I ever saw one."

Momma said, "Yes, sir. Mr. Dye, she sho' is something special."

Mr. Dye said, "Well, I want to see you at the big house in five days. I don't want you in those fields no more. I'll see if there is something we can find for you there. Bertha, that child sure has lost a lot of weight. I'll have some clothes sent down for her."

Then Mr. Dye walked out. Momma started to cry again. I couldn't figure out why Momma was crying so. Then Momma said, "Lord, they gon' take my baby. Lord, help me. Lord, she just came back to us. Lord, why? Lord, why? Lord, help me." Then Momma hugged me like I was a little baby. And she rocked me back and forth. Then Momma started to sing, "Yes, Jesus loves you. Yes, Jesus loves you. Yes, Jesus loves you, 'cause I heard him tell me so."

After a while, I fell asleep. Momma sure could sing. I always loved to hear Momma sing. I guess I was about sixteen years old when this happened. Momma, Daddy, Jimmy, Joe, Sister, and Dot didn't know what to think. None of us had ever gone up to the big house for much of nothing, except when Mr. Dye gave out extra food at Christmastime. So now everybody was sad. I didn't know what to think. I heard Momma and Daddy talking like I might be sold.

Then Daddy said, "Don't talk like that. Mr. Dye ain't sold none of us. He ain't like them other masters. He a good man."

Then Momma said, "No, he ain't, Zo." Momma and everybody called Daddy Zo. "There ain't no such thing as a good slave master. Anybody who own people and do the things these white folks does to us ain't good. Remember when that Willie Lynch man was going around teaching them slave masters how to stop them runaway slaves? You remember what he done to Master Burke's nigger, Henry? Henry was the biggest slave I had ever seen. He was three times as big as anybody around here. And Henry worked harder than all the slaves around these parts. Henry was black as night. He was mean as a rattlesnake. Henry's daddy was one of them Yisraelites. Folks say that's why Henry was so mean. Folks say his daddy filled his head with all that talk of keeping the commandments and being free. Folks say Henry always talked about being free and the Bible. They say he could read and write and read the Bible every day.

"Well, Willie Lynch came over to Master Burke's place and called all the slaves together out in that clear piece of farmland. Henry had just been brought back from running away. Henry would run away at least two or three times a year, and there was talk about other slaves running away. And there were other slaves running away from all around these parts, remember? Well, Willie Lynch went and got two of Master Burke's strongest horses. He had all the slaves in a big circle around Henry. White men with guns all around, just waiting to shoot. He went and got some tar. He put hot tar all over Henry. Then he put feathers all over Henry. He harnessed those horses like they were going to pull a wagon. He tied a rope around Henry's arm and leg on one side and then one on the other side. Then he had one horse on one side and the other horse on the other side of Henry. He had a slave holding each of the horses. Willie Lynch told those slaves to slowly walk those horses away from Henry. The slaves didn't want to do it till Willie Lynch put a gun to their heads. All the slaves seen it, women, children, and menfolks. They pulled Henry in two. Right there, then, those white men beat the menfolks something terrible. That is, they beat the slaves something terrible, remember? Only the men and boys got beat.

"They say they beat those black folks for six days straight. They say every last one of them almost died. And the women, the women were so scared, some say some went crazy. They called it crossbreeding. The women slaves who weren't crazy were crossbred with white men. They say they were putting good white blood into as many nigger women as possible. That's why they got all them light-skinned slaves over on Master Burke's plantation. And ain't none of them working in them fields. Only the real black slaves, like us, are working in the fields on Master Burke's plantation. Them slaves get beat with that "cat-o'-nine-tails." It ain't no regular whip like we get beat with. This one has nine long pieces of leather coming out the handle. It has pieces of steel and bone attached onto those long pieces of leather, so when they whip you with it, it snatches part of your hide from you. So don't be telling me about no good slave master."

"Now, Bertha, Mr. Dye ain't never done nothing like that to us. He don't even allow us to call him master. He say, 'Call me Mr. Dye.' He ain't like old no-good Master Burke."

Momma said, "He got us, don't he, and he can do whatever he want to us, and ain't nothing nobody gone do." I got real scared after I heard Momma tell Daddy all that. I didn't want to go to no big house.

All that week, everybody was being real good to me. Momma cooked my favorite: collard greens, neck bones, corn bread, fried chicken, and sweet potato pie. Jimmy and Joe were real nice to me. Jimmy was the baby boy. I was a couple of years older than Jimmy. Jimmy and I played after he got home from the fields, and Joe didn't run us away. Joe seemed to like us around. Joe was the oldest of all the kids. Joe was usually playing that fiddle Mr. Dye had given to him. Sister and Dot were combing my hair and putting pretty bows in it. Mr. Dye had a dress sent to me by Neal Henry. Neal Henry stayed in the house with Mr. Dye. Neal Henry did all Mr. Dye's running. Sister and Dot couldn't wait to put that dress on me. Sister and Dot got the big tub out that we used that to take baths in. They filled it with hot water and put me in it. All the bows they took out of my hair. They put some soap in the tub. And in I went. The girls were scrubbing like they were looking for gold. They scrubbed so hard, I thought they were going to take some of my skin off. They washed my hair and almost drowned me.

After all that scrubbing, they finally let me out of that tub. They dried me off. One got the comb, and the other got the dress that Neal Henry had brought. It was a pretty dress. It was white with a pink stripe around the neck. And it had baby's breath sewn into it around the bottom. Well, not real baby's breath but a picture. It was the prettiest dress I had ever seen. The baby's breath was a darker color of white than the dress. This dress was prettier than my Sunday best.

Sister combed my hair, and Dot put the dress on me. My hair was in two braids, one on each side of my head. Sister put a bow at the end of each braid. Dot fixed and pulled on that dress, making sure it fit. All the while, I was standing right in the middle of our little shack. Daddy was sitting outside. He seemed to be occupied. I didn't go anyplace that night. I guess everybody wanted to see how I looked. That's why Sister and Dot washed me and dressed me up. Momma said, "You look pretty as a peach."

No one seemed to be worried that I was going to the big house to work. Momma heard that Eppie Mae was going to teach me how to cook, clean, sew, and take care of Mrs. Dye's children. Eppie Mae did everything for Mr. and Mrs. Dye. She raised their children, cooked, cleaned, sewed, and kept house. Eppie Mae lived in the big house. Eppie Mae was old. She was older than Momma. Mr. Dye didn't let nobody cook or do anything in the big house without Eppie Mae knowing about it. At least that's what I heard Momma telling Daddy. And Momma didn't say much if she didn't know what she was talking about.

Early the next morning, Neal Henry came to get me. He was driving a wagon. It had a brown-and-white horse pulling it. Neal Henry knocked on the door. Daddy told him to come on in. Daddy woke everybody up. Sister and Dot got me ready. My hair was already fixed. Sister just put the bows back in my hair. Dot helped me get into the dress Neal Henry had brought by the other day. It had buttons in the back, big pink buttons. So Dot turned me around and buttoned the dress for me. Daddy and Neal Henry had sat down at the kitchen table. It was early Sunday morning, so no one was going to work out in the fields.

Neal Henry told Daddy, "I'm going to look out for Babe as if she's one of my own children. Eppie Mae's a real fine woman. Eppie Mae been in the big house longer than any other. She raised Mr. Dye, and now she raising his children. Don't you worry about a thing. Mr. Dye, he is a good man. And it's best for her to get out them there fields."

Daddy didn't say much. Daddy just told Neal Henry to let him know when Momma and all the rest could see me. Neal Henry told Daddy that I could come to slave row when I get finished with all my work. Momma and everybody walked me to the door. I didn't want to go, but Momma and Daddy said it was OK, I'll be fine. I didn't cry. I hugged and kissed Momma. Everybody seemed to gather to hug and kiss me at the same time. They all stood in the doorway. Daddy came outside. He walked me to the wagon and lifted me up onto the wagon. I sat down.

Daddy said, "Do what you are told, and don't talk back."

I said, "Yes, sir."

Then Neal Henry came over. He said something to Daddy. I didn't hear what he said. He shook Daddy's hand, got onto the wagon, and we left.

Chapter Two

Big House

Slave row had twelve little shacks on it. They were all in a row. Every shack looked the same on the inside. Slave row was east of the big house. All the shacks were on the far east end. They were lined up from west to south. The garden was on the south end of slave row. So when Neal Henry took me to the big house, almost everybody saw us. They must have heard the raggedy, raggedy of the wagon wheels. Momma and Daddy's shack was across from the garden, next to the outhouses. As we went by, folks came out their doors and waved. I didn't look neither to my right or left. I just stared straight ahead.

Up the pathway to the big house was a long red dirt road. It was wide enough for about two wagons. It had tall trees on both sides. The trees seemed to touch the sky. The leaves were green. I saw all kinds of pretty flowers along the path to the big house. I had never been to the big house before. I had never been in a wagon before either. Neal Henry didn't say a word. As I looked down the pathway to the big house, it looked as if the trees were making a tunnel. We rode under the shade of those trees. And it was so, so pretty. I don't think I had ever seen anything so pretty. All the trees, the flowers, the smells of that long red dirt road. Right then, I thought I liked riding on wagons. After a ways riding, my rump started to get sore from all the bumps and rocking back and forth. I wanted to get out that wagon. But I still liked riding on a wagon.

Soon, we were through the woods. There was a clearing. The grass was nicely cut. I had never seen grass like that before. I was coming into another world. Everything looked clean. Everything looked nice. I could see the big house from the pathway now. The big house was on a hill. As we rode closer, I saw a flower bed. It was pretty. I had never seen flowers arranged in different shapes. The bushes had shapes to them too. The big house was white. It had two big, long white poles in front of the door. Neal Henry said that this was the side entryway. I was only to come into the big house through this door. The big house had pretty windows. The windows were different colors and shapes. I later learned they were called stained glass windows. Neal Henry turned the wagon and stopped right in front of the side door. The door was closed. It had a big shiny doorknob. I sat on the wagon. Neal Henry jumped down. He walked to the big house, went up about two to three steps, and knocked on the side door. Eppie Mae answered the door.

She said, "Neal Henry, I been waiting for you. It don't take nobody that long to go down there and come back. I done fixed the child something to eat. Y'all, come on in."

Neal Henry came over to the wagon and helped me down. I didn't have anything. No bag of food. No clothes. No nothing. I was real shy. We walked to the door. Neal Henry walked into the kitchen. I didn't go in. I stayed on the porch.

"Where is Mary Lou?" Eppie Mae asked Neal Henry.

"She right behind me. Now, don't go making a big fuss over nothing. The girl ain't even got here good yet," Neal Henry said.

"Neal Henry, you get that girl in here now," Eppie Mae said.

Neal Henry walked back to the door and said, "Come on in here, girl. Ain't nobody gonna bite you."

He opened the door. I came on in. This room was bigger than Momma and Daddy's shack. It had a big table next to the door leading into another room. There was a big steel and iron stove. There was a wash sink built right into the wall. It didn't have no fireplace, though. I had heard Momma talk about how Eppie Mae cooked on a stove. But this was my first time seeing one. I was afraid of that thing. I wondered how Eppie Mae cooked on it. Eppie Mae was a big woman. She had a rag around her head

14

and one of them aprons around her waist. When she saw me, she smiled and said, "Come here, girl, and give me a big hug." I didn't want to, but I slowly walked over and hugged her. She squeezed me hard like Momma. She said, "You are a pretty little girl. I heard you was fat. You a skinny little girl."

"I lost weight after I was hit by lightning," I told her.

"Your hair always been like that?" she asked.

"No, that's where I was struck by lightning. I didn't feel anything after I was hit. But my hair had this patch of white in it when I woke up," I said.

"Well, we'll talk later. Right now, you sit down at that kitchen table and eat you something." She went over to the stove and brought me a plate of fried eggs, ham and grits, and glass of milk. I ate it all. Neal Henry had left. Eppie Mae took me through a door off the side of the kitchen. It had stairs that lead to a little room upstairs. There were a bed and dresser in the room.

"This is your room," Eppie Mae said.

I had never had a room before. I had never been in a bed by myself before. I had always slept with my sisters. The room had crosses over the beds. Eppie Mae told me that there were clothes in the dresser draws and sleepwear. Then Eppie Mae went over to the dresser and took out some clothes for me to change into. She put them on the bed. Then she got a white head rag out and said, "You must always wear this head rag, and keep it the same color it is now." Then Eppie Mae left.

I turned around and fell on my knees. I prayed, "Thank you, Jesus. Your loving kindness is better than life. From our first breath to our last, it is God who provides for all our needs."

Then I got up from my knees and hurried up and changed clothes. Just as soon as I had tied the head rag on my head, Eppie Mae called me, "Mary Lou, come on down here. Girl, we got plenty work around here. I got to show you how to do everything."

I ran downstairs and walked into the kitchen and stood right in front of Eppie Mae. Eppie Mae said, "You get that broom over there and sweep up this kitchen."

"Where the broom at, Ms. Eppie Mae?" I asked. She pointed to a little door.

"That's the broom closet. All the brooms, mops, buckets, brushes, rags, and cleaning stuff is in there. So whenever you are cleaning the kitchen, get the cleaning things out of there," she said.

"Yes, ma'am," I said. I started to sweep. It wasn't like sweeping dirt floors. The dirt came up, and the floor was wood. The floor was shiny wood too. I swept the dirt into a small pile. Then I went back to the little room in the kitchen and got a little thing called a dust pan. Eppie Mae told me to go get it and what it looked like, so I swept the dirt into the dust pan and threw the dirt into the garbage can in the kitchen. Then Eppie Mae told me to come with her. We went through the kitchen doors into what was called dining room. This room was beautiful. I had never seen such a room. There was a big long table in the center of the room with flowers on it. The table was clean and shiny. It looked like water was on it. There were pictures on all the walls, except where the windows were. This room had rugs over the wood floor. The rugs were soft to walk on. And the rugs had pretty red, green, blue, and yellow flowers on them with green leaves. There was a big shiny thing in the ceiling called a chandelier. It had candles in it, but none of the candles were lit. The light came in through the big windows. The windows had pictures of people around the top of them. And there were curtains in front of the windows. The curtains were the color of blood. This room opened up into another room.

Eppie Mae opened two large doors to another room. This room had a large fireplace that covered the whole side of the wall. There were stairs that went up to the top of the house.

"This is the parlor. This is where Mr. and Mrs. Dye entertain folks. You are going to learn how to wait on folks and how to clean. You are only to speak when spoken to. And then only say, 'Yes, sir,' and 'No, sir,' and 'Yes, ma'am,' and 'No, ma'am.' And there is Mr. and Mrs. Dye's youngens. There is Master William. He is eight years old. Call him Master William. And there is Miss Annite. Call her Miss Annite. She is eighteen years old. She's a little lady. I remember when she was born. She was such a pretty baby. She's grown into a beautiful young lady. Her momma and daddy call her Missy. Kathryn is about your age. She is sixteen years old. A real sweet little girl. Call her Miss Kate.

"Now, everybody done gone to church this morning. This ain't like the slave row where it ain't no slavin' on Sundays. Here, it's slavin' every day and every night, sometimes all day and all night. Now, Mr. Dye lets us go into the barn and sing and pray on Sunday nights. He lets us go mostly every Sunday night, unless there's lots of work. It's only the house slaves that go. You welcome to come. There is other slaves around. They out working. There is Uncle Buff. He drives Mr. and Mrs. Dye wherever they want to go and waits for them. You'll see him all the time. He always doing something for Mr. and Mrs. Dye around here. You met Neal Henry. He drives and fixes mostly everything that breaks. And he train Mr. Dye's horses. And there is Little Lizzy. She a little older than you. She cooks and cleans. She is in the barn now. And there is Billy Joe. He works with Neal Henry. And Neal Henry and Billy Joe don't come into the big house too much, unless to fix something. They stay in that little shack behind the barn.

"Now, if you have to call Neal Henry or Billy Joe, there is a big old cow bell right outside the kitchen door. Just ring it, and one of them will come. They always come, because I be feeding them. They try to eat all the food they come about. Mary Lou, what do they call you?"

"They call me Babe, Miss Eppie Mae," I said.

"I'll call you Babe too. Well, let's get into that kitchen and fix lunch. Mr. and Mrs. Dye and them children will be back from church soon," she said.

We went back into the kitchen, and no sooner had we entered the kitchen than a real pretty high yellow girl came in. She was carrying a turkey and a duck. They had already been cleaned and plucked. She said, "Eppie, I'm finished with these."

"Take them over to the sink and wash them, and cut up some carrots, onions, celery, and mix up some white bread stuffing. And show Babe what to do," Eppie Mae said. I went to the sink with Little Lizzy.

Little Lizzy said, "You must be the one who was struck by lightning. We heard about how the lightning went through you and into the ground. I'm Little Lizzy. What's your name?"

"I'm Mary Lou, but everybody calls me Babe," I said.

"OK, Babe. Everybody calls me Lizzy except for Eppie. Why do they call you Babe?"

"I don't really know. I used to be fat. But I lost lots of weight after I was hit by lightning. So Momma and Daddy might have called me Babe because I was fat like a baby. But, really, I don't know."

"Well, I'll call you Babe too."

"Why does Eppie Mae call you little Lizzy?"

"My name Elizabeth. But everybody calls me Lizzy. And I am little for my age. I am eighteen years old. And, Babe, you are just as big as I am."

"Little Lizzy, you the first slave I've known who know how old they is." Little Lizzy didn't say anything. She just kept on fixing the stuffing. What I didn't know was that Little Lizzy and Billy Joe were Mr. Dye's children. Mr. Dye had been known to visit slave row. The slaves would see Mr. Dye every once in a while, but I didn't know what he was doing in slave row. I'm sure the older slaves knew that Mr. Dye had fathered children by slave women. But there were no high yellow slaves on slave row. In fact, Little Lizzy was the first high yellow slave I had ever seen.

After Little Lizzy had finished stuffing the turkey and duck, she put the duck in the stove. The turkey she placed in the cold room, a little room off the kitchen where food is kept in. Then Eppie Mae told Little Lizzy and me to set the dining room table. I had never set a table before, so Eppie Mae and Little Lizzy told me where everything went. They had a plate and a bowl to eat out of. And next to each plate, they had three spoons, three forks, three knives, a napkin, a coffee cup, and two glasses, and we set six places at the table. I kept thinking, *Who needs all those knives, forks, and such to eat? These folks must not know how to eat a duck.*

After the table was set, I thought it was a very pretty table, so I asked Eppie Mae, "Does Mr. and Mrs. Dye eat this way every day?"

Eppie Mae told me, "No, usually on Sundays for lunch and dinner and every day during the week for dinner. Don't worry, Little Lizzy and me will teach you how to set tables, clean up, and wait on folks. Today, Mr. Dye invited Reverend Cole. Reverend Cole, he the pastor at Mr. and Mrs. Dye's church. I guess he wants to meet you, Babe. You know it's been lots of talk about you bein' struck by lightning and still livin'. Now, you and Little Lizzy will stand by the door, a little off to the side. You follow Little Lizzy, and she'll show you how to serve folks."

Eppie Mae went into the kitchen and checked on the duck and fixings. At about twelve o'clock, Mr. and Mrs. Dye rode up in a big shiny wood buggy. Mr. Dye had a black cowboy hat on. So did the man riding with him. I guessed that was Reverend Cole. Mrs. Dye had on a big white hat. It had pretty flowers all around it. Also, the girls wore hats too. The little boy, he just sat and didn't say a word. Everybody else was talking. Uncle Buff was a real dark slave. He had on a tall hat and a black suit with long coat. When they rode up, Uncle Buff jumped off the buggy and walked around the front of the horse. He tied the horse to a pole. Then he went and opened the door to the buggy. Mrs. Dye stepped down and then the girls and then Reverend Cole, and William, and Mr. Dye. Eppie Mae opened the door for them, and they all went into the parlor. Uncle Buff took the men's hats and coats. Mrs. Dye set her hat on the table next to the door, along with the girls'. Eppie Mae came and took the girls' hats and put them into the coat

19

room. The men were talking, and Mrs. Dye and the girls didn't say anything. Then Mrs. Dye said, "Pardon us, gentlemen." Then Mrs. Dye and the girls left and went upstairs. I was in the kitchen making lemonade. Eppie told me to take that lemonade along with the glasses into the parlor. I sat the lemonade and glasses on a server and carried it into the parlor. When I got to the parlor, I stopped at the side of the sofa.

Mr. Dye said, "Come in here, Mary Lou. Don't you be afraid. Ain't nobody gonna hurt you. This is Reverend Cole." Reverend Cole didn't say a word. He just glanced at me. I sat the lemonade down on the cocktail table and started to leave. "Mary Lou, Reverend Cole wants to meet you," Mr. Dye said. I stopped and put my hand behind my back and stood as straight as I could.

"So you the one who was struck by lightning?" Reverend Cole said.

"Yes, sir. I'm fine now, sir," I said.

Reverend Cole said, "I here you a God-fearing little girl."

"Yes, sir. Jesus has been real good to me."

Reverend Cole said, "That's right, Mary Lou, Jesus has been good to you. You are a very blessed young girl to survive a direct strike by lighting. Mary Lou, I want to ask you a couple of questions. First, does anything hurt you?"

"No, sir," answered Mary Lou.

"And has anything unusual happened since your accident?"

"Reverend Cole, sir, what do you mean by unusual?"

"Anything that's different than before you were struck by lightning."

"Yes, sir," answered Mary Lou.

"Well, go on, Mary Lou, tell me what you mean."

"Well, sir, since my accident, I seems to know things about Jesus."

"What do you know about Jesus, Mary Lou?"

"I know Jesus loved us very much. I know 'For God loved the world that he gave his only Son, so that whosoever believes in him might not perish but might have everlasting life. For God did not send his Son into the world to condemn the world, but that the world might be saved through him. And I am an Israelite of the tribe of Judah.'"

"Yes, Mary Lou, that's John 3:16–17. That's good. Did you hear that at church?" asked Reverend Cole.

"I don't know, sir. I just can remember things about Jesus."

"Thank you, Mary Lou. You can go back to your work. And you are a nigger. You're not an Israelite from the tribe of Judah. Do you understand?" said Mr. Dye.

"Yes, sir, Mr. Dye," I said.

"Well, Mr. Dye, I had previously thought the rumors were true," said Reverend Cole.

"What rumors, Reverend Cole?" asked Mr. Dye.

"You know my nigger Jim is the one who does the preaching for the niggers in the woods. The slaves have a little church in the woods, and nigger Jim preaches for them. I own a few choice niggers. I allow them to listen to me preach on Sunday mornings. There is a rumor that Mary Lou knows things about the Bible—you know, things that no slave should know."

"Well, Reverend Cole, I never heard any talk of no talk around here," said Mr. Dye.

"Mr. Dye, you know the slaves are real superstitious. The niggers mix Christianity with their own religion. They change the meaning of things. You know very well, Mr. Dye, if you tell a nigger to go left, he'll go right. And that's my point, Mr. Dye. My nigger Jim has been preaching confusion to the slaves in those woods.

"Now, there's a rumor that Mary Lou knows God's word. Mr. Dye, what I've just confirmed was that Mary Lou has been listening to my nigger Jim preach my old sermons. I preached John 3:16 for about a month. I

21

preached it every Sunday. I incorporated other scripture into that sermon to enhance the sermon. And nigger Jim was there. As you well know, I allow my niggers to sit in the room to the left of the pulpit to listen to my sermons. The door is closed, but they can still hear my preaching. It's either hear me preach or work. And, Mr. Dye, I hope that you and the other slave owners would allow their niggers to sit in the back of the church. You know, a God-fearing slave produces three times the labor as a heathen, no-God-having nigger. And the heathen is always trying to run off.

"But once you preach to a nigger, teach the nigger it's right for him to be a slave, explain that slavery is right in God's eyes, we must show the nigger that he is our property and why he is our property. That's the only way to eliminate the desire in the nigger to want to be free. And that's to put the fear of Almighty God into the nigger. Teach him what God's word says about slavery. That way, he'll teach other niggers about God, why they are slaves, and why it's right in God's sight.

"You know, Mr. Dye, none of my niggers run away. And I visit slave row twice a week to put good white blood in as many nigger women as I can. I'm inviting you, sir, to visit me at my home to observe how my niggers behave. Sir, I don't have the problems most of the owners have around these parts. And, sir, I apply the lash almost daily to any nigger who is unruly or slow to respond. Yes, Mr. Dye, my slaves respect me highly above all the owners in these parts. Just the other day, I overheard a nigger saying, 'Master Cole is the best owner around these parts.' Mr. Dye, it's the fear of God upon the nigger. The nigger must know his place in this world. And it's the white man's duty to put him in his rightful place before God Almighty, to make sure he stays there."

"Yes, Reverend Cole, you do have a point. God has placed a great burden upon the white race. Part of the burden is having the nigger fixed forever in his rightful place—a slave," said Mr. Dye.

"Mr. Dye, I did not come over here to preach, but, you know, when God calls a man to preach, he must preach. I want to share a piece of scripture with you today, sir. Would you pick up that Bible, please?"

"Now, Reverend Cole, you came over for lunch, not to preach."

"Mr. Dye, when the Holy Ghost calls, you must respond. Now, sir, open your Bible to Genesis 9:18. Now, Mr. Dye, this is why the nigger is our property. Let me read this to you, sir. 'The sons of Noah who came out of the ark were Shem, Ham, and Japheth (Ham was the father of Canaan).' These were the sons of Noah, and from them, the whole earth was peopled. Now, Noah, a man of the soil, was the first to plant a vineyard. When he drank some of the wine, he became drunk and lay naked inside his tent. Ham, the father of Canaan, saw his father's nakedness, and he told his two brothers outside about it. Shem and Japheth, however, took a robe, and holding it on their backs, they walked backward and covered their father's nakedness. Since their faces were turned the other way, they did not see their father's nakedness.

"When Noah woke up from his drunkenness and learned what his youngest son had done to him, he said, 'Cursed be Canaan! The lowest of slaves will he be to his brothers.' He also said, 'Blessed be the Lord, the God of Shem! Let Canaan be his slave. May God expand Japheth, so that he dwell among the tents of Shem; and let Canaan be his slave.' Noah lived 350 years after the flood. The whole lifetime of Noah was 950 years. Then he died."

"Now, Reverend Cole, that passage was written six thousand years or so. You can't possibly believe that just because Noah's youngest son saw him naked, he cursed his entire lineage," said Mr. Dye.

"Mr. Dye, let me explain a few things to you. First, Noah was a highly blessed man. He was the only one God found favor with. God was going to destroy the entire world, including Noah, but God found favor with Noah. So God saved Noah, his sons, and his son's wives. Mr. Dye, we serve a mighty God, and nothing wicked will stand in the presence of God. Now,

Ham is translated into what we call the nigger or black race. Shem is translated into the Jews, or the Semite, the lineage of which Jesus our Lord and savior was born. The term 'Japheth' is us, the white man, the Aryan race. We, sir, are Aryans, pure white out of Europe. We are a warlike race out of the European mountains, but our race has found God in the person of Jesus Christ, fully God and fully man. And God has delivered the nigger into our hands.

"Mr. Dye, let me explain. What I read to you was Noah's curse. The nigger is cursed. He's been cursed from the start. You see, Mr. Dye, Genesis 9:24 states, 'When Noah woke up from his drunkenness and learned what his youngest son had done to him, he said, "Cursed be Canaan! The lowest of slaves shall he be to his brothers."' Mr. Dye, this wasn't just about some little boy running into a room and seeing his daddy naked. No, sir, Mr. Dye. We are dealing with a rascal. The nigger is the lowest form of human form. Sir, Ham went into his father when he was drunk, and he thought it was funny. Yes, sir, he went and told his brothers, but his brothers couldn't look at their father. They walked backward and laid a robe on their father."

"Sir, you don't say."

"Yes, Mr. Dye, I do say. That nigger went into his father as a man would go into a woman. That's why his father cursed him. The nigger can't be trusted. His entire race is a rascal. There is no such thing as a good nigger. Mr. Dye, we have a huge burden. We have been given the entire continent of Africa. We are to make every nigger on the planet our slave and the slave of the Semite. The nigger is a coward. He is rotten, a rascal. So that little nigger girl you have in your house is not nothing special. Pure chance she lived through that lightning strike. She doesn't know nothing about the Gospel of Jesus Christ or the Bible than what she's been told. Some niggers think she's something special since she lived through that lightning strike. Mr. Dye, that is pure hogwash. That's a little dumb nigger. She don't know nothing about nothing. And more than likely can't learn nothing.

"There you have it, sir, a sermon free of charge. Maybe I should pass the plate around. Usually a sermon like that would fetch a good penny. Our job, sir, as God-fearing men, is to put these niggers in their rightful place, as the lowest of slaves. Mr. Dye, open your Bible to the book of Matthew 15:22. Read with me here, sir. 'And behold, Canaanite women of the district came and called out, "Have pity on me, Lord, son of David! My daughter is tormented by a demon.' But he did not say a word in answer to her. His disciples came and asked him, 'Send her away, for she keeps calling out after us.' He said in reply, 'I was sent only to the lost sheep of the house of Israel.'

"There you have it, sir. Jesus was not, I repeat, was not sent to the nigger. The nigger is our slave. The entire continent of Africa is ours. Yes, sir, every nigger in Africa is ours and his land. So, Mr. Dye, we have our work cut out for us. And we've been slacking. The nigger is to fight our wars, fix our meals, clean our houses, pick our cotton, and everything we can imagine. That's the nigger's job as long as he or she shall live. That's the word of God. And we are God-fearing men. You've read it for yourself—it's only left to believe. Christianity is based on belief. So, my friend, believe the Bible and know who you are as a Christian and why God has put the white race over the nigger.

"Our white people are white and innocent. But God has put it in our heart. We know the nigger. Yes, sir. We know they are liars. We know they are thieves. We know we can't trust none of them. They'll rape our women. The nigger is a rascal. Yes, sir. So keep your eyes open. Be ready to apply the lash at a moment's notice. And put as much good white blood into as many nigger women as you can. The good white blood adds stability to the nigger race. The yellow nigger hates the brown nigger. The black nigger hates the brown and yellow nigger. So they don't even trust themselves. They live in constant insecurity. The nigger can't trust his own kind, so he trusts us, the white race. We do what's best for him. That's why God has placed the rascal in our possession.

"Mr. Dye, excuse me for talking so much, but I've got the preacher spirit. I just can't help preaching, and the nigger is a good subject to preach on. We must maintain our way of life. There are some who disagree with our way of life. They don't fear God, nor do they believe in the teaching of the Bible on slavery. They are enemies of God. Slavery is in the Bible. All through the Bible, there are references to slavery and how to treat the slave. So, my Christian friend, we will do what's right in the sight of God. We will make every damn nigger a slave. And we will take Africa and all its wealth as is rightfully ours."

At that moment, Little Lizzy walked into the parlor and said, "Lunch is ready." Reverend Cole and Mr. Dye got up and walked into the dining area. Ms. Dye, Annite, Kathryn, and William were already seated at the table. The table was beautifully set. Eppie Mae opened the door to the kitchen with her backside and walked into the dining room, smiling from ear to ear.

She was carrying a baked duck stuffed with dressing. Eppie set the baked duck next to Mr. Dye. Mr. Dye was sitting at the head of the table. Mrs. Dye sat next to him, on his right. Reverend Cole sat directly opposite Mr. Dye at the other end of the table. Reverend Cole said, "Mr. Dye, you must have the best cook in this part of the country."

Uncle Buff was standing off to the side of the table. Uncle Buff approached the table and carved the duck. He placed equal portions on all the adults' plates. Little Lizzy and I went around the table and sat a plate in front of everyone with our right hand on the right side of the person we were serving. Uncle Buff gave the children a smaller portion as instructed by Mrs. Dye.

Mrs. Dye said, "Mr. Dye, did you have a pleasant conversation with Reverend Cole?" Mrs. Dye, when speaking to her husband in the presents of company, referred to him as Mr. Dye.

Mr. Dye said, "Yes, Queen Bee, we had a very enlightening conversation. Queen Bee, its men's talk. Nothing to concern you pretty little head about."

Reverend Cole said, "Mr. Dye, you have a beautiful family. God has really blessed you, sir."

"Thank you," said Mr. Dye. "Reverend Cole, can you please bless the table before we eat?"

"Yes, sir, I'll be happy to bless this beautiful table. May Almighty God, our sovereign King, bless this table. Bless this household. Bless the man of the house. Keep this family in your will, Almighty God and King. Thank you for the food we are about to receive. Amen."

"Thank you, Reverend Cole, for your blessing," said Mr. Dye. "Reverend Cole, you are indeed a preacher's preacher."

"Thank you, sir, but I give all glory to Christ Jesus, for he has anointed me to preach his word."

"Sir, you stand correct. Now, let's eat," said Mr. Dye.

After dinner, the two men went into the parlor. Uncle Buff served brandy. Reverend Cole said, "Thank you for the wonderful dinner. You have to let Eppie Mae come and cook for me sometime. That nigger has a gift for cooking."

"Yes, sir," said Mr. Dye. "Eppie Mae is in the process of training Little Lizzy and Mary Lou. I expect for one, if not both, of those girls to be excellent cooks under the supervision of Eppie Mae."

"Thank you, Mr. Dye, for your hospitality. The dinner was outstanding. And I hope I shed some light on the predicament of the nigger and Mary Lou."

"Yes, Reverend Cole, you were very enlightening. I thank you for gracing my home with your presence."

"Well, Mr. Dye, I hate to eat and run, but I have some pressing duty at the church. Can you please have my cart brought, sir?"

"Yes, sir, Reverend Cole."

Mr. Dye told Uncle Buff to have Neal Henry bring his cart to the front entrance. Uncle Buff went into the kitchen, opened the kitchen door, and rang the bell hanging outside. Neal Henry slowly walked up and said, "What you need, Uncle Buff?"

Uncle Buff said, "That evil reverend Cole wants a ride home. He wants you to take him home in Mr. Dye's cart."

"Well, I'm on my way," said Neal Henry.

Uncle Buff went back into the parlor. Mr. Dye said, "Uncle Buff, get the reverend his hat and wrap."

"Yes, sir," said Uncle Buff.

Uncle Buff went into the hall closet and got Reverend Cole's hat and wrap. Uncle Buff handed them to Reverend Cole and slightly bowed. Reverend Cole stood up, took the hat and wrap from Uncle Buff, quickly put the wrap on, and walked quickly to the door. Neal Henry was outside holding the reins on the horse.

Reverend Cole said, "Good day, sir. Thank you again for that wonderful meal." Reverend Cole walked to the cart, stepped up into the cart, sat down, and tipped his hat. Neal Henry hurriedly got onto the cart and said, "Giddy up now." The cart jerked forward, and they were off to the church.

Chapter Three

The Family

After lunch, Little Lizzy and I cleared the dining room table. Everyone had left the dining room. Little Lizzy and I were washing the dishes in the kitchen when William came into the kitchen. He stood near the door and then said, "Who is that?"

Little Lizzy answered, "This is Mary Lou. She is the new girl. She gon' be cooking, cleaning, and taking care all ya'll."

William walked over to me and said, "Hi, I'm Will."

I said, "Pleased to meet you, Master. I'm Mary Lou, but everybody calls me Babe. You can call me Babe too."

William said, "OK." Then he turned around and ran out the back door.

Little Lizzy said, "That boy is something else. When he around, don't take your eyes off him. Ain't no telling what he gonna do. He just bad. It seems like he's too little to be that bad. Can't nobody tell him nothing? He rip and run so, ooh."

"He just a baby," I said.

A few minutes later, William came back into the kitchen. He ran and stood next to Little Lizzy. Little Lizzy ignored him. William just stood next to Little Lizzy, pulling on her dress. Then he got on the floor and started crawling around the floor. I was standing on the other side of Little Lizzy. William crawled under Little Lizzy's dress. Little Lizzy kept on washing dishes. I stopped washing dishes and looked to see what William was doing. Then Little Lizzy yelled, "Will, come out from under there!"

William raised up Little Lizzy's dress and peeped out. Then Little Lizzy grabbed William by the arm and yanked him out. William ran into the dining room.

Little Lizzy said, "See, that boy is terrible. And he only eight years old." Little Lizzy went back to washing dishes.

I said, "Have you prayed for him?"

Little Lizzy answered, "No, ain't no prayer gonna help that boy! He just needs a good beatin', that's all, just like Mr. Dye beat us. Just one good beatin' will do William a world of good. I know once I'm beat, I don't do nothing wrong no more."

I said, "You know, Little Lizzy, there was a man who lived long ago. He lived in another country. He was a God-fearing man. His name was Elijah. Well, this man Elijah was human like us, yet he prayed earnestly that it might not rain, and for three years and six months, it did not rain upon the land. Then he prayed again, and the sky gave rain, and the earth produced its fruits."

Little Lizzy said, "You just making that up. How do you know about some man who lived a long time ago? He lived in another country. And why was he praying for rain to stop? Why would somebody be praying for the rain to stop?"

I said, "Well, Little Lizzy, Elijah the Tishbite, from Tishbe in Gilead, said to Ahab, 'As the Lord, the God of Israel, lives whom I serve, during these years there shall be no dew or raining except at my word.' The Lord then said to Elijah, 'Leave here, go east and hide in the Wadi Cherith, east of the Jordan. You shall drink of the stream, and I have commanded ravens to feed you there.' So he left and did as the Lord had commanded. He went and remained by the Wadi Cherith, east of the Jordan. Ravens brought him bread and meat in the morning and bread and meat in the evening, and he drank from the stream. Elijah is a prophet."

"Mary Lou, what do you mean Elijah is a prophet? I thought you said he was died."

I said, "He is dead. But he alive with the Lord. And he was against ungodly folks. That's why he had Elijah stop the rain. God showed them evil folks he is the only God."

Little Lizzy said, "Mary Lou, who been telling you these stories about Elijah and prayer?"

I said, "Nobody. I just seems to know some things. It's like I was there. I remember everything."

Little Lizzy said, "How do you know it's real and this Elijah man was a real prophet?"

I said, "I just know. I feel it in my bones. I hear these stories in my mind, and I sees them too. I know it's real."

Little Lizzy said, "Have you ever told anybody about what you hears and sees?"

"No, Little Lizzy, I don't tell nobody nothing. I just keep it to myself. I thought you is nice, so I told you about prayer and Elijah," said Mary Lou.

Little Lizzy asked, "Is this what happened to you when you was struck by lightning?"

I said, "I guess so. I didn't hear God's word before I was struck by lightning. Or maybe I heard God's word but not likes I hears it now."

Little Lizzy asked, "How can you tell if it's God's word or if you just making thangs up?"

I said, "God's word is warm. God's word seems to be in my bones. God's word is like you're getting a big hug from ya Momma, only it's in your

31

bones and God's word doesn't let go. Little Lizzy, I just know. Have you ever just known something? It's who I am now. I changed after I was hit by lightning. But I didn't want Momma, Daddy, and my brothers and sisters to know. I didn't want them to worry. I'm just blessed and highly favored, that's it. I'm blessed and highly favored."

All the while Little Lizzy and I were talking, we were washing dishes. Just when we finished the last dish, Mrs. Dye walked into the room and said, "Hello, you must be the new nigger. Do you know who I am?"

I said, "Yes, ma'am. You Mrs. Dye, Mr. Dye's wife."

Mrs. Dye said, "Yes, you are correct, and you are a talkative one, aren't you?"

I said, "No, ma'am."

Mrs. Dye said, "I expect everything around here to be perfect. Everything you do while working in this house shall be done perfectly. If not, that's your hide. I believe in beatin' the niggers. You are a lazy bunch, but I knows how to get the work out you. You will work every day and every night until everything is finished. And if everything is done correctly, there may be some extra food. Do you understand?"

I said, "Yes, ma'am." Then Mrs. Dye turned, went into the parlor, and sat down.

Little Lizzy said, "Mrs. Dye isn't that bad. She just talking. She just beat me three times since I been here, and I been here as long as I can remember. She wanted to beat me more, but Mr. Dye wouldn't let her. Mr. Dye came right up to her and snatched that whip right out of her hand. That's right. He snatched it right out of her hand and said, 'Queen Bee, you ain't gon' be beatin' the hide off the niggers. These niggers take care of the children.' That's what he said. He sho' did. Ever since then, I makes sure everything is done right around here. And that's the last time I was beat. But you know, I don't remember what I was being beat for."

I said, "That woman need prayer. She needs lots of prayer too."

Little Lizzy looked at me and smiled and giggled. Mr. Dye came down the stairs and went into the parlor. Mrs. Dye was already in the parlor. She was waiting for Mr. Dye. Mrs. Dye said, "Mr. Dye, what exactly did Reverend Cole want to talk to you about?"

Mr. Dye said, "Queen Bee, I told you it's menfolk business."

"Any business that comes into this house is my business too."

Mr. Dye said, "OK, if you must know, we were discussing politics. Currently, we have two political parties: the Whigs and the Democrats. Our Democratic Party is strong. We believe we can win the election. But there is talk about the northern states creating a new political party called the Republican Party. Some of them believe that if the northern states do create a new political party, they will try to eliminate our way of life in the south. We believe this is just another attempt to destroy our way of life. This Republican Party was once a strong party. Then it died. Now, some are trying to give life to a dead horse. So, my dear, don't worry."

Mrs. Dye asked, "Is this about slavery?"

Mr. Dye answered, "Yes. That's the reason I brought Mary Lou into the house. Since she didn't die in that lightning strike, the niggers are using any and everything to hold on to. We don't want to give them false hope."

Mrs. Dye answered, "I see, Mr. Dye. You act accordingly."

Mr. Dye said, "Don't I always do what's right, Queen Bee? Like I said before, it's men business."

Little Lizzy and I had finished the dishes. There was plenty of duck leftover. Eppie Mae yelled, "If ya'll wants some of this duck, come and gets whats you want! I fixed Neal Henry and Billy Joe a plate." Eppie Mae went to the back door, opened the door, and rang the bell. Little Lizzy and I went to the kitchen table and fixed huge platefuls of duck, dressing, and cranberry sauce. Eppie Mae came back into the kitchen and said, "You know ya'll ain't gonna eat all that duck and dressing."

I said, "Yes, ma'am, but I'm gonna try."

Eppie Mae said, "You girls take that food to your room."

Little Lizzy and I went upstairs to our room and sat on the edge of our beds facing each other. I tasted my duck and said, "This is the best duck I've ever had. It doesn't taste like chicken."

Little Lizzy said, "Mary Lou, is this the first time you had duck?"

I said, "Ya, how did you know?" The girls just started laughing and eating.

A few minutes later, Eppie Mae yelled, "Ya'll come on down here! It's plenty of work to be done. We has to get dinner started, clean up, and gets ready for church tonight. I can't do all the work by myself."

Little Lizzy and I went downstairs and washed our plates. Then Eppie Mae told me to get the turkey out and prepare it for roasting. I went and got the turkey from the cold room. I then asked Little Lizzy, "What do I do next with this turkey?"

Little Lizzy said, "It's already prepared. Just get a roasting pan and put it in there. We baked the duck. We're going to roast the turkey."

I asked, "What's the difference between baking a duck and roasting a turkey?"

Little Lizzy said, "When we bake a duck, we just put in the oven and let it cook. But when we roast a turkey, we put in a roasting pan and use low heat. It's right after lunch. By dinnertime, that turkey should be cooked."

I said, "It don't seem like much difference to me." I put the turkey in the stove. Eppie Mae told me to go and get the plates from Neal Henry and Billy Joe from the barn. I went out the back door and stood. I looked around to see what I thought looked like a barn. To the west of the big house stood a large red structure. I had never seen a barn, but that was the only other thing that could be a barn. So I decided to walk to the large red structure. There was a white fence around it, and it had a gate. I pushed the gate open and slowly walked to the large red structure. The doors were open. I stood in the doorway and looked in.

Billy Joe yelled, "Girl, what you doing!"

I said, "I come to get the plates."

Billy Joe said, "What plates? We ate them plates along with the duck."

Billy Joe said, "You must be the new girl. Neal Henry went to get you this morning."

I said, "That's right. I came here this morning."

Billy Joe said, "I'm Billy Joe. I works with Neal Henry. We fix things. We train horses. We just about do whatever fixing that needs to be arounds here."

I said, "My momma and daddy calls me Babe. You can call me Babe if you wants to."

Billy Joe said, "That's OK with me. I like Babe better than Mary Lou. So what are you going to do around here? Mr. Dye don't like lots of slaves around the big house. He says he can't watch them all, and he's not going pay for some overseer."

I said, "I'm gonna be working in the big house. I'm gonna cook, clean, and I guess do whatever I'm told to do, sunup until sundown. I thinks that's what Mrs. Dye said."

Billy Joe said, "I thought Eppie Mae and Little Lizzy was doing all that."

I answered, "They is. I'm just going to do whats they do."

"At least you out those cotton fields," said Billy Joe.

"I'm glad I'm out of those cotton fields too. I was struck by lightning in them fields," I said.

"No, you was not," said Billy Joe.

"Yes, I was. I was hit right in the top of my head," I said.

Billy Joe said, "You sho' don't look like you was hit by lightning. I never seen anybody who was hit by lighting before. Did it hurt?"

I said, "I don't know. At first, it was like getting hit by a sledgehammer right in the head. After that, I didn't feel anything. I was out. I woke up weeks later. But it was so fast, it was like I didn't feel nothing. At the time I was hit, I didn't know what had happened. It's kind of hard to explain. It's troublesome to me. I just don't understand it all. It happened so fast. But I'm not hurting now. And I wasn't hurting when I woke up. I lost lots of weight."

Billy Joe asked, "Did getting hit by lighting make you lose weight?"

"No, I thinks it's because I couldn't eat nothing when I was out. I couldn't feed myself. Momma and my sisters had to feed me."

"They must didn't feed you too much 'cause you ain't big as nothing," said Billy Joe.

"Well, I used to be fat. I thinks that's why everybody used to call me Babe. Well, they still call me Babe."

"Mary Lou, Mary Lou, Mary Lou, what you doing, girl? I told you to get them plates!" Eppie Mae yelled at me. "Come on, girl, we gots lots of work to do. Next time I tells you to do something, you go do it and get on back. I ain't got time to come looking for nobody, ya hear?" said Eppie Mae.

"Yes, ma'am," I said.

"Now, you get on back to the big house. Little Lizzy is cooking and cleaning all by herself," said Eppie Mae.

"Yes, ma'am," I said.

Eppie Mae said, "Now, Billy Joe, you know better. This her first day. She can't be talking to you about nothing. You going to get that girl a beating on her first day."

In the big house, Little Lizzy was fixing turkey dressing. I came in the back door. I set the plates in the sink and washed them. Little Lizzy didn't say anything. She kept on fixing the turkey dressing. After I had finished washing the plates, I walked over to where Little Lizzy was fixing the turkey dressing and said, "I'm sorry."

Little Lizzy said, "It's OK. Sometimes I go over to the barn and talks to Billy Joe. He don't do nothing but works. He's nice. We been friends since I came here. We both been here ever since we could remember. He's been my real only friend. He's not my boyfriend. He just ain't the boyfriend type. But I never had a boyfriend anyhow." Little Lizzy put the turkey in the oven. Then Little Lizzy and I went into the parlor and dining room to clean.

I said, "It's not much to clean in here."

Little Lizzy replied, "Mrs. Dye likes everything perfect. Everything must be dusted off. And everything must be put in its proper place, or else, Mrs. Dye gets besides herself and wants to beat us, even if the littlest thing is out of place."

Mrs. Dye, Kathryn, Annite, and William came down the stairs. They walked down the stairs as if they were soldiers in the army. As they went into the parlor, they walked in a straight line. The children lined up from shortest to the tallest. Mrs. Dye stood off to the side of the children. Mrs. Dye said, "Little Lizzy, Mary Lou, stop what you are doing. I want to introduce the children to Mary Lou, our new house slave. Mary Lou, this is Kathryn, Annitte, and William. I believe you've already met William."

Little Lizzy curtsied. I stood still and looked straight ahead. Little Lizzy nudged me slightly. I looked at Little Lizzy and attempted to curtsy. After Mrs. Dye observed my attempt at a curtsy, she told the children, "That's all, children." The children turned and exited the room in military form: from the shortest to the tallest. They walked up the stairs in the same manner.

Little Lizzy and I stood still with our hands at our sides. Mrs. Dye stood looking at us both. Her face was white as cake flour. She wore bright red lipstick. She didn't smile or make a sound. Her arms were tightly folded. I was calm, almost poetic in appearance. Little Lizzy was afraid. Her knees were beginning to slightly shake. Little Lizzy had seen this before, usually just before a beating. But Little Lizzy thought, *I hadn't done nothing, so I can't be about to get beat.*

Mrs. Dye said, "I expect the best from both of you. I expect you to treat my children with the same respect as me or Mr. Dye. Anything else will not be tolerated. Do you understand?"

Both of us said, "Yes, ma'am," at the same time.

Mrs. Dye continued. "There will be no foolishness. I will not tolerate anything but the best from both of you. Do you understand?"

Both of us again said, "Yes, ma'am." Mrs. Dye looked intently at us. She looked almost as if she wanted to cry. Then she turned and slowly walked upstairs. I went back to cleaning. I stopped and turned around. Little Lizzy was still standing there.

I called out, "Come on, girl." Little Lizzy turned and returned to cleaning. We cleaned in silence. I would look intently at Little Lizzy, but Little Lizzy looked like she was in another time and place. After we had finished cleaning, we went and set the table. This time, I knew exactly where everything went. I set the table by myself. Little Lizzy went into the kitchen and checked on the turkey. Eppie Mae was putting the last touches on an apple pie.

Eppie Mae said, "Mr. Dye's favorite, apple pie." Little Lizzy didn't say anything. She just looked at the turkey. As she turned around, a tear trickled down her cheek.

Eppie Mae said, "Girl, you better get back from that stove. It's hot." Just then, I came into the kitchen. I looked around to see what should be done.

Eppie Mae said, "Come on over here, both ya'll. I wants to show ya'll how to makes Mr. Dye's favorite, apple pie." We walked over and stood on each side of Eppie Mae.

Eppie Mae put peeled apples in the pie. She put beaten eggs, butter, goat's milk, sugar, nutmeg, and cinnamon into a bowl and whipped it all together.

"Goat's milk is the special ingredient. It adds a special flavor. Now, for everybody else, no eggs and no goat's milk. Ya'lls always to make two apple pies: one for Mr. Dye and one for the Mrs. Dye and the children. The apple pie for everybody else, use water instead of goat's milk. Now, pour one mixture over Mr. Dye's pie and the mixture without the goat's milk over the other. Roll out the dough and put dough over the top of both pies. Then ya'll just puts them in the oven. It don't takes long for them to cook." We all went and sat down at the kitchen table.

Eppie Mae said, "When the turkey gets done, the pies should be done too, because we started the turkey way before we put them pies in the oven. Now ya'll just always check on whats ya'll cooking all the time to makes sure it's ready. I'm not going nowhere, but Mr. Dye told me to teach ya'll how to cook. That's what I'm gonna do.

"Now, once everything gets done, we will serve the family just like this afternoon. But after serving and cleaning, we got church. Little Lizzy already knows how we does things, but I wants you, Babe, to know. When everything is finished, make sure you're finished with everything. Mr. Dye allows us to have church in the barn, just us slaves here. Uncle Buff will be a few minutes late. He has to serve after-dinner coffee and wine, whatsever they wants. But we gonna already be in the barn, waiting. OK, Little Lizzy, Babe, don't be taking y'alls sweet time to get ya'll work done."

Both of us said, "Yes, ma'am."

Little Lizzy and I went into the living room and parlor. We looked around to see if anything was out of order. Everything was fine. So we got the dust brushes out and began dusting and straightening everything in the room, making sure everything was perfect. When we had finished, we went back into the kitchen. The turkey was ready, so we got the turkey out of the oven, along with the pies. It was dinnertime now. The family was seated.

I brought the turkey into the dining area and set it exactly where the duck was placed earlier. Little Lizzy brought the pies into the parlor. Eppie Mae didn't do anything but tell us what to bring out and where to set it. Little Lizzy and I didn't serve any food. We stood off to the side, along with Uncle Buff. Mr. Dye carved the turkey and passed the plates around the table. When everyone had turkey on their plates, Mr. Dye sat down. He looked at everyone at the table and said, "Bow your heads, please. Lord, thank you for blessing our table this day. Amen. Let's eat."

"Pass the apple pie," William said.

"No, William, not until you've finished all your food," Mrs. Dye said.

"Look here, Eppie Mae has fixed my favorite, goat's milk apple pie. Eppie Mae, what's the special occasion?" Mr. Dye asked.

Eppie Mae came into the room and stood next to the kitchen door. "I thought you might like something nice today, sir."

"Well, I appreciate the thought. That's all, Eppie Mae. You can go now," Mr. Dye said.

Eppie Mae turned without saying a word and humbly left the dining area.

Annite said, "I'm not hungry. We just had duck for lunch a few hours ago."

Mrs. Dye said, "Annite, you watch your mouth and eat something."

"Please pass me some stuffing and cranberry sauce, please," Annite said.

Kathryn passed the stuffing and cranberry sauce to Annite and said, "Momma, I'm not hungry either."

Mrs. Dye said, "You all listen very carefully. Everyone will eat something. There will be no more discussion about it." Mr. Dye had already fixed his plate and was eating. He didn't say a word. Mrs. Dye said, "Mr. Dye, don't you have something to say?"

Mr. Dye said, "Mary Kate, I've told you that's your responsibility. You just have to put your foot down."

After dinner was over, Little Lizzy and I cleared the table as quickly as possible. Eppie Mae did the dishes. Uncle Buff served coffee to Mr. and Mrs. Dye in the parlor. Then Eppie Mae, Little Lizzy, and I went out the side back door. We walked side by side and headed toward the barn. It was a beautiful summer evening. The sun was just beginning to set. We women walked as if we were on a special mission. We walked quickly and quietly. No one said a word. Our eyes were fixed on the barn. When we entered the barn, Eppie Mae broke out in song.

Come, Holy Ghost, Creator blest,

and in our hearts take up thy rest

Come with thy grace and heavenly aid to fill the hearts which thou hast made,

to fill the hearts which thou hast made.

O Comforter, to thee we cry,

Thou heavenly gift of God most high,

Thou font of life and fire of love,

And sweet anointing from above,

Praise be to thee, Father and Son, And Holy Spirit, with them one;

And may the Son on us bestow the gifts that from the spirit flow,

The gifts that from the spirit flow.

Little Lizzy and I stood next to Eppie Mae as she sang. We closed our eyes. We saw every word Eppie Mae had sung.

I whispered, "Enter his temple gates with praise and his courts with thanksgiving."

Little Lizzy said, "Babe, we ain't in no temple, and there ain't no courts here."

I said, "When you go before the Lord, first begin to praise him. Then thank him for all he has done and for all he is going to do. I know ya'll been praising the Lord in this barn. I can feel his presence. Do you know that our Lord Jesus Christ was born in a barn? He became the least among us.

Who, though he was in the form of God, did not regard equity with God, something to be grasped? Rather, he emptied himself, taking the form of a slave, coming in human likeness, and found human in appearance. He humbled himself, becoming obedient to death, even death on a cross. Because of this, God greatly exalted him and bestowed on him the name of Jesus. Every knee should bend, of those in heaven and on the earth and under the earth, and every tongue confess that Jesus Christ is Lord, to the glory of God the Father."

"Babe, how do you know these things?" asked Little Lizzy.

I said, "Sometimes I see words and pictures of Jesus. It's hard to explain. I feels it in my bones. I gets warm, like I'm on fire. So I just say what's there."

Eppie Mae said, "Ya'll stop all that talking. We gon' have Church. Ya'll girls move those bundles of hay into a circle. Little Lizzy, you know what to do. Show Babe where everything goes."

"Babe, what do you mean by Jesus became a slave?" asked Little Lizzy.

I said, "You know, Jesus is Lord of Lords. Jesus is King of Kings. Jesus reigns in heaven above. Jesus has all power. Jesus is the bright morning star. Jesus is the Prince of Peace. Jesus is the first and the last. Jesus is all those things and more. Jesus has all riches. Yet Jesus left his place in heaven and became just like us. That's right. Just like us—a slave."

"He wasn't picking no cotton, and he wasn't cooking and cleaning, was he?" said Little Lizzy.

"No, that means that he was in heaven, with all glory and all power, and he became one of us. He was like us . . . just ordinary folk. And he lived like we live. He laughed like we laugh. He felt hurt and pain just like us. But he was God. He taught us how to love so we could go to heaven and be back with him, Jesus. And then we will live forever and forever," I said.

Little Lizzy said, "You sho' know a lot about Jesus. But what do you mean he became one of us?"

I answered, "He was all man and all God. He shared in our life experience."

"Did he get whipped?" asked Little Lizzy.

"Yeah," I said.

"Did he get slapped and spit on?" asked Little Lizzy.

"Yeah," I said.

"It seemed to me that if he was God, he could avoided all that whipping and getting spit on," said Little Lizzy.

Eppie Mae stopped moving the bales of hay around and looked to see what Little Lizzy and I were doing. Little Lizzy yelled, "All finished!" The bales of hay were all in a circle with a large area in the center of the circle.

Neal Henry, Billy Joe, and Uncle Buff all came into the barn. Neal Henry and Billy Joe went and sat next to Eppie Mae. Everyone was seated all around the circle on bales of hay. Uncle Buff was standing in the center of the circle. He looked around as if to see if anyone was missing. He stood tall and noble. His left hand was placed on his chest, open. His right arm, straight down at his side. His right hand was clinched into a fist. He turned and looked everybody in the eye and said in a loud voice, "Thank you, Jesus. Thank you, Jesus. Thank you, Jesus. Thank you, Jesus. I just want to thank you, Lord." His voice was salted. When he spoke, his every word rang in his listeners' ears. He spoke like a seasoned Baptist preacher. Yet he had never had any training, nor had he ever read a Bible. He preached from what he had heard from sitting outside the local Baptist church.

Uncle Buff said, "Lord, we've come to thank you. You've been mighty good. Lord, you see all. You knows all. There is no one like you, oh, Lord. Lord, you saw this child. This child, Mary Lou. 'How great are your works, Lord! How profound your purpose! A senseless person cannot know this; a fool cannot comprehend,' Psalm 92:6–7. Lord Jesus, you brought this child to us. Lord, we know she is blessed. Lord, there is no way anything on this earth is going to survive a lightning strike like that and live. Yes, Lord, we thank you. We thank you, Lord."

Eppie Mae, Little Lizzy, Neal Henry, and Billy Joe all stood up and yelled, "Thank ya, Jesus! Thank ya, Jesus!" They all seemed to raise their hands over their heads at the same time and yell, "Thank ya, Jesus!"

Eppie Mae started to jump up and down, yelling, "Thank ya, Jesus." I sat still. My eyes were bright and wide. I looked as though I was in shock.

Uncle Buff jumped up and down, yelling, "Thank you, Jesus! Thank you, Jesus! We gonna have church in here tonight. There is nothing better for a man to have than devotion to Jesus Christ. Yes, sir. We gon' abide in the word of God. Yes, sir. We gon' live in the word of God, because Jesus is Lord. I say, Jesus is Lord. Did ya'll here what I said?"

Everybody yelled, "Yes, sir!"

Uncle Buff stopped jumping up and down. He became calm, almost majestic in appearance and attitude, and said, "Everyone, please sit down. I want ya'll to know this day that Jesus is good. Jesus has been good to us in spite of our situation. We are slaves, the lowest of the low, or so they say we are. But Jesus has a plan for us. I know God has a plan for us. Yes, sir. I know God has a plan for us. You see, God speaks to us. I say God speaks to us. Every time we hear God's word, God is speaking to us. Ya'll didn't hear me. I say every time we hear God's word, God is speaking to you and me. God says, 'They shall be my people, and I will be their God.' Yes, sir, he sho' did. God says, 'They shall be my people, and I will be their God.' God is talking to you and I."

Uncle Buff shouted at the top of his voice. His voice rang with authority and power. "Ah, Lord God, you have made heaven and earth by your great might, with your outstretched arm. Nothing is impossible for you. You continue your kindness through a thousand generations, and you repay the father's guilt even into the lap of their sons who follow them, oh, God, great and mighty, whose name is Lord of Hosts, great in counsel, mighty in deed, whose eyes are open to all the ways of men, giving to each according to the fruit of his deeds, You see the wrongs committed against all God's children. Ah, Lord, we beg you to send your Holy Spirit upon this land. Yes, oh, Lord, send your Holy Spirit upon this land. Make the wrongs done into a right."

Eppie Mae, Little Lizzy, Neal Henry, Billy Joe, and I all stood up and shouted, "Yes, Lord, send your Holy Spirit upon this land and upon us too. Oh, Lord, we are your children!"

Uncle Buff said, "The spirit of the Lord is here. It's in this place. Thank you, Jesus."

Eppie Mae started dancing around the barn, yelling, "Thank you, Jesus!"

Little Lizzy started dancing around, shouting, "Thank you, Jesus!"

Then we all were yelling and dancing around the barn, shouting, "Thank you, Jesus!" We put our hands in the air over our heads, skipped, and jumped on one foot. We jumped up and down on two feet, shouting at the top of our voice, "Thank you, Jesus!"

Neal Henry threw his head back and shouted, "Thank you, Jesus!" Tears ran down his cheeks. He was jumping on one leg. The other leg was raised to his chest. Both fists were clinched as if he was holding on to something. Both arms were outstretched over his head. There was a rhythm to their movements. Everyone moved on one accord. Although there was no music playing or being sung, our jumping and shouting created a rhythmic sound. The shouting continued. Different sounds and utterances came from each one. It was as if we were all speaking different languages.

While we were still having church, Mr. Dye entered the barn and yelled, "All right, that's enough of this noise! I can hear you clear up to the big house." Silence fell over everyone.

Uncle Buff said, "Yes, sir, we gon' quiet down, sir." Mr. Dye turned and walked out the barn. Uncle Buff said, "The Lord is good. Yes, sir. The Lord is good. I want all ya'll to know that devotion to Jesus Christ is mightier than all else. We been washed in the blood of Jesus Christ. We been baptized, baptized by the Holy Spirit. Yes, I'm telling everyone here that Jesus Christ is with each and every one of you standing here. God is on our side. Yes, God is on the side of all who call on him in truth and sincere heart. Eppie Mae, can you lead us in song?"

Eppie Mae walked to the center of the barn. Everyone formed a large circle around Eppie Mae. Eppie Mae sang slowly and majestically. She sang as if this was the last thing she was ever going to do on earth. With a broken heart and sorrow coming from her voice, Eppie Mae sang "I Know That My Redeemer Lives!" As she sang, a tear trickled down her cheek. She continued.

What joy this blest assurance gives!

Christ lives, he lives, who once was dead, He lives, my ever living head!

Christ lives triumphant from the grave; He lives eternally to save;

Christ lives in majesty above; He lives to guide me in love.

Christ lives to silence all my fears; He lives to wipe away my tears;

Christ lives to calm my troubled heart; He lives all blessings to impart.

Christ lives to bless me with great love; He lives to plead for me above;

Christ lives, my hungry soul to feed;

Christ lives, to help in time of need.

Christ lives and grants me daily breath; He lives and I shall conquer death;

Christ lives, my mansion to prepare; He lives to bring me safely there.

Christ lives, all glory to his name! He lives my savior still the same;

What joy this blest assurance gives;

I know that my redeemer lives!

Tears ran down Eppie Mae's cheeks. Everyone felt every word she sang. No one said a word. There was silence for a moment. Then Uncle Buff said, "That was a wonderful song. I know that my redeemer lives. Yes, my redeemer lives. He lives in me. My redeemer lives in me. Jesus Christ, the son of the living God, lives in each one of us. He is the rock I stand on. We gonna close. I don't wants to. I can thank Jesus all day, every day. But Mr. Dye won't take too kindly to us being in this here barn all night. Does anybody wants to say something before we go?"

Little Lizzy said, "I just wants to thank the Lord for bringing Mary Lou. She's real nice. That's all I have to say."

Uncle Buff said, "Does anybody else have something to say?"

Neal Henry said, "Yes, I thinks Mary Lou is gon' do fine. I believe she was sent here for a purpose. I thanks the Lord for sending her to us. We gonna treat her just like she is our own youngen, and that's what I told her folks on slave row."

I took three steps forward and looked at everyone passionately. I spoke softly and slowly. I said, "Thank ya'll. God is good. He saved me. Jesus hears the prayers of the faithful. Thank ya'll for welcoming me." Tears ran down my cheeks. I started to cry and fell to my knees. I put my hands over my face and cried. Eppie Mae and Little Lizzy walked over and helped me to my feet. I kept on crying. Eppie Mae and Little Lizzy slowly walked me out the barn.

As Eppie Mae and Little Lizzy were walking me, I held my head down and kept on crying. Eppie Mae and Little Lizzy held on to me tightly. I seemed weak, as if my legs couldn't hold my weight. As the women were walking to the big house, Uncle Buff, Neal Henry, and Billy Joe slowly walked out of the barn. They stood in front of the barn and watched as I was taken to the big house. Uncle Buff and Neal Henry took out their corn pipes and filled them with smoking tobacco.

Billy Joe said, "Would you just look at them stars? The entire sky is filled with stars. What a night! I thinks God knows the names of all them stars. What do you think, Uncle Buff?"

Uncle Buff said, "God knows all things." Uncle Buff and Neal Henry looked up at the stars.

Neal Henry said, "Look, there is the Big Dipper, and that star over there points north. Yes, if you knew what you were looking for, you can follow them stars and go anywhere a man has a mind to go."

Uncle Buff said, "I've heard of runaway slaves following them stars all the way up north. And I heard of an African named Cinque who took a ship and tried to follow the stars back to Africa. Yes, sir, you are right. A man can go anyplace in this ole world if he can see the stars and know what he's doing."

Billy Joe said, "The stars change, and you can't see no stars during the day. So a man could only know where he's going at night."

"Well, don't you boys be getting no ideas about running away," said Uncle Buff. "I heard Reverend Cole preach on a man named Abram. God said he would change his name from Abram to Abraham. God took Abram outside and said, 'Look up at the sky, and count the stars, if you can. Just so,' he added, 'shall your descendants be.' Abram puts his faith in the Lord, who credited it to his as an act of righteousness. Yes, we are the descendants of Abram, you see. God's promise to Abram was based on Abram's faith. If we have faith in God, we are the descendants of Abram."

Billy Joe said, "So that means we are related to this man Abram."

"Yes, sir," said Uncle Buff. "We all spiritually related by faith. We believe in the same God, the God of Abraham, Isaac, and Jacob. So, Billy Joe, put your faith in God, and God will credit you as righteous in all you do," said Uncle Buff.

"What does righteousness mean?" asked Billy Joe.

"That just means that God is on your side," said Uncle Buff. "And if God is on your side, who can be against you?" Neal Henry replied.

Billy Joe continued. "So what is faith?"

Neal Henry said, "I heard a preacher say that faith is hoping for something real and not yet seeing it, but you keep on hoping and working for what you want to happen."

"I don't rightly understand you," said Billy Joe.

"I don't rightly understand what that preacher was all saying myself," said Neal Henry. "But I guess it's like breaking a horse. We know how we wants that horse to be. We wants to ride him. We wants him to pull a wagon. But that horse, he ain't got no mind to for us to ride him. And that horse ain't gon' pull no wagon. So we rope the horse, and we tame him. We work that ole horse until we can ride him and use him for work."

"Yes, sir, I see," said Billy Joe. "I thinks I knows what you means. So faith takes time. Faith takes work. You have to know what you want."

"Yes, that's it," said Neal Henry. "You got the idea. Only God is working with us. Yes, that's it. God is pulling the yoke right along with us. And sometimes God just pulls that thang by himself."

"Yes, sir," said Uncle Buff. "That sounds like faith to me. I'm calling it a night. Good night." Uncle Buff turned and walked to the big house.

Billy Joe and Neal Henry said, "Good night," and walked slowly into the barn, talking about faith. Uncle Buff went into the kitchen side door and sat at the kitchen table. The kitchen was empty. He crossed his legs and took out his corn pipe. He stuffed his pipe with cherry tobacco and lit it. The smell from the pipe tobacco slowly filled the room and rose to the upstairs slave room where Little Lizzy and I slept. Eppie Mae and Little Lizzy were upstairs preparing me for bed. Little Lizzy had lit a candle, and the room was dimly lit. The candle flame flicked back and forth. Eppie Mae and Little Lizzy took off my dress and shoes. I was exhausted. I lay on the bed, sleeping.

Eppie Mae whispered, "Bless her heart. The poor child is too tired to take her own clothes off."

Little Lizzy said, "I smell Uncle Buff's pipe smoke. He must be downstairs in the kitchen. He's probably hungry." Eppie Mae tucked me under the covers, and they both went downstairs.

Uncle Buff said, "That girl must be tired. She put in a good day's work. I think she'll do just fine. She's a good little girl."

Eppie Mae said, "That girl just as old as Little Lizzy. She a young lady, Buff."

Uncle Buff said, "I sure would like some of that turkey, duck, and stuffing that Mr. and Mrs. Dye had to eat today."

"That's right, you ain't ate all day, have you, Uncle Buff?" asked Eppie Mae.

"That's right. I ain't ate a thing. And bring me a piece of that apple pie."

Eppie Mae yelled, "Little Lizzy, you get up and fix Uncle Buff a plate!" Little Lizzy got up and began fixing Uncle Buff a large plate of turkey, duck, and apple pie. Little Lizzy didn't say a word. She was tired. Little Lizzy brought Uncle Buff a plate of food and sat it in front of him.

"Thank you," he said.

Little Lizzy said, "Good night," and she turned and went upstairs to bed. Eppie Mae sat down at the kitchen table opposite Uncle Buff.

Uncle Buff said, "Mr. and Mrs. Dye are sleeping now. They don't stay up late into the night, and that's a good thang. I'm going to bed just as soon as I finish eating."

"Buff, you sure did preach tonight. God really moved in a mighty way. I felt the Holy Spirit deep down in my bones. Everybody there must have felt God's presence."

"You know that's a real special thang to be able to worship and pray like we do here," replied Uncle Buff. "And God sent Mary Lou to us. I heard that she knows the whole Bible backwards and forwards."

"Buff, who told you that?" asked Eppie Mae.

"That's what her sister told Lil George," Uncle Buff replied.

"Uncle Buff, you can't be believing them old Negroes who don't know nothing about nothing. That old man just talking. She ain't said nothing to me about nothing except keeping this place and doing her chores. But I'm just an old woman. Who knows? Wouldn't it be something if God really touched that girl? She such a sweet girl. I ain't never known no one like her before. She sweet and nice. She don't mind working. She don't look like nothing but good things been done to her all her life. She just don't act like no field slave. She don't even look like she been out in them there fields since she was old enough to walk. And she seem to know how to behave. She is a wonder."

"Eppie Mae, you about to run me out of this kitchen. I just told you what I heard," said Uncle Buff. "Good night." Uncle Buff got up and went through the door off the side of the kitchen. Eppie Mae got up and cleaned up after Uncle Buff. Then she followed him to their room off the side of the kitchen.

Chapter Four

Raised the Dead

Eppie Mae was up at daybreak cooking breakfast. The house smelled of fresh coffee. She cooked bacon and eggs with toast and strawberry jam. The Dye family was up and all seated at the kitchen table. Eppie Mae set a plate of bacon on the table. Next to the plate of bacon, she set a medium-size bowl of eggs. There was a pitcher of fresh cold milk in the cooler. Mr. Dye drank his milk cold. No one served the family breakfast. Mrs. Dye set two pieces of bacon on William's plate and a small portion of eggs, with two pieces of toast and a spoonful of strawberry jam. Will sat there with his hands at his side.

Mrs. Dye said, "William, you will eat everything on that plate." William picked up his fork and scooped a hunk of eggs on his fork and shoved it in his mouth. William sat with his cheeks pushed out full of food. He looked around the table at his mother, father, and sisters. Then he slowly chewed his food. Mrs. Dye whispered, "That's a good boy. You see, if you eat all of your food, you'll be a big and strong man someday." William didn't say anything. He just continued to eat. Everyone else at the table was silent. Annite and Kathryn seemed to ignore Mrs. Dye's success at getting William to eat. This was the Dye's family routine.

Mr. Dye replied, "Queen Bee, will you stop making such a fuss about that boy eating? He'll be just fine." Mrs. Dye didn't say a word. She kept on eating her breakfast.

After breakfast was over, Annite and Kathryn hurried up from the kitchen table. Annite said, "Daddy, we are going to go riding this morning. It's a wonderful morning for a horseback ride."

Mr. Dye said, "You girls be careful." The girls quickly went out the back door and walked toward the stables. Mr. Dye and Mrs. Dye sat drinking their coffee.

Mrs. Dye replied, "Mr. Dye, you should be sterner with those girls. They just do whatever they want."

Mr. Dye replied, "Well, Queen Bee, it is a wonderful morning for a horseback ride. I remember when you would join them."

Mrs. Dye replied, "I still ride. Just not as much as I used to."

Mr. Dye said, "I remember when you were probably the best lady rider in these parts."

William sat next to Mrs. Dye looking intently at his mother. His eyes were wide and big as he was picturing his mother riding a horse. She looked at William and said, "William, you're finished. You can leave now." William got up from the table and pushed his chair in. He went into the parlor and sat pouting.

Mr. Dye interjected, "I'm going to take a ride over to Reverend Cole's plantation I believe we still have some business to discuss." Eppie Mae came into the kitchen and poured Mrs. Dye a cup of coffee. "No more for me, Eppie."

Eppie Mae replied, "Yes, sir."

Mr. Dye stood up from the table and ordered, "Eppie Mae, have Billy Joe bring my horse around to the front of the house. I think I'm going to take a little ride over to Reverend Cole's place."

Eppie Mae walked to the back door, opened the door, and rang the bell. Billy Joe slowly walked over to the back door of the big house. Billy Joe lightly knocked on the back door. Eppie Mae opened the door, shouting, "Mr. Dye wants his riding horse in front of the big house right now! He's gon' riding over to Reverend Cole's place." Eppie Mae handed him a plate of bacon and eggs with a cup of black coffee.

Billy Joe said, "Thank you. I'm pleased to get some of your good cooking. You know this ain't enough for Neal Henry too."

Eppie Mae said, "Well, wait a minute and I'll get you another plate. You boys sure can eat. And bring me any eating wares ya'll may have."

"Yes, ma'am," replied Billy Joe.

Eppie Mae shouted, "Little Lizzy! Mary Lou!"

Little Lizzy and I came walking from the barn carrying a bucket of milk in each hand. We had been milking the cows and storing the milk in the milking containers. When we had reached the back door, we poured the milk into a large barrel. The barrel had rope handles on each side of it. We each grabbed a handle and took the barrel inside the kitchen.

Eppie Mae cleared the table from where the Dyes had eaten and set two large plates of bacon and eggs with toast and jam. Eppie Mae said, "Ya'll take those plates and go sit on the back steps and eat."

We took our plates of bacon and eggs with toast and jam and went and sat on the back steps. Eppie Mae came out carrying two large cups of cold milk and gave them to us. We sat and ate without saying a word as if we were in deep thought. Then I asked, "Is Mr. Dye your daddy?"

Little Lizzy said, "No, well, I don't know who my daddy is. I don't know. Why did you ask me if Mr. Dye is my daddy?"

"I don't know," I said. "You just look like him."

"Well, I heard that if a man starts to feed a child and takes care of them, they start to look like him."

"That don't make no sense at all."

Little Lizzy replied, "I've been here on this plantation ever since I can remember, so I'm bound to look like Mr. Dye."

"I'm sorry, don't pay me no mind. Little Lizzy, you know that ain't nothing but one of those ole Negro stories. You know you can't believe everything you hear on slave row. Them folks don't know what they're talking about."

54

"Well, they said that you was struck by lightning and lived."

"Yeah, I was struck by lightning, but that ain't no ole Negro story made up on slave row."

Little Lizzy said, "Well, to folks who don't know it's the truth, it's an ole Negro made-up story, right? And that's the same thing with menfolk feeding and raising kids that ain't theirs. Them kids start to look and act just like the menfolk who've been taking care of them."

"That ain't got no truth to it."

"Well, you just believe what you believe, and I'll believe that if men feeds and raises kids that ain't theirs, them kids gon' look like that man that's feeding them and act like the man raising them."

"I can see I ain't gon' get nowhere with you."

Little Lizzy stood up and shouted, "And I ain't never been on slave row!" Then she turned and walked into the kitchen.

I got up and followed behind Little Lizzy. Little Lizzy went to the sink and started to wash her plate. I stood next to Little Lizzy and washed out her plate. "Why do you think that if men take care of kids, they gonna look like that man that's taking care of them, Little Lizzy?"

"Because I looks like Mr. Dye, and that's what Eppie Mae told me. And she ain't gonna tell me nothing wrong." Little Lizzy's eyes were watery. She was a heartbeat away from crying. Tears slowly burst from her eyes. Little Lizzy didn't know why she was so upset. She didn't want to think about being Mr. Dye's daughter. She had never thought she could be Annite, Kathryn, and William's sister. Mr. Dye didn't treat her like a daughter. He didn't talk to her like he spoke to Annite, Kathryn, and William. And he came to her room at night. And he had been coming to her room ever since she started to become a woman.

Little Lizzy said, "Billy Joe looks like Mr. Dye too. Do you thinks he could be Mr. Dye's child too?"

Mary Lou said, "I don't know. I was just asking. I didn't mean to make you feel bad."

Little Lizzy cried, "I don't feel bad. I just never would think I could have a daddy. I never had a daddy or a momma. All I know is Eppie Mae, Uncle Buff, and the other slaves around here. I ain't never been off this plantation. That's all I know. I heard about slave row. But I ain't never been down there. When something needs to be done for the slaves on slave row, Neal Henry usually does it. What does slave row look like? Is it nice?"

"Girl, slave row ain't nice," I replied. "The shacks got dirt floors. The youngens run around naked and without shoes until they're old enough to work out in the cotton field. And ain't never enough to eat. Or it just feels like it. We have a little garden, though. And we gets the leftover of the pigs and cows that Mr. Dye ain't gonna eat. And when it rains, some folks' shack ain't got a good roof. So the rain comes in the shack and gets the floor all muddy. And some folks ain't got beds, so they sleep on the floor. And everybody old enough gon' work from sunup to sundown every day but Sundays.

"Sunday is our day to go out in the woods and pray. We got a praise shack out there. That's how I got hit by lightning. It started to rain. And some of us youngens started to run in the rain back to slave row. I was running in the rain and got struck by lightning. And when I woke up, I was skinny. I used to be fat. And I don't remember nothing when I was sleeping.

"I slept for a long time. They say I slept for weeks. But I don't remember. But when I woke up, I could remember or see things that I didn't know before I was hit by lightning. Like I remember Bartholomew. Bartholomew was one of the twelve disciples."

"What's a disciple?" asked Little Lizzy.

"Well, I'm talking about one of the twelve men who followed Jesus," I answered. "Bartholomew preached about Jesus. And there was this king named Astyages. And King Astyages threatened Bartholomew. He said, 'Unless you stop preaching Jesus Christ and make sacrifices to the god

Ashtaroth, you will be put to death.' 'You can be sure of this, King Astyages. I will never sacrifice to your idol. I would rather seal my testimony with my blood than do the smallest act against my faith or conscience.' Upon hearing this, the king ordered, 'I want this man to suffer severe torture.' First, they beat him with rods. After that, held him upside down on a cross and skinned him alive!

"Following the king's command, Bartholomew was beaten, hung on a cross like Jesus, and they skinned him alive. He didn't die right away. He kept on telling folks to believe in Jesus and worship the true God. And after this, they wanted him to stop talking. So the king's men took an ax and cut off his head. Now, Bartholomew is with Jesus his Lord and God. And I remember all the apostles. There was Simon, whom he named Peter, and his brother Andrew, James, John, Phillip, Bartholomew, Matthew, Thomas, James the son of Alphaeus, Simon, who was called Zealot, and Judas the son of James, and Judas Iscariot, who became a traitor. I feel them. It's like they are with me. It's like they are my family."

"Mary Lou, you ain't making no sense," said Little Lizzy.

"It makes good sense to me. And sometimes I just want to tell somebody about Jesus. I feel all warm inside. It's like I'm hot. It's like I'm on fire. God told me in a dream, 'Before I formed you in the womb, I knew you. Before you were born, I dedicated you. To whomever I send you, you shall go. Whatever I command you, you shall speak. Have no fear before them, because I am with you to deliver you,' says the Lord. Then the Lord extended his hand and touched my mouth, saying, 'See, I place my words in your mouth!'

"And I can remember that dream just like I can see you," I said. "I just know I have to tell somebody about this fire in my bones.

Little Lizzy said, "It sure sounds like you should be telling somebody about Jesus. Why don't you tell us? Uncle Buff tells us what he hears Reverend Dye preach. But it sounds like you can preach too."

"But I ain't never preached before. I don't know the first thing about preaching."

"It sounds like it's just telling folks about Jesus, and you can do that, can't you, Mary Lou? You tells me about Jesus. Just act like you telling me when you tell folks about Jesus," explained Little Lizzy.

"Well, I can try. Sometimes I feels as though I can burst open if I don't tell folks about Jesus Christ, the King of the Jews, son of David."

"Well, when we have church, maybe you can preach or just tell us about Jesus," explained Little Lizzy.

"I can do that. It's just talking. And we talks. But I ain't never talked about Jesus to nobody but you," I said.

"Sometimes we have a time for prayer. Uncle Buff or Eppie Mae gets everybody together in the barn. And we pray. We pray for everything that's troubling us. We don't do it all the time. But if we have prayer, why don't you try to preach us something? And you don't have to be afraid 'cause ain't nobody here gonna do nothing. And I think they would like to hear what you got to say," said Little Lizzy.

"Well, Little Lizzy, I'm gonna pray about it. I know that if I takes it to God in prayer, he'll answer me. God hears the prayers of the poor. Our prayers pass through the clouds and goes straight to the throne of the Almighty. Our prayers are a sweet smell to our Lord Jesus. So I'm not gonna think about it. In all my ways, I'll be mindful of the Lord, and he will make straight my paths," I said.

"We been sitting out here for a while. We best be getting back to work before Eppie Mae comes looking for us," said Little Lizzy.

Eppie Mae came the back door and said, "I heard what you two have been talking about. And we don't mind you saying a few words, Mary Lou. We all no different than anybody else. So don't be shy. Now, come on in here. Ya'll been wasting too much time doing nothing. There's plenty of work to be done. Now, get that bucket and fill it with water. I wants you two to scrub this floor real nice. And when you scrubbing, I don't want all that talking. You and Little Lizzy done talked enough for one day. We works around here."

Little Lizzy and I went into the kitchen. Little Lizzy went to the closet and got the mop bucket out. She called to me, "Come on, girl. I'm going to the well, and I'm gonna need some help carrying this bucket of mop water." We went out the back door.

The morning dew was still on the ground. It was cool. But it was a beautiful summer morning. We walked quickly. we didn't say a word. The well was in the back of the big house on the west side. Little Lizzy set the bucket under the pump, and I pumped the water. When the bucket was full, I picked it up. Then Little Lizzy came over and grabbed the handle. We both carried the bucket.

As we were walking back to the big house, a snake was slowly moving in the thick of the grass. We didn't see it. The snake crossed right in front of my path. I stepped directly on the midsection on the snake. The snake struck at my heel. I kept on walking and stepped on its head and killed it. I kept on walking without realizing that I had killed it. Little Lizzy turned her head around a few feet past the dead snake and said, "Look, a dead snake. Somebody must have killed it. Maybe Billy Joe killed it. You know those snakes been known to kill folks who gets bit by them."

"No," I said. "I ain't never known for nobody to get killed by them ole cottonmouth snakes."

"Them cottonmouth snakes done killed lots of folks around here before. That's what I heard Mr. Dye say," said Little Lizzy.

"Well, I hope don't nobody around here gets bit by one of them ole cottonmouth snakes," I replied.

"Mr. Dye says that they lives by the swamp. And that's why nobody goes near that ole swamp. That swamp is supposed to be full of them cottonmouth snakes. And I ain't seen many so far, and I don't want to see none," said Little Lizzy.

"Well, maybe this one got lost, because he a long way from that old swamp," I said.

"Yeah, Mr. Dye don't like none of them cottonmouth snakes around here. There was one around way back. And Mr. Dye killed it. Mr. Dye, he gon' have Neal Henry and Billy Joe looking around to see if there is any more around," said Little Lizzy.

When the girls got back to the big house, Little Lizzy ran into the kitchen and told Eppie Mae that she had seen a dead cottonmouth snake close by the well. Eppie Mae went into the parlor and stood at the bottom of the stairs, looking up the stairs to see if she saw Mrs. Dye. She didn't see Mrs. Dye. So Eppie Mae called Mrs. Dye in a polite and humble voice, "Mrs. Dye, Mrs. Dye, Mrs. Dye."

Mrs. Dye came to the top of the staircase and said, "Yes, Eppie Mae, what do you want?"

"Well, ma'am, Little Lizzy saw a dead cottonmouth down by the well."

"Get William and keep him in the house!" shouted Mrs. Dye. "And tell Neal Henry and Billy Joe to go and find them nasty cottonmouth snakes and kill them."

"Yes, ma'am," said Eppie Mae. Eppie went to the back door and looked for William. But she didn't see him. Then she went into the living room. William was standing in the living room looking out the window. Eppie Mae yelled, "Come over here, William! I been looking for you." Eppie Mae grabbed William by the arm and took him into the parlor to the bottom of the stairs. She called to Mrs. Dye, "Mrs. Dye, Mrs. Dye."

Mrs. Dye came to the top of the stairs and said, "Where did you find him?"

"I found him in the living room looking out the window," replied Eppie Mae.

"Come up here, William," Mrs. Dye said sternly. William slowly waved up the stairs holding his head down as though he had been scolded.

When he reached the top of the stairs, Mrs. Dyed grabbed him by the arm and snatched him, saying, "Come on, William, hurry up." William broke away from Mrs. Dye and ran into his bedroom. Mrs. Dye ran behind William, shouting, "Come here, boy, I'm not going to have none of this behavior in my house."

William was trying to crawl under his bed. But his mother grabbed him by the back of his pants and pulled him back. William was almost under the bed when his mother grabbed him. His hands were outstretched. He was trying to grab onto the bottom end of the bed. When he grabbed the bed, he screamed at the top of his lungs. A cottonmouth snake had gotten into William's bedroom. William had been bitten on his right arm. He screamed and screamed. Mrs. Dye pulled him back and saw the snake still biting William. She screamed, "Oh, no!" She reached with the other hand and yanked the snake off William. She screamed, "Eppie Mae! Eppie Mae!"

Eppie came running up the stairs and ran into William's bedroom. Mrs. Dye was holding William in her arms, crying. She cried, "A cottonmouth snake is under the bed. It bit William."

Eppie Mae screamed, "Oh, no!"

Mrs. Dye carried William into her bedroom down the hall. Eppie Mae followed Mrs. Dye, crying. She cried as though she was William's mother. Eppie Mae had nursed William during his infant and toddler years. Mrs. Dye examined William and saw a mark on his forearm. The bite was turning red and beginning to swell. She didn't know what to do. She screamed at Eppie Mae, "Get me some hot water!" Eppie Mae ran out of the bedroom and went into the kitchen.

Little Lizzy and I were standing in the kitchen looking bewildered. Little Lizzy asked, "What happened?"

Eppie Mae said, "William done got bit by one of them old nasty cottonmouth snakes. The snake was under his bed. Little Lizzy, get me some bandages and some iodine, and, Mary Lou, get me some hot water." Little Lizzy went to the medicine cabinet and got the bandages and iodine. I boiled some hot water and poured it into a silver pitcher. Eppie Mae went out the back door, screaming, "Neal Henry, Billy Joe, come quick!"

Uncle Buff was in the stables grooming the horses. Uncle Buff walked slowly out of the stables and asked, "What's wrong, Eppie Mae?"

She screamed, "William done got bit by a cottonmouth!"

Uncle Buff asked, "Where is the boy?"

"He's in Mr. Dye's bedroom," Eppie Mae said.

Uncle Buff said, "Go get Neal Henry. And send Billy Joe over to Reverend Cole's to fetch Mr. Dye."

Eppie Mae ran into the barn and told Neal Henry what Uncle Buff had said. Neal Henry and Eppie Mae came running out of the barn. Uncle Buff was already at the back door. Billy Joe quickly got on a horse bareback and rode out to Reverend Cole's plantation.

Eppie Mae, Uncle Buff, and Neal Henry all ran upstairs to Mr. Dye's bedroom. Little Lizzy and I were already in the room. Mrs. Dye was on her knees, crying, holding William's hand. Uncle Buff slowly stooped on one knee and gently lifted Mrs. Dye and took her away from the bed.

Neal Henry said, "I'm gonna have to cut him and suck out the poison."

Mrs. Dye said, "Do it, do it. Do what you have to do."

Neal Henry took out his pocket knife, bent over William, and got on one knee over the bed. He lifted William's arm and made a long cut on the puncture wounds that the snake had infected. Then he put his mouth over the cut and sucked as hard as he could. Then he spit the poison out on the floor. Neal Henry did this about five or six times. Then he said, "I think I got all of it. But the poison was in the boy for too long. I done seen these nasty cottonmouth take down horses before." Mrs. Dye stood and cried, holding on to Eppie Mae for comfort.

Uncle Buff said, "Ain't nothing we could do now but wait."

Mrs. Dye cried, "Neal Henry, ride over to Dr. Johnson's plantation and tell him to get over here as fast as he can. He can help." Neal Henry left the room. He went to the stables and saddled a horse and headed out to Dr. Johnson's plantation.

William was sweating and moaning. The wound had swollen and become red. The room was silent. Eppie Mae helped Mr. Dye to a chair in the bedroom. Mrs. Dye sat down and slowly rocked back and forth. Hope had left the room. Mrs. Dye and Uncle Buff knew well how deadly the cottonmouth snake was. The mood had changed from any hope of him recovering to one of death. Death was present in the room.

Mrs. Dye, Eppie Mae, and Uncle Buff were crying. Tears were running down the cheek of Little Lizzy. I stood motionless. My eyes were watery, but I wasn't crying. I was sad and brokenhearted.

Mr. Dye and Billy Joe rode to the big house and jumped off their horses and ran upstairs to the master bedroom. Mr. Dye ran over to the bed and screamed, "What happened!"

Mrs. Dye said, very sorrowful, "A cottonmouth snake bit him. It was under his bed."

Mr. Dye put his head down on the edge of the bed and cried. Mr. Dye asked, "Where is Dr. Johnson?"

Mrs. Dye replied, "I sent for him. He should be here soon."

William was motionless, sweating, and breathing very slowly. There was nothing anyone could do. Mr. Dye poured some water into a wash pan and soaked a rag in the water that I had brought and wiped the sweat from William. Mr. Dye put him under the covers. William was getting cold.

Mr. Dye asked, "Where is the snake?"

Mrs. Dye said, "I don't know. I guess it's still in William's room."

Mr. Dye said, "Billy Joe, get that snake out of this house."

Billy Joe left the house and went over to the barn. He got a gardener's hoe and went back into the big house. Billy Joe went into the master bedroom and screamed, "Where's the snake?"

Mr. Dye screamed, "It's in William's room."

Billy Joe went into William's room very slowly. He stood in the middle of the room and looked around. Then he looked under the table and then under the dresser. He slowly turned around. The bed was directly in front of the dresser. He stared at the bed. Slowly he bent down to look under the bed. He didn't see anything. Then he walked over to the side of the bed. He carried the hoe in his right hand like a club or hammer.

Intently at the bed, he stepped back and looked under the bed again. He saw it. An adult cottonmouth snake. He knew very well how deadly the snake was. Sweating profusely, and scared, he opened William's closet and grabbed one of William's shirts. Billy Joe slowly and cautiously walked over to the bed and extended the hoe. He held the hoe by the handle and extended it under the bed.

Without seeing the snake, he pulled the snake slowly out from under the bed until the snake was in full view. The snake tried to get back under the bed. Billy threw William's shirt over the snake. The shirt landed over the snake's head. Then Billy Joe chopped the snake with the hoe, killing it. He chopped and chopped until William's shirt was blood red and the snake was in a number of pieces. Then Billy Joe gathered all the pieces in William's shirt and took the dead snake outside, walked over to the wooded area, and threw the dead snake wrapped in William's shirt into the woods.

Dr. Johnson rode up to the big house in his carriage. Neal Henry was riding besides his carriage. Dr. Johnson quickly got out of his carriage and rushed upstairs to the master bedroom. Dr. Johnson had been into the Dyes' home many times. He had delivered all of Mrs. Dye's children. He was an elderly man with a heavy Southern dialect. Everyone was in the bedroom except Billy Joe and Neal Henry. They had returned to the stables.

Dr. Johnson asked, "How long has it been since the snake bit him?"

Mrs. Dye answered, "About two to three hours."

Dr. Johnson checked William's eyes. Then he checked his pulse. He looked at the wound and said, "It's good you got the poison out of him."

Then Dr. Johnson said, "You all can leave the room now." Everybody slowly walked out of the room except Mr. Dye.

Eppie Mae helped Mrs. Dye to her feet. Uncle Buff and Eppie Me assisted Mrs. Dye down the stairs and into the parlor room.

Mr. Dye said, "Now, Dr. Johnson, tell me the truth. How is he doing?"

Dr. Johnson said, "He's not going to make it. If you had left the poison in him, he would already be dead. The only thing you can do now is to make him comfortable. And you and your family can say your good-byes in a godly manner. I'm sorry."

Mr. Dye asked, "Is he in any pain?"

Dr. Johnson said, "No. He's in a coma. He doesn't feel anything. I'm truly sorry."

Mr. Dye closed the bedroom door and wept bitterly. Dr. Johnson hugged him as if he was his son. Dr. Johnson had also delivered Mr. Dye. He knew the family well.

Mr. Dye asked, "Is there anything you can do? And what am I going to tell Mary Kate? This is going to destroy her. We've never lost a child before. And William—he is our only son."

"I'm truly sorry," replied Dr. Johnson. "Maybe you would like me to break the news to the family."

"No," replied Mr. Dye. "I'll inform the family of the tragedy."

Mrs. Dye was sitting on the sofa crying when Annite and Kathryn walked into the parlor. Kathryn said jokingly, "The next time we go riding, I'm going to be the better rider and beat you back here to the big house."

Annite said, "Oh, no, you won't. No little girl is going to beat me riding." Annite noticed Mr. Dye crying and said, "What's wrong with Will, Daddy? What's wrong with Will?"

"Go downstairs and take your sister with you. I'm not finished talking with Dr. Johnson!" shouted Mr. Dye. Annite turned and grabbed Kathryn's hand. And they both walked out of the bedroom and went downstairs into the parlor. They sat on the sofa next to Mrs. Dye.

Mr. Dye and Dr. Johnson came down the stairs together. Mr. Dye walked Dr. Johnson to the door. Dr. Johnson handed him some medicine and said, "This will make him comfortable." Then Dr. Johnson put his hat on and left. Mr. Dye closed the door behind him slowly and went into the parlor and sat in the chair opposite his wife and daughters. Eppie Mae, Little Lizzy, and I were upstairs in the master bedroom washing William with cold water.

Mr. Dye spoke to his wife and daughters sympathetically with a great deal of sorrow in his voice. He leaned over and grabbed his wife's hands and held them and said, "William is very sick. Dr. Johnson has informed me that William isn't going to make it." Mrs. Dye fell off the sofa onto her knees into her husband's arms and wept deeply.

Annite said, "What do you mean, Daddy? What do you mean, Daddy? Will is going to be OK, right?"

Mr. Dye said, "No, dear, William is dying."

Annite and Kathryn fell off the sofa onto their knees and cried, hugging their mother and father.

"Oh, no, oh, no," sobbed Mrs. Dye.

Mr. Dye hugged his wife and daughters, comforting them in their time of sorrow. Then he said, "Let's go be with William." They all walked slowly upstairs, hugging each other. As they walked, they saw Eppie Mae, Little Lizzy, and me washing William in cold water. Mr. Dye said, "Thank you. Can you please leave us alone with William?" Eppie Mae pulled the blankets up close to William's shoulders and tucked him in bed. Then we left the room and went downstairs into the kitchen.

Mr. Dye hugged his wife and daughters, who were crying and moaning. Mrs. Dye fell to her knees and wept and prayed at the bedside. Annite and Kathryn did the same, and Mr. Dye sat in his chair in the master bedroom. Soon, William began to slowly stop breathing. Finally, he stopped. William was dead. Mr. Dye sat in the chair and placed his head in his hands and cried.

Mrs. Dye slowly stroked William's head and face. Then she kissed him. Mrs. Dye and the girls got up and left the room crying. They walked down the stairs, crying and holding on to each other. Eppie Mae was standing at the bottom of the stairs, looking sympathetically at them. Eppie Mae had tears in her eyes, and Little Lizzy and I were standing in the kitchen doorway.

Eppie Mae asked, "Is William all right?"

Mrs. Dye said sorrowfully, "William is dead."

Eppie Mae shouted, "Oh, no!" and ran into the kitchen and sat at the kitchen table crying with her head on the table with her arms folded on the table. Little Lizzy and I came and stood next to Eppie Mae and rubbed her back, comforting her. Mr. Dye and the girls sat in the parlor, crying in a state of agony and bewilderment.

It was a sorrowful day. There had never been such sorrow in the Dye family. Sorrow was in the air, and everyone in the house was crying. I slowly walked to the stair case as if drawn by an unknown force. I had my head down. My heart was broken, and my eyes were full of tears. I never had field hands die of overwork, and I wasn't troubled in my soul. But this troubled me. William was a child and innocent. I loved William in the brief time that I had known him. I knew he was a good boy.

I slowly made my way up the stairs, taking each step cautiously and slowly as if I was being moved by an unseen force. I entered the bedroom and stood at the door and looked at Mr. Dye. He was still crying. His head was still in his hands. He didn't notice me enter the room. I walked over to the bed and stood over William's body, looking compassionately at William. William looked as though he were asleep. But he was dead. His body was still warm. He had the face of an angel. I started to cry. Tears slowly ran down my cheek. I pulled back the bedspread and got into bed with William and hugged him. I gently kissed him on the jaw and said, "Come back, Willie, in the name of Jesus Christ the Nazorean." Then I squeezed William's body. I gently let him go and stood up next to the bed. I looked lovingly at his lifeless body. I reached over and grabbed his hand and squeezed it. William turned his head and looked at me. I pulled him out of the bed, and he stood up. He didn't say a word. His eyes were filled with water. Then a single tear came streaming down his cheek.

Mr. Dye was still weeping with his head in his hands. He hadn't seen or heard me, for God had caused him to be unaware of the accuracy of the facts. William and I walked over to Mr. Dye, holding hands. Mr. Dye looked up and saw William and me standing in front of him holding hands. He was shocked. He couldn't say a word. His lips were trembling. And his eyes were full of tears. He grabbed William and hugged him, squeezing him.

William said, "Daddy, I can't breathe. You're squeezing me too tight."

Mr. Dye let him go and kissed him frantically on his cheeks and head. Then he screamed, "Mary Kate, Mary Kate, Mary Kate, come quick!"

Mrs. Dye slowly got off the sofa and walked sorrowfully up the stairs. When she reached the top of the stairs, she saw William standing next to Mr. Dye, holding his hand, and me standing in the back of them. Mrs. Dye screamed, "William, William, my precious baby! My baby! Oh, God, oh, God, thank you, thank you." William ran to his mother and jumped into her outstretched arms.

Annite and Kathryn came running up the stairs to see what all the noise was. They saw William hugging his mother and his mother crying and kissing William frantically on the cheeks, face, and head. The girls paused for a second and stared. Then they ran over to William and hugged and kissed him.

William said, "Why is everybody so happy to see me? I just woke up. I was asleep."

Mrs. Dye said, "That's right, William. You were asleep and now you are awake."

Mr. Dye turned and looked at me in bewilderment. He was at a loss for words. He didn't know what had happened. He knew William was dead. He had seen many dead folks before. And he knew that William hadn't taken a breath in at least two hours. He wanted to talk to me.

I seemed just as happy as the family was. I crying in the doorway, mumbling softly to myself, "God is good. God is good. My soul proclaims the greatness of the Lord. My spirit rejoices in God my Savior. The Mighty One has done a great thing for me, and holy is his name."

Mr. Dye asked, "Mary Lou, did you see what happened?" I stood motionless and silent with tears streaming down my face.

Mrs. Dye said, "Douglas, leave the girl alone. We got our baby back." Mr. Dye walked over to where the family was hugging William and hugged his wife.

Eppie Mae said, "Is ya'll all right upstairs?" She stood at the bottom of the stairs and looked intently up the stairs to see what everyone was so excited about.

Mrs. Dye shouted, "William is all right! He's standing right here."

Eppie Mae ran up the stairs and stood in shock looking at William. She couldn't believe her eyes. She knew he had died. She knew also that I had something to do with him being well and alive. She looked at me standing in the background. I had the face of an angel. I was glowing. It was a heavenly glow. The Dye family didn't notice my appearance. Everyone was occupied with William's miraculous recovery. I walked past the family hugging William and fell into the arms of Eppie Mae.

Eppie Mae was crying and asked, "You all right, Mary Lou? It's all right. It's all right. It just wasn't his time." I didn't say a word. I just cried.

Little Lizzy had come to the bottom of the stairs and was looking up to see what all the excitement was all about. She didn't see William or the family. She saw Eppie Mae and me hugging and crying. Then she ran up the stairs anxiously to see why we were crying. Then she saw William, alive and well, being embraced by his family. Little Lizzy was speechless. She placed her hands over her mouth and said, "Oh, Jesus Lord, help us all." Little Lizzy continued to whisper, "I thought . . . I thought he . . . I thought he was dead."

No one heard her excitement except for Eppie Mae, who said, "You hush now. That boy don't know nothing about what happened to him. He thinks he's been sleeping and everybody's just happy to see him."

Mr. Dye said in a very calm voice, "Little Lizzy, go tell Billy Joe to ride over to Dr. Johnson's plantation and have him get over here as soon as he can." Little Lizzy ran down the stairs frantically and ran into the kitchen.

Mrs. Dye shouted, "Don't you run through this house, ya hear!"

Little Lizzy ran out the kitchen back door and ran over to the stables and yelled, "Neal Henry, Billy Joe! Neal Henry and Billy Joe!"

Neal Henry and Billy Joe were feeding the horses and grooming them. They both stopped and ran over to Little Lizzy, shouting, "What's wrong? What's wrong? You act like you done seen a ghost."

Little Lizzy could barely get the words out. She was mumbling, and spit was dripping from her chin and from the sides of her mouth. She was out of breath and panting something terrible. She said, grasping onto each breath, "William, William . . . he's . . . he's well. He's up talking, walking, and hugging everybody. I seen it. I sure did. He ain't dead. And Mr. Dye wants Billy Joe to ride over to Dr. Johnson's right away."

Neal Henry dropped the bucket of feed and calmly sat down on a bale of hay. He was lost speechless. He rubbed his beard and stroked his head and said, "I don't rightly know what to say. I ain't never heard of nobody getting bit by a cottonmouth that big and live. Well, Billy Joe, you go on over to fetch Dr. Johnson." Billy Joe went on Mr. Dye's fastest horse and rode him bareback and headed out for Dr. Johnson's.

Dr. Johnson had just arrived at his plantation. As he rode up to his door, he noticed Billy Joe riding a midnight-black horse as fast as he could down the long road leading to his plantation. One of Dr. Johnson's slaves was holding the reins onto his horse and buggy.

Billy Joe rode up next to Dr. Johnson's buggy and said, "Mr. Dye wants you to come right away."

Billy Joe replied, "Mr. Dye's boy is well. He's up walking around and talking. And ain't nothing seems to be wrong with him."

Dr. Johnson replied, "That's impossible. That boy was as good as dead when I left. Well, I've got to see this for myself." Dr. Johnson said, "Let that horse go. I'm going back over to the Dyes' plantation."

Billy Joe rode up. Dr. Johnson slowly made his way back down the road leading to the Dyes'. Billy Joe arrived in a full gallop and jumped off the horse. He walked the horse over to the stables and put him into a stall. Neal Henry was still in the barn. He was grooming the horses and smoking his corn pipe.

Billy Joe asked, "Why ain't you over to the big house looking at Mr. Dye's boy?"

Neal Henry replied, "You know, we done had lots of youngens die around here. On slave row, folks' youngens been bit by cottonmouth snakes, rattlesnakes, and been kicked in the head by mules. They done died in every way you can think of. And if they didn't die, they was put out in the fields to work just as soon as they was strong enough to carry a hoe or pick cotton. And the little girls, when they reached a womanly age, old Mr. Dye ran on down there and laid up with them. So, no, no, I ain't gonna go over to Mr. Dye's big house and smile and grin 'cause Mr. Dye's boy is well. I'm gon' stay right here and take care of these horses. You go smile and grin. I ain't gonna go."

Billy Joe replied, "I ain't gonna go. I just . . . I just—"

Neal Henry interrupted him forcefully, "I just nothing. You old half nigger." Billy Joe walked out the stables and walked over to the barn. He went up to the loft sat.

Neal Henry was angry. He hated Mr. Dye. He hated Mr. Dye's wife. He hated Mr. Dye's daughters, and he hated Mr. Dye's son. In Neal Henry's eyes, Mr. Dye was evil, wicked, and his offspring were the same. Neal Henry had never known anything good to come from whites. He was treated like an animal all his life. There was the horse, the cow, the pig, the nigger, and the dog. And all belong to the white man. And Neal Henry hated it. He hated all that Mr. Dye was. And he didn't understand why a just God would allow people like Mr. Dye to keep on doing evil and wicked things all their lives and grow rich off the blood of black African slaves with no bitterness in their life. On hearing that William was snake bit, Neal Henry felt a sense of relief. He felt that, finally, Mr. Dye would get some of what's due to him because of his wicked and evil ways.

Dr. Johnson rode up to the Dyes' plantation. He got out of his buggy and tied it. He knocked on the door, and Uncle Buff answered the door. Mr. Dye, Mrs. Dye, and his daughters were upstairs. They were in William's bedroom. William had eaten and went to bed. And the family was in his bedroom, comforting him. Uncle Buff informed Dr. Johnson that the family was in William's bedroom. Dr. Johnson replied, "I'll see my way to William's bedroom." Dr. Johnson walked upstairs and found his way to William's room.

He found the family standing around his bed. Dr. Johnson asked, "How long has he been asleep?"

Mr. Dye replied, "He just fell asleep."

Dr. Johnson leaned forward and called out quietly, "William, William." William woke up and smiled at Dr. Johnson. Dr. Johnson said, "I just want to ask you some questions. How do you feel?"

William said, "Good. I feel good."

Dr. Johnson put his head to William's chest and grabbed his wrist to check his pulse and heart rhythm. Then Dr. Johnson checked the snake bite on his arm. The wound was there, but it wasn't swollen. It's like two minor scratches. Dr. Johnson rose up and said, "He's fine. He's as healthy as a horse." The family and Dr. Johnson left the room and closed the door. William went back to sleep.

Dr. Johnson said, "I'd like to speak with you alone, sir." Mrs. Dye and her daughters went downstairs. Dr. Johnson said, "I don't know rightly how to explain this, but that boy should most likely be dead. I never seen or known of anyone to recover from a cottonmouth snake bite like that before. That is nothing less than a miracle. Mr. Dye, you should be on your knees thanking God, because nowhere has anyone recovered from such a serious snake bite."

Mr. Dye said, "Thank you, Dr. Johnson, for coming over. I had given up on William. Then the next things I knew, he and Mary Lou were standing in front of me holding hands. William was standing right in front of me. I didn't even see him get out of bed. I couldn't believe my eyes."

"Well, he's fine now," replied Dr. Johnson.

Dr. Johnson said, "Well, I'll best be getting on back. God bless you. Good day."

Chapter Five

Calling to Preach . . .

The days turned into weeks, and the weeks turned into months. My life seemed to be set. I was in a routine. I was a slave, a piece of property, nothing more than a pig, a horse, a dog, or any other farm animal in the sight of my owners. Yet God had called me. God had called me to minister to the nations. I didn't know how to fulfill my calling, but I knew I had a gift. I knew things I didn't know before the accident. So I waited. I waited. I did what I was told to do. I didn't complain. I worked harder than any of the other slaves. I did the work of both the slave men and the women. I was strong. I awoke early in the morning and went to bed late at night.

Soon, Mrs. Dye began to look on me with favor. Mrs. Dye noticed my willingness to work and the good work I produced. Mrs. Dye knew the niggers believed in God. Or at what the niggers believed to be what God is. And Mrs. Dye knew that every Sunday night, the niggers would get together in the barn and have a shouting and yelling time. At least that's what Mrs. Dye called it. So on this particular Sunday, nothing had changed. The niggers would get together and shout and yell and go to bed. But this Sunday night, Mrs. Dye noticed something different. She heard the voice of a girl. Usually, it was Uncle Buff who did all the so-called preaching, which he had overheard Reverend Cole preach. But this night, it was different. Mrs. Dye had never seen or heard a woman preach before. All the menfolk had done all the preaching she had heard. So upon hearing a female's voice coming from the barn, it interested Mrs. Dye. So she stood intently and slowly and cautiously walked over to the barn, and these words stood out.

"Who is the King of Glory? Who is this King of Glory? I says ya'll don't hear me. The Lord of Hosts is the King of Glory. The Lord, a mighty warrior, the Lord, mighty in battle. Yes, that's who he is. That's who he is. The Lord of Hosts is the King of Glory. A mighty warrior. Don't ya'll know that ya'll ain't alone. We got the Lord of Hosts on our side. And he says this to all ya'll and to let this be ya'll prayer. The Lord is my light and my salvation, whom do I fear? The Lord is my life's refuge, of whom am I afraid? When does evil doers come at me to eat my flesh, these my enemies and foes themselves stumble and fall."

Eppie Mae, Uncle Buff, and the rest of the slaves all shouted, "Go on now. You preach, ya hear me!"

I continued. "Though an army encamp against me, my heart does not fear. Though war be waged against me, even then do I trust. One thing I ask of the Lord's house all the days of my life, to gaze on the Lord's beauty, to visit his temple. For God will hide me in shelter in time of trouble, God will conceal me in the cover of his tent, and set me high upon a rock. Even now my head is held high above my enemies on every side! I will offer in tent sacrifices with shouts of joy. I will sing and change praise to the Lord."

Eppie Mae shouted, "Glory, glory to our God! He gone help us. Yes, Lord. Yes, Lord."

All the while, I continued to preach. "Hear my voice, Lord, when I call. Have mercy on me and answer me. Come, says my heart, seek God's face. Your face, Lord, do I seek! Do not hide your face from me. Do not repel your servant in anger. You are my help, do not cast me off. Do not forsake me, God my savior! Even if my father and mother forsake me, the Lord will take me in. Lord, show me your way. Lord, show me your way. Lead me on a level path because of my enemies. Do not abandon me to the will of my foes. Evil and lying folks have come against me. But I believe I shall enjoy the Lord's goodness in the land of the living. Wait for the Lord, take courage, be strong of heart, wait for the Lord!"

Mrs. Dye heard my preaching and was cut to the heart. She fell to her knees and started to cry. No one knew she was listening. She gathered herself and slowly made her way back to the big house. The veil was torn on Mrs. Dye's heart. She no longer thought of Eppie Mae, Uncle Buff, and the rest of the niggers as animals no more than a cow or goat. But she saw them as people. Mrs. Dye had never heard a woman preach before. And I had preached with power and conviction, being moved by the Holy Ghost. Mrs. Dye had never dreamed a woman could be so passionate and express herself so profoundly. What I said was beautiful. Every word I had spoken rang in Mrs. Dye's ears. Mrs. Dye knew she wasn't dealing with a beast anymore but people, a God-fearing people. She thought, *How could I have ever treated these people in such a cruel and harsh manner?* But she was raised to think of the nigger as such. Now her entire understanding of her perception of the Negro had changed in a matter of seconds. She felt compassion for a people whom she had never felt before. She remembered how she had beaten them, spit on them, and believed that they were a no-good-lay, good-for-nothing lot that needed to be treated as such. She went into the parlor and sat quietly looking bewildered and profoundly sad. Mrs. Dye felt she had wronged generations of slaves. She believed herself to be a good person. She thought, *How could I have treated these people so cruel?*

Eppie Mae, Uncle Buff, Little Lizzy, and I came in to the kitchen in the back door. Uncle Buff asked, "Is there anything a man could eat?"

Eppie Mae replied, "Sho' is. I made some peach ice cream. And there is plenty. Mr. Dye told me earlier that we could have some. I'll get it." Mrs. Dye came in. Uncle Buff, Little Lizzy, and I stood still and didn't say a word. Eppie Mae finally stepped forward and said, "Mr. Dye said that it would be all right if we ate some peach ice cream."

Mrs. Dye replied, "I don't care about no peach ice cream. I was there. I heard Mary Lou preach—"

Eppie Mae quickly interrupted Mrs. Dye, saying, "She didn't mean no harm. She was just talking."

Mrs. Dye stood silently glazing at Eppie Mae. Fear shook Eppie Mae. She had seen that look many times before and never with a good outcome. Mrs. Dye walked over to Eppie Mae. Eppie Mae instantly looked down at the ground and braced herself for a slap. All the slaves' eyes were looking intently at Mrs. Dye. Mrs. Dye placed her hand on Eppie Mae's cheek and gently wiped the teas away that were running down her face. Eppie Mae looked up and looked into Mrs. Dye's eyes. Mrs. Dye's eyes were full of tears. Slowly, the tears swelled in her eyes and trickled down her pink cheeks.

Mrs. Dye said, "That was amazing. I never heard anything so beautiful in my entire life." Then Mrs. Dye turned and walked out of the kitchen.

There was complete silence. Eppie Mae, Uncle Buff, Little Lizzy, and I didn't know what to say. Mrs. Dye went into the living room and slowly climbed the stairs. Eppie Mae followed as if to see where Mrs. Dye was going and if there was going to be any punishment for me. She heard Mrs. Dye's bedroom door close. Eppie Mae went back into the kitchen. The others were still standing in the middle of the kitchen as if in shock.

Uncle Buff said, "Well, I guess I don't really wants no peach ice cream. I'm going to bed." He slowly walked down the back hall to his room. Eppie Mae followed Uncle Buff without saying a word. They moved slowly and cautiously, as if expecting to be beaten or punished. Their mood was sorrowful. Their secret was out. Mrs. Dye had heard me. Little Lizzy and I went the back stairs and went to bed.

I prayed, "No weapon formed against me shall prosper. Every tongue speaks evil against me shall be condemned. This is the heritage of the servants of the Lord, and their righteousness is from me, says the Lord." Then I climbed into bed and got under the covers. Soon, Little Lizzy and I were asleep.

I was awoken from my sleep by the sound of a man's voice. I didn't know who it was. I kept on hearing someone saying, "Get up, get up, get up." Mr. Dye was standing over me with his privates in his hand.

I awoke and cringed into a corner in the bed. I started to cry. I whispered, "Touch not my anointed and do my prophets no harm." Tears were streaming down my face.

Little Lizzy awoke and stood next to my bed. Little Lizzy said, "Mr. Dye, I'll go. I'm ready."

Mr. Dye turned and grabbed Little Lizzy by the arm and pulled her out of the room and dragged her down the stairs. Little Lizzy was silent. She knew where she was going. She had been there many times before. Mr. Dye led her to the barn. She was pulling away. Mr. Dye yelled, "Come on here!" He smelled like whiskey. She heard the voices of men talking and laughing coming from the barn. In the barn, she saw the usual, Reverend Cole, Master Burke, and the others.

Little Lizzy was only wearing a white gown. It was a summer night, but it was cool. Little Lizzy was sweating and afraid. Mr. Dye wasn't a caring man, nor did he have any compassion for the nigger. And he showed his contempt in his actions. He slung Little Lizzy into the middle of the barn. She fell onto her knees. She began to weep. She stood up and dried her eyes and said, "Well, I'm here. Who first?" Then she walked over to the hay pile and took off her gown.

Mr. Dye said, "Well, here she is. Ya'll have some fun. Go on the bitch."

Earnest said, "Well, I might as well. It has to be done." He went over to the hay pile where she was standing and pulled her into a corner of the barn where there wasn't any light. Master Earnest had his way with Little Lizzy. She was silent.

Reverend Cole, Mr. Dye, and Mr. Burke stood over by the hay wagon talking and sipping on whiskey. Reverend Cole said, "You know, it's our duty to put as much good white blood into as many nigger women as possible. Burke, you wasn't here the other day. I explained the importance and the responsibility for the white man to cultivate the nigger. Yes, we need many shades of niggers. You see, the nigger don't trust themselves. The dark nigger don't trust the light nigger. And the light nigger don't trust the dark nigger. And the ones in the middle, the middle-shaded niggers, are just as good as the field hand. And this is how we keep control over the nigger. We must keep the nigger confused, dumb, uneducated, and stupid."

"Yes, sir. The nigger is ours, boys. That nigger will depend on us for everything for hundreds of years. The nigger is only one step higher than the ape. And the more we put some good white blood into these nigger bitches, the better worker we'll produce. So, boys, we got a duty to do tonight. And if we are lucky, she'll get pregnant. And that's more money."

"Jonathan Burke, you sly dog. Your wife is pregnant!" yelled Mr. Dye.

"I didn't know that," replied Reverend Cole.

"Yes, sir. She should be giving birth any day now," replied Mr. Burke.

"So what you gonna name this one?" replied Mr. Dye.

"I don't know. You boys know I don't concern myself with naming no youngens," replied Mr. Burke.

"Earnest, Earnest, you come on now, boy. I'm next," said Mr. Burke.

"Now, you boys just take your time," replied Reverend Cole. "We're going to do a good job."

"So where is that new nigger of yours?" asked Mr. Burke. "The niggers think she got some kind of special powers. And I'm anxious to put some of this good white blood into those special powers," replied Mr. Burke.

"She's in the house," replied Mr. Dye.

"I was under the impression that you was going to bring Mary Lou instead of Lizzy. Lizzy just may be incapable of childbearing. Because as much good, fine white blood we done put in her, she should have brought forth a litter by now," replied Reverend Cole.

"Mary Lou's time is coming. That's for a special night," replied Mr. Dye.

Earnest came walking toward the other men. His shirt was unbuttoned, and he was carrying his black jacket under his arm. Sweat was dripping from his forehead, and he was out of breath.

"Earnest, it's about time!" yelled Mr. Burke.

"I believes she's starting to enjoy it some. She used to be full of fight. She's done stopped all the crying. She just lays there now," replied Mr. White.

"Yes, sir. I remembers when I had to give her a few good slaps. You know, it's just like breaking a good old stubborn mare," replied Mr. Burke.

"Go on, man, and get to it. I can't be out in this barn all night," Mr. Dye said.

"That's good. Soon, everybody will be able to ride this young mare," Reverend Cole interjected. "And that's profitable to us all. The more off-spring we can breed, the more money for us all."

"Douglas, you seem a bit distracted tonight. Now, Douglas, you very well know the purpose of these actions. We all are going to deposit our seed into the wench. And that's the best way. That way, when she does get pregnant, none of us will be the worst," replied Reverend Cole.

"And we all have these high yellow niggers on our plantation, and they are usually kept in the house around our wives and children. So let's get to it," interjected Mr. Burke.

"Douglas, you're next. I insist," replied Reverend Cole.

"Fine."

Mr. Dye went on over to the spot in the barn where Little Lizzy was lying. It was dark, and he didn't see her at first glance. She was lying in the corning of the barn holding her knees to her chest. She was rocking back and forth, sobbing. He sat on the hay next to her and said, "You know why we does this. It's our duty to keep the colors of the niggers in all different shades. You know I ain't never let nobody hurt you. And I ain't gonna hurt you none either. But it has to be done. So come on now. Get to it."

Little Lizzy rolled over and cried. She put her back toward him. She was broken. She said, "Daddy, why you doing this to me?"

Mr. Dye said, "'Cause you a nigger. And this is what happens to all niggers."

"But I'm your daughter," said Little Lizzy.

"That don't matter none. You still a nigger girl. And this is what got to be done," replied Mr. Dye.

Reverend Cole was standing off in the distance listening to their conversation. He didn't trust Mr. Dye. He knew Mr. Dye cared for Little Lizzy. But to Reverend Cole, Little Lizzy was not more than a cow or farm animal that needed to be pregnant to make a profit. Reverend Cole yelled, "Douglas, you take care of your business. Because I need to take care of my own business. You hear me?" Mr. Dye finished with Little Lizzy. Then Reverend Cole completed their cycle.

Early the next morning, I awoke and ran down the back kitchen stairs. I didn't see Little Lizzy. So I kept on running and ran out of the back kitchen door and ran over to the barn. Little Lizzy was lying in a corner of the barn unconscious. I grabbed Little Lizzy and held her. I started to cry. I whispered, "It's gonna be all right. It's gonna be all right." I rocked Little Lizzy back and forth in my arms, crying.

Little Lizzy was dirty. She looked like she had been rolling in mud naked. Her nightgown was lying next to her. I shook her, trying to wake her. She awoke and started to cry. I said, "Come on. I'm going to get you all cleaned up. I'm gonna take good care of you."

Little Lizzy said, "It's OK. I'm all right. Help me up and give me that gown. I just need to gather myself some." I helped her put on her nightgown and helped her to her feet. I held on to her and helped her walk to an empty stall. Little Lizzy stood leaning against the railings. She said, "Go get me a bucket of water, some soap, and my clothes." I ran to the big house and got the things she asked for. Little Lizzy washed herself from head to toe using the water I had gotten. I ran back and forth filling buckets of water for Little Lizzy to use. After Little Lizzy had finished cleaning and drying herself, she put on her clothes and tied a rag around her head. "Now I'm ready to get back to work."

I was standing looking confused. I wanted to say "I'm sorry." I wanted the men who did that to her friend to die. I felt hurt and ashamed. I felt that it had happened to me. I had heard of the things slave masters did to the womenfolk, but I had never seen. Now, I was afraid. I thought, *How could God let this happen to my friend?* And I knew it was Mr. Dye who had done this to Little Lizzy. Little Lizzy seemed to be unaffected by what had happened. And I was puzzled and confused why Little Lizzy wasn't angry and hurt by last night's events.

I asked, "How could you act like ain't nothing done happened to you?"

Little Lizzy replied, "There ain't nothing I can do. Everybody knows what Mr. Dye and his friends do. They have been doing it for years. They goes to each other's plantation and gets the slave womenfolk with child. You know that old no-good Reverend Cole is one relations to that old slave maker Willie Lynch. And Mr. Dye and all the white folks around these parts listen real close to what Reverend Cole says when it comes to the Negroes around here. It's been like that as long as I can remember."

"I'm scared," I said. "What if they come for me?"

"Well, if they comes for you, all I can say is to don't fight. If you fight, they'll beat you something awful. I know. I used to fight. But I just can't take beatings. I heard they beat one of Master White's slave girls to death because she was fighting so."

A tear slowly ran down my cheek. I walked over to Little Lizzy and hugged her. Little Lizzy was stunned. Her heart was broken. She began to cry. Soon, we both were passionately crying. We fell to our knees and continued crying.

Billy Joe came into the barn to finish his daily work. As he walked past the stall, he heard the crying and looked inside. He said, "What ya'll crying so? It's too early in the morning for all this here crying and such. Ya'll act like somebody done got a beaten this morning or somebody done passed away. So what's wrong?"

"Nothing," replied Little Lizzy.

"Come on, let's get back to the big house," I replied. We got up and ran to the big house, holding hands as if nothing had happened.

I went upstairs and changed clothes. Little Lizzy had begun her work, and she behaved as if nothing had happened. But I was cut to the heart. I was in mourning for Little Lizzy as if she had died. I came down the stairs and began my daily work as usual. But it wasn't usual. I'd seen and felt the terrors of this awful life I was living. Something had to change. This wasn't right. Slavery wasn't right. What happened to Little Lizzy wasn't right. As Little Lizzy had been abused, I knew that any one of them could be abused in the same way or much, much worse.

I prayed, "Dear Lord, God of heaven and earth. Father, you know the plight of the Negro. You know all the things. Lord, we need you. Help us, oh, Lord. Help us, oh, Lord. In you, Lord, I take refuge let me never be put to shame. In your justice deliver me. Incline your ear to me. Make haste to rescue me! Be my rock of refuge, a stronghold to save me. You are my rock and fortress. For your name's sake, lead and guide me. Free me from the net they have set for me, for you are my refuge. I will rejoice and be glad in your love. Once you have seen my misery, observed my distress, you will not abandon me into enemy hands but will set my feet in a free and open space."

She meditated on the words of her prayer over and over again. Then fear left her. Grace, peace, and love of Jesus Christ covered her like a blanket. She did her tasks without worry or dread. I prayed again, "Lord, give me a word for my friend. Lord, just a word from you. Father, my friend needs you. Father, she is good. Shouldn't no one be treated like that. Jesus, what can I do? Jesus, what can I say?"

We went over to the barn to milk the cows. We milked the cows daily. But this day was unusual. We knew what had happened in the barn. On the way to the barn, we were silent. We dreaded the barn. That old red barn had become a place of avoidance. Little Lizzy thought she could keep it unknown to me what had happened in the barn. Now I knew Little Lizzy's secret. Little Lizzy believed and felt that's how things were supposed to be. She had known nothing else. We sat down and milked the cows in silence.

After we filled a couple of buckets of milk, I broke the silence. I said, "It ain't your fault."

Little Lizzy shouted, "What you talking about!"

I said, "You know, what happened last night."

"I just slept in the barn, that's all."

I said, "It's not your fault. No one has the right to treat people like that. You know something? You are a child of God, and God loves you. Yes, he does. And God don't like ugly. Jesus gonna help us. Because he loves you. He died for you. It's not your fault. They were wrong. And folks can't just do God's children an old way and think God ain't gonna fight for them. God knows they're wrong."

Little Lizzy leaned over and hugged me and cried. She said, "I'm scared. I can't do nothing. They hurt me."

I held on to Little Lizzy and cried in a loud voice, "It's not your fault. You a child of God. Oh, help us, Lord. Oh, help us, Lord."

Chapter Six

The Stigmata

Almost a week had passed since Little Lizzy was abused by the slave owners. Sunday evening was here. All the work was completed, and the slaves
headed over to the barn for church. Once in the barn, everyone was silent.
Usually, Sunday night meeting was a joyful time. But everyone knew what
happened to Little Lizzy. And it was like a heavy weight was on the heads
of each of them. Uncle Buff, who was usually the leader, sat quietly. In fact,
everyone sat quietly. Then Eppie Mae sang. She began in a low whisper.
"Holy God, we praise thy name! Lord of all, we bow before thee!"

As Eppie Mae whispered the first verse, the other slaves joined in and
sang. "All on earth thy rule acclaim. All in heaven above adore thee."

I stood up and shouted, "Praise his holy name! Let everything that
has breath praise his holy name. Sing praises. Sing praises in good time and
in bad time." Soon, the barn rang out with the praises of the Lord. As they
sang the Lord's praises, the barn seemed to be filled with a holy cloud.

Uncle Buff shouted, "I feel the Lord's presence! That's right. Sing of
the Lord's goodness while you still have breath in your body."

While they were singing the Lord's praises, the barn door opened,
and Mrs. Dye walked in. Everyone stopped singing and stared at Mrs. Dye
as if they had done something wrong. Mrs. Dye walked over and sat next
to Eppie Mae and began to sing, "Holy God, we praise thy name." After she
began singing, the slaves started to sing again. Soon, everyone was singing.

Eppie Mae continued on to the next song. "Soon, and very soon,
we are going to see the King. Soon, and very soon, we are going to see the
King." The Lord's presence was with them. It was like a great cloud had
entered the barn.

I went into the center of the barn and said, "Close your eyes. Feel the Lord's presence. Be still and know that this is God." I began to speak to them in a low voice, almost a whisper. Eppie Mae hummed "He Is Lord." I said, "I saw the Lord seated on a high and lofty throne, with the train on his garment filling the temple. Seraphim were stationed above. Each of them had six wings, with two they veiled their faces. Each of them had six wings, with two they veiled their faces, with two they veiled their feet, and with two they hovered aloft."

They sang, "Holy, holy, holy is the Lord of Hosts!" They cried one to the other. "All the earth is filled with his glory!"

At the sound of that cry, the frame of the door shook, and the house was filled with smoke.

"Holy, holy, holy is the Lord God almighty, who was and who is, and who is to come."

I cried in a loud voice, "Worthy is the Lamb. Worthy is the Lamb that was slain to receive power and riches, wisdom and strength, honor and glory and blessing. To the one who sits on the throne and unto the Lamb be blessing and honor, glory and might forever and ever." As I cried unto the Lord, I raised my hands. I didn't notice. I cried louder, "Worthy is the Lamb. Worthy is the Lamb that was slain to receive power and riches, wisdom and strength, honor and glory and blessing. Worthy is the Lamb."

Soon, there was a constant flow of blood running down my arm. But, still, no one noticed. The barn was dimly lit. I was seemingly dripping sweat. But it wasn't sweat. There was blood running down my forehead. My feet were also bleeding. I cried louder, "Worthy is the Lamb. Worthy is the Lamb. Worthy is the Lamb that was slain to receive power and riches, wisdom and strength, honor and glory and blessing."

While I was worshipping the Lord, Neal Henry opened his eyes and looked at me. I was swaying back and forth, seemingly in a trance, crying out, "Worthy is the Lamb. Worthy is the Lamb." Tears were streaming down my face mixed with blood from my head. Neal Henry walked over to me and grabbed my outstretched arms. I continued to sway back and forth, crying out, "Worthy is the Lamb. Worthy is the Lamb. Holy, Holy, Holy is the Lamb."

Neal Henry looked at one of his hands and noticed it was blood. Everyone in the barn stopped praying and praising the Lord and stared at me in shock. Neal Henry picked me up and carried me into the big house. Everyone in the barn ran behind Neal Henry, hoping to see what had happened to me. He took me upstairs to my room and laid me on the bed.

Mrs. Dye came into the room and lifted her hand up and saw a hole in the center. Blood was flowing from the hole. Mrs. Dye ripped part of her dress and wrapped her hand to stop the blood flow. She lifted the other hand and saw another open hole in the other hand. She tore another piece of her dress and wrapped the wound. Mrs. Dye was stunned. She had never seen nothing like it before, and she didn't know what to make of it. She yelled, "Get me some clean water!"

Little Lizzy ran down the stairs and brought a bucket of clean water to Mrs. Dye. Mrs. Dye looked at my dress and noticed it was wet on the right side under my arm. She rubbed it with her hand. It was blood. She frantically took my dress off and stripped me down nude from the waist up. There was a deep cut under my arm. Blood and water flowed from the wound. I was unconscious. And I seemingly wasn't in any pain or discomfort. But I was sweating and breathing very heavily. Mrs. Dye took a rag and dipped it in water and slowly cleaned the blood from my forehead. I slowly opened my eyes. I tried to sit up, but Mrs. Dye said, "No, Babe. You better be still."

I lay back down and said, "I'm all right. These are the wounds of Jesus. I offer my body as a living sacrifice, holy and pleasing to God. And I guess God saw and he's just showing us his power and might."

Mrs. Dye was stunned. She was speechless. She leaned over me and held my hand and kissed it. Then she laid her head on my chest and cried. Eppie Mae and Little Lizzy bent down on both knees behind Mrs. Dye and prayed. Neal Henry, Billy Joe, and Uncle Buff were standing at the door, seemingly in a trance, motionless and wide eyed. After a brief pause, they all bent on both knees and prayed.

I said, "This ain't for me. It's all for you all. Jesus wants you all to see his suffering. He went to the cross for us. He loves us."

Mrs. Dye lifted her head. Tears were running down her cheeks, and blood smeared over her face. "I'm sorry, Mary Lou. I'm so sorry. I treated you all so awful."

I replied, "Jesus forgave you before you were born. He knows. You just have to accept. And you have." She laid her head onto my chest and wept bitterly.

Eppie Mae stood up and helped Mrs. Dye to her feet. Her clothes were bloody, and her hands and face were smeared with blood. "Let's get you cleaned up. We don't want Mr. Dye seeing you like this here." Eppie Mae escorted Mrs. Dye to her bedroom.

Little Lizzy went over to me and began to wash blood off me. I got off the bed and stood up. My body was covered with blood. I bent down and got a rag and began washing the blood off. I wasn't afraid. I was filled with the Holy Spirit. I looked like an angel.

I asked, "How is Mrs. Dye?"

Little Lizzy said, "She is a little broken up. We ain't never seen nothing like this before. I guess we all kind of afraid. You look a little scary to me."

I said, "Don't you all worry none. Jesus is showing you all his wounds. He wants you all to know that he freely, willingly, lovingly gave all of himself for us, for everybody who believes in the son of man."

Eppie Mae came into the room where I was. She said, "Well, Mrs. Dye is in her bed sleeping. The presence of God is here. And when God is with us, he comes to set things right. Yes, he does. I knows it." She went over to me and began to wash the blood off of me along with Little Lizzy.

Eppie Mae said, "Girl, you sure something special. We ain't never seen or heard about the wounds of Jesus Christ getting on anybody before. Did it hurt?"

"No, ma'am. I didn't feel nothing. And I still don't feel nothing. I just feel the warm blood running down my arms and face."

"Well, it's about stopped now. But the wounds are still in your hands, feet and side. But it ain't bleeding like it was. We just about thought you was going to bleed to death," said Eppie Mae.

Eppie Mae looked around and noticed Neal Henry, Uncle Buff, and Billy Joe still on their knees praying. Their hands were bowed. They didn't look up to see me naked from the waist up. They kept their heads bowed as if afraid to look at me. Uncle Buff spoke. "Is it all right for us to go now? We don't wants to be here for so long."

I said, "It's good, for you all stayed and prayed. It's for you that Jesus gave me his wounds."

All the while I spoke, they kept their heads bowed. After I finished speaking, Neal Henry, Uncle Buff, and Billy Joe went backward on their knees out the door. Never once did they look up. When they got clearly out of view of me, they stood up and walked slowly down the stairs. Uncle Buff went to his bedroom in the big house. Neal Henry and Billy Joe walked slowly out of the back door and went to their shack. They were all silent, mostly from shock at what had happened. Something great had happened. Something beautiful had happened. Something wonderful had happened. Something amazing had happened. They knew it.

After I was all cleaned up, Eppie Mae and Little Lizzy went to bed. It had been a very tiring day. They were spiritually exhausted. My hands and feet were bandaged. The wounds on my side and around my head seemed to vanish, which made Eppie Mae and Little Lizzy doubtful.

The next day was just like any other. The slaves did their work as usual. I did all of my work with my hands and feet bandaged. The bandages were wrapped tightly around the palms of my hands. The bleeding had stopped, and there were just red spots in the center of my hands. No one noticed my feet because the house slaves wore shoes.

When Mrs. Dye saw me, she asked, "Are you all right? I never seen anything like that in all my natural born days. And I just wanted to let you know that I haven't told anyone. And that includes my husband, Mr. Dye. I just don't know how he would respond to something like that. So if he asks about your hands, I'll tell him that you grabbed a hot pot and burned both hands. He's less understanding than I am."

I said very politely, "Yes, ma'am."

"And, Mary Lou, I don't want this getting around to all the slaves. I certainly don't want a circus around here. And I don't want doctors and such taking you away. That's been on my heart. So nobody says nothing. And I'll talk to the rest."

Mary Lou said politely, "Yes, ma'am."

Then Mrs. Dye went to the back door and rang the dinner bell. All the house slaves came to the back door of the big house. Mrs. Dye said, "Now, all ya'll know what happened last night. We don't have to talk about it. It's best not to tell no one. And I don't want you to talk among yourselves about it. Do I make myself absolutely clear? This is for Mary Lou's best interest. We don't want her being took away from here, now, do we?" The slaves all said yes. The slaves walked away with their heads bowed down as if depressed for not being able to tell all the other slaves on slave row about me.

Mrs. Dye went back into the house and told me, "I wants you to keep out of sight of Mr. Dye until you are healed up. And I want you to have prayer every night in the barn. I believe God wants you to pray for us and teach us how to pray. Can you do that, Mary Lou?"

I responded, "Yes, ma'am, I can do that."

It was a beautiful summer night. The moon was full, and there was a gentle breeze coming from the west. There was a peace or calm in the air.

And the calmness seemed to be in every breeze, every movement; the trees and brush swayed in perfect poetry. The night was right for preaching.

Word has spread among the house slaves that Mrs. Dye enjoyed my preaching and she wanted me to have a prayer meeting among the slaves every day. When I entered the barn, the house slaves were already there. I went and sat next to Eppie Mae. When I sat down, Eppie Mae put her hand on my knee and said, "We here for prayer meeting, and you're leading the prayer meeting. Well," said Eppie Mae, "you better pray about it."

I stood up and turned around. Then I knelt on both knees and prayed. "Dear Jesus, teach me how to pray with everybody here." As I stood up and turned around, Mrs. Dye entered the barn. She brought William, Annite, and Kathryn. Mrs. Dye walked rigidly as if she was leading an army troop into battle. Her children followed her like they were soldiers. Mrs. Dye sat away from the slaves on the bales of hay. Her children sat next to her. They all directed their attention to me.

I said in a whisper, "I ain't a good singer. But we gonna start this here prayer meeting with a song." I sang, "To him who sits on the throne, and unto the Lamb. To him who sits on the throne, and unto the Lamb. To him who sits on the throne, and unto the Lamb. Be blessing and power forever." They all stood and sang the song that I sang. The barn was filled with praise and worship unto Jesus the Lamb of God. I said, "Sing with all your hearts onto Jesus. Lift your hearts unto the Lord." I continued. "For he is worthy. For he is worthy. Oh, come, let us worship and bow down. Let us kneel before the Lord our Maker."

As they sang, a peace entered the barn. They were neither slave nor master, for the presence of the Lord had entered the barn. All was calm. The animals didn't make a sound or an abrupt movement. They all continued the song. Then I said, "Be still and know that he is God." The song stopped. I whispered, "Lift your arms above your heads, for the Lord is here." I raised my hands above my head, and the bandages were bright red. Blood slowly ran down my forearms and dripped to the ground. She sang,

"Hal-le-lu-jah, Hal-le-lu-jah, Hal-le-lu-jah, Thank you, Lord." Everyone in the barn repeated the song exactly the way I sang it. Tears slowly welled up in every eye in the barn. They began to sway back and forth, singing, "Hal-le-lu-jah."

I took off the bandages. There were holes in both of my hands. I said in a loud voice, "These are the wounds Christ our Lord and King. And I am wounded for your benefit. So you can see and know that Jesus was born, lived, suffered, and died for all of us. The slave and free. The white people and the Negro people. He gave his life freely for all mankind. Did you know, Jesus the Christ could have called legions of angels at his death? But he didn't. He was obedient unto death. Come, all of you. Come, come and see the wounds of Jesus Christ. Put your hands in them. Touch and see what Jesus is revealing to you."

Mrs. Dye stood up and took William by the hand and slowly walked over to where I was standing. William was reluctant. He pulled back. But the more he pulled back, the more Mrs. Dye pulled on his arm. Annite and Kathryn slowly followed their mother.

Neal Henry stood, and the other slaves all slowly followed him over to me, except Little Lizzy. She stood and cried profusely. Then she covered her face and ran out to the barn. Everyone thought that she was so overwhelmed with joy that she just couldn't control herself.

When everyone reached me, all formed a circle around me. They were afraid to touch me and stood aloof. I extended my hands. I said, "Look and touch."

Uncle Buff slowly extended his hand and grabbed me by the wrist. He took hold of me with a firm hold. He pulled me toward him. He seemed to take charge of me. I didn't resist. I was like clay in his hands. He held my hands close to his face, peering into the wounds, perplexed. Eppie Mae gently put her right hand on my shoulder. Then all the others came close and stared intently at me.

Mrs. Dye extended her hand and held on to my hand along with Neal Henry. Blood slowly dripped to the ground. Neal Henry asked, "Does it hurt you any, Babe?"

"No, sir."

Then Neal Henry did the unexpected. He took my hand gently from Mrs. Dye. He held my hand in both of his enormously large hands. Then he gently put his pointer finger into the open hole in my hand. I shirked as he put his finger slowly into the hole. He pushed harder, deeper into the hole. He pushed his finger completely through the hole in my hand. My eyes were wide as silver dollars. I was just as astonished as all who watched. Blood flowed from the wound onto Neal Henry's hand. Neal Henry took his hand out of the wound and said, "It's all the way through the hand." Then he took the other hand and did the same. He said, "It's through this one too." He wasn't afraid anymore, nor were any of the others who saw. Fear had left. There was an atmosphere of acceptance. The room was filled with peace. There was a calmness there like they had never felt before.

Everyone slowly began to touch my hands and inserted their finger into the wound. I stood perfectly still. Annite and Kathryn each held on to my hands and inserted their finger. Afterward, they looked at their hands and fingers, and they were covered with blood. Mrs. Dye held on to my elbow with her right hand, and with the left hand, she inserted her pointer finger into the hole from the back to front. Then she slowly leaned over and kissed me on the cheek and hugged me.

William stood by aloof. Then he slowly walked and extended his hand. I extended my hand and grabbed William's hand. I leaned forward and took a hold of William's hand. I extended his pointer finger and placed it into the hole. William stood perfectly still. He stared straight into my eyes. He slowly looked at his finger go slowly into my hand. His hand was bloody, but he didn't care. He didn't understand. He was compelled to touch and see.

I slowly smiled. They didn't recognize that I bathed in inexpressible joy. My face was the face of an angel, for the presence of the Lord was upon me. Never in my short lifetime had I ever felt such joy and peace. I raised both hands over my head and shouted, "Hal-le-lu-jah, Hal-le-lu-jah, for the Lord God Almighty reigns, Hal-le-lu-jah, Hal-le-lu-jah, for the Lord God Almighty reigns!" as I fell to my knees. I continued to praise God, shouting, "Holy, holy are you, Lord God Almighty. Worthy is Lamb. Worthy is Lamb."

Everyone in the barn fell to their knees as someone had pushed them down. Their knees buckled as if it was the natural thing to do. They raised their hand also and shouted along with me, "Hal-le-lu-jah, Hal-le-lu-jah, for the Lord God Almighty reigns!" They repeated every word I said. The barn was filled with praises of the word I said. The barn was filled with praises unto the Jesus the Lamb of God. This went on for over an hour. Everyone was sweating profusely. There were sweat, blood, and tears running down my face. Everyone was still on their knees. And I said slowly and calmly, "The Lord has heard and seen our cry. He knows what you desire. Ask the Lord for what you need, and if it's according to his will, it will be done."

I stood up and walked out of the barn and walked to the big house. Everyone in the barn was still on their knees praying. No one noticed me leave. When I entered the big house, I saw Little Lizzy washing dishes. I asked, "Why didn't you stay in the barn?" Little Lizzy didn't say a word. She just kept on washing dishes. She was anxious, nervous, and annoyed. I whispered, "There is nothing to be ashamed of. You haven't done anything wrong. It was never your fault what happened to you."

Little Lizzy said, "I just wanted to get my work done. I'm OK. I just couldn't stay. Maybe I'll stay next time."

Uncle Buff and Eppie Mae entered the big house kitchen and stood at the kitchen door. Uncle Buff said, "Babe, we didn't know what happened to you. One minute we were praying, and then you were gone. Girl, you had us worried for a spell."

Mrs. Dye and the children soon followed behind and entered the kitchen door. Mrs. Dye was out of breath. She gasped for a breath of air, saying, "You all say something before you decide to end pray."

I said, "Yes, ma'am. I'm sorry. I just wasn't thinking."

"And, Mary Lou, I just want you to know that you are a very special person. I never met anyone like you. God is using you in a very powerful way," replied Mrs. Dye.

"Thank you," I said. "But it's not me. It's Jesus working in me to help folks see things better. I don't know why Jesus chose me."

Mrs. Dye stepped toward me and hugged me. Her children also came over and hugged me as well. Tears slowly ran down Annite's and Kathryn's cheeks. William just held on to his mother's dress and hugged her. Mrs. Dye kissed me on the cheek and whispered, "Thank you."

Annite and Kathryn also kissed me on both cheeks and said, "Thank you."

Uncle Buff said, "Well, everything is all right. If it's OK, I'm going to bed."

Mrs. Dye replied, "It's late. We all had a long day. Everybody, go straight to bed. No more work tonight." Everyone quietly went in three different directions and retired for the night.

Chapter Seven

Jonathan Burke's Plantation

The next day, early in the morning, Uncle Buff screamed at me and Little Lizzy, "Get up, you all, and get up and pack a change of clothes." The girls didn't know what to pack or get together since they had never packed anything before. They both put a head rag and a dress in a rag that they use to wash up with. They put on their clothes and went downstairs and sat at the kitchen table. The sun still had not risen. Eppie Mae had cooked breakfast for them. She cooked bacon and eggs, with a glass of milk.

Little Lizzy asked, "What's we supposed to be doing?"

Uncle Buff said, "Well, I was told to get you dressed, fed, and ready for travel. But I believes that you all are going over to Master Burke's plantation. I heard from the grapevine that the Master Burke needs some extra workers because of the cotton picking season done started. But you all shouldn't worry none. Mrs. Burke done had a baby. And Mr. Burke wants you two to help out some with Mrs. Burke and the baby and the cooking and cleaning. It seems Mrs. Burke don't want none of her own niggers around. She scared of them. That's all I know." The girls finished eating and sat quietly at the table.

At sunrise, a coach pulled to the front of Mr. Dye's big house. Mr. Burke's driver Eli drove the coach. He was alone. Eli was a short slave. He didn't smile or talk much. He seemed to not care or notice anything. He was considered a good nigger by Mr. Burke. And Mr. Burke trusted Eli not to talk to anyone or run away. Eli stepped off the coach and knocked on the front door of the big house.

Uncle Buff opened the door and said, "Eli, how you been?"

Eli looked intently at Uncle Buff with compassion and said, "Fine."

Uncle Buff said, "You must be here to pick up the girls."

Eli replied, "That's right. I'm here for Mary Lou and Little Lizzy. I guess Little Lizzy ain't so little anymore."

Uncle Buff replied, "Well, you go around to the kitchen door and I'll send the girls out." He closed the front door and walked through the house into the kitchen. The girls were sitting there looking bewildered. A few moments later, a short older dark slave stood at the back kitchen door. He didn't say anything. He just peeped through the kitchen door.

Eppie Mae noticed Eli peeping through the door and said softly, "Eli, you come on in here." Eli opened the door and slowly walked into the kitchen. Eppie Mae said, "This here is Mary Lou. She's something. So you be sure to take good care of Mary Lou. Everybody calls her Babe. And you remember Little Lizzy."

Eli replied, "Yes, I do. The last time I saw her, she was knee high to a chicken. She sure has grown. She's a young lady. And she is pretty as can be." Uncle Buff just stood at the doorway and smiled.

Then Eppie Mae said, "Why didn't you tell me Eli was here? I could have fixed him something to eat."

Uncle Buff replied, "He just got here."

"Still, you should have said something. Eli, you just sit right down. I'm gonna cook you something."

"No, I don't want to be any trouble. And, besides, I have to get right back right away."

"Well, you take some of these buttermilk biscuits with you," replied Eppie Mae.

Eli said, "Well, Eppie Mae, you still the best cook in these parts. A man would have to be crazy not to take some of your famous buttermilk biscuits." Eppie Mae went into the oven and took out eight large biscuits. She wrapped them in a white clean rag and put them in a basket and

handed it to Eli. Eli said, "Thank you. I'm gonna share these with the girls."
Eli walked out the kitchen back door.

Uncle Buff shouted, "Mary Lou and Little Lizzy, you all go with Eli.
And take care of each other."

Eppie Mae hurried to the girls and hugged them and said, "Both of
you come back safe. It's going to be just fine. Just keep you mind on Jesus."
We just waved good-bye and walked out the kitchen back door.

Eli had gotten onto the coach and took hold of the reins. Little Lizzy
and I climbed onto the coach and sat upright and proper. Eli whispered,
"Come on. Let's go." The coach jerked forward, and they headed off.

It was a long journey to Master Burke's plantation. And it was still
dark when they left. Along the way, we talked. As the sun began to rise,
we noticed its bright reddish-orange color and marveled at the wonders of
God. I said, "Look at that. What a pretty sight. Our God is wonderful. He
makes the sun rise and the sun set. Can you imagine the power, the glory,
the honor, the praise due to our God?"

Little Lizzy just sat back and said, "No. I just see the sun rise. And I
see the sun rise almost every day. But sometimes I wonder where it comes
from. And who makes it rise and set every day. But I thinks that those
things are too much for me to worry about. I can't do nothing about the
sun rising or setting. But it is pretty, though. Mary Lou, you see God in
everything. When I look at the sun, I just see the sun. But you think about
God and Jesus."

"Well, that's who made the sun, the stars, and the moon, and everything else," I replied.

Eli didn't say a word. He ignored us and drove the coach. He seemed
to be in deep thought or preoccupied.

We slowly pushed forward toward the Burkes' plantation. Time
seemed to drag. As the sun rose, it got hotter and hotter. It seemed like the
road we were on went on forever in a straight line, just heat and the hot sun

beaming down. As we continued, we came upon a lake. Eli stopped. Eli got out of the coach and asked us if we wanted to stretch a bit. We jumped out of the coach and went and stood barefoot in the water. Eli went and sat under a shade tree next to the river and opened the bundle of buttermilk biscuits. He shouted, "If you all wants some of these biscuits, come on and get some!" We ran over. He handed us two biscuits each. We sat under the tree next to him and ate our biscuits. Eli said, "That Eppie Mae, she sure can cook. This here trip was worth the ride just to get some of Eppie Mae's famous biscuits."

Little Lizzy replied, "I know how to cook biscuits. Eppie Mae showed me."

"Can't nobody cook buttermilk biscuits like Eppie Mae," replied Eli.

Eli stood up and walked over to the coach. He unhitched the horses. He led them over to the water and stood next to them. After the horses were refreshed, he hitched them up and climbed in. This was the most fun we had ever had. On this day, we weren't slaves. We didn't feel like slaves. We felt a freedom we had never known before. We could run and play. We could laugh and joke. Everything we said or did was funny. Eli just watched us. He knew the feeling of freedom. And he didn't want to take it from us. But he knows that we couldn't come to the Burkes' plantation like we were. He knew Master Burke would whip us until we passed out if we came to his place laughing and playing.

As we were riding back on the trail, Eli said very sternly, "Both of you gonna have to stop all that laughing and playing. He gon' beat you. Now, understand me. You slaves. Ain't no more laughing and playing. So you might as well stop right now." We were shocked. Our eyes got large as silver dollars. We looked at one another and sat back in the coach and became perfectly still. Eli knew what was going to be expected of us. He knew that Master Dye was considered a good slave master. And he knew that we were treated fairly well on Master's Dye's plantation. But Master Burke wasn't a good slave master. The life we knew on Master Dye's plantation was over.

As we drew closer to Master Burke's plantation, we began to see slaves on the side of the road hoeing and slaves in the open fields picking cotton. We saw white men on large horses with whips and guns riding back and forth between the slaves, shouting orders and directions. Continuing on the same road, we came to a fork in the road. Eli said, "We go right. We go to Master Burke's plantation, but if we go left, we go north. And up north, there is freedom." Eli tugged on the reins, and the horses turned right.

This wasn't like the first time when I was on a wagon riding to Master Dye's plantation. This was a hot, dry, tiring, lonely trip. Even though Eli and Little Lizzy were there, this was different. This was strange. I didn't see the beautiful trees or the lovely flowers on the side of the road. I thought Mr. Dye's place was better. I prayed. As I prayed, peace came upon me. I heard a voice say, "To whomever I send you, you shall go. Whatever I command you, you shall speak. Have no fear before them, because I am with you."

Worry seemed to leave me like removing a blanket on a hot summer night. I knew God wanted me there. I thought, *It's for your glory, Lord.*

Little Lizzy sat perfectly still. She looked around with her eyes, not moving her head. Although Little Lizzy was slave, she was extremely beautiful, she had a grace, a disposition, a dignity that was uncommon among slaves. Although she was uneducated and couldn't read and write, she carried herself as if she was highly educated.

As we road along the road to Master Burke's plantation, the slaves stopped working and stared at the beautiful high yellow girl. Little Lizzy fixed her gaze on the road straight ahead. The stares made her uncomfortable. The white men on the horses yelled, "Get back to work! Ain't you ever seen buggy with niggers on it before?" The slaves had never seen a woman as beautiful as Little Lizzy. She was dressed nicely. And she didn't look like she had been in the fields plowing or picking cotton. I glanced at Little Lizzy. I knew Little Lizzy was considered proper and upright to the slaves. But I also knew that Little Lizzy was a slave, and in some ways, her slavery was worse than the slavery in the fields.

When we rode up to the Burkes' big house, we noticed that it was three times larger than Mr. Dye's big house. There were slaves all around the house working and hoeing, unlike Mr. Dye's plantation, where he didn't allow any of the field slaves close to the big house. We road on a brick road, and Eli said, "This here is a soldiers course. Mr. Burke's daddy was a military man." The bricks were large shiny, smooth, polished red rocks. We road along the soldiers course around to the front of the big house. The coach stopped, and a large house slave named Jesse stood on the porch.

Jesse said, "We been waiting. You must have stopped off at that little watering hole."

Eli said, "Yes, sir. It's a long, dry, dusty road to Mr. Dye's. A man has got to take a rest."

Jesse walked to the side of the coach and extended his hand. "Well, come on now. My arm gonna fall off if I hold it out any longer." Little Lizzy extended her hand and grabbed Jess. He helped her down from the coach. I slid over and extended my hand, and Jesse extended the same courtesy. We stood on the large porch looking at the large Ionic pillars that held up the roof. Jesse said, "Come on in. Mr. and Mrs. Burke been waiting for you."

We followed Jesse through the two large doors into the forum. The floor was white marble. It looked the same as the Ionic pillars. But there were Ionic pillars inside too. We followed Jesse to the large spiral stairway. We looked around at the art, the decoration of the room, and the beautiful royal-blue carpet on the stairway that was trimmed in gold. When we reached the top of the stairs, we turned left. We walked past large oil paintings twice as large as we were. Paintings of soldiers, paintings of women in long beautiful dresses, paintings of men in distinguished clothes. We walked directly behind one another as if marching in army formation. We became rigid with fear and anticipation. This wasn't the Dyes' plantation. This was different, new, and awe inspiring.

We came to the end of the hall. We stood before two large wooden doors. Jesse stood to the side and pulled something on the side of the door.

A man's voice said, "Come on in. The door's open." When we entered the room, we saw the room was more beautiful than what we had previously seen. Mr. Jonathan Burke stood next to a large bed with a large canopy over the bed and a beautiful petite woman lying in bed holding a newborn baby. Jesse stood off to the side, motionless. We stood perfectly still and looked straight forward.

The woman lying in bed said in a very soft voice, "Come here." We slowly walked over to the side of the bed. She said, "Hello, I'm Mrs. Burke. You girls have been recommended to assist me with my baby."

Mr. Burke stared at both of us, looking to see if there were any signs of discomfort or ill will to come from us assisting his wife with the newborn. Mr. Burke said in a very polite and dignified voice, "I'll leave you ladies alone to get acquainted." He left the room, and Jesse left after him, closing the door behind him.

Mrs. Burke continued. "I haven't been too well since I had the baby. And it's been a strain for me to take good care of her. This is Ashley. She is my fist. Here, hold her."

I stepped forward and took the baby from Mrs. Burke's arms. I said, "She is pretty."

"Yes, she is," Mrs. Burke responded. "And you must be Mary Lou," Mrs. Burke continued.

"Yes, ma'am, and this is Little Lizzy," Mary Lou replied.

"I heard good things about both of you. And I can see that Ashley likes you already. I just don't trust any of the slaves around here. Sometimes they just downright fearful to me," replied Mrs. Burke.

"Well, you don't need to worry none. We gon' take real good care of you and Ashley," replied Little Lizzy.

Mrs. Burke was exhausted. After I took Ashley from her arms and the greeting we exchanged, Mrs. Burke slowly drifted off to sleep. I stood next to the bed holding Ashley, and Mrs. Burke was sound asleep. She lay there with the face of an angel. I whispered, "Poor Mrs. Burke, she don't even got the strength to take care of her baby. And she living like this."

"Yeah, I guess you can have all the money and good things and not really have nothing. If I had a baby, I'd sure rather take care my baby than have all this stuff," replied Little Lizzy.

I paced back and forth rocking the baby. And Little Lizzy paced step for step with me, talking and playing with Ashley. We treated Ashley as if it was ours, although we hadn't had much experience. I had taken care of babies on slave row. But never had I taken care of any of the Master Dye's kids when they were infants.

After a while of pacing and rocking Ashley, the door opened, and Master Burke and Jesse entered the room. There was a baby's crib on the far wall of the bedroom. Mr. Burke said, "You can place Ashley in her crib. If she wakes up, my wife will take care of her." I carefully placed the baby in her crib and covered her under her pink and white blankets. Mr. Burke told the girls to follow Jesse.

Jesse walked slowly out of the bedroom and headed down the stairs. At the bottom of the stairs, he turned to his left, and about halfway to the kitchen, he stopped and pushed on the wooden side of the wall. The wall opened like a door. In fact, it was a door. It was made into the wall not to look like a door. All three of us entered the room, and there were two beds, a dresser, a mirror, a vase, and several candles about the room.

Jesse said, "This here is where you'll be staying. And you see that there bell over in the corner? If you hear it ring day or night, you come on out of here and go straight to Mrs. Burke." Lying on each of the beds was a white dress and a white head rag. Jesse told us to put on the dresses and come and stand at the bottom of the stairs when we were changed. He left the room. After we had changed, we came and stood at the bottom of the stairs. He was standing there waiting for us. We were dressed in white from head to toe. Jesse said, "You girls gon' help Mrs. Burke with her baby. That's why you here. And there is some cleaning and cooking you gon' be doing too. But, first, I want you all to know that anytime you hear a bell ring, that's for you to go straight to Mrs. Burke. If you ain't taking care of Mrs. Burke and the baby, you gon' be cooking and cleaning. And there's ringing bells every room around here. So you both listen for Mrs. Burke's ring."

Both of us said, "Yes, sir Mr. Jess."

Jesse said, "No, I ain't no Mr. Jesse. Jesse, that's my name. Now, come on, I'll show you where everything is around here."

Jesse took us from room to room explaining to us how to clean each room and that we were going to help Ms. Bell cook. We walked through large rooms in amazement. The rooms were large with high ceilings. The rooms were filled with large paintings and statues of every sort. This wasn't the Dyes' plantation. The Dyes' plantation and big house were small compared to this.

The last room we entered was the kitchen. It had two stoves and a large brick oven built into the wall, and there were pots and pans hanging from the ceiling all around the kitchen. In the center of the kitchen, there was a large table called an island. Off to the side of the kitchen, there was a small room. In the room, there was a table with eight chairs around it. Jesse said, "This is where you'll be eating your meals."

When we left the slave dining room, we saw a heavy female slave. She said, "My name is Ms. Bell. How are you all doing?"

"We fine," Little Lizzy quickly responded.

"Well, this is where you gon' to spend lots of your time. The other girls been sent to the fields to pick cotton. You know, Mrs. Burke didn't want them around her baby. She sure is crazy about that baby. And you girls been cooking with Eppie Mae, I hears," replied Ms. Bell.

"Yes, Ms. Bell, Eppie Mae been showing us how to cook and clean ever since I been there," I replied.

"OK, I see. You know, Eppie Mae supposed to be the best cook around these here parts. We gon' see, we sure gon' see if you girls can cook," replied Ms. Bell.

Jesse yelled, "Come on! I haven't shown you all around." We followed him out of the kitchen, through the living room and dining rooms of the big house, to the front door. Jesse opened the door and said, "Come on now." We stood at the opened door and looked out. We went out on the porch and stood tall, strong, and erect. There was pride in his eyes as he looked around the plantation. He said with pride in his voice, "You see that big red road that goes down yonder there? That's a soldiers course. That road goes all around the big house and down to the main road. You rode up on it over there to the left of the stables. That's where the Master Burke keeps his prize horses. You two ain't got no business over there. Look there. Straight ahead. That's Master Burke's prize flower garden. Folks come from all parts just to look at the arrangement of the flowers and the special flowers he's got. He's got specially trained slaves in that garden. Just to keep the garden just right. You see, Master Burke has got to have the best of everything. You know, horses, flowers, cotton, livestock, slaves, everything. And over there to the left, down that hill, is the barn."

I asked, "Where do you have church?"

Jesse looked deep into my eyes as if looking for something in one of them. Then he responded, "We don't have church around here."

"Well, don't you all believe in God and pray?" I continued.

"Well, I guess I believe in some things. Otherwise, we don't. We mostly work and do what we have been told."

"Well, at the Dyes' plantation, we had church every Sunday night," Little Lizzy replied.

"You know, you not on the Dyes' plantation. We work around here. And that's all we do. But maybe it's a good thing to have church service, and the one to talk to about a church service is Mrs. Burke. When she was well, she went to church every Sunday. Master Burke, he not a churchgoing man," Jesse replied.

"We just going to have to talk to Mrs. Burke," I replied.

Chapter Eight

A Miracle

As the days turned into weeks and the weeks turned into months, the daily routine of the Burkes' plantation set in. Mrs. Burke became used to Little Lizzy and me helping with the baby. Little Lizzy and I did our daily work with pride and care. The cotton picking season was over. It was a beautiful fall evening when one of the slaves from the valley came to the back door of the big house. It was Bo. Bo was a field hand. He was tall, strong, and black as night. He looked like he could lift a bull with ease. Only, he was dignified. He was polite. And many of the female slaves considered Bo a good catch.

Bo stood at the door, barefooted and sweating, wearing overalls. He huffed and gasped for breath. I opened the back door. I stared at Bo as he stood there gasping for air. He fixed his mouth to speak, but he couldn't catch his breath. Finally, he said, "Come quick. We think he might die. I was told to get you."

I whispered anxiously, "What happened?"

"Just come on, you hear!" Bo replied.

Jesse walked to the door and shouted, "What you want, Bo? You know you don't supposed to be here at this here back door. You just asking for a beating."

"It's Billy. They done caught him. And he been beat. He been beat bad," replied Bo.

"Come on, Mary Lou, we got to go. You get some ointment and bandages," replied Jess.

I hurried around the kitchen getting everything he told me. Bo stood outside waiting.

Jesse went upstairs to Mrs. Burke's bedroom door. He knocked softly. Mrs. Burke said, "Come in." He slowly walked into the bedroom with his head bowed. Little Lizzy was changing Ashley, and Mrs. Burke was sitting on the sofa in the bedroom, sipping coffee. Mrs. Burke said, "Yes, Jesse, what do you want?"

"If it's OK with you, Mrs. Burke. Well, Mrs. Burke Billy been found. And he's been beat bad."

"OK, you go and see what you can do. It's OK. But you be back here before sunrise," replied Mrs. Burke.

"Yes, ma'am." Then he slowly and politely left the room. He walked down the stairs in a dignified manner and went into the kitchen.

I was pacing back and forth in the kitchen, anxiously waiting for Jesse return. Jesse walked into the kitchen and quickly said to me, "Hurry, let's go." I followed behind. Bo followed behind. All three of us marched in a straight line over to the stables, and Bo harnessed a horse and wagon. Jesse and I sat up front. Jesse drove. Bo sat in the bed of the wagon.

The valley was about a mile from the big house. It's where the slaves live. Long ago, it was said to have been a lake bed. Now, it was dry. It probably had some of the best soil around. The slaves planted their gardens there. They raised their children there. At least until the children were old enough to work or be sold off. Master Burke had no problem with selling slaves, beating, or using them for anything he felt.

As we rode to the valley, no one spoke. Only the clinging, clanging of the wagon and heavy breathing of the horse could be heard. As we rode closer to the valley, the smell of humans living in filth filled the air. I knew the smell well. To Bo, it smelled of warmth, compassion, and safety. There in the valley, he knew he was safe. At least for the night. Rarely did the white slave masters visit the valley at night. Under nightfall, there was protection, safety, and Bo knew it well.

As we rode up, we saw lights from lanterns and slaves standing outside their shacks waiting for Bo and me. When we rode into the valley, Red grabbed a hold of the reins to the horse and stopped the wagon. Red was an older slave. He was light skinned. But he was a field hand. Red was an elder in the valley.

The valley had taken on the character of an African village in the way it was organized. Everyone knew and respected Red, from the youngest to the oldest in the valley. Red yanked the reins and tied the horses, shouting at Jesse, "They didn't have to beat him like that! They know the boy ain't got good sense."

Jesse replied, "Where is he?"

"He's in my shack. My missus is looking after him. But he been beat bad. He bloody from head to foot. I told him. I told him. I told him they'll kill him," replied Red.

Red tied the horse and buggy to a tree stump. Bo jumped down from the bed of the wagon and hurried to the front of the wagon to help me down from the wagon. Bo extended his right arm, staring into my eyes, just like he had seen white men help white women down from their buggies. I looked deep into Bo's eyes. I said, "Well, thank you very much."

By the time I had gotten down from the wagon, Eli and Red were walking toward a clearing in the woods. Red's shack was just before the clearing. When they entered the shack, Billy lay still on the eating table. His feet were bare and bloody. They hung off the table also. The blood on his body was drying. Billy lay perfectly still.

Red's wife, Cece, was washing Billy's face and applying cool water to the open cuts, brushes, and beat welts on his body. The water dripped down to the dirt floor of the shack, red as blood, slowly turning the hard dirt to mud. Cece knew that Billy was dead, but she kept on cleaning his wounds.

I entered the room. The room was dimly lit by candlelight. The candlelight flickered back and forth to a gentle breeze. I stood back and stared at Billy's body. His face and head were swollen. His mouth was full of blood. The blood slowly oozed from his mouth and nose. The beat welts had swollen and disproportioned many areas of his body. His clothes were dirty, ripped, and torn, loosely hanging on to his body. Where his clothes were still on his body, blood had dried and stuck the clothes to the open wounds and dried blood.

When I stepped forward, I looked down into Billy's face. His eyes were staring directly into mine. I whispered, "It's OK, Billy." Then I slowly raised my right hand and gently stroked Billy's face. I softly whispered, "It's going to be just fine." Then I leaned over and kissed Billy on the forehead.

Jesse and Red stood on each side of Billy's body. Jesse whispered, "He's gone. Ain't nothing to be done now. Just to clean him up. We don't want the folks to see him like this." Red, Eli, and Cece washed and cleaned Billy's body quietly. No one questioned my request. They moved poetically and in unison as they cared for Billy's remains.

I drifted off to a corner of the room and prayed. I prayed, "Father in heaven, you know all things. You can do all things. There is no one like unto you, oh, Lord. Father, this child of yours became perfect in a short while. He reached the fullness of a long life. For his soul was pleasing to you, oh, Lord, therefore you sped him out of the midst of wickedness. But the people saw and did not understand, nor did they take this into account. Yes, Father, the just man dead condemns the sinful who live, and youth swiftly completed condemns the sinful who live, and youth swiftly completed condemns the years of the wicked man grown old. Oh, heavenly Father, I pray that you fill your servant with the breath of life. Yes, oh, Lord. Use this youth Billy."

When I finished praying, I quietly walked over to where Billy was lying. They were still washing his body. But most of the dried blood had been washed off. Billy's body lay naked on the table with his hands hanging off the table, almost to the floor, and his legs hanging off the ends of the table. Cece had placed some of Red's overalls and a cotton shirt on a chair. I softly, almost in a whisper. I said, "Please leave me alone with him." Jesse,

Red, and Cece looked bewildered at me and quietly left the room. They went and stood outside.

I stood next to Billy's naked body. I looked at him. Then I lowered my head and placed it over Billy's heart. I lifted my head and looked at Billy's face. He looked as though he was sleeping. Then I placed my left hand over Billy's heart. I placed my right hand on Billy's forehead. I prayed, "Father in heaven, you alone, by your power, love, and grace, can do this. Father, put your immortal spirit back into this empty shell. Father, by the power of your might, put your spirit into this empty shell."

Tears slowly ran down my face. I gave a deep groan and moaned. Billy lay still. I began crying profusely. Tears and sweat ran down my cheeks. But Billy still didn't move. He was dead. A calmness came over me. I stopped crying. Then I picked up the clothes that Cece laid out for his burial. I slowly dressed Billy in them. When I had finished, I took a chair and placed it in the corner of the shack and sat down. I put my head into my lap and cried. I felt that I was asking too much of God. I felt that I was somehow offending the God of heaven and earth. Then I cried, "Devil, you have no place here. In the name of Jesus Christ, the King of the Jews, I claim the victory in Jesus, the mighty name."

After saying that, I fell to the ground. I seemed to be in a trance. I closed my eyes and lay still. There was a peace. A calmness. I had prayed with all of my heart and soul. I was drained. I felt as though I couldn't move a muscle. All of my strength was gone. I lay on the dirt floor of the shack weak and broken.

I turned and opened my eyes. I glanced over toward the table where Billy lay. The table was bare. I raised myself up on one arm and glanced around the room. There stood Billy. Billy stood there adjusting the overalls I had dressed him in. I forced myself to my feet. Billy didn't say anything. He continued to adjust the overalls. I slowly walked over to Billy. I stood directly in front of him and looked directly into his face. Billy stopped fixing his clothes. He looked at me. Billy looked into my eyes. An overwhelming sense of love filled Billy's heart. He couldn't control himself. He fell to his knees and cried. He clung on to my dress like a child. Then he put his head at my feet and cried.

I knelt on both knees and hugged Billy with all of my strength. I cried. "It's all right. It's all right. Everything is all right. We gonna be just fine."

Billy couldn't raise his head. He kept his head and face buried into my breasts. He cried as if he were a newborn baby. But the tears weren't the tears of sorrow. They were tears of joy. Joy, sweet joy. His soul burst to the brim with love. His face radiated unconditional love. For the love of Christ, Jesus filled Billy. The resurrection power of Christ dwelt in Billy's heart, mind, and soul. Billy wasn't just raised from the dead. He was born again. He was a new creation.

I put both of my hands on Billy's cheeks and slowly raised his face. I looked into Billy's tear-filled eyes. Billy looked into my tear-filled eyes in bewilderment, for Billy didn't know what had happened to him. The last thing he remembered was being beaten. He tried to fix his lips to speak, but nothing came out. He mumbled something, but I couldn't understand. He tried to speak again. He pressed his lips together. "Was . . . was . . . was . . . I dead?"

I said softly, "The Lord Jesus says, 'It's not your time. You are my child. And you have work to do. My work.'"

Billy stared into my eyes and shook his head in agreement, saying, "Yes, Lord. Yes, Lord. I hear. I hear you. Yes, I hear, and I obey."

"Come on," I said.

Billy stood up, for Billy hadn't lost any of his strength. Billy was strong. There wasn't any sign of him being beaten. He had grace. Grace had radiated from him. After Billy stood up, he helped me to my feet, for I was still weak and drained. I said, "The people are mourning for you. They are waiting outside. And they been told that you were dead. So we gon' go see the people and show them that you all right."

Billy said, "Yes, ma'am, I'm fine."

I walked outside the shack. I stood silently glazing at the slaves all huddled around Red's shack. The night sky was beautiful. Stars filled the sky. The slaves stood silently holding torches. I held out my hand, reaching behind me. Billy was afraid. He didn't want to come outside of the shack. All the slaves looked intently at me. But I just stood still. A moment later, Billy slowly walked out of the shack. Billy looked at all the salves. Then he lowered his head, looking at the ground.

I screamed, "It's not his time! The Lord has got work for him to do. God's work."

Cece yelled, "Thank you, Jesus! That boy was dead. I done seen him dead. It's a miracle. It's a miracle. Thank you, Jesus. Thank you, Jesus."

Jesse yelled, "That's right! I saw. I saw him dead."

Billy, overwhelmed with joy, fell to his knees. He cried. He threw up both hands over his head and yelled, "Thank you, Lord Jesus! Thank you, Lord Jesus. I was dead, dead and gone. But Jesus done brought me back. Jesus done brought me back."

All the slaves rushed toward Billy and hugged him. Many just wanted to touch him. They began singing, "Jesus done brought him back. Jesus done brought him back. Jesus done brought him back from the dead. He once was dead, but now he's alive."

The slaves pulled Billy all around the valley, singing and praising God. There was great joy in all the hearts of the slaves, for they had witnessed a miracle and believed. As they sang and praised God, they seemed to be drunk or intoxicated. The screams and yells grew to higher and higher levels, and soon everyone was feeling the presence of the Lord.

I walked into the midst of jubilation and began to sing. I sang in a low, almost whisper, "Thank you, Lord. Thank you, Lord. Thank you, Lord. I just want to thank you, Lord." I repeated the song over and over again. Then Cece joined me in the middle of the jubilation and sang the song. Red followed, and soon the entire valley was singing "Thank you, Lord" in a low almost whisper.

Billy knelt down in the center next to me. He raised both arms and hands above his head and sang with all his heart. "Thank you, Lord. Thank you, Lord. I just want to thank you, Lord."

Time seemed lost in the glory of the Lord, for all the slaves worshipped, praised, and thanked God with all their hearts. Never had any one of slaves witnessed the power of God in such a wonderful, powerful, and glorious manner. The night was soon coming to an end. The sun was slowly rising.

Jesse yelled, "Mary Lou, we better be getting on back to the big house. The sun is coming up, and we got work to do."

Bo heard Jesse's call to me and pushed his way through the slaves, for the slaves had all surrounded me as if capturing me for themselves. Bo put his arm around my waist and escorted me through the crowd. I leaned onto Bo's shoulder and chest with my head buried deep under Bo's arm. I was faint from exhaustion and felt my legs buckle under my own weight. Bo escorted me to the wagon. Jesse followed behind. Jesse climbed onto the wagon and sat down. Bo helped me onto the wagon. I seemed to not notice getting onto the wagon or who was there. When I sat down, I leaned over and rested my head on Jesse's shoulder. Bo untied the horse and walked the wagon around to head in the direction of the big house.

Jesse said, "You take care now," and yelled, "Come!" to the horse. The wagon jerked forward, and we headed back to the big house with me sound asleep, leaning on Jesse.

I slept all the way back to the big house. Jesse woke me. I climbed down from the wagon, almost in a daze. I stumbled to the back door, tripping over my feet as if drunk. Jesse took the horse and wagon back to the stables. When I reached for the door handle, Little Lizzy opened the door quickly and hugged me. Little Lizzy walked me through the kitchen and to our room. I sat on the edge of the bed and slowly leaned backward. As

I rested my full weight onto the bed, the Holy Spirit came upon me, and I fell sound asleep.

Little Lizzy took off my shoes, my dress, and put me under the bedspread. There was a bowl of water next to the bed and a towel that we use to wash in. Little Lizzy soaked the towel in water, wrung it out, and tenderly washed my face, arms, and hands. After she had finished caring for me, she left and went into the kitchen and continued with her work.

Jesse soon came to the back door. He asked, "Where is Mary Lou?"

Little Lizzy responded in a whisper, saying, "She's sleeping."

"Yeah, she sure was tired. She slept all the way back from the valley. And I know you all got plenty of work to do around here."

"That's sho' right. We got everything to do. And she 'sleep. I can do it all myself, though. I know it must have been something mighty important for all of you to go to the valley in the middle of the night and stay to sunrise the next day," replied Little Lizzy.

"Well, you don't know Billy, do you?" asked Jesse.

"No, I don't know Billy. I ain't never been to the valley," Little Lizzy replied.

"Well, Billy had run away. He runs away. He tries to follow the drinking gourd up north. That boy done run away more times than you can shake a stick at. I'm surprised he's still alive. They sure to kill a runaway nigger just as sure as I'm standing here. And last night, Billy was caught. He was beat bad. I saw him. He looked dead as a dead rat. He looked like he ain't have no life in him at all. I still don't know what to make of it. That boy lay on an old eatin' table looking something awful. You could have set fire to him and he wouldn't have budged. He was bloody. His body was swollen. His eyes was wide open, just looking. And it looked to me that most of his blood was on the floor. Like I say, I still don't know what to make of it.

"Mary Lou asked me, Red, and Cece to clean him up. We cleaned him up. Cece even put some of Red's clean overalls on a chair for the boy.

And I was thinking that we just getting him ready so the slaves could look at him without acting a fool. 'Cause, you know, we sure don't need no more dead niggers around here. Then we left and went outside and talked to the slaves. We had done told everybody that Billy was dead.

"Then Mary Lou came and stood outside of Red's door. That's where he was, in Red's shack. She reached behind her. Billy walked out and grabbed her hand. It scared me something awful. And he was wearing Red's overalls. That boy looked dead to me. Yes, he sure did. Then everybody started to thank Jesus. I even thanked Jesus. Everybody was caught up, just thanking Jesus. And we must have spent the night thanking Jesus. And in all my days, I ain't never seen or hear of nothing like this. Billy walked out of that shack just as alive as I'm standing here talking to you. And his face was shining. He didn't look like had been beat to death. In fact, he didn't have a mark on him. Something real special happened last night. And I don't rightly know what to think of it. Maybe it ain't for me to know. But Billy was dead and gone. I know that," replied Jesse.

Little Lizzy stared at Jesse with her mouth open. She gasped to speak, but nothing came out. She went and sat down at the kitchen table. Then she said, "I believe that boy was dead. You don't know Mary Lou like I do. Mary Lou is a gift from God. That girl should have been dead herself from being struck by lightning. But God has shown up and shone out in Mary Lou's life. Billy, I believe, was dead just from what you just told me. Mary Lou prayed for Billy's life. Jesus heard her prayer and brought Billy back from the dead. I believe that's what's done happened."

"Well, whatever it was, I believe that boy was dead and now he's alive," replied Jesse.

Little Lizzy got up and finished her cooking and cleaning. Then she went to check on me. I lay asleep in bed. Just as Little Lizzy was leaving, she heard Mrs. Burke call, "Mary Lou, Mary Lou, come here."

Little Lizzy rushed up to Mrs. Burke's bedroom and slowly eased the door open, saying, "Yes, ma'am, you called?"

Mrs. Burke replied, "I didn't call you. I called Mary Lou. Now, go on. Go on and get her for me, would you, please?"

"Yes, ma'am," replied Little Lizzy. She turned and politely left the room then quickly ran down the stairs and hurried into the room. She went over to the bed and shook me, saying, "Wake up. Mrs. Burke wants you right now."

I lay still on me back, with white sheets draped over me pulled up to me shoulders. I looked like an angel. Light seemed to radiate from the bed. But it was the grace of God upon me that radiated through the entire room. I rose up on me elbows and looked at Little Lizzy.

Little Lizzy said, "Mrs. Burke wants you now."

I hurried out of bed and stood barefooted next to the bed in a white under garment that extended to the floor. I reached and quickly put a housecoat on. Then I retied the head rag on my head and quickly went to see what Mrs. Burke wanted.

I stood at the entrance of Mrs. Burke's bedroom door barefooted and in a housecoat. I shifted my weight back and forth from foot to foot. I didn't know what to expect. I hadn't done my daily work. I had stayed in bed. A glimpse of getting beat crossed my mind. I pictured myself being beaten like Billy. I gently knocked on the bedroom door.

"Come on in." A gentle voice came from within.

Tears welled up in my eyes. I put my hands together, closed my eyes, and prayed. As I prayed, tears slowly ran down my cheeks. Mrs. Burke said, "Now, now, you don't need to go on crying like that."

"I can't help it, Mrs. Burke. You been real good to me. I just don't know what to say. It's like a dream come true."

"I think you done a fine job with Ashley. And this old house has turned into a home since you've come. I didn't do that. You did. So I'm gonna give you a wedding," replied Mrs. Burke. Mrs. Burke walked over to me and put her arms around me and held me. I buried my face into Mrs. Burke's shoulder and cried tears of joy.

The next day, word spread quickly that I was getting married in the big house or in the flower garden. The women living in the valley seemed more excited than me. And everyone wanted to help plan the wedding. But this wedding was going to be different. Usually, when a slave gets married, the elder women plan the entire event, except the entertainment—that's left to the men. But I wasn't going to be getting married in the valley; I was going to be married properly. And this caused a confusion in the valley because no one had ever had a proper wedding.

Later on during the day, Mrs. Burke called me into the lower library to discuss the wedding plans. The lower library was in the southwest corner of the house. It is lavishly decorated in royal-blue and gold trim. The carpet is deep dark blue, while the curtains, walls, lighting fixtures are all royal blue or gold. The few statues in the room are also gold, which makes the entire room look extremely rich. I rarely entered the lower library. Only when I was called to enter it, and this was one such occasion.

When I entered the room, I noticed a man dressed in black with a white collar around his neck sitting on the royal-blue couch with gold leaf embroidered into it. He sat with one leg crossed over the other, leaning back into couch, resting comfortably. Mrs. Burke sat next to him, sitting on the edge of the couch, sipping tea. I stood at the open doorway, not knowing what to do.

Mrs. Burke gestured with her head, and she cautiously walked over to the couch and stood directly in front of both of us. Mrs. Burke said, "This is Father Phleiger. He is a Catholic priest. We've been discussing your wedding."

Father Phleiger stood up and extended his right hand and said, "How are you? I have heard nothing but good things about you, and I've wanted to meet you for some time, but my schedule didn't allow me to."

I extended my hand and gave him a firm handshake. I looked into his eyes and quickly averted my eyes to the ground because I had never seen a priest before and was uncomfortable about meeting him. Father Phleiger sat down.

Mrs. Burke said, "Sit down, Mary Lou. We want to discuss the wedding with you and some other details." I politely sat down. My face radiated a calmness, a peace that showed complete acceptance.

Father Phleiger spoke directly and asked, "Around how old do you think you are?"

"I don't really know. But I guess I could be of the age of marriage."

"Yes, I can see you are old enough for marriage. The question had to be asked. You see, Mary Lou, marriage is a very big step. As you already know, not many slaves have a formal wedding in the Catholic Church."

"No, sir, I ain't never hear of any slave having any sort of marriage in no church," I replied.

"Well, Mary Lou, you may be a bit confused. But don't you worry none. I'll explain everything. First, I want you to know that Jesus Christ is the head of our church. It's in his name that you will be married. And I understand that you've been struck by lightning and you've been blessed with certain spiritual gifts. Well, I want you to tell me all about the things of Jesus you know and about all your gifts."

I explained all the things I knew about Jesus. I told Father Phleiger about my feet, hands, side, and blood running down my face when I sometimes prayed.

He said, "Yes, that's called the stigmata, or 'the wounds of Christ.'

I continued explaining about my baptizing the slaves. Father Phleiger interrupted, "How many slaves did you baptize?"

"We own over five hundred slaves."

I told the priest about the apostles Paul, James, and John. Then I said, "I can go on and on. I don't know why I know these things, but I do. Jesus is real, and he loves us all."

Father Phleiger said, "Yes, you have had a profound spiritual experience, and Jesus has truly revealed himself to you. You are truly a blessed young lady, and there isn't any problem with you being married in the Catholic Church. Although a lot less of a dramatic appeal would have been liked." Mrs. Burke turned and placed her hand over her mouth and gently laughed. I sat straight on the couch, not resting my back on the back of the couch, and stared at both of them, not finding the humor in his joke.

Father Phleiger said to both of us, "I would like to tell the bishop about all you've told me. This is extremely rare, and if you have been truthful, I believe there have been some miracles."

"Yes, there have been, but I don't believe they can be proven," replied Mrs. Burke.

"Regarding your marriage, Mary Lou, I was considering baptizing you and your husband to be. But considering what you've just told me, I don't think it's necessary."

"I was already baptized. I was baptized in the name of the Father, the Son Jesus Christ, and the Holy Spirit. It was when I was young, before I was struck by lightning. And don't mind me none about telling the bishop about how much Jesus loves me. I think it's good to tell folks about the goodness of the Lord," I replied.

"Well, thank you, Mary Lou. I will certainly explain everything you've told me to the bishop." Father Phleiger stood up and bowed to both of us and said, "Good day, ladies. I'll see myself to the door," and slowly walked to the door, and Mrs. Burke quickly caught up with Father Phleiger and led him to the door. I stood as well and watched both of them without saying a word. After they left the room, I quickly returned to my duties.

When Mrs. Burke returned, she called me back into the lower library. Mrs. Burke was sitting in the library, waiting patiently for me. I came and stood at the entrance of the door and looked around the inside of the room, expecting to see someone else.

Mrs. Burke said, "Sit down, please. We need to talk." She sat quietly looking into my eyes. Mrs. Burke continued. "I want you to understand that you are very special. In fact, you are a blessing. I was told that your nickname is Babe. Can I call you Babe?"

"Yes, ma'am. I have been called that in a while."

"Well, Babe, I plan to give you a wedding just like I would for my own daughter. I am a God-fearing woman even though my husband is not a God-fearing man. I'm going to plan everything."

"Yes, ma'am."

"Don't you worry about nothing. You'll wear white, and your Bo will wear a tuxedo. All the slaves will be given clean white clothes, and you will be married in the flower garden. It's extremely beautiful in the summertime. I spoke with Fr. Phleiger, and he's available this summer. And I don't care whether the bishop knows about you or not, or approves or not. Fr. Phleiger is a good friend of the family, and he'll marry you. Is that OK with you?"

"Yes, ma'am. I don't know what to say. I couldn't ask for more. But I just wants to know, is my momma, daddy, brothers, and sisters gonna be here?"

"No, they are not. I'm sorry. I wish they could, but it's not possible," replied Mrs. Burke.

"Thank you, Mrs. Burke. I thank God for all you're doing for us slaves. I know it was you who talked to Master Burke for us to have the baptizing and picnic. You are really a blessing," I replied.

Mrs. Burke extended her hand and grabbed my hand and gently rubbed it affectionately. We looked into each other's eyes, knowing that we shared something special, something divine, a trait not usually found among many. We shared faith, hope, and love—traits uncommon between slave and slave owner.

Mrs. Burke continued on explaining the plans of the wedding. She seemed more excited than me. She explained about the color of the roses and how she wanted pink, white, and red roses arranged in the garden. She explained how she wanted the exterior of the house decorated with red roses and how she wanted little Negro slave girls carrying bushels of roses and placing them around the gazebo. She explained that she was going to have the gazebo covered in white roses.

All that she explained to me was astonishing. I sat listening with my mouth wide open, staring into Mrs. Burke's mouth, lingering on every word. When Mrs. Burke finished explaining all she had planned for the wedding, I put my head in my hands and bent forward, placing both head and hands in my lap and cried. I rocked back and forth, crying tears of joy.

"It's gonna be fine. It's the least I can do. I've never agreed with slavery. I'm gonna make sure you have a beautiful, wonderful wedding that folks gonna talk about for years to come."

During the next few weeks, Mrs. Burke was exceptionally busy. There were added chefs—chefs from the finest cities. There were cleaning and painting going on, both inside and outside of the house. The flower garden was being prepared exactly the way Mrs. Burke wanted. And all the while, I watched and waited in anticipation of the big event.

Nothing changed in the valley. Bo worked the fields in the valley, and I continued my duties inside the big house. Yet there was a sense of excitement in the air. Never had anyone, slave or free, known for a slave holder to give a wedding for a slave. And the anticipation grew day by day.

Yet Bo grew more and more angry toward me. During their evening walks, he would ask, "Why is Mrs. Burke fixing up everything and giving you such a big wedding? We are slaves. Ain't nobody ever know for no slave master to give a wedding for a slave. They don't even allow us to get married most of the time. We have to sneak and jump the broom. I was planning on us jumping the broom right down here in the valley."

I didn't know what to say. Bo's words were true and direct. In fact, I hadn't even heard of such a thing being done for a slave. I wondered, was it right? Should we? What were the other slaves goin' to think? Could we not get married in the garden and just jump the broom in the valley? Yet I wanted it. I saw all the fixing and doings. I wanted it. It was more than a dream come true. I hadn't ever dreamed that I could have such a wedding.

But Bo. He was scared. He didn't understand the goodness of the Lord. During our evening walks, I explained that God wanted all good things for man. I told Bo that he did not spare his own Son but handed him over for us all, how he will not also give us everything else along with him. The more I explained the goodness of the Lord, the more Bo became comfortable with the wedding. Soon, Bo wanted the wedding. He wanted everyone to see what the Lord has done for him.

Father Phleiger came by occasionally and discussed marriage with Bo and me. He explained that God's plan was for a man to be fruitful and populate the earth. He continued saying that once a man and woman were joined together in marriage that the marriage was until death do us part. We accepted all that was said and happily awaited the day of our wedding.

When Father Phleiger talked about marriage vows, neither of us knew what they were. So he asked, "How do you feel about one another?" Still, we seemed confused. So he went on and said, "Bo, tell Mary Lou how you feel about her."

Bo looked into my eyes and said, "Ms. Mary, I want you to be my wife."

"That's good, Bo, but you have to say what's in your heart and soul."

Bo looked into my eyes again. This time, he reached out to me and held my hand. He cautiously and affectionately said, "Ms. Mary, I love you. I want to take care of you. I want you to be happy and free. Every time I look into your eyes, my heart jumps for joy. I want to have a family with you. My heart, my life, all that I am belongs to you. You are who I live for, every day, every hour, every minute."

"That's good, Bo. Real good. Real good," Father Phleiger responded.

Bo and I continued to stare into each other's eyes as if in a hypnotic trance searching and finding the love we so much saw in each other. We believed that it wasn't our natural desire for each other but a heavenly call of God. It made our hearts burn with great passion and desire. Almost unbearable. I didn't express my marriage vows that day. We both decided I would wait until the day of our marriage.

The day of the wedding drew quickly. The bishop didn't respond to my special gifts, nor was he against the wedding. Mrs. Burke was alarmed that the bishop didn't do more inquiry into her miracles, but she was pleased he didn't prevent the wedding. Mrs. Burke informed me, and word spread like wildfire.

On the day before the wedding, Mrs. Burke had Jesse and Eli take a wagonload of brand-new pure white clothes to the valley. White was the color of summer, and Mrs. Burke was determined to create an atmosphere of peace, unity, and beauty in my honor. The women were given white gowns that stretched to the ground. They were cotton and looked similar to wedding gowns but in fact were cotton summer dresses. The men were given pure white cotton shirts and pants of all sizes. The children were given the same as adults. Never had it been known for a slave to have such a lavish wedding. Excitement was high in the valley. The slaves picked and chose their right size by trying on this one and that one. All were smiling, forgetting they were slaves. They danced for joy while trying on the garments. There was peace and excitement throughout the valley. Everyone was happy for me and Bo.

Later that evening, there was a special ceremony for the bride and groom. The women held theirs inside Cece's shack, and the men held theirs outside in the clearing. Both ceremonies were based on ancient African tradition. All that was not forgotten was both men and women tried to perform. The women sang songs. They sang, "Everybody all too know what love is. Everybody all too know what friendship is. Everybody all to know what peace is. Everybody all too know what marriage is." They sang, clapped their hands, and danced for joy. They danced around in a circle; even the young girls joined in the celebration.

The men celebrated similar to the women. They sang, "Marriage is coming, and it won't be long. A son is coming, and it won't be long. Land is coming, and it won't be long. Prosperity is coming, and it won't be long." As they sang and danced, they danced to the rhythm of the stomping of their feet onto the ground. Usually, they would have played a ceremonial drum. But they weren't allowed to have a drum. But all in all, the message was conveyed. Prosperity was coming.

Everything had changed since my arrival. The slaves embraced it with a passion. For the first time, since they left Africa, a wedding, a formal wedding was going to take place. Although it wasn't an African wedding, the excitement, joy, and all the feelings that came with their tradition were present.

Finally, the day of the wedding was at hand. All the preparation, planning, and excitement had finally come to beautiful white cloud puffs in the sky. It was a perfect day for a wedding. The slaves had arrived early. This was a Sunday to be remembered. The slaves all sat in white chairs, which were in neat rows designed to accommodate up to five hundred plus slaves, for the record showed they owned five hundred, but they weren't 100 percent correct. Everyone was dressed in the white clothes that Mrs. Burke had provided.

Mr. and Mrs. Burke sat in the front row alone. No one sat next to them or near them. They displayed the grace and dignity of the Southern rich of the time. Ashley sat next to Ms. Bell in the second row along with the house slaves, behind the Burkes. The gazebo was beautifully decorated with the exact specification of Mrs. Burke. Fr. Phleiger had arrived early, which was the custom of a Catholic priest. He stood in liturgical dress with a Roman collar. He looked extremely plus.

The ceremony began with the orchestra playing a slow rhythmic melody, "Wachet Auf," by J. S. Bach. As the orchestra played, the flower girls began to march to the music. One step, hold, and then another step. The girls were all dressed in white, each holding three roses, red and pink, either two pink with one red, or two red with one pink. The girls were slaves, which seemed to add to the beauty of the ceremony in an odd way. They marched side by side, one on each side of the aisle. As the girls approached the gazebo, each girl turned and went onto each side of the gazebo and stood with their roses in hand. The girls completely encircled the gazebo except for the aisle in which the bride and groom were to walk. The slave girls looked completely beautiful and majestic.

After the girls had finished their approach, the orchestra played a new song. Mrs. Burke was abreast of the current music and books of the time. She heard a song from England that she liked. It was "Here Comes the Bride." The orchestra played, and I, the bride, slowly walked down the aisle. Bo stood next to the priest on the gazebo. Billy stood next to Bo as his best man. Little Lizzy stood on the other side as the maid of honor. Every head was turned. Every eye was on me as if in a trance. I majestically graced the aisle. I was beautiful. Only the music could be heard. I took a step, paused, and then another. I did exactly what Mrs. Burke had said. This was the first time any of the slaves had seen a formal Christian wedding. They were astonished at the beauty, the dignity, the eloquence, the majesty of it all.

Mary Lou looked like an African queen. I had baby's breath in my hair. It was formed a crown. I didn't have a head rag on. My hair was combed back and oiled with chicken fat, which made it glisten in the sunlight. The streak of white from where the lightning had struck me added to the dignity and beauty. I looked amazingly beautiful. The slave women were astonished. The mouths of some of the slave women were wide open, like a trout out of water. Nothing they had ever seen or heard could compare to the event that they were so much an intricate part of.

When I reached the gazebo, Eli stepped to the side. I walked up the three stairs alone holding a bouquet of roses next to Bo, who stepped forward and extended his left hand. I grabbed it and stood eloquently next to Bo. Eli went and sat next to Ms. Bell.

Fr. Phleiger stepped forward and said, "In nomine Patris, et Filii, et Spiritus sancti."

Mr. and Mrs. Burke stood up and quietly said, "Amen." After Mr. and Mrs. Burke stood, the slaves also stood. The ceremony was in Latin. No one spoke or understood Latin except the Burkes.

Fr. Phleiger continued, saying, "The marriage ceremony is a sub rosa, in the strictest confidence." He explained that most of the service would be in Latin and that he would inform the slaves on what was being said.

Bo and I stood with our backs to the crowd. Fr. Phleiger gestured for the slaves to take their seats. After everyone had taken a seat, he began. He spoke in Latin, and whenever he needed response from Bo or me, he repeated it in English. Bo repeated his marriage vows he had spoken earlier, and this brought tears to many slaves. After Bo had finished his vows, I softly said, "I take this man as he is in sickness and in health, through good times and bad times, whether slave or free. I solemnly swear to love, cherish, and obey Bo as long as I shall live, until death do us part."

As I finished my vows, tears slowly ran down my cheeks. I squeezed Bo's hands and passionately lost myself in his eyes. Every word I said entered Bo's heart. He was left speechless. His heart, mind, and soul were passionately, romantically, spiritually forever linked to mine. He knew it. I had become his, and he had become mine. We were no longer two but one. The words we spoke became spirit and life. The words became a reality. No longer could we ever think of ourselves as individuals again, for we were one—one mind, one body, one spirit—yet living in separate bodies dedicated to serve Jesus Christ. The spirit of Lord Jesus Christ had covered the entire wedding ceremony like a blanket. There seemed to be a cloud magnifying the glory of the Lord resting upon everyone there.

As Fr. Phleiger continued the service, the glory of the Lord grew and grew. As Fr. Phleiger spoke, a slave filled with the Holy Spirt cried in a loud voice, "Thank you. Thank you, Jesus. Jesus is Lord."

Then another stood and cried, "Alleluia, alleluia. Praise our God, all you, his servants, and you who revere him, small and great."

Fr. Phleiger stopped in the middle of giving the closing wedding vows and looked off to his left into the crowd. The shout of Bible scripture took him by surprise. He was astonished. He felt the move of God upon the ceremony like no other ceremony he had ever attended. He stopped speaking in Latin and said, "I now pronounce you man and wife. You may kiss your bride."

As he spoke the closing words, the shouts of joy increased. Tears of joy ran down many cheeks of both the male and female slaves, both old and young. To them, this was a sign of hope. A sign of freedom. A sign of what could be. A sign of a future full of freedoms not yet imagined or dreamed of. As the tears of joy flowed, shouts of joy filled the air. Everyone stood, shouting, dancing, jumping up and down, hugging each other, and spinning around and around in excitement.

Fr. Phleiger softly said, "You are now married."

Celebrating in the aisles, we slowly walked between the crowd. Mrs. Burke secretly had rice passed out among the slaves. As we continued our slow walk down the aisle, rice rained down upon us as coming from the sky. The men reached out, patting Bo on the shoulders and quickly shaking his hand.

As we continued our departure down the aisles, the flower girls walked behind us. There had been dozens of roses placed onto the base of the gazebo. The flower girls had each grabbed handfuls of long-stemmed roses and threw them into the crowd. The women and children eagerly grabbed and struggled to catch as many roses as possible. It was a beautiful sight. A wedding fit for the riches of the South given to a lowly slave.

At the end of the wedding march, there was a white coach along with a white horse waiting there for us, the newly married couple. Eli was standing there opening the coach door for us. I was no longer to live in the big house, but now, I would live in the valley. I would have to walk to the big house for work, come rain or shine. Eli was to deliver us to our new home in the valley.

We arrived at the valley. Our shack was beautifully decorated with flowers around the door and white cotton draperies. The slave women had given me pots, pans, tin plates, and cups. Our shack was fully furnished with a table, two chairs, and a bed. It was Bo's shack that he had formally shared with the other field slaves. Now, it was going to be our home. They had placed all kinds of beans, greens, fruits, and smoked meat inside our shack.

Bo jumped down from the coach, eager and excited. He extended his hand the way he had noticed Eli assist Mrs. Burke from the coach. I eloquently grabbed his hand. I stepped from the coach with the dignity of a princess. Bo had heard of men carrying their bride across the trash hold into their new home. So when I stood in front of the doorway, he lifted me into his arms and carried me into our new home.

The old dirty, smelly slave shack that he had shared with other slaves had transformed into a home. A home. Yet we hadn't lived in it a single day. A home. Yet we hadn't slept in it for one night. For the blessings of the Lord preceded us. Neither of us knew of the surprises the slaves had placed inside the shack. So upon entering it, we both were exceedingly overjoyed at the cleanliness, the foods, and the colors, and some slaves gave gifts. Some slaves had acquired a ring, a necklace, a bracelet, something bought, something found, something that had been passed down from generation to generation. And to the slaves, these things were exceedingly valuable. Yet they were placed on the table, the bed, and in the windowsill. Everyone wanted to show their appreciation old enough to know the depth, the honor, and the importance of her wedding.

When I saw all the salves had done, I fell into Bo's arms and cried. All the joy had come to a climax. I overflowed with love, care, humiliation, care, and respect for Jesus because I attributed everything to him. I held on to Bo as one flesh and cried, "Thank you, Jesus. Thank you, Jesus."

Bo slowly rocked his new bride from side to side in triumphant joy. Tears streamed down my face. Bo dried my tears with his gentle kisses. As he kissed me, he slowly unbuttoned the dress I wore. When the last button was undone, the dress slowly dropped onto the floor. I stood glowing in a promise of love. I wanted all the marriage entailed, and Bo wanted the same.

Bo slowly, gently, passionately kissed my entire face. Then he triumphantly kissed me. We lost ourselves in each other's love. Bo lifted me slowly into his arms. Slowly, he carried me to the bed. He gently laid me down, still passionately kissing me. The marriage was totally and completely consummated in the fear of the Lord.

The next day, we both awoke and began to get ready for work as usual. But upon leaving our shack, there stood the adult slave men and women. When we walked out, the crowd let out a loud cheer. Bo and I were so embarrassed that we lowered our heads and quickly rushed through the cheering crowd and headed in separated directions to work. The days after our marriage seemed to go faster now. Every day was blessed to the newlyweds.

Chapter Nine

They Come in Threes

The news of their marriage spread among the slaves like wildfire. Not only did the slaves in Georgia know about their marriage, but also it was heard through the grapevine as far north as New York City. Not only of our marriage but also that I was the girl struck by lightning who bled from my hands and feet. A few of the miracles followed through the grapevine, but mostly of my wedding.

I continued preaching the Gospel of Jesus Christ. God had softened Mrs. Burke's heart in such a way that I had been allowed to preach in the barn on Sunday mornings to all the slaves the Burkes owned. The news of the wedding spread also among Southern whites who held on to strict racist views, who didn't believe I should be preaching or any of the stories of miracles.

Early one Sunday Morning, I was preaching in the barn. The barn was full, which was the custom. I preached with fire in my belly. A burning desire of the Holy Spirit drove me. The anointing flowed like a river upon every word that came forth from my lips. I preached with fire and anointing, saying, "Believe in the Body and the Blood of our Lord Jesus Christ. Shall you not believe? God says, 'I raise the dead. I give sight to the blind. I call forth things into existence as they there already were. I made the heavens and the earth. I will judge the living and the dead. Shall you not believe that I have the power and love to give you my body and blood forever. I am not symbolic. I will love within my people, and my people will live with me. Did you not believe? I am the living bread that came down from heaven. Whoever eats this bread will live forever, and the bread that I will give is my flesh for the life of the world. I say to you, unless you eat the flesh of the

Son of Man and drink his blood, you do not have life within you. Whoever eats my flesh and drinks my blood has eternal life, and I will raise him on the last day. For my flesh is true food, and my blood is true drink. Whoever eats my flesh and drinks my blood remains in me and I in him.'"

When I had finished preaching those words, some of the slaves didn't believe that Jesus gave us his own body as food and drink. The barn became deftly silent. I wore a white head rag, and I preached in my dress. I seemed to radiate the Holy Spirit, truth and life. I broke the bread into small bite-size pieces and put both hands above the broken bread, which I had laid onto a covered barrel.

The clouds became gray, black, blue and purple with flashes of lightning radiating from within.

Bo stood to the right of his bride, staring straight at the crowd of slaves. He slowly stepped forward and ushered the slaves into two lines. He slowly stepped forward and ushered the slaves into two lines.

I held a broken piece of bread and said, "Receive the body and blood of Christ."

Slowly, one by one came up. Bo ushered them to me. I looked the first slave in the eyes. He humbly bent down on both knees in front of me. I took a piece of broken loaf and placed it inside his mouth. I poured wine into a tin cup and said, "Drink." Red slowly took a small sip of wine. Then he rose to his feet and went and knelt down and prayed.

Everyone watched Red as if in a trance. Then, slowly, each slave went and knelt in front of me. I placed a broken piece of bread into each one's mouth and gave a sip of wine.

The storm continued to rage. The sound of thunder boomed and echoed throughout the barn.

I continued to give each slave the body and blood of Jesus Christ. As they received the heavenly food, they knelt and prayed. Many slaves lay completely prostrated upon the ground, for Christ dwelt in them, and they dwelt in Christ.

And the storm continued to rage outside the barn.

But unknown to me and the slaves, a group of racist white men had been observing among the slaves. The group was headed by Captain Burris. He was a self-proclaimed captain He hadn't served or thought to serve in the military. He had only one goal—he wanted my death. He didn't believe any of the miracles. He didn't believe I was struck by lightning. He didn't believe that I miraculously knew the entire Bible. He believed that these things were lies told so that white men would view the nigger as people. Captain Burris believed that the nigger was a little higher than the ape. He believe they had no rhyme, no logical reasoning ability. He believed that I was a complete hoax and that I must be watched and eliminated, along with all the niggers who were so-called witnesses to anything I had done.

Captain Burris had devised to plan to kill me and all the slaves of the Burkes' plantation. He and his men planned to kill us during our Sunday morning church services. He knew that all the slaves would be there, young and old, sick and well. They all looked for a miracle. The plan was to watch and wait until all the slaves were in church and the service had reached its height so that none would notice any other activity except the church service. The scheme was to block the church doors and pour kerosene all over the barn and then set the barn on fire with all the slaves trapped inside. This was one swift and thorough act of terror designed to kill me and all the slaves who had witnessed any miracles.

On this Sunday morning, Captain Burris was informed that such an opportunity had finally arrived. He and his men mounted their horses and rode hard and fast to the Burkes' plantation. They hid in the surrounding thicket. They watched and listened.

Captain Burris told Shawn McDuff, "Go sneak a peep. See if we can kill the bastards."

Shawn was a skinny, pale redhead flunky. He was a follower, and he took orders well. He hated niggers because they were different. He hated them because they were black. He saw them as a threat to his livelihood. Shawn was poor. On some days, he couldn't feed his family. He knew that the niggers had food, and he hated them for that. He hated them because they sang while they worked. He hated them because they prayed and danced. He didn't understand them, nor did he care to. He wanted them dead. He felt that if the niggers were dead that he'd have more work, more money, a bigger house, and plenty of food.

Shawn crept and hid in the thickets of the bushes until he was close enough to the barn. There was a maple tree next to the barn. He climbed up the tree to get a better view of what was going on inside. He saw the slaves were kneeling in prayer, and many lay prostrated upon the ground. He hurried down the tree and ran to Captain Burris, tripping and stumbling over his untied boot straps. He, quietly gasping for breath, said, "It's our time, Captain. We can kill them all."

Captain Burris ordered McDuff to get a couple of men and block the barn door with wooden planks leaning against the door in such a way as to lock the slaves inside. He ordered Patrick Gallenger, another of his men, to fill as many buckets of kerosene as he could.

Patrick was a lot younger than McDuff. But he hated niggers as well. He hated them because his father hated them. He hated them because he was told that niggers had tails and that niggers rape white women, and he believed all that he heard.

Patrick hurried to a wood shack where the Burkes kept their kerosene. He didn't fill any buckets. He was in such a hurry that he grabbed all the bottles of kerosene that he could carry. After bringing them, he went and grabbed more.

Captain Burris ordered each man to pour the kerosene onto the barn. All of this activity went completely unknown to the slaves inside the barn. They were still very much in prayer and worship, for they had just received the body and blood of our Lord Jesus Christ. The slaves made sounds and words unrecognizable by man. Many seemed to speak in a foreign language, a heavenly language. As they prayed, their prayers rose up, piercing the clouds, going straight to the thrown of God Almighty.

Captain Burris gave the orders, "Set the niggers on fire." McDuff, Patrick, and the others made torches. They lit the torches and quietly set the barn on fire. Smoke slowly seeped into the barn.

The slaves started to panic. Many ran around trying to get out, pushing the barn doors to no avail. The situation seemed hopeless. I and many of the slaves huddled in a corner of the barn with the least smoke. We covered our heads and faces. Some tried to dig their way out to no avail. Screams reached a high. The screams reached the big house. But only Mr. and Mrs. Burke and their baby remained in the big house, for everyone else, except Jesse and Ms. Bell, were in the barn. Mr. and Mrs. Burke ran to the barn, but they were unable to come near because of the flames.

Thunder cracked and boomed. Lightning struck behind the barn. Lightning struck the barn. Lightning struck again on the road leading up to the barn. After the lightning had finished flashing and booming, there walked three angels toward the barn. The angels were invisible, unknown and unseen by anyone. Only the appearance of death and destruction loomed over me and the slaves. The angel Raphael walked tall and strong. He was sent to heal any of the wounds the slaves had. Also, the angel Jophkiel was sent to guide the slaves out of the burning flames. Finally, the angel Barak was sent, because they were to leave the barn praising the Lord of Hosts.

The angels walked directly through the fire into the barn. Once in the barn, the angels took on the appearance of slaves. Jophkiel walked and stood directly in front of me and the slaves huddled in the corner of the barn. He said, "Come, I have found a way out." I and the slaves could hardly see him because the barn was filled with smoke. The smoke was gray and burned our eyes when we tried to see. As we sat rubbing our eyes, trying to clean them of smoke to see more clearly, the angel Raphael walked up and stood next to Jophkiel. Raphael gently waved his right hand in the air in the direction of the slaves. Our eyes were opened, and everyone in the barn saw clearly. When everyone looked up, we saw three slaves dressed the way we were, but unknown to us.

Barak said in a soft yet strong voice, "We shall leave praising the Lord, for he has done great things." Everyone's attention went onto Barak. Time seemed to freeze. The smoke didn't move. We breathed freely, unhindered by the smoke. We saw clearly in a barn full of smoke and completely burning.

Barak cried, "Worthy is the Lamb who sits on the throne." Then he ordered the slaves, saying, "Sing, sing. Worthy is the Lamb. Worthy is the Lamb. Hallelujah. Worthy is the Lamb who sits on the throne."

Everyone repeated the praises exactly. Soon, the entire barn was full of the Lord's praises. Mr. and Mrs. Burke heard the singing and didn't know what to think because they didn't believe anyone would be able to survive the barn fire.

Jophkiel cried amid the Lord's praises, "Follow me and stay close together."

Unknowingly, the slaves walked directly through the fire. The fire didn't harm them, nor did it have its quench. The barn doors seemed to open by themselves. Smoke filled the sky, and the flames leaped wildly, consuming the barn. But the praises continued.

Ms. Bell cried, "Look, look!"

The slaves emerged from amid the smoke and fire singing, unharmed. The smoke and flames seemed to part and fly away from the slaves. As the slaves moved through the smoke and fire, it seemed an unending stream of slaves. Both young and old, sick and well left the barn, unharmed and breathing easy like in the cool of a summer's evening.

Once the last slave had left the barn, it collapsed. The slaves all stood looking and staring to find a face they knew, making sure that everyone was safe. The praises had slowly quieted down, and the rain continued to fall. Soon, everyone stood soaking wet in the rain. Cece grabbed my arm and pulled me close and hugged me. Everyone found a friend or loved one and hugged. Hugs and kisses rained upon the slaves like the rain that fell from the sky, and peace filled the air.

Jophkiel cried in a loud voice, "Praise the Lord, for he has delivered us from death. Let us rejoice in the Lord always."

At the sound of his voice, I fell to my knees. I placed both hands over my face and wept bitterly. Just as quickly as the slaves found their loved ones, they wept with tears of joy. Their weeping became a praise unto the Lord of Hosts, because the Lord had delivered them from death.

As the slaves cried tears of joy, Captain Burris and his men watched in astonishment. Shawn McDuff knelt down lurking in the thicket of the high grass, pointing a rifle at me. He spoke just loud enough for Captain Burris to hear him saying, "I got a clear shot, Captain. I got a clear shot. Just you give the order."

"No. We don't want to been seen or known by anyone. But the time is coming."

Captain Burris and his men quickly hurried through the woods to their horses. They mounted their horses and rode hard and fast to the Burrises' ranch. If Captain Burris was lacking in anything, it wasn't patience. He didn't get me today, but he knew he'd have another chance. He had become obsessed with me. He wanted me dead. He didn't understand the ways of God. In fact, he hated God and all who called themselves believers. So he hurried to the security of his ranch, until another opportunity appeared.

Chapter Ten

Be Fertile and Multiply

After the barn fire, the slaves united in an amazing way. Care, love, peace, and joy flourished among the slaves, both house and field niggers. When they worked in the fields, they sang songs of joy and triumph to Jesus their savior. They made up songs seemingly on a daily basis. And the songs they like, they sang over and over again. The slaves who worked in the house were no different. When they greeted each other, a smile raced onto their faces. They felt an amazing warmth and togetherness.

There were a few slaves who didn't share the same depth of joy. Bo was one of them. While Bo worked in the fields, he spoke to Ben. Ben was a little smaller than Bo. But they both worked equally hard, and for them, hard work was a sign of dignity and respect. Bo told Ben, "You know I heard they found some kerosene bottles around the barn. I believes that someone had set that old barn afire. Barns just don't burn like that. It rained that day, and the rain didn't put the fire out."

"What you gonna do, Bo?"

"I don't know, but I'm thinking about running."

"What! Where you gonna run to?"

"I'm thinking about taking Mary Lou up north. I ain't gonna let no cracker hurt her."

"You sure, Bo?"

"The ways I sees it, I don't have no choice. If I stays here, something bound to happen. And I'll be dead and in my grave before I let something happen to Mary Lou."

"Bo, you can't let nobody hear of your talk of running away. You know these ole no-nothing cotton-picking niggers will tell everything they hear."

"Shut up, Ben, and put that cotton in that croker sack. A man got to do what a man's got to do."

"I heard everything you said," replied Billy. "I wasn't trying to listen, but you know what Mary Lou done for me. And, Bo, whatever you thinking about doing, I'm in," replied Billy.

"Billy, how long you been over there?" asked Bo.

"Well, I went and sneaked off to pee-pee a while ago. And just as sure is my name is Billy, as soon I started to pee-pee, I had to do-do real bad. So I hear everything you said. I been leaning against the other side of that old tree for a while."

"Billy, you about as crazy as they come. Boy, get your tail on over here," Bo told Billy. "Now, Billy, you two are the only ones who know what I am planning. I ain't even told Mary Lou." The three of them sat crouched down upon their knees in the thicket of the cotton field.

"Well, Bo, if you gonna take Mary Lou up north, I'm with you, and I'm taking my old Creasy with me. You know I love me some Creasy," replied Ben.

"Yeah, you sure do," Billy quickly laughed out.

The sun was slowly setting, and the sky was a beautiful reddish orange, which seemed to turn the entire sky reddish orange with sprinkle clusters of white clouds bursting through. Everyone was slowly walking back to the valley. They walked with their backs a bit bent forward from all the bending and cotton picking of the day.

Bo seemed unaffected by the hard day's work. He quickly walked past the slaves all grouped together and headed for his old shack. The thrill of his new bride drove him. Excitement pushed his every step. Desire and hunger ran rampant through his body. As the sun slowly set, a few stars twinkled in the approaching night.

Bo had finally made it home. He didn't go directly into the house. He sneaked a peek through the wood-framed window. He saw me busy, bent over the fireplace, tending to some fried chicken, Bo's favorite food. The smell rose up his every sense. He stood there staring at his bride. I was simply beautiful. I wore a white head rag that highlighted the structure of my oval face, and my big brown eyes twinkled with stardust. I moved completely femininely. My femininity was absolutely amazing to Bo. He loved to watch me walk. The sway of my hips moved with grace and sexual excitement that caught the attention of most men of the day. I had a beautiful hourglass shape with extremely beautiful breasts. And Bo loved my every movement. I completely captured his entire being. My hands were soft and petite. I wore a brown-and-white maid's uniform worn by the slaves of the day. But it clung to me like pure silk, moving in a rhythm of femininity and sensuality that shamed the most beautiful women of her time. Bo's heart rose up his throat. He was proud of his bride. He could have peeked through that window all night, thinking I wasn't aware of his presence. But from the very beginning, I knew he was there.

Bo quietly entered his shack. I completely ignored Bo's coming and kept to my cooking. Bo glanced around, amazed at the cleanliness of his shack, and humbly took a seat at the eating table. I knew he'd worked hard, and I was thankful to have a man who prided himself in his work.

But I still didn't look in his direction. After turning the chicken and stirring the greens, I walked over to the end of the bed and picked up a pitcher of cool water and a washbasin. I took the pitcher of water and the basin over to Bo and knelt down on both knees in front of him. I rested upon the back of my legs and feet, supporting myself. I still didn't look at Bo; I seemed to be fixated on the task at hand. I untied Bo's old smelly boots. He didn't wear socks, and his feet had sores and blister in several spots. I slowly and carefully took off his boots one by one.

I had a rag draped over her shoulder. Still not raising my head to look into my husband's eyes, I gently, slowly lifted his feet and placed them into the washbasin. I slowly poured the cool water over them and washed them. Bo, amazed at the humility of his bride, sat erect in the chair, watching my every movement. I rolled his pant leg up and slowly washed his calves. My hands were so small and petite, they couldn't completely grab his calves. My touch was sensual and loving. I cared for Bo like none other he had ever known, including his own parents, whom he briefly had known. As I washed his calves, I slowly raised my eyes. My eyes met his in majestic sensuality.

Loved filled the room. We both felt a warmth deep into the depth of our souls. Our eyes seemed to water in the hope of compassion we both expected. Time seemed to stand still. Although for only a moment, our eyes, hearts, minds and soul became one. As we looked in each other's eyes, nothing else mattered. Only love. A love complete. A love of faith of compassion and care. No words could possibly describe the love we felt, and yet we expected more.

I said in a low romantic voice, looking into his eyes, "Bo, Mrs. Burke been real nice to me. I only works from sunup to sundown now. That's why I been able to cook you a good meal. I had Cece watch my greens for me."

Bo, gazing deeply into his bride's eyes, leaned over and slowly took hold of both my hands. He slowly and passionately pulled me forward. We both moved toward each other in majestic harmony. Then we kissed. I quickly pulled away, saying, "Bo, we got to eat something. I runs home to cook you something to eat, and you don't want to eat nothing. Come on, Bo, let's eat."

I leaned back and lifted Bo's feet out of the water one by one and dried them. I quickly put the wet washcloth in the dirty water and draped the dry rag onto my shoulders. Quickly, I stood and dumped the dirty water out of the window. Bo sat looking at the majestic beautiful sway of his wife's movements.

The smell of the fried chicken, greens, corn bread, and candied yams filled the room. I quickly set the table, placing one large wax candle in the center of the table. I fixed one plate and then another, setting them on the table, one in front of Bo and the other directly across from Bo. I moved quickly and quietly. Then I sat.

Bo's eyes, full of anticipation, looked upon the meal as if it were set for a king. His eyes moved from chicken to greens to corn bread to candied yams. Then he looked deeply into my eyes as if asking for approval to eat. He quickly grabbed a piece of chicken.

I blurted, "Bo, we supposed to say grace." He put the chicken down and bowed his head. I prayed, "Dear Lord Jesus, thank you for the meal that you have given us." I looked up, meeting Bo's eyes in anticipation of his prayer.

Bo quickly prayed, "Jesus wept. Now let's eat." We ate quietly, occasionally gazing romantically into each other's eyes.

After dinner, Bo sat leaning back into his chair, gazing into the fireplace, seemingly completely content. I slowly cleared the table, gazing into Bo's eyes each time I picked up a dish or walked by.

Bo, staring into the fire, said, "Ms. Mary, I'm gonna take you up north. I don't think that fire just started by itself. You know that they found some kerosene bottles around the barn? I thinks somebody trying to hurt you, and I ain't gonna let nobody hurt you. I couldn't live with myself knowing that something happened and I could have stopped it."

"Bo, what you saying ain't so? Master Burke and his missus been real good to us. They done gave us a wedding fit for one of their own family. I don't believe Master Burke would hurt us."

"I ain't talking about no Master Burke. It's somebody else. You know, we live in the dirty south. These white folks will just as well kill us than kill a coon. We ain't nothing to these folks. They don't care nothing about you being blessed by God."

"Bo, you should say such a thing. God hears every word you saying."

"Well, God surely knows these folks don't mean you no good. And we gonna run away up north." After Bo finished talking, silence filled the room. I was completely silent. I slowly washed the dishes, staring at them as if in a trance. Bo sat staring into the fire.

Later that night, we made love. An ancient love that sprang from the beginning of time. A love that held both life and death in a bond of harmony and unity that produced all creation in the explosion of passion. Unknown to both of us, I conceived a son that night.

The next day, I woke early. I wanted to get to the Burkes to get a fresh start on breakfast and taking care of Ashley. I had been feeling guilty lately because Little Lizzy had been mostly taking care of Ashley since our marriage.

The sun hadn't yet risen. The haze from the approaching sunrise had barely begun to light the sky. As I walked through the woods with the dew still wet on the ground, I noticed a shadow following a ways back. I kept walking and hurried my pace. It was one of Captain Burris's men. I didn't see him, but I know someone was following me. As I cleared the grassy plane leading onto the main road, leading up to the big house, I saw one of the slaves who helped us out of the burning barn.

Jophkiel was walking toward me, seemingly coming from the big house. He was dressed like a field slave. I thought he must have come from visiting Little Lizzy. Jophkiel was amazingly strong in stature. He was bald headed with deep eyebrows and a kindly disposition—all the qualities that I knew Little Lizzy liked in a slave.

As we drew closer, I noticed him smiling. I said, "What's so funny this early in the morning?"

He replied, "It's just a nice morning for a walk."

"It's too early to be out walking. You must be coming from visiting Little Lizzy."

"Oh, no," replied Jophkiel. We both stopped in the middle of the road. A moment of silence passed between us. Then Jophkiel said, "You are going to have a son, and listen to your husband. He's going to take you up north. Don't worry."

I looked into his eyes, staring, trying to somehow understand how he knew about what Bo wanted to do. I blurted out, "So I'm gonna have a baby? Well, I hope so. I really wants one."

"You'll make a good mother," replied Jophkiel.

"Yeah, I think I'll be a good mother. I better be getting on up yonder. Master Burke, he'll be getting up soon." Unaware to me, I still didn't know the true nature of Jophkiel. Upon arrival at the big house, I did my usual duties for the day and went home.

The weeks seemed to fly by. Bo and I finally conceived. I told all on slave row and the big house that I was pregnant. For the most part, all who knew me was pleased to hear the good news. Yet Bo seemed to be worried.

During our evening talk, Bo said, "Beloved, you know I love you. I want a baby just like you do. But I don't want no child of mine to be a slave."

"What you saying, Bo?" I replied.

"I been talking to Billy and Ben, and we decided to run."

"Now, where we gonna run to, Bo?"

"We going up north. That's right. On the next rainy evening. You get just what you need. And don't you tell nobody. You hear me? Don't you tell nobody."

"Bo, you know that slave that helped us out of the fire? Well, he told me a while ago that we was going up north and that I was going to have a baby."

"Somebody must of told him, but that don't change nothing. We still gonna run."

"I'll be ready. I just wants to tell my friends good-bye."

"No, no, no, we can't tell nobody. We have to go without anybody knowing."

"But what about Little Lizzy? I done met some good folks, Bo. They should know."

"I ain't gonna say no more. If I'm gonna be able to take you up north, nobody can know . . . I ain't gonna have my child being nobody's slaves," replied Bo.

During the next few weeks, I began to show. My belly seemed to grow day by day. The bigger I got, the more Bo worried.

Chapter Eleven

Run Away to Freedom . . .

It had been a hazy day. The wind blew from the north to south. To most of the slaves, it was an ordinary workday, but to Bo, Billy, and Ben, it looked like the day that was going to forever change their lives.

I worked as usual, occasionally looking at the sky, thinking, *If it rains, we may run, and I'll never see Little Lizzy again.* Little Lizzy didn't know of the plans Bo had made. But she was aware of me being really nice lately. She thought it was because I was pregnant.

I had been wearing a beautiful silver pen in my head rag that I had received as a wedding gift. As we continued preparations for dinner, I took the pendant from the head rag and stood face-to-face with Little Lizzy, saying, "Thought you might like it."

"Oh, no, girl. You better keep that thang. It's a wedding gift. It's yours."

"I wants to give you something. Here, take it. I want you to have it," I replied. I continued to move and arrange the pendant into Little Lizzy's hair and head rag.

"How does it look?"

"Girl, you look good. You know you look good in everything you put on."

Little Lizzy walked back and forth in the kitchen, holding her head stiff, showing off the pendant and teasing me. The sound of thunder echoed through the kitchen, startling us two.

"It sounds like it's going to be an awful storm," replied Little Lizzy.

"Yeah, I'm gonna be heading on home or else I might not make it."

"You better talk to Mrs. or Mr. Burke before you go running off."

She hurriedly took off her cooking apron and quickly went into the parlor. There sat Mr. and Mrs. Burke. Mrs. Burke said, "What is it, Mary Lou?"

"Well, Ma'am, it gonna rain something awful."

"You can leave. The others will do just fine," replied Mrs. Burke.

"Thank you, ma'am," I replied. I quickly left the room went into the kitchen and wrapped myself into my shawl and quickly headed for the valley without saying good-bye to anyone.

As I reached the dirt road leading to our shack, I saw the field slaves all grouped together walking from the fields. I saw Bo, Ben, and Billy walking in the midst of them. It gently began to rain. Bo hurried into the shack and said, "I want you to get everything ready. We gonna run tonight. We ain't never gonna be a slave again." I quickly went around packing changes of clothes and getting food items together. Bo quickly put on double his clothing and stared out the window. After we got everything ready, I quickly prepared a meal. That evening was going to be our last as slaves.

During our evening meal, we sat quietly. Candlelight flickered throughout the room, and a sense of anticipation filled our hearts. After dinner, Bo sat looking out of the window. He patiently waited for Billy and Ben's signal. The wind continued to blow north to south, and rain started to pour. Soon, the entire valley was soaked. The roads were muddy, which seemed to Bo to be a blessing. Bo said, "I guess Billy and Ben must be eatin' something too."

"I hope they eatin' something. We gonna need all our strength. Bo, you know I'm pregnant, and I don't know why you couldn't wait until I had the baby?"

"Don't you go fussin' with me, woman. I didn't tell you to get pregnant," replied Bo.

Bo sat staring out of the window, looking for a signal. After it had gotten good and dark, Bo raised a kerosene lantern up to the window and waved it back and forth. A few seconds later, he looked toward Billy's shack. He saw another lantern being waved from Ben's shack. The time had finally arrived. All the preparations and waiting had finally arrived. All the preparations and waiting had finally come to a climax.

Bo and I gathered all we could carry without being overloaded. We blew out our lantern and quietly snuck out of our shack. We quickly ran around the back of the valley and headed to a cluster of trees. It continued to thunder and lightning, and the rain poured. We were soaking wet only after being in the rain for a few minutes. As we huddled under a large tree, Billy, Ben, and Creasy snuck up upon them. Bo said, "We going up north. We ain't gonna run. We gonna walk and keep a good step. Come on. Let's get the moving."

During the previous few months, Bo, Billy, and Ben had plotted a route up north. During the clear summer nights, they plotted a course following the drinking gourd. They had planned a route to freedom through the woods and bush that they believed no one could follow. They believed the rain would wash away their shoe prints by the time they'd be missed. They would be many miles away. Their plan was to travel by day and by night.

It was hard traveling. The ground was muddy and soaking wet. Our clothes were soaked completely through. A chill ran through our bodies. Each step seemed a labor of love. Although we were tired, we kept on moving. Although we were chilled to the bone, we kept on moving. An inner warmth kept us warm. Deep in our souls, a burning desire pushed us forward and warmed our bodies. When the stepping was hard, our feet sank deep into the muddy ground. But it didn't hinder us or seem to be a burden, for we had fixed our hearts on freedom. And no one complained.

As the night ended and the early morning sunrise pierced the sky, I said, "Look a' here, Bo. We been moving all night long. I'm hungry. I'm eatin' for two."

"Well, we'll stop just a ways up."

We reached a cave that looked to be covered with growth. The cave was barely seen, but, somehow, Bo spotted it through the high grass and bush. It was on the side of a rocky high hill. Everyone thanked God, for the cave was the only dry place we had entered during our entire run. Once in the cave, we all sat huddled close together. I had packed some dried beef. I pulled some out and handed some to Bo. It seemed like we all had the same thought because every one of us ate dried beef we had packed.

When we finished eating, the men went out and stood looking around the area, surveying. It continued to rain, and everyone believed that was a blessing because the rain would wash away our scent. We stayed together and ducked down under the high grass and hid behind trees. No one could be seen or heard. When we came back into the cave, I asked Bo, "Where are we supposed to be running off to?"

"We're going to Ohio. Negroes is free in Ohio."

"Bo, I heard that Ohio is a long, long way."

"We can make it. It's a railroad out here. It's an underground railroad. That's right. There's white folks that going to help us. Once we get out of Georgia, we'll stop in Tennessee. There's a way, and I know it."

"Bo, you ain't never been out of Georgia, though."

"We all going to make it, and this here rain is washing our scent and footprints away. We couldn't have asked for a better day to run. It done rained all night long, and it done rained hard too. We stayed in the grass. We moved fast. No one would think anybody would run in this kind of weather. We be fine. We goin' to get some rest, then keep a moving while it's still rainin' heavy."

"I'm pregnant. I don't know when the baby is coming. We could be anywhere and he comes."

"You having a boy?"

"I don't know. I just said 'he.'"

149

"Ms. Mary, I wants you to pray. Pray for us to get through this and make it to freedom. God hears you."

"Bo, God hears all our prayers."

"Yeah, but you special. God has blessed you a little more than the rest of us."

"OK, Bo! I'll pray. You just get us to freedom." I went and sat down next to Creasy. Creasy was sitting in a corner of the cave, trembling from the cold weather. We both sat and hugged each other, trying to keep warm.

Ben said, "I can start a fire if I can find some dry wood."

"No, ain't no fire going to be burning around here. They'd be able to see the smoke for miles away. We'd sure to be caught," replied Bo.

"That's right," replied Billy.

"Smoke could be coming from anybody. It don't necessary have to be from us," Ben replied.

"Now, Ben, we the only runaways. We going to have to use some mother wit when it comes to this here. I don't plan on going back. They'll put trees with a whip on all our backs. We ain't having no fires. We be just fine," Bo replied.

We all sat huddled together, trying to get warm. The cave was dry and dark, but it kept us out of the weather for a while. The rain continued to pour down. Like a wave, peace entered the cave. A moment later, they were all sound asleep.

Later, Bo woke up. He peeped out of the cave and saw the sun just beginning to set, and the rain was still coming down hard. He woke the others, saying, "Come on. Let's go. It's almost sundown. We done slept the whole day away." Everyone stood up and arranged our clothes. We peeped out of the cave. Then Bo said, "Come on. It's this way." He was pointing north. We rushed out of the cave, following Bo. The sky was beautiful bluish red with streaks of white piercing its way thought the clouds. We set out headed north to freedom.

The rain felt like drops of joy on our faces. No one was afraid. It seemed a playful time. As we ran, they leaped and jumped for joy. We ran and ran, running without getting tired, just running in the rain of Georgia. As night quickly fell, we slowed our run to a very fast walk. We walked and walked, always going north. The rain stopped and the clouds cleared and the beautiful night filled the sky with a burst of stars. The going was a quiet going, following the drinking gourd.

As morning slowly came, we came to a large cotton field. It looked just like the ones down home. Everyone sat in the thick woods, looking, hiding, waiting to see if anyone comes to pick cotton. Just as we got seated good, slowly and surely the field slaves came. The sun slowly rose, and the south dry heat quickly dried the grass. We hid under the tall dry grass and rested. All but Bo. He slowly crawled to the edge of the cotton field, hiding in the tall grassy areas. He watched the slaves pick cotton and put it into croker sacks. He thought, *Nothing has changed. We slaves wherever we go.*

He'd been told that in two days' running by night that he'd come to a cotton field, and that in that cotton field, there was an old field Negro called Smiley. Smiley helped on the underground railroad. Smiley would help runaway slaves and feed them. He was also told that Smiley picked on the edge. He wore an old brown hat and smoked a corn pipe and that he was black as coal, blue black with all his teeth, and when you spoke to him, he smiled.

Bo lay in the thick grass, watching. He stayed out of sight. He peeped up and down, gazing all around. Finally, he saw an old Negro picking cotton to the left of him. Bo was surprised to see him because he didn't even notice him come up. He crawled on his belly through the thick grass as close to Smiley as he could. Smiley picked cotton, unaware that Bo was close enough to touch him. Bo lay in the cotton field, hiding in the rows. Finally, Bo whispered, "Smiley, Smiley." Smiley turned his head, looking around to see if any of the other field slaves were calling him. Then he ignored the call. It came to him in an instant. *It must be a runaway.* He kept his head down and kept on working. Bo whispered again, "Smiley, I'm looking for Smiley."

Smiley finally whispered back, "That's me. I'm Smiley. Where are you? I can't see you."

"I'm over here, lying in the dirt between the rows."

"I can't do nothing until the sun sets. When the sun sets, you go down to the creek. Hide in the brush by the old oak tree. I'll send someone to fetch you," replied Smiley. Smiley kept on picking cotton and moved away from the edge. He worked his way toward the center. As he worked his way toward the center, many slaves raised their heads watching Smiley. They knew he'd found runaway slaves.

Chapter Twelve

Good-Bye, Dear Friend . . .

Master Burke had slave hunters searching the surrounding area night and day looking for me and the other runaways. I was the talk of the South. Master Burke was humiliated. He treated me like his own daughter. Honor, respect, he held tight. Now, he was in complete dishonor. He sent for his dear friend Reverend Cole. Reverend Cole had a way of finding runaways.

Upon arriving, Reverend Cole quickly entered the house and went directly to the library. Master Burke sat quietly, sipping brandy. Reverend Cole walked over to the desk and poured him a glass of brandy. He said, "So your prize nigger has run."

Burke sipped on his brandy and gazed toward Reverend Cole, replying, "I treated that damn nigger like she was white. I gave her a wedding better than most white folks had ever seen. I can't believe she'd do such a thing."

"Well, sir, I've explained the nigger's mind-set from the start. You can't never trust them. You paid good money for her, and the others were good workers. So you're out of money, honor, and respect. Now I'd suspect that others are planning to run," replied Reverend Cole.

"God forbid."

Reverend Cole walked over and sat across from Master Burke and asked, "Are you still keeping company with the nigger girl that came with Mary Lou?"

"She's my property. I do what I want to her."

"I'd take that as a yes. Well, I bet she knows where your property is run off to."

"No. Lizzy is dumb as a rock."

"That's what she wants you to believe. You've already had, what, four or five run off. And this Lizzy was friends with Mary Lou. She knows more than she's told."

"I ain't asked her nothing about it."

"Let's see what she knows." Reverend Cole stood and quickly finished his brandy. He looked down staring into Master Burke's eyes and quietly said, "Call her. I have a few words for her. Jonathan, call her. I don't give a damn if she's the best ass you've ever had. You have to stop this thing right now. If you don't, every damn nigger you own will run off. She was Mary Lou's friend. She's the example. It must be set. Now call her."

Jonathon stood and slowly walked to the library door. He opened the door and screamed, "Little Lizzy, get your black ass in here right now."

Little Lizzy ran to the library, unaware of who was there or why she was called. When she saw Master Burke standing in the doorway entrance, she stopped and slowly walked to him. She stood close to him, looking intently into his eyes and batting her eyes. He said, "Come on in. We have some questions for you." She slowly and shyly walked into the library. She stood with her hands to her sides, completely still. She knew now what this was about. Fear rushed upon her like mighty wind. She saw Reverend Cole standing at the desk, pouring brandy into a glass.

"She was your friend," Reverend Cole quickly blurted out.

"Yes, sir. I come here with her."

"I suppose you don't know where she run off to or which way she took."

"No, sir, I don't know nothing about her running off. She had been real quiet lately. Since she got married, she didn't talk to me about nothing but Jesus and work."

"Jesus, Jesus, you talk about Jesus. What did Jesus do when the thieves and money changers came into his house?"

"I don't know, sir."

"Well, he beat them. That's right. He drove the thieves and money changers out of his Father's house. He beat them. Now, it's like this. You are my dear friend's property. You are the one who knows where the thieves and money changers done run off to."

"No, sir, I don't know nothing about no stealing, and I ain't never had no money."

"Well, Little Lizzy, you a slave. You are property, so is Mary Lou and the others. Also, she's your friend, so that makes you a thief just like her."

"No, sir, I ain't never stole nothing."

"Well, Little Lizzy, a apple don't fall too far from the tree. So you'll be the one who gets punished for your friend Mary Lou. So you better tell us where she's at, or I'll take the hide right off your back."

Little Lizzy burst into tears, falling on her knees, crying. "I don't know where she is. I don't know."

"Your friends stole their freedom. Good money was paid for them niggers. You see, we have to get our money. We not in this business for fun. Although that is a part of our business. Now, get up. Come on. Let's go to the stable." Little Lizzy lay on the floor, crying, trying to hug the floor. "Jonathan, get her up and drag her black ass to the stable!" shouted Reverend Cole.

Jonathan slowly walked over to her. He leaned over and grabbed her arm, lifting her off the floor. She refused to stand. Her legs were limp, unable to support her weight. Jonathan snatched her off the floor and flung her over his shoulder like a sack of cotton. He quickly walked to the door, kicking it open. Mrs. Burke heard Little Lizzy's screams and stood at the top of the stairs, watching him take her quickly through the house. Reverend Cole followed quickly behind him.

Once outside, Reverend Cold reached inside his carriage and quickly grabbed the cattail whip. Jonathan kept on walking. The slaves working outside stopped working and stared at Master Burke forcefully carrying Little Lizzy. No one said a word. Every slave who saw stood scared for their own lives, unable to move. They seemed to be in a trance watching Master Burke carry her across the yard to the stable.

Once in the stable, Reverend Cole shouted, "Get me a rope!" A few slaves were in the stable cleaning up. Upon hearing Reverend Cole's order, a slave immediately dropped a rack he was using and ran to the back of the wall and grabbed a rope hanging on the wall. He ran and handed it to Reverend Cole. Reverend Cole screamed, "Everyone, out of here right now!" He looked around the stable, making eye contact with every slave he could. Each one stopped what they were doing and left the stable.

Jonathan laid Little Lizzy on the ground in the middle of the stable. She lay there crying and moaning, unable to move, and desperately hoping in vain that no harm would come to her. Reverend Cole slung the rope over a beam in the stable. He tied one end of the rope to a post. With the end hanging over the post, he lifted Little Lizzy's arms up and tied her hands together at her wrist. Then he pulled her up until her feet were off the ground. Jonathan Burke walked around closing all the doors and windows. When he returned to the center of the stable, he walked quickly to Little Lizzy and ripped her clothes off of her. She hung there completely naked. Her eyes were streaming with tears. Her body was beautiful.

"It's a shame to scar such a beautiful young lady. But you brought it upon yourself. Take a good look, Jonathan. She's never going to look the same. That beautiful yellow skin is gonna come right off. You better tell me where they ran off to."

"I don't know," cried Little Lizzy.

"OK, I got something for you." Reverend Cole walked around looking for chicken fat, cooking oil, anything to oil his whip with. He shouted, "Where's the damn oil around here?"

"I'll get it. It's in the utility shack." Jonathan hurried back to the stable and gave it to Reverend Cole.

"Thank you, Jonathan. I'm gonna take the hide right off this nigger. I'll show you how to cut the head off this here runaway business before it gets worse." Reverend Cole slowly took the lid off of the cooking oil. He knelt down in front of Little Lizzy, staring up at her. He put his right hand into the cooking oil and slowly rubbed it onto his whip. After he finished, he stood up and slowly walked around her. He stood behind her, staring at her naked body. Tears ran down her face in an unending surge of emotion.

Reverend Cole raised the whip with its nine strips of leather and metal pieces attached to each strip dripping with cooking oil. He shouted, "Aw, nigger, I got you now!" Then he swung with all his might. The whip struck her. She felt a jolt like lightning surge through her body. Her breath left her body. She gasped for breath, unable to find it. Sweat immediately appeared all over her body. She jerked in an uncontrolled spasm and screamed at the top of her voice. The whip dug into her flesh, ripping and cutting into her flesh. When he jerked it back, he took pieces of her flesh and blood. Flesh and blood squirted upon Jonathan's and Reverend Cole's faces. He swung again, again and again. With every stroke of the whip, flesh and blood flew through the air. Her back was completely covered in blood. She hung there unconscious. Blood flowed down her legs and formed a puddle under her.

Jonathan shouted, "Stop! She's half dead."

"No, she ain't. The nigger is a tricky bastard."

"No more. She ain't no good to me dead."

"She'll survive this beating. OK, it's your nigger. I'm just here to help you stop this before it gets worse."

"I'll call the other slaves and let them see her and care for her."

"It better work or it'll be some dead niggers around here."

The house slaves and other slaves who worked around the plantation were all standing around, listening and hoping that Little Lizzy wasn't beat to death. Silence filled the air. It seemed like the wind told the story. Every crack of the whip echoed throughout the plantation. No one was unaware of the terrible deed being done.

Master Burke came out of the stables spotted with blood. He took his handkerchief out of his back pocket and slowly wiped the blood off his face. He looked around and stared into the eyes of each slave standing. "Compared to what's going to happen when I find the others. Let this be a lesson to you. If you run or know somebody who done run, this is what you'll get and worse. Now, go and get her out of my stables and get it cleaned." He continued to stare each slave in the eyes. Then he shouted, "Come on, Reverend Cole, let's get this nigger blood off us!"

He and Reverend Cole walked directly to the big house. None of the slaves moved. The ones there stood in a trance like statues. They were numb, afraid, unable to move. When Master Burke and Reverend Cole entered the big house, Eli and Jesse ran to the stables. They saw Little Lizzy hanging from a rope tied to the rafters. She was unconscious. Blood was dripping onto the ground. Her beautiful fair skin was smeared in blood. There were whip lashes on her breasts, legs, and stomach. Eli cried, "Oh my god. Get Ms. Bell in here right now."

Jesse stopped dead in his tracks and ran to the big house back door. Ms. Bell stood staring toward the stables. Jesse cried frantically, "Come on. It's Little Lizzy. Come on. It's Little Lizzy. Come on."

She hurried behind Jesse as fast as she could. When she entered the barn, Eli held Little Lizzy in his arms, crying. She lay there limp, unconscious. Her back was beaten raw. There were large rips and cuts left from the cat-o'-nine-tails. She was covered in blood.

Ms. Bell shouted, "We got to get her wounds covered and stop the bleeding! Get me one of those horse blankets. We can wrap her in it."

"Bell, we gonna sure enough get beat if we use Master Burke's horse blankets!" shouted Eli.

"You let me worry about that. You just do what I say."

Eli ran over to one of the horses and snatched the blanket off of it. He quickly gave it to Ms. Bell. She wrapped Little Lizzy in the blanket, completely covering her. "Get me some axle grease, and plenty of it!" shouted Ms. Bell.

Jesse went out to the utility shack and grabbed a large canister of axle grease. On the way back to stables, he saw Eli carrying Little Lizzy, walking behind Ms. Bell. They were walking toward the big house. He followed. Once in the big house, they took her to her room. Eli laid her onto her bed. "Get me some hot water," ordered Ms. Bell.

Jesse went into the kitchen and brought a wash pan, rag, and a pitcher of hot water. Ms. Bell soaked the rag in the hot water and gently washed the blood from Little Lizzy. Little Lizzy lay unconscious on her bed completely nude and unaware. Ms. Bell shouted, "You two can go. Ain't nothing you can do. She'll be fine. She's gonna be scared. She's got a tree on her back, and it's branches stretch around to her breasts and stomach. I'm gonna put some axle grease on her and lay her on her stomach."

Eli and Jesse left the room, and Ms. Bell turned Little Lizzy onto her stomach and put large quantities of axle grease inside whip wounds and all over her back and the areas where she was whipped. Ms. Bell whispered, "God loves you, baby. It's gonna be all right. You just hang in there. You'll be fine. I'm gonna take good care of you." She gently stroked her hair and ran her hand gently across her face.

Little Lizzy lay still motionless with a glow of an angel radiating from her. No sooner had Ms. Bell finished talking than Little Lizzy breathed out her last breath. She lay there motionless, peaceful, radiant, seemingly resting. She was beautiful—beautiful in life and beautiful in death.

"You gone home now. Ain't nobody gonna ever hurt you again. Good-bye, sweet Little Lizzy."

Chapter Thirteen

Lily in the Valley . . .

Bo, Billy, Creasy, Ben, and I all lay in the bush next to the old oak tree. The bush was high and we couldn't be seen. We had waited all day. The sun set in a beautiful burst of colors of reds, oranges, blues, and whites that seemed too peaceful for description. As we watched the sunset, peace covered us. There was a warm breeze blowing from the south. As the breeze rested upon us and filled our lungs with the breath of life, I became teary eyed. Tears ran down my cheek. Bo asked me, "What's wrong? Something done blown into your eyes?"

"No, Bo. It's Little Lizzy. I can feel it. She's . . . she's dead."

"How do you know that?"

"I don't know how to explain it. The wind blew a word from the Lord into my spirit."

"I believe you."

"She's with Jesus. Come on. Let's pray and praise the Lord." I lay on my stomach as best as I could. I placed my face into the dirt and prayed. I wept for my friend and prayed for freedom. The others all sat still, looking and mourning the loss of Little Lizzy in the bushes.

After a while, a whisper was heard. Everyone sat quiet and fearful. Fear filled our minds and hearts. We thought it might be a bounty hunter. It sounded again. Ben crawled out from under the bush. The sun had set; it was dark. He couldn't see anything. Then he looked toward the old oak tree down a ways, and he saw a lantern rocking back and forth. He hurried back into the bush and told the others.

Bo whispered, "Ben, you go see. It could be Smiley, or maybe he sent someone to fetch us."

Ben hurried from under the bush and crawled on his belly, always staying hidden to the place where he saw the lantern. He lay on the ground, looking around. Then he heard it again. "You all out here? Anybody out here?"

"Yeah, I'm here," Ben answered.

"I been sent by Smiley to fetch you."

"I need to see you. Show yourself."

A blue-black slave slowly came from hiding behind a cluster of trees. He walked slowly and clutched over. He walked up to where Ben was hiding and said, "I'm here. Where are you?"

Ben slowly came out of hiding and said, "Who sent you?"

"Smiley sent me to fetch you and take you to hiding." They stood there bent over, looking into each other's eyes, searching for any hint of deceit or treachery. They both were fearful of each other. This gave them adequate confirmation that they both could trust each other.

Ben said, "Come on. Follow me." They both hunched over and quickly hurried to where the others were hiding. Ben and Lil George crawled under the brush to where the others were hiding.

Lil George whispered, "I'm Lil George. Smiley sent me to take you to hiding." We all stared at first, wide eyed and unsure. He looked around at us. Then he whispered, "You must be Mary Lou. We heard it was you that was running. Word spread far and wide and how you was struck by lightning and all."

Bo quickly interjected, "We ain't got no time for that. We need to get to where there's food and shelter. My wife is pregnant. So if you gonna take us, let's go."

"Come on. We ain't got far. We hides you all in the big house. Master Davis's wife is against slavery. She show enough against slavery. She's got hiding places for you."

We all crawled from under the brush. We followed Lil George, all hunched over, running in a slow trot. We ran and ran. It seemed like hours. The only one who knew the way was Lil George. A clearing appeared. "We here now. That's the big house over there. I'm gonna take you all to the barn later. We hides slaves in the barn."

Lil George whistled like a bird, and someone opened a small door at the end of the barn. It was barely big enough for one man to enter. We all hurried and ran into the barn. We were guided into horse stalls. We all fell on the ground and huddled together. Lil George hustled up some food that was hidden around the barn. Everyone was pleased to be out of the night weather into a dry place. There were blankets and hay in the stalls. We covered up for the night.

Early the next morning before dawn, Lil George came and brought some bread and milk. We quickly ate, while Lil George stood and watched in amazement. When we had finished eating, Lil George told them, "Get ready. Master Davis is going for his morning ride soon. He rides every morning. That's when we can sneak you all into the big house. The stables is on the other side of the plantation. You all stay put. I'll go and watch Master Davis to ride past. Then I'll come and get you."

"You sure we gonna be fine in here?" asked Billy.

"He ain't caught no runaways yet." Lil George quickly turned and left the barn.

We all stood and gathered in one stall and waited. Soon, the door opened. A man with a hat on and a pipe in his mouth came into the barn. He looked in our direction. Fear rushed upon us. We all backed into a corner of the stall and sat down, putting hay quietly upon ourselves, hoping to hide. The man slowly walked over to the stall we were in until he opened the stall door. He stood there, smiling from ear to ear. He took out a wooden match and lit his pipe, slowly puffing and drawing smoke in and out of his mouth.

Bo stood and quietly asked, "Smiley, is that you? You scared us something awful."

"Yes, sir, it's me. Come on. I'll take you into the big house. Mrs. Davis is excited that you all made it this far. We heard a Captain Burris is looking for Mary Lou and the rest of you."

"I suppose some of everybody is looking for us," Bo replied.

"Come on. Follow me."

Smiley went to the secret barn door that they had entered the barn in. He opened it and held it until everyone had left the barn. He followed behind us and took the lead. He led us to an outside basement door of the big house. Smiley looked around to see if anyone was looking. He lifted the basement door and gestured for us to go into the basement. Everyone quickly scurried into the basement. The basement was dark and musty. There were no windows. Smiley followed behind and closed the door behind him, locking it. He knew his way around in the dark, while everyone else stood close together, afraid and worried.

Smiley lit a wooden match. He held it up to his face, smiling. He seemed to enjoy himself. We didn't know why. Smiley seemed happier than we were. He found a lantern and lit it. He motioned for everyone to follow him. Everyone walked slowly, ducking down as if the ceiling was low. A sense of suspense filled the air. We walked directly to a large number of shelves on the wall. Smiley raised the lantern and moved his hand along the edge until he found a long nail sticking out of the wood. He took a strong hold on the nail and lifted. He pushed the shelves backward, and a roller opened up behind the shelves of preserved goods.

The room was completely dark. He held the lantern and motioned for us to enter the room. We all stood there, afraid to enter. Our eyes were wide and bucked. Smiley motioned again, and Bo, slowly holding onto my hand, walked into the room. Smiley extended his hand that held the lantern into the room. Bo and I saw straw beds on wooden planks lined against the wall and a small table in the center of the room. He handed the lantern to Bo. Bo motioned for the others to follow. They slowly entered.

Smiley whispered, "You all will be fine in here. Don't talk loud. Keep everything to a whisper. There's another lantern here too. It's food and clothes in there too. I'll be back later." Smiley closed the secret door behind them. He went to the basement door and opened it. He slowly looked out and quickly hurried out of the basement.

In the hidden room, there was plenty of room. The room looked to be an old storage shed that had been converted into a hiding place for runaway slaves. We felt safe and secure for the first time since we had begun to run. Bo quickly lit the other lantern, and the room burst with light. The floor was wooden. Also, the walls were wood and brick. The room was exceptionally clean. On the table were a pitcher of water and a small washtub. There were four chairs around the table. In fact, the room looked better than our shacks on slave row, and it was larger too.

On the top of each bed were a blanket and some food wrapped in brown paper, clothes, and a pair of boots. Each one sat on a separate bed and unwrapped our items. There were a couple of pieces of fruit and two jam sandwiches.

Creasy opened hers and took it over to me. "You eating for two. I'm not hungry. I want you to have this."

"I can't take your food. You needs to eat too."

The others all looked in our direction, listening to my refusal. Slowly Ben, Billy, and Bo came over to my bed and handed me a piece of fruit or a sandwich. I looked into each one's eyes, wanting to cry. I felt compassion and love from each one, feeling ashamed to turn them down. I took an apple from Bo's hand and ate it. The other items I wrapped in a shirt that was in the bundle.

Billy and Ben unwrapped the clothes and held them up to their bodies, looking to see if they fit. They quickly took off their smelly damp clothes and put on the dry clothes. Soon, everyone followed.

After eating, I lay on the straw bed and fell sound asleep. Billy, Ben, Creasy, and Bo sat around the table. The lantern sat in the middle of the table. The other lantern sat on the floor next to the hidden entrance. They sat relaxed and calm, glaring into each other's eyes. Bo calmly said, "I told you we were going to be just fine. I could feel it in my bones. I can see old Master Burke looking and hunting everywhere with them hound dogs and can't find a thing." Everyone smiled.

"Yeah, we still got a ways to go. We ain't gonna be free until we in Ohio, a free state," Ben replied.

"We gonna make it. I can feel it too, Bo. It's in the air. I can smell it," replied Creasy.

"What you talking about, woman?" Ben quickly whispered.

"I'm talking about freedom. I can feel it. I can smell it. We all gonna be free. I know it."

"Billy, you must feel something. You done ran away more times than you can shake a stick at," whispered Ben.

"She's right. I ain't never got this far before. I'm usually caught by now. And I ain't never had no one to look after me. How did you find out about Smiley and that underground railroad? You must know somebody, boy." Everyone sat quietly staring at Bo.

Bo looked into each one's eyes, searching for a word. He thought, *I'll just tell them. It's as good a time as any.* "You remember them three fellas who helped us out of that burning barn? One day, I was walking back from the fields. It was hot, and I was tired. I must have been dragging my being. Well, one of them caught up with me. He must have been the last one to come from the fields. He walked a spell with me. He said he was Jophkiel. I ain't think nothing of it at the time. I just thought he had one of them

African names. Well, he told me some things. I don't know if I should tell. But I'll tell.

"He said, 'The fire wasn't no accident. It was set by a captain Burris and his men. These men want Mary Lou dead. They been watching her and all she's done. They are up to no good and will do just about anything to kill her. She got to go north. There is a woman known as Harriet Tubman. She's what they've called the Black Moses. She's been taking slaves up north. I've walked with her. I know the way up north. You just follow the North Star, point to it, then, in rain or shine, you'll know the way. Just remember.'

"Then he told me about Smiley and the others who would help us run. He even told me to run before she has the baby. I didn't even know she was gonna have a baby. We walked a ways. Then he just left. I didn't see which way he went or nothing. He was talking. It got quiet. I looked for him, and he was gone. He must have ducked into the woods or something. I believed him, though. That night when I got home, she told me she was having a baby. I knew I was gonna run. We had already talked about it anyway."

"Bo, that don't make a bit a sense. If I'd a know what you told me, I would've not run," replied Ben.

"Well, I would have still run. I ain't nobody's slave. Man born to be free. Freedom. That's all I dream about. That's all I think about. I'd be dead in my grave before I'd be a slave. It's only right for a man to want freedom. Wise people. We ain't supposed to be beat like no mule or be killed like no chicken. I'd run again and again. I'm starting to think that we might be here too long," replied Billy.

"Billy, that's the difference between me and you. You'd run without knowing which way to run. You'd just run. Me, I have to know the way. I needs me a plan. Without a plan, we just running around like chickens with our head cut off. And I got too much sense to be putting Creasy and me in harm. You know they'll kill us rather than have us free. You should know better than anybody. You been dead before."

"Now, don't go talking about that. Don't remember nothing about that."

"Well, you were dead—dead as a dog. If it wasn't for Mary Lou, you'd be pushing up daisies."

"Now, let's not fight among ourselves. We got a ways to go. We need to love as brothers if we gonna make it. I ain't gonna let nothing happen to my Mary Lou," replied Bo.

"So where do we go from here?" asked Creasy.

"We gonna take the Mississippi River as far north as we can. Then we'll have to walk. Then we'll take the Ohio River. Then we'll be in Ohio. But I'm not sure on everything. I'm gonna talk to Smiley. Maybe he can talk to Harriet Tubman on the proper route north. It's a railroad. We'll have stops like this one, and there's others who will help us. We gets directions as we go. At each stop, we get new directions north and where to stop. Nobody knows the entire underground railroad except, probably, Harriet Tubman, and then it's liable to change anywhere along the way. I've been told it's white folks who'll help us. We may even take a real train ride. It's lots into this. We made it this far. God did not bring us out to bring us back again," answered Bo.

"That's right. He brought us out of slavery to bring us into freedom. I heard of Harriet Tubman, Fredrick Douglas, and mens they call abolitionists. It's lots of folks who are against slavery. I bet they done heard of your wife too. They know she blessed, and they sent those men who helped us out of the burning barn," replied Creasy.

"Whatever the reason, we still got a ways to go. And we got a pregnant lady to look after. So whatever we do, we have to make sure it's planned. There can't be no mistakes or any guessing," Ben answered.

"We come this far by word of mouth. I believe that fellow Jophkiel, he one of the reason I decided to run. It's just something about him. He's believable. He don't talk like he's a fool. He makes perfect sense to me. This journey is all about word of mouth. Can't none of us read except Mary Lou. So we have to trust folks along the way."

Ben interjected, "OK, Bo, we came this far. But lets me talk to whoever gives us directions north. I don't trust nobody except for all you in this room. You seem to be emotional about getting your Mary Lou up north. I got my Creasy to look after. Billy, he just plain don't care. He'll run anyway he can." Everyone looked at Billy and laughed.

"Ben, I ain't no fool now." Everyone laughed harder. Billy looked at the smiling faces of his friends and could no longer keep a straight face. He smiled and laughed with them and laughingly said, "I always run north."

Ben looked into Billy's eyes and, smiling, said, "Which way is north?"

The laughter slowly died down, and a still quiet fell upon them. They all glanced into each other's eyes, searching for direction. Bo finally broke the silence, saying, "I'm going to get some rest. We done come along ways. I'm just about too tired to sleep."

"Yeah, that's a good idea. We've ate. We've changed clothes. We're in a dry, safe place. I'm going to get me some rest too. Come on, Creasy. We can rest together and keep each other warm."

"OK, Ben. Let's push one of those beds together."

"I ain't pushing nothing together. Come on, woman."

"You all get some rest. I'm fine," Billy replied.

Billy sat quietly looking at the candle flicker in the dark. Everyone else slept in a bed for the first time since their journey began. Time raced. Billy pondered in his heart about the last time he'd run. He remembered getting beaten. He pictured the faces of men striking him with the ends of their rifles, kicking him, punching him, and then nothing. He remembered that he'd awoken in a shack and then crying.

He glanced over at me. His heart felt a deep warmth he couldn't explain. He loved me. Not a love that he'd feel for a girlfriend or wife; no, this was deeper. His soul was connected to mine in a majestic and mysterious way. He couldn't even imagine a thought that would express the connection he felt. He knew he couldn't sleep or rest until I was safe. My safety was all he wanted. He no longer wanted freedom for himself. He wanted freedom for me and my unborn child. He'd stopped thinking about himself long ago. He wasn't afraid. He felt a perfect love, complete and all consuming. He thought about the life Bo and I would have as free Negroes. No matter how hard he tried, he couldn't think of his life of freedom. He reflected on his old thoughts before the beating. They didn't matter. He'd changed. He knew it.

He heard a noise coming from the hidden entryway. He quickly blew out the candle and waited. The shelf slowly opened. He grabbed the chair he was sitting on and quietly stood by the hidden entrance. He was determined to kill anyone who would harm me.

The shelf opened, and a petite white-haired white woman entered the room holding a candle. She was alone. The candle light flickered back and forth upon her face. She had the face of an angel. Her small frame added to her beauty. She wore a pink full-length dress with a white cotton shawl draped over her shoulders. She stood there seemingly glowing from the candlelight. Her eyes raced across the room. Everyone was sleeping. She counted. She thought, *One's missing.*

Billy stood holding the chair over his head, ready to strike. She turned and looked in his direction. She couldn't see his eyes, but he saw hers. He stared into her eyes as he'd seen an angel. She smiled. He stood towering over her, ready to protect his beloved Mary Lou. He heard a whisper, saying, "She loves you, Billy." He jerked forward as if his breath had been snatched out of his lungs. He slowly put the chair down. She continued to look for his eyes, searching. Then she raised the candle to his face. She smiled and said, "Hello, I'm Mrs. Davis. What's your name?"

"I'm Billy."

"Billy, that's a good name. You know a good name is better than gold and silver. Yes, a man with a good name, he can go places."

Billy stood there confused, lost for words. He stared wide eyed at the beautiful white-haired, blue-eyed white woman. Her voice seemed to calm all through he'd had of violence. He gently called the others. They woke and stared, amazed at the aura, beauty, calm, and grace of the gentle soul that stood before them.

"I'm Mrs. Davis. You all don't have a thing to worry about. I'm so pleased you all made it. I prayed and prayed. Now, you must be Mary Lou. I heard good things about you. Billy, step outside there and bring in those baskets of food and the bucket of milk." Billy stood there in shock, staring around the room. "Billy, you get those things now. I got some buttermilk biscuits, fried chicken, ham, candied yams, and some greens and corn bread. It's dinnertime around here, and there's plenty for everybody. And don't you give old Smiley none. He'll come around just to eat."

Everyone looked in awe. They had never seen such power and compassion come from such a small frame. She overwhelmed them completely within a few minutes' span. They trusted and respected her without hesitation.

Billy brought the food and milk into the room and set it on the table. He looked through the baskets, and finally grabbing a hold on a chicken leg, he took a big bite and smiled. "That's good chicken." The others quickly hopped out of bed and rushed to the table.

"There's plates for you all to eat from."

Creasy set the plates around the table and distributed equal portions of food onto each plate. Bo lit the lamp and placed it on the center of the table next to the food. They all sat down and ate. I made Christmas trees with my greens and corn bread and gently placed one into Bo's mouth. He smiled, looking into my eyes, and ate.

Mrs. Davis sat on the edge of one of the straw beds and quietly watched them eat. The sight of them eating warmed her gentle heart. She felt a sense of pride and accomplishment. She hated the peculiar institution. She didn't understand how a human being could be so cruel and treat another person so inhumanly. She wanted slavery stopped, and she wasn't about to sit around and pray about it without doing nothing. She believed that when you pray about something, you better do everything to work your prayers into reality. And that's just what she did.

I prepared her a plate of food and quietly whispered to Bo, "I'm gonna show our friend some kindness." I slowly and poetically took the food over to Mrs. Davis and sat on the edge of the bed. Without saying a word, I handed her the food and passionately, gently looked into her eyes.

Mrs. Davis took the plate. She set it in her lap and gently crumbled some corn bread over the greens and made a Christmas tree and ate. She looked at me and said, "Green taste much better when you eat them with your fingers."

I held my head down, looking into my plate, and ate with my fingers just like Mrs. Davis. "Yes, ma'am, they sure do. I've always eaten greens with my fingers."

"It's only proper to eat greens with our finger," Mrs. Davis said, smiling, slowly chewing on a mouthful of greens.

I felt a compassion I had rarely felt before. I knew Mrs. Davis fully understood our situation and would do what it took to ensure our freedom. I felt it. I had learned to listen to the Holy Spirit. It was a gentle voice that spoke to my mind in my innermost being. The voice whispered always. If I missed it, the whisper came again. I had learned to welcome the voice. It led and guided me.

After we had finished eating, I took the plates and set them on the table. I came and sat next to Mrs. Davis and asked, "How you planning on getting up north?"

Mrs. Davis smiled and looked deep into my eyes and spoke softly, saying, "I'm not new to this. I've been doing it awhile. There's always changes, and some things just simply stay the same. But I knows a few people who share our hope of freedom. I've met Frederick Douglas and

Harriet Tubman and quite a few others. I'm not just name-dropping. We are serious. We will make every effort to ensure your freedom."

"We? What you mean we?"

"Mr. Davis is just involved as I am. You don't think I'd be able to do all this by myself without my husband knowing?"

"We'd been thinking that it was just you. I believe Smiley told us that."

"Well, my husband is a silent partner. He doesn't want the slaves knowing what he's doing. It's his way of protecting everything. That way, if something happens to one of us, the other would continue."

"Yes, ma'am. I see. So you all keeps everything a secret."

"That's right."

"Then why you telling me?"

"Well, Mary Lou, you something special to us. You know folks up north done heard about you. Now, hold out your hand. Let me see it."

I stared deeply into Mrs. Davis's eyes. I knew what Mrs. Davis wanted to see. I never showed my hands to anyone. I learned ways of covering them. I slowly stretched my right hand. I wore black cotton gloves that women of dignity wore.

Mrs. Davis slowly extended both her hands. She embraced my hand and gently rocked back and forth. She closed her eyes and prayed, "Thank you, Jesus, for bringin' this dear child to our home. Help us to care for her properly and respectfully. Let her be free, Lord Jesus. It's by your grace she sit here before me." Mrs. Davis slowly pulled on the tip of my index finger and grabbed the tip of the cotton glove. She very gently and slowly removed the glove. My hand was wrapped in a white rag. It had traces of blood around the edges. Mrs. Davis very gently unwrapped the rag. The rag was wrapped around the center of my palms. Upon each unwrapping of the rag, it became more heavily stained with blood. Soon, the spot that laid upon my hand was fully saturated with my blood.

I looked deep into Mrs. Davis's eyes and whispered, "Praise covers my soul like a warm blanket on a winter night. It warms me from the inside through and the depths of my soul."

Mrs. Davis looked amazingly upon my face. She seemed to glow from within. She looked at my hand. She saw a deep indentation. It was bloody red. It appeared to be pressed into my hand by a nail or spike. It seemingly went completely through my hand. The front and back of my hand was bloody red. Yet she couldn't see through the wound.

"What happened to your hands?"

A voice spoke to my spirit in a whisper. It said, "These are the wounds of Christ. That's all I know, and I believe."

"So you didn't hurt yourself and no one hurt you?"

"No, ma'am. They just comes and goes. So I try and keep my hands covered at all times."

"I see. You don't have any control over it."

"No, ma'am. But usually when I give glory to God, they more likely to come. I even eats with my hands covered."

"I can see why. Let's get you some new gloves. We can cut the fingers out of them. That would keep your gloves from getting so messy when you eat."

"That's a good idea. I never thought about that before."

"I'll get you some clean bandages too."

"Thank you, ma'am. You're being too kind."

"I'm here for you all's safety and to get you up north. Now, you wash up in that washbasin. I'll get you some clean bandages, and I'll get you a pair of clean gloves. I'll cut the finger out for you."

Mrs. Davis left the secret hiding room. She closed the hiding shelves. The others all stared at me, wondering what all was said between us two women. I returned their stare and said "She's coming back. She's going to get some bandages and gloves. I'd been wearing those for so long that I must have didn't realize how dirty they were." I thought, *I can still wear these gloves. All they need is a good washing.* I went over to the table and took the pitcher of water and the washbasin. I thought, *I'll wash up. Then I'll wash these old gloves.*

I poured and scrubbed. The water quickly became a deep red. I carefully took the washbasin to the corner of the hiding place. There was a whole dug into the floor. The place was partially hidden. It was our restroom. I dumped the bloody water into the hole and took the basin back to the table. I looked at my hands. They were still smeared with blood. I filled the basin again.

No sooner had I filled the basin than Mrs. Davis slowly pushed open the secret opening. I stood at the table washing my hands. The others stood around the table watching me. No one said a word. They watched. Mrs. Davis quickly came over to the table. She set the bandages on the table. She looked at the bloody wash water in amazement.

"You're not still bleeding?"

"No, ma'am. I suppose the blood had caked on my hands and fingers. We been running and hiding so much that I ain't had a chance to take a proper cleaning."

"Well, you can clean yourself as much as you want," replied Mrs. Davis. "Here." Mrs. Davis had brought some soap wrapped inside the bandages.

I took the soap and used one of the cotton bandages, soaked it, and began washing my hands with soap. "This is real nice. I can clean up real nice now." I continued to wash my hands and face, leaning down and splashing water onto my face. Soon, I was finally clean.

After I had finished, Mrs. Davis took hold of my left hand and led me to the straw bed. She'd brought the bandages and gloves. "Here, give me your hands."

I placed both my hands upon Mrs. Davis's lap. The others all sat around and looked patiently at us two women. Mrs. Davis slowly and gently wrapped my hands. She showed the same care she'd shown for her own daughter. She'd cut the fingers from a pair of black silk gloves. She gently put the gloves onto my hands and smiled.

"There, now you're as fit as a fiddle." A warmth swept through the hidden room. Everyone felt secure.

Mrs. Davis jokingly replied, "You are the lily of the valley." Everyone erupted in gentle laughter.

Chapter Fourteen

I've Got a Baby . . .

That hiding room became like home. The days turned into weeks and the weeks into months. Time seemed to fly. We'd learned to live comfortably. Over the few months hiding, Mrs. Davis allowed us to make a fireplace. It was dug out of the concrete side of the hiding place. We had pushed and broken the wooden beams on the floor and curved an area around the fireplace. We had also placed bricks on the floor around the edges of the wooden floor to keep the fire contained. The fireplace was dug directly under the one inside the mansion. It's ventilation ran directly under that of the large fireplace above it. It seemed a stroke of genius, but it was completely a necessity. With the fireplace there, we could cook our own food. It would keep us warm in the winter, and it provided a source of light.

I was good and pregnant. We would have liked to put some distance between Captain Burris and his wicked men, but we were safe. It was right for me to finish out my pregnancy in safety.

We rarely left the hiding place. Smiley brought food and other provisions. After he'd worked the fields, his other duties were around the big house. He'd chop firewood for winter. He'd garden, clean, shovel snow during the winter, and do whatever was needed. So him going in and out of the big house's basement went unnoticed. He was also the only slave Master Davis allowed into the basement. He'd take and stock wood in the basement, also carry boxes for Mrs. Davis into the basement almost twice a week. The boxes were filled with food, clothing, milk, water, and anything else the hiding slaves might need.

This went on for months. Winter began to set in, and Bo became worried. Early one cold winter morning, Smiley was placing wood and provisions in the basement. Bo, Billy, and Ben quietly came and helped him, which had become their custom. Bo asked, "Smiley, we has plenty of food and other thing here, but what if something happen to you? What are we supposed to do? My wife is pregnant."

Smiley, his usually cheerful self, laughed almost at the top of his lungs, saying, "Remember Lil George, Mrs. Davis, and there are others."

"I thought this here was a secret."

"It sure is. But we got a backup plan."

"If you all got such a backup plan, how come we don't know nothing about it?"

Smiley grinned, saying, "It's a secret too."

"I needs to know your secrets around here. What if we can't get no food, water, wood, you know, the things we need every day to live on."

"Well, if it gets that bad, you better sneak on out of this basement and find what you need."

"That does it. I can't stay in here locked up not knowing nothing, just waiting. I'm coming out and help."

"Help? What you gon' help with, boy? You better stay put. You know, since you all been hiding in here, we've had other runaway slaves. We just ain't putting them in here. We wants to make sure you and the others make it up north, and your wife is due anytime now. We've three runaways now. They been asking about you all. They got funny names—names hard to say. Sounds like them old African names. One of them is called Barak. Then there's Jophkiel. The last one name is Raphael. Do you all know these fellows?"

"One of them sounds familiar. It's been a long time. I remember. There is a fellow I remember. That boy Jophkiel. I remember him. He's the boy who spoke with me on the road. So he's done run. Ain't that something?"

"And he's got two others with him. You want to see him?"

177

"Sure. He's a good fellow. You know, I think I remember him in the barn fire."

"What are you talking about, Bo?"

Ben quickly interjected, "Them three boys. They was in the barn. They the ones that helped us out."

"He sure right," Billy quickly interjected.

"Maybe they'd just come, you know, like Mary Lou and her little friend Little Lizzy."

"That could be it. I just don't remember them. And I don't plan on getting caught by some ole cotton-picking nigger! Rather be dirty and picking cotton all his life than free."

"Billy, I know that boy Jophkiel. He's the one I told you about. If it wasn't for him, we wouldn't have made it this far. And his running friends must be all right. They're running."

"You boys are safe. I just asked did you know them. I'll try and bring them around and sneak them in."

"Yeah, that's good, Smiley. I want to thank that boy Jophkiel. Almost everything he told me done come true. All but my Mary giving me a son."

"Bo, you mean to tell me that the boy Jophkiel told you that you were going to have a son?" Smiley replied.

"Yeah, that's right. What's wrong with that?"

"You sure have been picking cotton all your life. Bo, you either gon' have a boy or girl."

"Yeah, but—"

"Bo, you either gon' have a boy or girl. Ain't nothing special about that."

"It just something about him. I believed him."

"Well, I'll tell you this. I'll come around after the sun has set, and I'll take you to see him. I ain't gonna take all of you, just Bo."

"OK, Smiley, I'll see you this evening," replied Bo.

Smiley slowly and quietly eased out the basement in his usual manner. Bo, Billy, and Ben put a few items they needed into the hidden room and closed the secret shelf.

After the sun had set, Smiley came to the secret hiding place. Bo was eagerly waiting. Smiley whispered, "Come on, Bo." Bo quickly grabbed his coat and an old hat and quickly left with Smiley.

Upon entering the barn, they couldn't see anything. The barn was dimly lit. It had an oil lantern in the center, which didn't provide much for light. It was cold, but the barn was warm. The heat from the horses and other animals kept it warm. Smiley and Bo looked around the barn. They saw farm animals and their shadows. They heard the sound of horses moving and rustling of ducks hurrying out of the way of their footsteps.

Smiley whispered, "You boys here. It's me, Smiley. I brought a friend to see you." Smiley thought, *They could be hiding anywhere. They're probably scared to death. We'll just come back later when it's daylight.*

Bo whispered, "Smiley, ain't nobody in here, only horses and ducks. Come on, let's go. I could be taking care of Mary Lou."

Jophkiel, Barak, and Raphael were standing directly in front of them. They were invisible and could be heard when they spoke.

Bo and Smiley quietly and slowly looked around the barn. Smiley whispered, "They got to be around here somewhere. I know they ain't trying to run without knowin' which way to go."

Raphael said in a strong and gallant voice, "We should show ourselves and work with them. That's why we're here."

"No, we're not here to be friendly with the humans. We're here to love them and protect them," replied Barak.

"We have freedom. So let us consult the Lord in prayer," replied Jophkiel. The angels prayed.

Smiley and Bo continued their hunt. Smiley heard a squeaking sound. He'd heard it many times before. It was the secret barn door. Smiley whispered, "Bo, come here."

Bo quickly hurried over to Smiley, and they both hid in a horse stall, keeping watch on the secret hiding door. The door slowly opened. They watched three tall dark figures slowly sneak into the barn. Smiley whispered, "Jophkiel, is that you? It's me, Smiley. I brought Bo."

Jophkiel quietly replied, "Yes, sir, boss. It's me."

Smiley and Bo walked gallantly from the horse stall, proud and unafraid. Jophkiel, Barak, and Raphael walked into the dim light of the barn. Bo and Smiley joined them. They all stood in the center of the barn, looking, smiling, and searching for words to say. Smiley finally asked, "Where you boys been off to?"

"We been searching the area. If we have to run, we want to know which way to run."

"Jophkiel, boy, you look good," replied Bo.

"It's been a while. We been hiding in this barn a spell. Smiley been real good to us."

"Smiley is a good man. Me and Mary Lou been well taken care of. In fact, she is about to have a baby. That's why we ain't run no further," replied Bo.

"That's good. She's gonna have that baby boy you been wanting."

"I'm Barak, and this is Raph. We run with Jophkiel. We've heard good things about you and your wife. She's the one who was struck by lightning."

"That's right," replied Bo.

"We sure is hungry," replied Barak. Jophkiel and Raphael looked into each other's eyes and smiled, because they didn't eat the food the slaves eat; they ate heavenly manna, which God gave his angels.

Bo paused for a few seconds and then said, "We have plenty of food. I don't see why you all can't eat with us tonight. What you think, Smiley?"

"Don't be puttin' me in this. If you wants to feed them, you can."

"OK, come on. Let's get back to the big house. We can get you boys a change of clothes too. You boys look like you ain't had a decent meal in a while. My Mary Lou done turn out to be a good cook."

Smiley stared at Bo in unbelief, thinking, *He don't know these boys to be takin' them around his pregnant wife and the others. He must see something in them I don't.* Smiley glistered and said, "Come on. We can use the secret door and take you to the big house."

They all quietly followed Smiley, imitating his every move as he moved through the secret door and ducking and dodging his way to the big house's basement door. Once at the door, Smiley said, "I'm not coming in. You all go on. I'll let Mrs. Davis know." He held the basement door open, and they all followed Bo into the basement.

Bo couldn't see his hand in front of his face. The angels saw as clear as day. They followed Bo unhampered by the dense dark of the basement. "Come on. Stay close by," Bo whispered. Bo pulled the secret hiding shelf open, and light from within shone the way. They all entered the room.

I was shaped like a pear with legs, ready to give birth. My face radiated with love. I glowed and swayed from side to side when I walked. I still wore the gloves Mrs. Davis had given me, and I sometimes experienced the stigmata when I was pregnant.

Barak, Jophkiel, and Raphael smiled with great joy at the sight of me. They all stood in the center of the room, wondering what to do next. Bo hurried over to me and hugged me as best he could. My belly made him keep his distance. I smiled and whispered, "Who are your friends? They sure do look a mess."

"These are runaways. You remember Jophkiel?"

"No, I don't remember Joph . . . Which one is that?"

"Come on over here, boys. Let me introduce you to my wife."

The other slaves sat wide eyed and quiet while Bo introduced Jophkiel, Barak, and Raphael. Ben quickly said, "Come on over and sit down. We ain't had word from runaways since we been here."

Bo introduced them to me. They smiled and repeated their names in rhythm. They kept their eyes on me and slowly took a seat at the table.

"You boys hungry? I've got fried chicken, collard greens, and neck bones. It's Bo's favorite."

"Yes, ma'am, we sure is. We ain't had a good hot meal since we been running," replied Barak.

"Mary Lou done turn out to be one of the better cooks I've ever had the honor of eating with," replied Ben.

"He says that every time he sats down to eat," Creasy quickly interjected.

"That's right. Ben don't turn down nothing he can eat. That's included his collar," replied Billy. Everyone smiled and laughed. We felt a connection rarely felt. We all accepted each other, and a connection of unity was made. We were all runaway slaves who shared the same background, or thought we did.

Bo, Billy, Creasy, and I didn't realize the three runaways were angels. Nothing in their appearance implied they were anything but runaway slaves. They looked like slaves. They smelled of human musk. They spoke a broken form of English that the slaves spoke. When I brought them food, they even appeared to eat. They even ate with their fingers, making Christmas trees out of collard greens and eating the fried chicken with their fingers. As the angels ate, there was silence. The angels appeared to eat so fast that it was baffling to the others.

Ben whispered, "You boys eating like you ain't ate in a year, licking your fingers and all that smacking and eating with your mouth open. I can see everything in your mouth and I'm over here." Ben had moved, and he was sitting on his bunk. After they'd finished eating, Ben asked, "How long you boys been on the run?"

No one said a word. They glanced in each other's direction. Barak replied, "It's been a while. I done lost count of the days. You know how it is when the days turn into weeks and the weeks turn into months. It's freedom we want."

"Yes, sir. You said something, then. You the kind a man we needs around here."

"Ms. Mary Lou, that was the best meal I've ever ate," replied Raphael.

"Thank you. I'm sorry. What's your name?"

"I'm Raph."

"Raph, that's a good name. You seem to fit your name."

"Well, thank you," replied Raphael.

Although the angels didn't eat the food that I had prepared. The food that they ate was the heavenly manna. Although it looked and smelled like my fried chicken and collard greens, it was actually manna, the food of angels, and they ate everything on their plates.

Ben continued to ask questions about which way they'd run, how Red is doing, and how the other slaves are doing. He'd missed the company and nonsense the field slaves usually pulled. His questions seemed to fall on deaf ears. They listened but no response. Soon, Ben began to grow angry. He blurted out, "You boys didn't talk much. I thought you boys knew something. I might as well talk to Creasy."

"Let's get you boys cleaned up. There's clean water and clean rags on the wash table," I replied.

The three slowly went over to the table. They took off their raggedy shirts and began to wash. Bo, Ben, and the other sat around the eating table and discussed their three new friends. The three laid their dirty shirts on the floor. Creasy went behind them and picked up the dirty shirts. She placed clean white shirts off Billy's bunk for the boys. Billy's bunk was next to the wash table.

As the boys were washing, I asked, "Can you boys stay the night? We'd love to have you."

Bo quickly interjected, "Woman, you suppose you should have asked us?"

I ignored Bo's words and ordered, "You boys can sleep on the floor. We've got plenty of room. We have blankets for you all, and there's plenty food. After you all finish washing, we have evening prayer. We pray every night. We'd love to have you join us."

"Thank you, Mrs. Mary Lou. We'd appreciate staying. It's warmer than that old, dirty, smelly barn," replied Raph.

"And we love your company too," Barak quickly interjected.

Later that night, after everyone had finished eating and it was close to bedtime, they had talked and laughed and told stories of picking cotton in the hot summer's day. I stood and raised both of my arms over my head and stretched and yawned. I said, "It's my bedtime." As I finished the last word, Bo, Billy, Ben, and Creasy all stood and clasped hands. Jophkiel, Raphael, and Barak sat quietly looking at the others.

"It's our evening prayer time," replied Creasy, looking directly at the three sitting down.

We stood and all clasped hands. I prayed, "Thank you, Lord Jesus, for our new friends."

As I continued to pray, a demon lurking in the shadows became extremely angry at the prayer. He ran and attached himself onto Ben. He dug his talons into his chest and face. He wrapped his long tail around Ben's waist. He squeezed. The demon was invisible. He couldn't be seen, felt, or heard by humans. Barak, Raphael, and Jophkiel stood amazed watching the demon.

The demon's tail rose up around Ben's throat. The demon yelled, "You want her! I hate you. Think thoughts of sex." Thoughts of lusts filled his mind.

Ben blurted out, "Come on, finish praying. I'm tired."

At the sound of Ben's voice, many demons slowly came lurking out of the darkness. Another demon ran and jumped onto Ben. He gorged his talons into Ben's spine and back. In an instant, demons were attaching themselves to all the slaves, except me, Jophkiel, and Barak.

Ben slowly, completely lost focus on my words. He slowly began getting sexually aroused. He thought of Creasy. His mind was picturing her nude. He stood completely unaffected by my prayers.

Barak yelled, "God of Hosts, Lord of Lords, Prince of Peace, send us into battle!" Barak's voice couldn't be heard, nor did his mouth move. He stood head bowed, as were everyone in the prayer circle.

A voice echoed. "Go forth into battle."

Barak stepped forward. His physical form stayed. His angelic spirit came forth. His body was draped in amazingly white garment. It was white as the whitest snow. His face shone of chrysolite. His hair was white as his garments. He wore a woven gold belt around his waist. He wore golden sandals with laces that went to his knees. Attached to his belt was a golden sheath. It held a four-foot-long sword made of diamond and other precious minerals. There was a gold cross on his garment. Jophkiel and Raphael followed, dressed exactly the same, except Raphael's face shone of beryl and Jophkiel's face shone of chrysoberyl. Their stature grew. They stood erect.

The demon ran into the darkness and yelled, "Murder!" He leaped up, attempting to attach himself onto Billy. In an instant, Barak drew his sword and cut the demon in half as he flew through the air. Raphael's sword was immediately slicing the limbs from Ben. There was a loud screeching sound that filled the room. Jophkiel stepped forward with sword in hand and, in a twinkling of an eye, killed the demons. The battle was over. I continued to pray.

Lurking in the shadows, there was a huge evil presence. Unseen by the angels, the demon spread its wings and fled in fear of being seen. It was the prince of Egypt. He flew high into the sky and screamed, "They've killed all my minor demons I brought with me! I'll bring more. I'll return. I'll have my vengeance. I kept the children of Joseph in slavery for centuries. This is a minor setback."

I prayed, "Thank you, Lord, for your protection. You bless us as we come and as we go. We give you, Lord Jesus, all honor and praise."

As I continued to pray, Ben immediately regained focus. He meditated on the words that came so poetically from my mouth. With his head still bowed, he whispered, "Thank you, Lord Jesus. You been real good to us." Soon, the others were praising and giving thanks unto the Lord. The angels had returned into their physical bodies and were giving thanks and praises along with the slaves.

After evening prayer was over, we all hugged and shook hands. The slaves were unaware of the battle that had moments earlier took place. Smiles were on everyone's faces, and joy filled our hearts. Bo said, "It's good to have you all. I think we gonna be just fine."

Creasy and I spread the blankets on the floor around the fireplace. They moved the bed close to them over to provide more room. The three said their good nights to the slaves and lay on their blankets for the night. The slaves got into their beds and retired for the night.

During the night, the three quests took their angelic form. Their human form lay motionless on the floor, seemingly sleeping. The angels stood tall and alert, guarding the slaves from any demons that may return. Barak filled the air with his constant songs of praises. "To the one who sits on the throne and unto the Lamb. Be blessings and honor and glory and power, forever." He sung in perfect harmony and joy that the sounds of God's praises burst through the plane between the spiritual and the physical reality. The song echoed throughout the room in a very small, amazingly beautiful whisper. The song comforted the sleeping slaves throughout the night.

The prince of Egypt hid in a lofty tree. He watched the house, thinking wickedly how to destroy me. His demonic essence raced wildly. There

was a complete absence of peace and warmth in him. He felt he'd have better success with Captain Burris. Captain Burris had always been a willing
vessel for hatred, murder, and all sorts of evil. In an instant, he flung himself into the air. A moment later, he'd reached Captain Burris's campsite.
He landed in a tree, staring at the camp. There were many demons of lesser
rank surrounding the campsite. Many were attached to Captain Burris and
his men. The prince of Egypt watched and devised a plan to lead Captain
Burris to me and the slaves.

Early in the morning, I woke up to a bed full of water. My water
broke. Bo lay sleeping next to me, unaware that he was lying in water. I
immediately got out of bed and slowly walked over to Creasy. She looked
into my eyes. "What, girl? The sun ain't even up. We got time to sleep,"
Creasy slowly whispered.

"It's time. It's time. My water done broke."

Creasy's eyes grew the size of silver dollars. She quickly got out of
bed and helped me to a chair at the table. She stoked the fire, adding wood
and putting a pot of water on. She slowly walked back to me and said, "We
need to get you out of those clothes."

I slowly tried to stand. Creasy took hold of my left arm and helped
me to my feet. We slowly walked to the foot of my bunk. I sat on the edge
of the bunk. Creasy hurried over to her bunk and reached under it and
grabbed a clean gown. I grabbed Bo by the leg and shook him. He quietly
and softly whispered, "It's too early. I'm not getting up."

"Bo, it's time. Bo, wake up! I'm having the baby now."

Bo sat up on the bunk wide awake. He placed both hands on my
stomach. He felt odd, a feeling he hadn't felt since he was a child. He looked
down. Then he removed the covers from himself. He was soaking wet. He
thought he'd had an accident. He looked embarrassed and startled.

I whispered, "It's me, Bo. My water broke during the night."

Bo hopped out of bed and quickly began putting his pants and shirt on. While Bo stood dressing himself, Creasy returned with a clean gown and clean bed linen. Bo helped me to my feet. He and Creasy pulled the wet gown over my head and threw it on the floor. I stood there nude and excited that it was finally time. Bo grabbed the clean gown and helped me into it. Creasy pulled the wet linen off the bed and replaced it with clean ones. She doubled everything on the bed. Everyone else was sound asleep and was completely unaware of the morning's activity.

I carefully climbed into bed, and Creasy tucked me snuggly under the covers. Bo went and shook Ben and Billy, saying, "Get up. You all get up. It's time."

Billy replied, "Time for what? We ain't picking no cotton."

"She's having the baby."

"She ain't having the baby now, is she?"

"Yes, she's having the baby now. Her water done broke. Ben, Ben, get up. She's having the baby." Ben immediately got out of bed and frantically put on his pants, boots, and shirt.

Creasy quietly whispered, "Bo, come here. We gonna need some private time. I'm thinking that we can turn these old beds on end and dump the inners out of them."

"OK, anything you want. I'll do."

"Well, get to moving, then." Bo grabbed the end of one bed and quickly flipped it over.

Jophkiel, Barak, and Raphael heard the noise and commotion and immediately stood by the fireplace, holding their linen in their hands. They stood looking utterly confused and bewildered. Bo quickly told them, "Mary Lou's having the baby. I'm trying to make a private place for her to have it."

The three laid their blankets on the table and grabbed another bed and set it on end. Soon, they had three beds on end and were placing sheets and linen covering the bunk. They'd sectioned off the room, only leaving a small aisle leading to the exit.

Creasy stoked the fire and removed the pot of hot water she placed over the fire. She poured some hot water in a clean tub and refilled the pot and returned it to the fire. She returned to me, who hadn't started labor.

The men all sat around the table looking confused, anxious, and hungry. Bo impatiently decided to cook breakfast. He'd cooked for himself many times when he was single. But since he'd married, he almost never cooked. The men all watched Bo breaking eggs, frying bacon, and making coffee, and none moved or said a word. Bo finally blurted, "Get up and do something." The men all stared at Bo and said nothing.

Creasy quickly came from behind the partition and said, "I want my eggs over easy, and your wife wants a hot cup of coffee." She smiled and quickly returned behind the partition.

Bo quickly made me a cup of hot coffee. He slowly approached the partition and whispered, "It's me, Bo. I got your coffee."

Creasy forcefully replied, "Come on in here against the wall."

My face glowed of love and joy. I smiled gently and reached both arms out stretched in Bo's direction. Bo quickly leaned over the bed, holding the coffee away from me, and leaned forward. I reached up and passionately hugged him around his neck. He leaned over, almost falling onto the bed, not returning the hug. Creasy reached over and took the coffee from his hands. Then he leaned forward and passionately kissed me. After the quick kiss, he asked, "Are you hungry? You shouldn't be having a baby on an empty stomach."

"Yes, Bo, I'll have a plate of bacon and eggs."

Bo left the partition and quickly fixed a plate of bacon and eggs. Upon returning, he found me breathing heavily and in labor.

Creasy replied, "You can leave that breakfast with me. Now go."

Bo handed her the plate and clumsily left. He returned and sat with the other men and quickly ate his breakfast. After they'd finished eating, they all sat quietly and listened to any sound of a baby. After a while, Bo began pacing back and forth. It seemed like hours had passed and still no baby. Then, finally, a tiny cry. Bo ran behind the partition and saw me, his beautiful Mary Lou, holding a baby. I lovingly wiped the baby's face and with a clean cloth.

Bo stood frozen. He finally asked, "What is it?"

"It's a baby, Bo."

"Is it a boy or girl?"

"It's a boy. Here, you can hold him." Bo walked closer. He continued to gaze in amazement. He reached over and gently lifted the baby. Gently, he held his son. His mind was racing thinking of a name. Beyond his control, tears filled his eyes. His heart raced. His breathing slowed. His eyes were completely fixed upon the infant in his arms. He gently kissed his cheek and slowly and carefully returned his son to the mother. A smile I had never seen before filled his face. I knew. He slowly left the partition and announced to everyone, "I gots me a son." He stood smiling as proud as he could be.

Chapter Fifteen

Description

The partition was removed, and the hiding place was restored to its former form. The men all stood around the bed, gazing at the new addition. Ben whispered, "That baby got more wrinkles than I do."

"I heard that. He ain't got no wrinkles. He's just beautiful," I replied.

I lay holding my baby. I glowed of joy, love, and peace. I never loved another human being the way I loved my baby. I was completely and totally consumed by my baby. I loved his smell. I loved to touch him. I loved his cry. I loved the way he fidgeted back and forth. I knew I had something special. A gift. An honor. A respect I had never fully comprehended. A mother.

What in the entire world could be more fitting for me? I thought. The gifts of Jesus Christ raced through my mind. *How am I goin' to do what Jesus wants me to do? I've got to take care of my baby.* A flash of warmth filled me as I lay holding my son. I thought, *I haven't even named him yet.* "Jesus is a way maker. My yoke is easy" flashed through my mind. I knew deep within my soul that I was never going to worry. God's perfect plan will always be fulfilled as long I accepted his plan for my life.

Later that evening, miles away in the country, Captain Burris and a reckless lot of men were camped out looking for any sign or hint to capture the runaway slaves. They'd been looking for months without any sign. Many of the men were getting discouraged and angry. The living outside in the cold and rain, the long months without any pay, the lack of proper food were indeed taking a toll on many men. Many of them had left. Yet there was a still a substantial number. Some had taken to drinking and gambling to pass the time.

Captain Burris had issued spies. Men were assigned to visit farms and plantations in groups of threes or fours. Also, these spies would visit towns and purchase supplies, always looking and asking questions about me and the others.

Completely unknown to Captain Burris and his men, they were constantly and completely surrounded by demons. Captain Burris and many of his men were possessed by demons—demons of hatred, lust, addiction, false pride, murder, envy, and all other ungodly spirits. These men were open to them all.

Pakaaret the evil was the head of them. He was a hideous and grotesque figure. He was ancient. He'd brought many souls to hell. His arrogance preceded him. His rebellion was unlike any other. He destroyed many of the lesser demons for not carrying out his orders, and the other demons were intoxicated by the way he killed them. Each demon was always attempting to cause another demon to fail. If a failure occurred, they'd see Pakaaret's evil. Yet they wanted much more to please Pakaaret, for he gave them what they wanted, and their desire was only for pleasure of any kind.

Unknown to Pakaaret and the lesser demons, they were being watched. The prince of Egypt watched from a distance, always knowing that he'd take over them and lead them to me.

This night, there was a full moon. The demons were going wild attaching themselves onto the men. Outbursts of anger and fights routinely broke out in camp. Some men had brought prostitutes into the camp. They were selling them to the men. Lust rode rampant. All sorts of evil took place this cold winter's night.

Captain Burris sat in his tent drinking whiskey, thinking, *It's been a long time. I'm running out of money. My men will revolt against me if I attempt to stop their fun. A break. I need a break.* He sipped his whiskey and watched the fire. He saw something flash by. He thought, *I'm seeing things.* He continued to watch the fire.

Invisible to human eyes were the demons, yet they could be felt. And if they attached their talons to a person, they could sometimes completely control that person through their impulsive nature. Their demonic thought would fill the person's being and influence them to act without any thought, always in a detriment to the person's life and soul. The demons hated humans. They wanted them in hell.

Many of the demons were once angels. They know the glory of the almighty God. Yet they rebelled against the love that creates everything. They rebelled against the word made flesh Some had stood in the presence of the King of Kings and the Lord of Lords. These demons hated everything that is beautiful. They hated everything that is pure. They hated everything that is love and created out of love. Humanity has no concept of the evil that wants them dead, and these were the demons that Captain Burris and his men unknowingly accepted.

On the Davises' plantation, I lay holding my newborn. I was completely exhausted, falling in and out of sleep. My baby slept quietly in my arms.

Bo searched his heart and soul trying to find a name for his son. He thought, *I can name him Daniel or maybe one of them old African names like Obadiah. It's got to be a name that fits him. I'm his daddy, and a man is supposed to name his son. If it was a girl, I'll let Mary Lou name her. But I gots me a boy. Maybe I could ask them new fellows? No, I'll ask Mary Lou.*

Bo took a chair and set it next to the bed. He lovingly and thoughtfully looked at me and son. He whispered, "I been thinking about a name for you. What do you want to be called?" He gently reached out and touched his son's tiny hand. A name shouted in his mind. *Zechariah! I'm Zechariah!* Bo continued to hold his son's hand.

I sleepily opened my eyes and whispered, "What's wrong, Bo?"

"Nothing's wrong. I'm trying to find a name for him."

"What do you want to call him?"

"I'm gonna name him Zechariah. We can call him Zech for short."

"Bo, that ain't no name for a boy."

"It's done. His name is Zechariah. We call him Zech for short."

"OK, Bo, it's your son. I can get used to Zechariah. He just little Zech."

The others were sitting staring into the fire, quietly listening as best they could. Bo quickly and proudly walked over and stood in front of the fireplace and rubbed his hands together, making friction to warm his hands. He proudly said, "I done name him Zechariah. You can call him Zech too. That's his nick name."

"Well, you must feel mighty proud of yourself," Creasy sarcastically blurted.

I slowly walked over to the eating table carrying Zech. I stood looking lovingly upon my husband, who was standing toward the fire.

"Come on and sit here, Ms. Mary Lou," Raph quickly interjected upon observing me. Raph got up and held the chair for me to sit.

I sat and loving said, "I got something to tell you all." Every eye fell on me. I slowly and carefully said, "I've had a terrible dream. I know the Lord wants me to tell you all. I had already known that folks wants us dead."

"Now, you don't have to be talking like that," Bo blurted out.

"Let her talk, Bo. You done named your son," Creasy replied sarcastically.

"I dreamed that there was an evil presence who's on a mission to destroy us all. He's evil. He's from hell. He's old. He's the one who held the children of Israel in slavery. And in my dream, I saw him."

"You just had a bad dream. You were worried about the baby and all," Creasy answered.

"No, I had been having these visions and dreams for a while. I kept them to myself because I thought the same thing. I thought it was because I was pregnant and worried. But I kept on praying. The Lord showed him to me. We have to pray constantly. There is an evil out there who is straight from the pits of hell. He hates us. He wants every bad thing to happen to us, and I saw him."

"Go on, tell us."

Everyone listened carefully to every word I spoke. They hung on to every word, fearful and amazed at what they heard. I said, "He's not a man. He doesn't look like a man, but his body is like a man's. He has legs like a goat. He stands up straight like a man. He's got wings like a bat. Only they are a lot bigger, and he flies. He flies like the fastest bird you can think of. He's got deep red eyes, and he feeds on fear, hatred, and all the things that against God's goodness. But he especially likes slavery, bondage of any kind. And he's about three times the size of a man. And there is a slime or something covering his body. It's sin. It's sin covering him."

They all stood motionless and stunned. No one knew what to say or think. They looked into each other's eyes, but no one doubted me. I continued. "But God has sent us protection. We have angels all around us. When we pray, they go forth into battle against the foe. I've seen the angels, too, in my dreams. They are beautiful. They are about nine feet tall. They are in light. They wore white gowns, and they had a gold belt around their waist. And each angel had a long sword made of diamonds, topaz, jasper, sapphire, emerald, and every precious mineral. They wore gold sandals with gold shoelaces that went up to their knees, yet I couldn't see their faces because their faces glowed of bright light. And they praised God constantly. Then I woke up."

"That's some kind of dream," replied Bo.

"Yeah, that's some kind of dream," Billy responded.

"So what are we supposed to do, since we got some kind of monster after us?" Ben replied.

"We are to stay together. And we should leave this plantation as soon as possible. It's not safe here. That thing knows we're here, and it also knows about the angels who are helping us."

195

"Mary Lou, we ain't seen no angels."

"That's because we can't see them, Bo."

"So these angels are here now and we can't see them."

"That's right."

"It's in the dead of winter, and the farther north we go, the colder it gets. We Southern folk. We ain't used to all cold and snow. I think we should stay right here. And I don't believe in no monsters," replied Ben.

"Ben, you were always the one who wanted to keep moving. You didn't even want to stop here, and when we did, you didn't want to stay."

"That's right, Bo. He sure the one who didn't want to stay here."

"She just had the baby. I'm not talking about yesterday or last month. She just had a baby this morning. It's only evening, and you all talking about taking her and the baby out in the weather. No, we ain't going nowhere. It's way too soon. She and the baby will catch their death of cold!" Creasy quickly shouted.

"I was just telling you all my dream. We ain't got to pack up and move right now. I'm sure God knows our needs."

"Well, how long are we to wait here—until we're found" asked Ben.

"Ben, we already been found. This monster, as you call it, it's evil. It's from hell, and it's real. It's known about me and us probably since we were born. It's only now realized that we are on Jesus Christ's side. And the work we've done for Jesus by baptizing and witnessing to the Gospel. We are its main enemy. It can't hurt us as long as we stay in the will of God. And it can only hurt us if we give in to our flesh, the worldly desires, or give in to him. So we safe for a while. I should have spoken more clearly, I'm sorry."

"OK, so it's settled. When she and the baby are strong enough, we leaving," Bo replied forcefully.

"We gonna need a really good plan. Traveling with a baby isn't going to be easy. I think we should start to plan now. We planned our first run. Now, this run is going to get us into the land of freedom. All that talk about an underground railroad and not knowing where we gonna stay ain't gonna hold water. Everything we do has to be planned, and that's including where we stay," replied Ben.

"I agree with you, Ben. But I think we should first pray before making any decisions. Second, we need to talk to Mrs. Davis about our situation. After all, she's been helping us all along. And she's a part of the underground railroad," Bo urged.

"Where is Mrs. Davis? We ain't seen her in weeks, and ain't no word or tell about what's going on. We could be in danger," Ben passionately replied.

"No, we ain't got nothing to worry about. I looked into that woman's eyes, and I know. She'd rather give her life's breath than let something happen to us. She's on our side. Now, Ben, don't go badmouthing her," Billy angrily replied.

Chapter Sixteen

Healing in the Name of Jesus

No sooner had Billy finished speaking than the sliding door slowly slid open. Mrs. Davis sheepishly peeped in. The area was well lit, and everyone was clearly seen. I sat facing the fireplace holding my baby, unknown to Mrs. Davis. Mrs. Davis cautiously entered the room. She kept her gaze on the three unknown strangers standing around me. She was carrying a wicker basket and wore a pink shawl draped over her head and shoulders. She lowered the shawl from her face, and her smile warmed the room. She quickly came over to the eating table and placed the basket on the table. She reached into the basket and took out an entire turkey and placed it on the table. She slowly glanced up and saw me holding a baby.

With a loud shriek, she cried, "Oh my god, a baby!" She stepped in front of the fireplace and looked on the beautiful sight of me holding me baby. She slowly reached down and gently removed the blanket surrounding the infant's face. She asked, "Is it a boy or girl?"

"It's a boy. His name is Zechariah. His daddy name him. We gonna call him Zech for short."

"How old is he? He can't be more than a few days old?"

"He only was born this morning. He ain't even a day old yet. He been asleep all day. He woke up. I feed him, and he went right back to sleep."

"Can I hold him?"

"Sure, you can."

Mrs. Davis slowly reached for Zech, and I carefully handed him over. She gently held him. She pressed her lips to his cheeks and smelled, saying,

"I love the smell of babies. He's beautiful, and he's born free. That's what it's all about. You being free, Little Zeke."

"He is little. Is he too small?" I asked.

"No, he's not too small. He stayed full term. He's just fine."

"Mrs. Davis, his name is Zech."

"Didn't I say Zech?"

"No, you said Zeke," Bo interjected.

"Oh, I'm sorry. It's a good name too."

"I liked the sound of Zeke. It's still short for Zechariah," Bo continued.

Mrs. Davis stood holding Zeke. She walked back and forth, whispering something in his ear. Then she sat next to me and said, "You belong with your mom." She slowly returned Zeke to me and explained, "We've been on slave row. It's a sickness like nothing I've seen before around here. Slaves are dying, especially the older ones and the sickly. They've been catching a cold. Then they get sweaty and chills. They fall into a coma, and they're gone. And it's spreading. Many of the children are coming down with it. Old Dr. Johnson haven't done nothing. He gave them something for the cold and fever, but it's not working."

"Mrs. Davis, how long has this sickness been going around?" I asked.

"It started when it rained and rained so. It was around the time you came. Soon afterward, some folks got sick. It's no wonder. Those poor souls living in damp and muddy shacks. Some even sleeping on the floor. It's damp, cold, and wet. And who knows, it could be something from the old river done made them sick."

"It's the first we heard about it."

"That's right. With you being with child, I didn't want to worry you or any of you."

"I needs to get down to slave row right away. Mrs. Davis, I may be able to help."

199

"You just had a baby. You need your strength."

"I'm fine."

"Well, if you're OK, I'll take you to slave row tomorrow."

"That's fine with me. I'll be ready."

Mrs. Davis stood and leaned over and kissed me and placed her hand on Zeke's hand and replied, "You all enjoy the turkey and the rest of the fixings here. I'll be back in the morning and get my basket."

Mrs. Davis poetically left. Bo followed behind her and closed the hiding door. He came and sat in the seat she had just left and whispered, "You just had a baby. You need your strength. I don't think that you should be going to slave row."

"I'm fine, Bo."

"Who gonna take care of Zeke? Who gonna feed him? What about if you get the sickness?"

"Creasy can look after Zeke right here while I'm gone, and I ain't gonna be gone that long. Folks are dying. I can help."

"Woman, you getting besides yourself. I'm your husband."

"Bo, folks are dying."

"Yeah, well, what about Zeke? Who gon' take care of him if you get what them folks has got?"

"Mrs. Davis was there, and she don't look sick."

"Well, then, you go and come right back, you hear me?"

I peered passionately into his eyes and lovingly said, "Yes, sir."

I had felt all along that Bo's manhood would sometimes appear to be threatened by my gifts of the Holy Spirit. I knew he didn't understand things, nor did I. I willingly submitted to the will of God in my life. I always kept in mind Bo's heart, mind, and soul. I had seen the treatment of Negro men. I had witnessed the loss of dignity of many Negro men. I had witnessed the harsh treatment of Negro women upon their menfolk, and I always allowed Bo to feel and think that he was the man and in charge. Yet I know he wasn't in charge over nothing. Not even his own life.

Early the next morning, I was feeding Zeke. I heard the sliding of the secret door opening. I thought it was Mrs. Davis and took Zeke over to Creasy. I had already dressed and eaten. When the door finally opened, I saw a large shadow coming. I rushed over to Bo and woke him. A tall white man stood holding a lantern. He looked around the room. Now, all the slaves were awake and peering at the stranger standing before them. He spoke in a very strong and forceful manner. "My name is Ed Davis. This here is my plantation. I guess you already know my wife, Bridget Davis."

"No, sir, we only know Mrs. Davis," Ben respectfully replied.

"One and the same. She's my wife." His voice softened as he continued. "I'm here to escort Ms. Mary Lou to slave row. We got some mighty sick folks down there. I know you folks haven't seen me. Bridget and I thought it would always be best to keep ourselves separated in this underground railroad business." No sooner did he finish speaking than Mrs. Davis smiled gently, confirming her husband's sincerity.

"We are led to believe that you were on the side of slavery," Ben blurted out.

"Oh, no, I've never sided with that peculiar institution. We'd give our very lives for the destruction of it. I apologize for keeping myself away from you all, but it was for the benefit of everyone involved. Every liberty and freedom we now enjoy did not come through ease and convenience for all. Someone had to have faith and vision for the generations to come. Some even made the ultimate sacrifice. These are the history makers. From the early American settlers who fought against the tyranny of Great Britain or the American slaves who now fight against the cruel, inhumane horrors of slavery, to any and all people who fight against oppression of any kind. These are the history makers.

"You see, you can't win unless you compete. You can't conquer unless you invade. You can't triumph unless you do battle. You can't have victory unless you fight. Victory is never given. It is won! History records the quitters, the spectators, or the critics. But those who stand in the face of insurmountable odds, those who overcome impossible obstacles and boldly, courageously, faithfully, and fearlessly meet the challenges of life head-on—these are the history makers. So which are you? A history maker or history waster? What will tomorrow's history record about what we're doing today? I didn't come here to preach. But I want you to know that I'm on your side. Feel secure. I'll bring your precious Mary Lou back to you as soon as I can, hopefully in a few hours. I hear she's got a baby to care for."

The slaves stood amazed at the words he'd spoken. They felt pride and self-assurance. Mrs. Davis stared loving upon her husband, knowing his heart. She felt proud of him. She loved him ever since they'd first met. She'd never known a better man.

"Well, we better get going. Them folks are only going to get sicker. And I'd like to get back and feed Zeke."

"You take care of her."

"I will take care of your wife like she was my own daughter."

I grabbed a shawl and wrapped it around my shoulders, adjusted my head rag, and hurried to the hiding door.

Mrs. Davis, speaking softly, said, "She's fine. Don't you all worry. She'll be back before you know it. Now, let's get breakfast going. I'm hungry. I'm staying here. I can help cook and take care of Zeke."

Mr. Davis followed behind me and pulled the door shut. Outside the basement door, there was a horse and carriage. It was Mr. Davis's personal carriage. He helped me onto the carriage and mounted the carriage and shouted, "Giddyap!" The carriage jerked forward, and we headed to slave row.

Upon arriving in slave row, it looked isolated. The shacks were run down. There was uncleared-away snowfall around the shacks. It wasn't the slave row of the Burkes' plantation, nor was it the slave row of the Dyes' plantation she remembered. Master Davis pulled up to shabby shack. An old Negro woman opened the door and stood in the doorway. Master Davis tied the horse and carriage to the frosted tree.

Upon entering the shack, she saw several men and women lying on straw beds. They were covered with blankets. A fireplace in the center of the shack kept the shack warm. The shack was larger than most. It had a wooden floor, and there were three large rooms attached to the main room with the fireplace. I walked around, looking at each person. I saw that they had the same symptoms.

The older Negro woman said, "I'm Kora. You some kind of Negro doctor?"

"No, I'm no doctor or nothing. My name is Mary Lou. I'm here to help."

"I don't know what you can do. We done tried everything, and nothing seems to work. Old Dr. Johnson was here. He ain't do nothing. I seemed like folks got worst since he came. He gave folks castor oil and aspirin. I guess that's what he called it. Whatever, it didn't do nothing. I did better by rubbing their chest in fish grease."

"Oh, so that's what I smell."

Mr. Davis replied, "Can you do anything?"

"I don't know. I'll see."

"There are others in the other rooms. I usually take care of sick folk. So when folks started getting sick, they just came. I couldn't turn them down. I kept 'em."

"God bless you. You done a real good thing."

I took off my coat and shawl and laid them on the eating table. Mr. Davis's eyes stayed glued on my every movement. I sat at the eating table and folded my hands in front of me and prayed. Mr. Davis noticed that I kept on my gloves. I laid my head on the table and cried, "Lord Jesus, help me." Tears ran down my face. I felt warmth all over my body. My hands felt hot.

I heard a gentle whisper, saying, "Take off your gloves and make the sign of the cross on each sick person's forehead in your own blood." I slowly lifted my head from the table and glanced around the room. A gentle smile graced my face. My face glowed with love, peace, and kindness. I slowly stood and gently removed my gloves. Mr. Davis noticed that my hands were both wrapped in bandages and the palms of my hands were red with blood.

Kora stood by the fireplace, staring and lost for words. Kora thought, *What is wrong with this child? She must have cut both hands.*

My eyes slowly moved upon my hands. I began to undo the bandages from my right hand. Once I had finished, I laid the bloody bandages on the eating table while blood slowly trickled down my hand. Then I undid the left hand. I went and knelt by an elder man who looked to be close to death. I prayed, "Be healed in the name of Jesus," in a loud voice. I laid both hands on each side of his head and gently raised it up. Then I made the sign of the cross upon his forehead in my own blood, which flowed from the wounds on my hands. The man lay there smeared in my blood, seemingly unchanged. I moved on to each sick person in the shack and did the same.

Mr. Davis and Kora stood in shock. Both were lost for words and thought. Yet they were completely captivated. The shack seemed to get increasingly warm. Sweat began pouring down my forehead. I walked around the shack and lifted both hands over my head and yelled, "Thank you, Jesus! Thank you, Jesus. Send your Holy Spirit upon this place." Tears rolled down my face.

The first man I had touched began to cough violently. Kora went over and grabbed a bucket of drinking water and gave the elder man a cool drink. She placed her hand on his head after he'd drank and yelled, "The fever is broke!" He tried to sit up, but Kora lovingly whispered, "Be still.

Lay here awhile. You been sick for a while." The man slowly laid his head back down with eyes wide open the size of silver dollars.

Moments later, everyone who was sick began coughing violently. I joined Kora in giving them drinking water. Some stood up and got water for themselves. They were the ones who were less sick. Some of the lesser sick began helping me and Kora distribute water and wash the smeared blood from their heads and forehead.

Mr. Davis still hadn't removed his coat. He stood watching in amazement and wonder. He'd never seen anything like what he'd just witnessed, nor did Kora, yet they didn't question me, nor did they doubt what had just happened. They had witnessed a miracle of healing, and they felt healed as well and renewed in their faith.

Mr. Davis softly whispered, "Well, young lady, you are something very special. I've never seen or known of anything ever happening like what I've just witnessed." I glanced toward Mr. Davis and continued to care for the recovering sick.

"Well, our business here is finished. Come, young lady. You need to get back to your newborn."

I had practically lost all sense of time caring for the sick, but upon mentioning Zeke, I immediately dropped everything I was doing and slowly walked over to the eating table and put my coat, hat, and gloves on. I smiled and said, "I'm ready. These sick folk will be just fine. They'll be hungry and need plenty of drinking water."

"Who's going to help me? I'm going to need somebody to cook, clean, and get these folks on their feet."

"I'll send someone to help you, Ms. Kora. I suppose my wife may come to help. She'll want to see the miracle Mary Lou has done."

"It wasn't me, Mr. Davis. It was Jesus's working. I can't do nothing. I'm just like you or anybody else. It's Jesus. I can't take none of the credit."

"Well said, little lady. I like you. You really are something. Now, let's get you back to your baby."

Mr. Davis quickly hurried outside. He stood in the cold air and stared at the sun. He told me, "It's afternoon. Time sure did fly. It only seemed like we were here for a few minutes. I didn't even take off my coat." I stood beside Mr. Davis. I glanced at the sun, not knowing what I was looking up for because I didn't know how to read the sun and determine the time.

Unknown to either of us, the demons of sickness, despair, hopelessness, hatred, and all other ungodly spirits lurked outside. They had been driven from the sick inside the shack. Now they waited, looking for an opportunity to return.

Moved by the Holy Spirit, I prayed, "Jesus, send your protection upon this place. Send your angels to protect these your people."

"Why the prayer? They're healed, aren't they?" asked Mr. Davis.

"It's not a regular sickness these folks had."

While I was still talking, angels descended upon the shack in the sun's rays. Unseen to me and humans, the angels stood next to me and Mr. Davis with swords drawn ready for battle. The demons stood still and watched. The angels posed for battle kept guard. Mr. Davis and I got into the carriage and headed back to the plantation feeling secure of the victory won in Jesus's name.

Once back at the big house, they entered the secret hiding place to cries from Little Zeke. Mrs. Davis paced back and forth, lovingly holding Zeke and rocking him. I cried, "Oh, there's my baby. He must be hungry. Come to Momma. I'm ready to feed you." I quickly took off my shawl and coat. The front of my dress was wet with breast milk. I quickly sat at the eating table and fed Zeke.

Everyone watched her, and no one said a word as to what had happened on slave row. Mr. Davis spoke up, saying, "Come on, Bridget. Let's let these folks get settled. Slave row is clear of all sickness and disease. I'm taking you back there. Maybe you can help them. They need someone down there."

"I'd love to go to slave row and help any way I can. I'm gonna take two of these new fellas with me." She looked around the room searching for Raphael and Barak. Resting her eyes on the two, she said, "Come on. I'd like you, Raph, and you, Barak, to attend me."

Raph and Barak immediately stood, and Barak replied, "We'd need some warm clothes if we gonna be riding in a fancy carriage."

"Well, I don't see nothing wrong with that. Bo, can you let the new fellas wears some of you all winter clothes?"

"Yes, ma'am. We got plenty of winter clothes they can wear."

Creasy rushed looking under beds and pulled out heavy coats, gloves, boats, hats, and scarves. She took the things over to Raph and Barak.

"I didn't even know we had all that stuff!" Ben shouted.

"I sent these things when it started to get cold," Mrs. Davis responded.

"That woman will hide anything she gets her hands on. I swear she something else," Ben blurted out.

Raph and Barak quickly put on the warm clothes and stood posed, ready to leave. Mrs. Davis politely asked, "Can either of you drive a carriage?"

"I can drive," Barak cautiously replied.

"Well, that settles it. Mr. Davis, you can stay here. These fellas will do just fine." They all left the hiding place, including Mr. Davis. He returned to the big house, while Mrs. Davis, Raph, and Barak mounted the carriage and headed for slave row.

As they rode in the carriage, the wind picked up and the snow blew across the dirt road and whistled in the trees. It was a beautiful afternoon. The sky was clear. The snow clung to the branches of the trees and created a serene winter day. It couldn't have been a more beautiful winter's day.

As they approached slave row, unseen to Mrs. Davis were many, many demons. They were covered in slime and hideous in appearance. They had long talons and bulging eyes with horns coming from their heads. Their legs and feet were similar to that of a goat or ass, yet they had the body of a man. As the carriage passed, the demons hissed and cursed and spewed all sorts of profanity.

Raphael and Barak watched their every movement. They looked for a leader. a major evil one who controlled the lesser demons. They knew if they destroyed the major evil, the rest would flee. Raph and Barak kept their human form, and they were unknown to the demons. As they drew nearer to the shack, there were more and more. Demons were on the roof of the shack. On the main road leading into slave row, they made a stronghold.

As the carriage slowly came near the shack, Kora came and stood outside and watched as they pulled up. She stood there shivering in the cold and said, "I'm sure enough in need of help. These folks are cold and hungry."

"Well, we're here now, and I brought plenty of food."

Mrs. Davis eased onto the snow-covered ground and cautiously walked into the shack with Raph and Barak holding on to her, one on one side, and the other side holding on to her arms. Once in the shack, she glanced around the room and said, "We've got twice as many sick as before."

"They're not sick anymore, Mrs. Davis. They're getting well," Kora respectfully replied.

"Swell, they look sick to me!"

Barak and Raph glanced around the room and noticed that there were no demons in the shack. They began to take off their coats. Then they saw two angels coming from one of the side rooms. The two angels saw Raph and Barak. Barak gracefully bowed his head, unknown to Kora and Mrs. Davis. The two angels realized who they were and immediately fell to one knee and lowered their heads in reverence for the awesome task Barak and Raph had been entrusted with. The awesome task of escorting me to freedom and the ending of slavery in America—this is Jophkiel, Barak, and Raphael's mission from the King of Kings, Christ Jesus. No one knew my role in slavery's demise, not me, not the abolitionists, nor any other man, woman, or child. Only the heavenly hosts of the angelic rank.

Mrs. Davis ordered, "You boys go out and bring in the food and other supplies. Then I want you two to cut some wood and bring it in here. We gonna get this place nice and warm." The two followed her orders. After they'd brought in a good supply of firewood, Mrs. Davis prepared a large amount of ox tail soup.

While the soup was cooking, she helped Kora in the caring for the sick. She noticed blood smeared on many of them and asked, "What's all the blood from?" Kora told her all what I had done and explained that many of the slaves she now sees helping and sitting up were near death. Mrs. Davis didn't respond; she kept on caring for the sick. After the soup had cooked, she and Kora took to each person a large bowl along with bread and goat's milk. The ones that were still too weak to eat, she spoon-fed.

Raph and Barak sat at the eating table, seemingly staring blankly around the room. Unknown to Mrs. Davis and Kora, they were in constant communication with the other angels there. They spoke a heavenly language. Amazingly beautiful. The angels told of my praying and how they were sent and found the demons causing sickness among the slaves. Barak explained what was going on at the plantation. Also, he told of the wonderful baby that had just been born. The angel replied, "We know of the baby. His soul was brought to the baby by Naph. Talking of the heavenly host, the boy is to be the father of a king. Through the boy's lineage, freedom for the slaves will begin its completion. The boy's soul was designed in the chamber for souls for greatness throughout the ages."

"Thank you, my countryman. We were unaware that the boy's soul came from the chamber of souls, nor were we aware of his part in history. We were only aware of Mary Lou and freedom for the slaves. We know now that our mission is not just for Mary Lou and the slaves but for the benefit of all humanity," replied Barak.

Kora noticed Raph and Barak staring off into space. She asked, "What's wrong with you two? You act like you ain't never sick folks before."

"We done seen many sick folks. But ain't none of them ever got well from no touch," Raph quickly replied.

"It just wasn't no ordinary touch. Mary Lou laid hands on these people, and that's why they are well."

Mrs. Davis raised her voice. "This isn't to be talked about. Do you hear me! I don't want no one to know anything about this. It's too dangerous for Mary Lou and everyone involved. Every one of you in this here shack must keep quiet. That woman's life is in jeopardy, and she's just had a baby. Now, God has decided to work through her. So we give thanks to God for her, and we'll just forget she was ever here. Is that clear?" Silence filled the air. No one moved. Everyone froze in a desperate attempt to comprehend the severity of the words and force Mrs. Davis had used. "Is that clear!" she screamed again.

Kora quietly, almost afraid, whispered, "Yes, ma'am."

Slowly, everyone in the shack said, "Yes, ma'am."

Unknown to Mrs. Davis or any of the others in the shack, Kora had told her friend Missy.

Chapter Seventeen

The Move

Unknown later that evening, Mr. and Mrs. Davis visited me and the others hiding with me. Mrs. Davis rejoiced in explaining all that had happened on slave row. She said, "When I arrived on slave row and entered that shack, I looked with my eyes and thought with my mind. I saw sick folk, and there were more than before. But as I walked around the shack and cared for them, I noticed they were smeared with blood. So I asked why! I was told. It didn't affect me none. Then I noticed the faces of the folk. They were smiling and joking. Joy was running wild in that shack. It seemed like a heavy burden had been lifted. I felt like electricity was flowing through my body. I'd never felt nothing like it before. Then I looked again. I guess I didn't see right the first time I looked, but the folks were healed. They were well. They were regaining their strength."

"Mrs. Davis, that's the Holy Spirit. I'd know it anywhere. Yes, ma'am, I felt just like that. And you can't explain it unless you done felt it. I know what you talking about," Billy cautiously explained.

"Well, we really didn't come to say much. We come to thank you. After all we'd seen today, we forgot to properly thank you," Mr. Davis replied.

"You done already thanked me. I said it's not me but Jesus."

"Well, we'd like to invite you and the rest to stay upstairs in the big house with us."

"We're fine. We're doing all right here," Bo replied.

"Well, we think that it would be better if all of you move upstairs with us. Now, Bo, I understand how you feel. Just think. You've got a new baby. It's not right for you all to be in this wet and musty room. It's the least we can do."

"OK, it's settled. We're moving up to the big house," Ben blurted out. Everyone smiled and looked at Ben. He stared back in excitement and anticipation of moving into the big house.

Mr. Davis said, "It's settled. You'll all move up tomorrow. Now, I want you all to know right now, it's not going to be a walk in the park. We discussed it and came up with this. You all will be acting like our house slaves. You'll be expected to do all the things a house slave does. Only you won't be slaves. If one day you don't want to work, then fine. I'm am not a slave master, nor will I ever be. We making this decision for the benefit of you all. Now, if you don't want to live in the big house, you can stay right here, just like before."

The next day arrived full of anticipation. Before dawn, Creasy was wrapping the items they'd accumulated in a bed linen. By the time the others had woken, she'd packed and wrapped almost everything.

Ben, slowly waking up, replied, "Woman, you must have got up in the middle of the night and worked all the way to daybreak."

"It needed to get done. Now all you menfolk has got to do is move it right on into the big house."

Smiley had a secret knock that he'd come up with to let the slaves know it was him. As they were putting on their clothes, a knock came from the secret entrance. It was Smiley. Smiley came into the hiding place, his usual slow-moving self. He was smoking his corn pipe with cherry tobacco. The smell filled the room and was very much welcomed by everyone except me. I forcefully said, "You shouldn't be smoking. Suppose my baby gets a whiff of that old tobacco."

"I ain't never heard of no tobacco smoke hurting no one. I just came to get me a peep at the little one."

"Well, I don't know if I'll let you see him with that pipe."

"Bo, you sure enough got yourself a wife here."

"That's my Mary Lou, and you better set that pipe down if you ever want to see Zeke."

"OK, I'll put it down." He set the pipe still smoking on the eating table and went over to me. I was nursing Zeke. I pulled and gently pulled the blanket away from his face. He looked, smiled, and said, "He does look like a wrinkle." Everyone smiled and watched Smiley. Smiley was known for his reputation of getting a laugh out of the best and worst of situations. He sat at the table, puffing his pipe, saying, "Mrs. Davis wants you all in the big house right now. I see you all have packed. You can move, but you don't have to go outside. I've set a lantern next to the stairs. Just take the stairs upstairs to the big house. Come on, I'll show you." He slowly walked to the secret entrance and whispered, "Make sure you carry something with you. It will save you a trip." Creasy and Ben followed behind him, carrying heavy bundles of clothes, linen, food, pots and pans, and their personal items.

Ben asked, "So how many slaves does Mr. Davis own?"

"I guess you already know. We ain't slaves. I work because I wants to, and I'm helping runaways, like you all. That's why I stay. I could have been up north years ago. But helping slaves get to freedom, that's what's important."

"Smiley, you're a strange man. I would have been free years ago."

They continued to carry their things upstairs, following behind Smiley. At the top of the stairs, the door was shut. Smiley knocked his secret knock. A few seconds later, Mrs. Davis slowly opened the door. She stood there smiling, wearing a beautiful pure white dress with lace fringes.

Ben and Creasy yanked and pulled their things into a large room with hardwood floor. It was the most beautiful thing Creasy had ever seen. There were three large oil paintings directly in front of her. The walls were a deep red with gold vertical lines that stretched from the floor to the ceiling. Her eyes moved to the left, and she saw a huge black piano. Behind the piano, there was a huge window. There were royal-blue velvet draperies on each side of the window. Creasy's mouth flopped open. She stood amazed. She dropped the things she was carrying and said, "Oh my god. I never."

She slowly and hesitantly walked toward the oil painting, gazing upward at the enormous size and beauty of it.

Mrs. Davis lovingly said, "That's my great-grandmother. She was such a pretty woman." Creasy walked to the next oil painting. She cautiously touched the gold frame. Mrs. Davis replied, "That's my great-grandfather. He was a preacher. He's holding his Bible. I don't think I can ever recall him without it."

"Your grandparents look like fine folks, ma'am."

"Well, thank you, Creasy. They were. They long passed. My granddaddy was against slavery. It's probably where I picked up my view on it. He owned slaves, yet he did treat them nothing like slaves. Only around strangers he asked them to call him Master Davis. They usually called him sir. I always thought that was odd. I understand it better now. My grandmother was the same as granddaddy. In fact, when I was a little girl, I grew up, played, and slept in the same bed as the slave children. They'd spend many nights in this old mansion. We'd rip and run playing and had ourselves a ball. It wasn't until I was almost in my twenties that I fully understood the horrors of slavery."

Everyone was captivated by Mrs. Davis. She spoke with love and care completely feeling the predicament of Creasy and the others. While she was still talking, I came up and stood next to Creasy, carrying baby Zeke, and the others followed, carrying the remainder of their things.

Mrs. Davis continued, saying, "Her name was Elsie. We grew up together in this house. I taught her how to read, write, and do math. She was as sharp as anyone I'd met. I'd known her all my life. I can't even remember a day without her. She was my sister. She was a Negro. Although I didn't have a sister by my parents, Elsie was my sister. Well, we'd wend into town shopping. I used to love to buy things. And whatever I bought for myself, I bought for Elsie. Many times we'd be standing side by side wearing the exact same clothes. I'd never thought it wrong or anything. This particular day, we was shopping." Tears welled up in her eyes. Her voice cracked in anticipation of every word. She continued, "She was standing outside the boutique. The store didn't allow Negroes to enter. I can remember like it was yesterday. She was beautiful. I love to see her dress up. She was extremely dark skinned. She had a smile that brought joy to my heart. My friend and sister.

"Well, some men were walking down the street, and she didn't get off the sidewalk soon enough. I heard one of them yell, 'Nigger, you think you better than us? Get your black ass off this sidewalk!' After that, it's awful. One of the men slapped her. She turned and tried to walk away. Another grabbed her hand and yelled, 'We gone one of them uppity niggers who needs to be taught a lesson!' They took her over to a light post. They must have been drunk. I smelled whiskey on their breath.

"I screamed, running out of the boutique, 'Don't you dare touch her! She belong to me!' It was too late. By the time I reached her, they'd gotten a rope and hung her from the light post in the middle of the fashion district. I was completely heartbroken. I'd never imagined something so horrific happening to anyone. She was more dear to me than my own soul."

Tears slowly rolled down her cheeks. She took out a cotton hanker and dried her eyes. Everyone was completely silent. Bo let out a deep gasp. "I'm sorry for your loss. No one should ever have to go through anything like that ever again."

"Bo, you're right. That's the reason I'm in this business. I knew it was wrong then, and I know it's wrong now. Come on. Let's get you all to your rooms." She held her headlight and gently replied, "Follow me." She boldly and proudly walked through the lavishly decorated room, not noticing the beautiful things around her.

The slaves followed, turning their heads to and fro, looking and glancing upon all the beauty in the room. None had ever seen such beauty, including me. They marched through the room and walked through two gigantic wood doors. The doors reached completely to the ceiling. They had brass handles and were a deep dark wood like they'd never seen before.

They walked into another room with a huge crystal chandelier. The floor was a beautiful white marble. There was a huge marble spiral staircase that led to the upper rooms. The stairs were draped in a deep dark red carpet. The arm railings were made from the same wood as the huge door. They stood motionless and glanced around the room. There were paintings and sculptures throughout the room.

Billy looked upward and said, "Who live up there?"

I whispered, "That's the upstairs. Folks usually sleep up there."

"Is that where we're going to sleep?"

"No, we have quarters on the first floor for guests. We don't have slave quarters. You'll all use the guest quarters."

As they walked through the large forum, a young and petite girl wearing a black-and-white maid's uniform came down the hall. She politely asked, "Are we to be having guests, madam?" She spoke in a strange accent that none of the slaves had heard before.

"Yes, Ingrid. Our guests will be staying. I'll take them to their rooms, and I'll speak with you later. They will be assisting you."

"Yes, madam." Ingrid did a 180-degree turn and returned in the same way she'd come. Every one of the slaves was amazed. They'd never seen a white person serving.

Bo asked, "Is that your slave, Mrs. Davis?"

"Oh god, no! She is our hired maid. She cooks and cleans and does the duties of a maid."

"That's what we do, Mrs. Davis."

"Yes, Bo. We pay her, and she lives here. She free to come and go. She's not a slave."

"I see. She works and gets paid. Ain't that something?"

"You all will get a salary."

"What's a salary?"

"It's getting paid for our work."

"We getting paid?"

"Of course. We will pay you for every bit of work you do. I strongly suggest that you save your money. You'll need it when you all decide to continue on up north."

"Yes, ma'am. I'm ready to start work right now. I never got paid for working before."

"Well, it's about time you all received an honest day's pay for an honest day's work."

They walked through the library. The library had a huge wooden desk in it. It was shaped in a huge oval. There were books from the floor to the ceiling. There were huge paintings of Mr. and Mrs. Davis and others whom the slaves had never seen. Unlike the other room, almost everything in the library was made of wood. They continued through the library and exited onto another hallway, which didn't have any paintings on the walls and was extremely narrow. As they continued, they noticed closed doors.

Mrs. Davis said, "These are the guest quarters. It will be a big change from that old damp and dusty basement."

They walked past the first couple of doors and came to several wooden doors unlike the rest. They had crystal handles instead of brass, and they weren't as fancy as the others. Mrs. Davis opened the door, and there was a large canopy bed, a dresser, a desk, and beautiful white linen on the bed.

Mrs. Davis said, "This is Bo and Mary Lou's room. It's a big old house, and all the guest rooms are the same. They just have a different color. This is the white room. We have a blue room, a green room, a red room. I chose this one for her and Bo since they are newly married and with a newborn. It's the closest to the kitchen. The rest of you can choose your own rooms." She politely turned and left the same way she led them into the hall that contained the guests rooms.

Bo and I stood in the hallway looking into their new room. The others stood watching Mrs. Davis. As soon as she reached the end of the hall and turned the corner, they dropped the things they were carrying and ran from room to room, opening the doors, looking in, and running back into the hall, screaming, "This is the green room!" "I found the blue room!" "There's two beds in this room!" The excitement of their newfound living arrangements was pure joy. They loved it. They had never stayed in such luxury and beauty. This was a dream come true.

Barak cried out, "Come on, Raph, let's take the room with two beds and plenty room." They grabbed their bags and ran to the room like children. Once through the door, they came to a full stop. They dropped their bags and stood completely still.

Tzedakahi, the captain of the giving, stood in front of the fireplace. He was arrayed in pure beauty. The light from his being filled the room like the sun's rays. The sun's rays passed through him in beautiful colors of blues, reds, greens, crystal, yellows, and all colors of the spectrum. He was invisible to humans. He said, "You are called to give completely of yourselves, even your mortal bodies. Also in your duties here, you are to work abundantly, not as slaves but as freed men. Also, you are to do the duties of the others, because some still have a slave mentality. You are to be the example of duty, giving, loyalty, and self-sacrifice." Just as soon as Tzedakahi had finished speaking, his essence entered the sunlight coming into the window. He, poetically, in unspeakable beauty, became the rays and rose into heaven.

Barak and Raph looked passionately into each other's eyes. Without saying a word, they both walked out into the hall. Jophkiel was standing outside of his room. He said, "We have our orders. Things have changed. Let us worship God in them." They returned to their rooms feeling joy, peace, and love.

All the slaves were in their rooms, arranging their things and getting settled. Billy and Jophkiel had roomed together. Ben and Creasy had taken the red room because Creasy's favorite color was red. While they were unpacking, Ben heard a noise in the hall. He peeped outside of the door. He saw a large man carrying suits and a tall woman carrying maid's uniforms. He quickly closed the door and ran to the window, saying, "I think they done found us. Come on. We can climb out of this window. I ain't about to be nobody's slave again."

"Ben, ain't nobody done found us." Bo calmly walked over to the door and opened it. She stood in the doorway. She saw the two walking down the hall.

They walked up to her and said, "Good morning. I am Ivan. I am the butler. This is my wife, Elizabella. She is the maid. I believe you've met my daughter, Ingrid."

"Not sure. I ain't met no Ingrid."

"Oh, it doesn't matter. You will meet her soon enough. I was told to bring you some uniforms for your working clothes."

Elizabella stood off to his right. She gently smiled and handed her the maid's uniforms, saying, "Please choose one of your size. They are all the same, just different sizes."

Creasy took one and held it next to her and said, "These are some fancy clothes to be cleaning in. They look like Sunday meeting clothes. Ben, come on over here and pick out you one of these uniforms."

Ben calmly strutted over to the door and looked Ivan directly in his eyes. Ivan firmly said, "Please choose one, sir."

"Sure, I'm a sure. OK. I thinks I'll take this one."

Ivan handed him his choice and replied, "Please try it on, sir. It's important that you have a good fit."

Ben and Creasy took the uniforms and went back into the room. Ivan and Elizabella went to the other doors, knocked, and implored each one to choose a uniform of the right size. Once they finished, they stood at the end of the hall looking very dignified, even more so than Mr. and Mrs. Davis.

One by one, as we changed into their housekeeping attire, we came out into the hall. We stood looking and gazing at each other as if we had changed by putting on different clothes. Billy's uniform was too big and Ben's uniform was too small. They were both big men, but the fit just wasn't right. They stood looking at each other, and Billy said, "Let's change jackets."

"OK, Billy. Only if we could change pants too." They changed, and the fit was a lot better. Creasy and I yanked and pulled on our skirts and rearranged our head rags.

All the while, Ivan and Elizabella stood at the end of the hall staring. Ivan finally said, walking down the hall, "I will explain your duties," in a heavy accent that none of them had ever heard except from the younger girl they'd seen earlier. "First, I want you to stand still." This was a bit difficult since the excitement and the news of the rooms and clothes seemed to make them extremely anxious. Ivan forcefully said, "Be still, please." Everyone looked at him in shock at the sound of his voice and his behavior, since none of them had ever met anyone like him. They stood motionless and stared at Ivan. He walked down the aisle and strongly said, "Men on my right and women on my left." They all stood still, looking.

"Elizabella, would you please help me get them in order?" She quickly ran on her tiptoes to the women and gently placed her hand on their shoulders and put them in the positions that he wanted. She did the same to the men.

"This how you are to line up every morning. Had only been my wife, my daughter, and I. Now we have you. My wife did the cooking. Mrs. Davis also loves to cook. Can any of you cook?"

I politely said, "I can cook."

"OK, you will help Elizabella, and, you, you'll help my Ingrid."

Creasy and I both replied, "Yes, sir."

He walked back and forth and asked, "What's your names?" He pointed first at Bo and then Ben and then to the others. Each one gave the same response right down the line.

"I'm Ben."

"I'm Bo."

"I'm Creasy."

"I'm Mary Lou."

"I'm Raph."

"I'm Billy."

"I'm Barak."

"I'm Jophkiel."

Billy asked, "Where are you all from? You all sure do talk funny."

"We're from Russia."

"Russia? Where is Russia?"

"It's in another country. It's a longs ways from here."

No sooner had Ivan finished answering Bill than Ingrid gracefully entered the hall. Billy's eyes fell upon her. She was extremely beautiful. She had green eyes and reddish-blond hair. She looked amazingly like her mother. You could see where she'd gotten her beauty from. Billy's eyes followed her every movement as she gracefully walked up to her dad. She whispered something in his ear. Then she turned and left just as gracefully as she'd entered.

Ivan quickly said, "That's enough for today. We have work to do. Tomorrow you will start. Be standing here in the same places you are now at dawn."

Billy wasn't listening. He seemed to be preoccupied. He was daydreaming about Ingrid. He thought, *She's the prettiest girl I've done ever seen.* He imagined how her voice sounded. He dreamed of talking to her. Then he felt a tug on his arm. He quickly looked. It was Jophkiel.

"Let's take a walk around the place." Billy was still dreaming of Ingrid. "Billy, you listening? Let's take a look around. We work here now. It's all right."

"OK. You go first."

Jophkiel followed the path they'd come. Billy followed. They came into the library. Billy was just as amazed as the first time he'd walked through it. He slowly walked around the oval room, looking at the books, paintings, and sculptures. "Do you think Mr. and Mrs. Davis done read all these books?"

"I don't think so. I heard it takes a while to read a book. Maybe if they was a hundred years old, they could have read some."

"Jophkiel, have you ever read a book?"

"No, I can't read. Can you read?"

"No, but I know how to look like I'm reading. I just hold the book in front of my face and look at the pictures for a long time. Folks don't know no better. They'll think you're reading."

"I heard Mary Lou can read," Jophkiel replied.

"Yeah, she sure can read. She can do math too. Mrs. Burke taught her. She's smart."

Mrs. Davis walked into the library and stared at the two. She asked, "Are you two interested in books?"

"Yes, ma'am," Billy replied.

"We have books from all over the world. My husband loves to read, and so do I." She walked over toward them and reached right next to Billy. She picked up a book and said, "This book is about a Moor."

"A Moor? What's that?"

"Moors are people from Africa. Your people are originally from Africa."

"Mrs. Davis, I don't want to be disrespectful, but I ain't never been to Africa."

"I could assume as much. But maybe your great-great-grandfather was. And you probably have never met him. He might have been a Moor. And this book is by a writer named Shakespeare. He was a great writer. He wrote this book about an African slave who became a general in the army. His name was Othello."

"Othello. I ain't never heard tell of no Othello."

"I wouldn't imagine that you would have unless you read some of his books."

"Oh, no, Mrs. Davis, I can't read. I was just looking at the books. I would imagine a man would be mighty smart to read and write."

"You only need the desire to want to learn."

"I have plenty of that, but mostly I used my desire to work in the fields."

"Well, we're going to change that. If any of you want to learn how to read and write, I'm going to provide a way for it to happen."

"Mrs. Davis, I think it's against the law to teach slaves to read and write."

"Remember, Billy, you're not a slave anymore. You are free. Don't you ever forget that."

"Mrs. Davis, do you think we could look around the place?" asked Jophkiel.

"Sure, you can. How you ever going to know your way around if you don't look around? In fact, I encourage it. Tell the others. I'll let Mr. Davis know what you all are doing. And feel free to look at the books." She gracefully left the room just as poetically as she'd entered.

Billy and Jophkiel stood, wondering what to do next. Jophkiel replied, "I guess we should tell the others."

"Yes, that what the lady said." They went back to the guest quarters and knocked on the other's doors and explained what Mrs. Davis had just said.

Ben said, "That's good. I don't want to be trapped in here with this woman. Come on. I'm going with you all."

Creasy stood at the door, listening, and replied, "You all make sure we get wood and such for this here fireplace. These rooms are big as shacks that whole families live in."

"You better make sure you ask Mrs. Davis before you go start building a fire," Ben blurted out.

"OK, I'm going to visit Mary Lou and see if she wants to walk."

Creasy quickly walked past the men and went to my bedroom. She knocked on the door, and I answered, "Just a minute." I opened the door holding Zeke, rocking him back and forth.

"You want to walk around the house?"

"Sure, I do. Let me tell Bo." I told Bo and left with Creasy.

Bo came and stood at the door and watched me as I strolled off with Creasy. Billy, Ben, and Jophkiel were standing in the hall. Bo asked, "Where you boys headed off to?"

"We're just gonna walk around and see things," Ben replied.

"I might as well join you." He walked out into the hall and closed the door behind.

They all followed behind Creasy and me. We walked from room to room in a very orderly and dignified fashion. Creasy and I walked and talked about the beauty of the mansion, seemingly unaware of Bo, Ben, and the others. They followed us ladies from room to room, seemingly ignoring us. When the ladies stopped, the men stopped. When the ladies talked, the men talked. This went on throughout the house for some time.

We came to two large double doors. Creasy and I stopped in front of the doors and discussed whether to enter. Creasy opened the door and cautiously looked inside. She said, "There's another part of the house in here. Come on. Let's see what it looks like."

Creasy entered, and the others followed. The hall looked just like the one on the other side of the mansion. As we looked around, we noticed that everything was the same. The walls, the doors, the windows. But the colors were different. The paintings were different. The sculptures were different.

As we continued, Ingrid quickly walked by. She didn't say a word. She glanced at Billy and smiled. His eyes followed her as she continued on down the hall. She breathed deeply with every step she took.

We continued, stopping at each and every painting and sculpture, discussing what it was. Ivan saw us and immediately came directly to us and asked, "Who gave you permission to roam around?"

"Mrs. Davis said we could go wherever we wanted," Jophkiel answered.

"Well, you are now in the south wing of the house."

"South wing. What's a wing?" asked Bo.

"The mansion has four wings: north, south, east, and west. It's a very big place, but because the Davises don't have any children, they are very easy to care for. My wife and daughter have managed well."

No sooner had he finished speaking than he heard a heavy knock. He excused himself and went to the main entrance. A man with an army uniform stood at the door. He said, "I am Captain Burris. Can I speak to the owner of the place?" He spoke with a deep Southern accent and smelled of horses and dust.

Chapter Eighteen

No Weapon Formed . . .

"Who may I say is calling?"

"I'm Captain Burris of the United States Army."

"Please wait, sir."

Ivan closed the door and went directly to Mr. Davis, who was in his study room adjacent to the library. Ivan knocked and waited. A few seconds later, Mr. Davis emerged from the study room and asked, "What is it?"

"There is a Captain Burris here to see you."

"Please show him into the library."

Ivan returned to the door and said, "Please follow me."

Captain Burris cautiously walked into the forum. He stood amazed at the sheer size and beauty of the forum. He scanned the entire surroundings as his military training would allow.

Ivan kept his slow and steady pace, seemingly unaware of Captain Burris's amazement. Ivan opened the library door and showed Captain Burris to a high-back leather chair directly in front of Mr. Davis's desk. Captain Burris took off his hat and crossed his legs. He took a large pipe full of cherry tobacco. He struck a match and lit his pipe. The aroma immediately filled the room along with his arrogance. He settled back into the chair and relaxed.

A few minutes later, Mr. Davis entered. He quickly and quietly walked to Captain Burris. He extended his hand and said, "I'm Ed Davis. What can I do for you?"

"My pleasure to meet you. Your reputation precedes you, sir. I'm Captain Burris of the United States Army. I'm in the area looking for some runaway slaves. They are a murdering lot who set a barn on fire and killed several white people during their escape. They are led by a nigger named Mary Lou."

"So you're asking my help?"

"No, sir. I'm asking if you've seen them or heard of any tell of runaway niggers in the area."

"I haven't. If they were such deadly niggers, my own niggers would inform me. I run a tight ship."

"Yes, I've heard of your plantation and the tight ship you run."

Mr. Davis turned and walked behind his desk and sat down. He peered into Captain Burris's eyes, searching to find any hint of suspicion. He opened a cigar box on his desk and took one out. He lit it and said, "These are the finest cigars in the world." He drew a large amount smoke and blew it into Captain Burris's face.

Captain Burris stood up and said, "Well, I won't take any more of your time. I can see you are a busy man."

"No, sir. I'm not busy. B-u-s-y is used to refer to being under Satan's yoke, and we are a Christian family, my wife and I."

"Oh, I see."

"Ivan, please show Captain Burris to the door."

Ivan immediately entered the room and stood next to Captain Burris. Captain Burris respectfully said, "Thank you for your time. I'll call again." Captain Burris stood up and gentlemanly extended his hand.

Mr. Davis stood and stared him directly in his eyes and placed both hands in his pockets and said, "Good-bye, Captain Burris."

Ivan showed him to the door. He quickly got onto his horse and suspiciously rode off Ivan stood at the door and watched him, wondering what he wanted. He turned around and saw Mr. Davis standing behind him. "Ivan, bring all of our guests to me right now."

Ivan, without saying a word, respectfully lowered his head in respect and walked past him and went to the last place he'd seen us. When he got there, we were not there. He headed toward the small chapel. He quietly opened the door and saw us kneeling in the last pews.

Fr. Joseph had finished Mass and extended one hand over Mrs. Davis's head and said, "May the Holy Spirit shine upon you and deep within your heart and radiate from you. May you be a guide to all God's children. In Jesus Christ's name, we pray."

After he'd finished the blessing, Mrs. Davis rose from her knees and looked in the back of the small chapel. She saw us the slaves all kneeling. We rose just as soon as she glanced in our direction. She turned and quickly went to us. She said, "How long have you been here?"

"We just got here," Billy responded.

Ivan stood, listening and hoping for a break to inform us that Mr. Davis wanted to see us.

Fr. Joseph, dressed in violet, came and stood next to Mrs. Davis. He asked, "Who do we have here?"

"These are our guests, Father. They will be staying with us for a while."

Ivan grunted to break any more conversation between the two and said, "Mr. Davis would like to see our guests immediately." Everyone looked at Ivan as he stood in his usual dignified manner. He immediately turned and said, "Follow me." The slaves left the small chapel and followed Ivan. Mrs. Davis stayed in the small chapel and explained, talking to Fr. Joseph about her guests and why it was important to keep our visit confidential.

Upon arriving to the library, we found the door wide open and Mr. Davis sitting behind his desk, smoking a cigar. He stared at everyone as we entered the library. His stare was strong and forceful, dispelling any thought of folly. We all respectfully stood in front of his desk like soldiers.

Ivan turned to leave, and Mr. Davis called him and asked him to join the group. He looked each one in the eye and said, "I've been visited by a captain Burris. He told me some disturbing things. He's looking for you, Mary Lou, and the others. He's made you all out to be murderers. He doesn't know you are here. Your being here must be kept completely secret. Ivan, do you understand? Our guests have been here for years. In fact, if asked, tell anyone they are house slaves."

"Yes, sir," Ivan respectfully answered.

"Also, refer to Mary Lou as Babe from now on. No disrespect, little lady. But I don't think anyone knows your childhood nickname except a very special few, and Captain Burris isn't one of them."

We all stood there shocked. Frustration filled the air, and words seemed miles away. Everyone's mind raced back and forth, remembering what happened to Billy, remembering our long run in the rain, remembering our long stay in the basement of the bails. Bo slowly fidgeted back and forth and asked, "Mr. Davis, are we gonna be safe? I don't want nothing to happen to Mary Lou—oop, I mean Babe."

"Bo, you have a right to be concerned. I don't know what I'd do if my wife had just given birth and some shady character is wanting the worst for my wife. But I can assure you this—you're safer here than you are on the run. If I was you, I'd be patient. I'd wait here where I know it's safe."

Bo looked at each one standing there. We all glanced at him. He looked into my eyes. I gently smiled. My smile always warmed his heart. And this was no different. He felt secure. He looked into Mr. Davis's eyes and said, "If it's OK with you, we'd like to stay here."

"That's a good decision, Bo. I take it you are speaking for everyone." Bo glanced into the other's eyes. We looked back into his like sheep looking for a shepherd.

I replied, "He speaks for all of us, sir."

"Well, it's settled, then. Everyone will, from this day forth, refer to you as Babe, and everyone is staying."

Ivan interjected, "Is there anything else you need, sir?"

"Yes, Ivan. Please inform your wife and daughter that there is to be absolutely no discussion of our guests with anyone."

Ivan paused and respectfully glanced into Mr. Davis's eyes. He knew Mr. Davis, and he knew this was matter of grave importance both for the slaves and for his wife and daughter. Ivan replied, "I will inform them immediately."

"Thank you, Ivan." Ivan left to inform his wife and child.

Captain Burris rode hard and fast. He headed toward slave row. Something in him didn't feel right. He didn't believe Mr. Davis. He'd known plantation owners, and most of them hated niggers just as much as he did. But he didn't get the same feeling from them as he did Mr. Davis. That worried him. The sun was shining brightly, and planting season was just around the corner. Captain Burris thought, *This time next year, the fields will be full of niggers.*

As he rode on, he passed two women. He rode a few yards in front of them and then abruptly yanked on the reins and came to a quick stop. The women were carrying baskets of food on their heads. He forcefully yanked the reins and rode around the women, looking down on them. They stopped and maneuvered out of the way of the horse jerking back and forth. Looking down on the two slave women, he said in a heavy Southern accent, "You niggers seen or heard of any runaway slaves? You two wouldn't be lying to me now."

"No, sir. We ain't got no reason to lie. We ain't never seen a runaway before."

"Anybody been real sick and then all of a sudden getting well?" He jerked on the reins, and the horse screamed and came to a violent stop.

"Yes, sir. Folks was real sick the other day. Then a woman visited them and prayed for them, and they were healed."

"Well, you don't say."

"That's God's honest truth. My friend Kora told me she was there and she seen it."

"Well, little lady, what's your name?"

Smiling, looking into Captain Burris's eyes, she sheepishly replied, "My name is Missy."

"Missy. That's a pretty name. So where can I find this Kora?" His tone was hard and strong. Care had completely left his voice. His voice was cold and forceful.

Fear ran down Missy's spine, and goose bumps covered her entire body. She thought, *What have I done? He don't mean no good to nobody.*

"Where can I find this Kora? I'm not goin' to ask you again. I'll shoot your friend straight between the eyes if you don't tell me right now."

"She lives on slave row. She takes care of the sick folk. Her shack has the withered tree in front."

He yanked the reins. The horse stood on its hind legs and screamed. He yelled, "Giddyap!" He headed straight to Kora's. Excitement filled his heart and mind. Hatred rushed through his veins like life-giving blood. His heart raced. Sweat burst from his forehead in anticipation of finding me.

The snow had melted, and the ground was muddy. Mud flew from the horse's hooves as he raced off. Upon arriving at slaves row, he slowed and slowly entered. He looked hesitantly around. His military mind raced. He looked for exit routes. He looked for hiding places. He looked for any sign of danger.

Slowly and cautiously, he rode up to Kora's. Kora's house looked deserted. He dismounted his horse and tied it to an old dead tree. He cautiously walked to her door. Before he could knock, Kora opened the door. She stood fearful and worried, peering into his eyes, hoping to find some hope or compassion. There was none. He gentlemanly took off his hat and bowed his head and politely said, "I'm Captain Burris. I was told that you knew where a nigger was who called herself Mary Lou. She is a runaway and greatly wanted."

"I ain't never heard of no Mary Lou."

"Can I please come in?"

"Come on in. She ain't here."

He walked and stood just in the doorway. He looked around and saw all the recovering sick. His heart became hard. He hated what he saw. Anger rushed upon him like a great wind. He slowly and quietly walked in between the recovering sick, looking at the dried blood on their heads and clothing. He walked from room to room in silence. The slaves looked into his eyes, trying to ignore him, but fear filled them. Many moved out of his way as he walked. Some simply turned their backs to him. Silence filled the shack. They knew he was up to no good. His presence told the story. He hated them. He hated their skin color. He hated them because they were different. He hated them because he didn't know them. He hated them because they were slaves. Everything about them he hated.

After he'd walked around, he stood at the door and said, "I don't see how you can stand the smell."

She looked intently into his eyes and said, "I've smelled worse."

"I know you know something about Mary Lou. These niggers were sick. I see they're well. You know, this Mary Lou I'm looking for is supposed to have some magical powers to heal folks."

"Sir, I don't know what you're talking about. I been here taking care of these sick people. I haven't left. And ain't none of them left."

"I'm going to take my leave, Ms. Kora. I know you're a liar. Every nigger is a liar. When I return, you gonna pray that you die quickly."

Fear filled her heart and mind. She was lost for words. She wanted to cry, but pride wouldn't let her.

He left the shack and walked directly to his horse. He smacked the reins from the tree and forcefully mounted his horse. He rode hard and fast to his camp. He thought, *I'm gonna get my men and tear this place up. She's here. I know it. She's one dead nigger.*

After a long, exhausting ride, he entered his camp. Men were cooking and cleaning their rifles. The camp smelled of musk and filth. The smell filled his nostrils. He was used to it. It pleased him. He thought of the treachery of his men and what they would do upon command. His face stayed frozen, expressionless and distorted. He slowly rode to his base command. He stopped, and one of his men ran to his horse and grabbed the horse's reins. He looked at the man with the same expression that he'd greeted Kora with. The soldier had known the expression well. He welcomed it. He knew the captain was well and focused. He dismounted and quickly entered his command tent. He looked around the tent, peering into each man's eyes. He slowly took off his hat and said, "The nigger is near."

The men were drinking whiskey, smoking and gambling. McDuff took a long pull on his cigar and blew smoke in Captain Burris's direction. He said, "Let's ride, Captain. Hell, I ain't winning no way. This game is over. Let's kill us some niggers."

Patrick yelled, "There's no way I'm quitting! I'm winning. It's the first time I won. Come on, guys, just one more hand. Come on."

McDuff threw his hand in and stood up. He said, "Let's ride. Captain done found a lead. Come on now. Let's ride." The others threw their hands in and stood.

Patrick yelled, "No way! I'm not leaving." The others walked past him and followed Captain Burris, who had turned and exited the tent.

The soldier was still standing there, holding his horse. Captain Burris snatched the reins from him without looking at him and quickly mounted his horse. He leaped upon his stead and gallantly rode through camp. McDuff and the others leaped upon their horses and followed. As they rode through camp, the other men stopped what they were doing and stood.

McDuff shouted, "Half of you men, mount and ride!" The younger men immediately dropped what they were doing and frantically mounted their horses and followed. They grabbed their rifles and handguns, food, and other provisions that were quickly accessible. A dark cloud hovered over the camp. Evil was present. The captain wanted blood, and his men shared his ambitions.

They rode out side by side. Pride and arrogance filled their hearts and souls. This was an unholy army on a mission straight from hell. The air was thick and cold. Steam blew from the horses' noses in a steady and angry pace. Every face was pale and emotionless. Only the sound of the horses' breathing and hooves could be heard. They headed directly to Mr. Davis's plantation.

At the Davises' plantation, Mr. Davis sat at his desk reading Psalms 91. He read it over and over again. He thought, *Security under God's protection.* He couldn't stop reading it again and again. He felt compelled. He loves Psalms 91. As he read, he felt a great surge of peace and strength. It filled his heart and mind. Each word sank into his inner being. His body became warm. Large drops of sweat appeared on his forehead. He read out loud, "You who dwell in the shelter of the Most High, who abide in the shadow of the Almighty, say to the Lord, 'My refuge and fortress, my god in whom I trust.'"

He leaned back into his chair and closed his eyes. He drew a large breath of life's juices. He thought, *God is on our side, and no weapon formed against us shall prosper, and every tongue that speaks evil against us shall be condemned. This is the heritage of the servants of the Lord and our righteousness from him, says the Lord.* "We are safe." He picked up a cigar, lit it, and called, "Ivan, come here."

Minutes later, Ivan entered the library with the grace and dignity of king. He stood before Mr. Davis in complete silence. Mr. Davis slowly walked from behind his desk and stood directly beside Ivan. Ivan's gaze was fixed. He didn't flinch. He pulled a long draw on his cigar and blew the smoke across the room. With one long puff, the room seemed to fill with smoke.

"This smoke reminds me of when the praises began in Solomon's temple that he'd built for the Lord. Cloud entered the temple, and the glory of the Lord filled the temple. The priests could no longer minister because the glory of the Lord had filled the temple. You know, Ivan, I understand it's distorted, but cigar smoke reminds me of God's glory in Solomon's temple. I'm just funny that way. Ivan, did you or anyone of your family tell Captain Burris of our guests?" Mr. Davis stood motionless, staring directly at Ivan.

Ivan, without blinking an eye, replied with great confidence and assurance, "Sure, I am dedicated, first, to Jesus Christ and then to you. Me and my entire house serve the Lord of heaven and earth. Your guests are here to give glory to God. My family and I haven't betrayed you, nor will we ever. Please pardon my rudeness, but why question my family's and my loyalty?"

"Please forgive me, Ivan. I should have known better. It's just that I feel that we are in grave trouble."

"Then, sir, maybe our guests would feel better if we hid them."

"Yes, I think you are right. But where?"

"They could return to their previous place."

"No, I believe we have to take special means."

"Special means, sir?"

"Yes. Our enemy is on the rampage. I can feel it in my bones." Ivan turned and faced Mr. Davis. The two men stood face-to-face, inches apart. Mr. Davis whispered, "I want you to quickly get a horse and ride as fast as you can to Buddy Smith's ranch. Tell him to prepare for our friends. He'll know what you're talking about."

Ivan quickly left the room and headed directly to the barn. He harnessed Black Beauty. It's the fastest horse in the county. He rode fast and hard. Buddy Smith's ranch was just through the meadow and past the creek. He saw Buddy's place in the distance. It looked like a tiny speck in the distance, but Buddy owned over fifty thousand acres. Through the meadow and the creek was the nearest and closest possible link between the two plantations. As Ivan rode, one of the hired hands noticed him.

Buddy owned and raised cattle. He raised the largest Herefords in the south. He sold Herefords for beef all throughout the friends. They were slave owners. Buddy and Mr. Davis were good. States and everyone respected him. Buddy was a Catholic. They were best men at their respective weddings. And they both were intricate parts of the underground railroad, and they both owned slaves. Secrecy was their biggest weapon against slavery. No one knew of their friendship except their closest friends. They'd planned from the beginning that if one of them would get suspected of hiding slaves or found out, the other would hide the slaves. The time had finally come.

Ivan rode directly to the big house. He stopped in front of the main mansion's entrance. He dismounted and eloquently walked to the double doors. There were huge brass knockers in the shape of cherubs. He grabbed one and raised it. He released it, and the thud echoed throughout the mansion.

A few moments later, a very beautiful African slave answered the door. She spoke in a heavy African accent, saying, "May I help you?"

"Yes, I'm here to speak to Buddy."

"May I ask who's calling?"

"Please tell him Ivan."

"Thank you. Please wait here." She closed the door, and Ivan stood outside waiting Waiting impatiently he stood erect.

A few minutes later, a large man with whitish-gray hair opened the door. He looked extremely brutal. His stare was cold. He looked through Ivan as if he wasn't there. He spoke in a hard, coarse tone. "I am Buddy. You are?"

"I am Mr. Davis's butler."

"I heard he had gotten real fancy and all hiring foreigners to cook and clean his house."

Ivan stood patiently and fixed his gaze directly upon his eyes and said, "Mr. Davis needs your help."

"What kind of help does he need?"

"It's concerning your friends."

"I don't have any friends. You need to be more specific."

"Captain Burris approached Mr. Davis concerning slavery."

"What's that got to do with me? We're both slave owners."

"Captain Burris is hunting a runaway slaves by the name of Mary Lou, and Mr. Davis believes Captain Burris will return with additional men and search for runaways on his plantation."

"Why didn't you say so? Don't you ever beat around the bush when talking to me. It's a big waste of time. Be direct. You understand me, boy?"

"Yes, sir."

Buddy quickly turned and yelled at the top of his lungs, "Felix! Felix, get down here right now." He turned and faced Ivan and said, "Now, what are you waiting for?" Ivan stood staring like a deer in shock. "You get back to Davises' place as quickly as possible. Tell him I'm right behind you."

"Yes, sir." Ivan quickly mounted Black Beauty and dashed off.

Seconds later, a short African slave rushed to the door holding two rifles. "Get the horses and those special wagons I had built. We need to leave here in five minutes."

Felix rushed off without saying a word. He ran to the stables. He entered the stables and yelled, "Get them special wagons harnessed and ready to go. Right now!"

Everyone working in the stables dropped what they were doing and with the precision of well-trained soldiers had the wagons ready. Felix climbed onto a horse and grabbed Buddy's prize mare Precious by the reins and slowly trotted out the stables.

Buddy stood waiting on the mansion's porch. Following Felix, there were four wagons driven by slaves. Buddy screamed, "That's damn good time!" He lit a large cigar and then walked to the center of the walkway toward the stables. He snatched the reins out of Felix's hands and mounted his horse. Within seconds, he was in a full gallop directly behind Ivan. Felix and the wagons followed as best they could. Ivan headed back the exact way he'd come. It was the quickest. Buddy followed. Soon, they were in sight of the Davises' plantation. Buddy thought, *That's damn good. Doesn't look like any army troops around.*

As they rode up to the house, Ivan leaped off his horse and ran to the main door. The door was wide open. He never saw the mansion's door open before unless he opened it. His heart raced. He frantically looked down the empty halls of the mansion. A second later, Buddy slowly walked into the huge forum and stood next to Ivan. They both kept deafly silent. Nothing could be heard. They peered into the deepest recesses of the mansion. The place was completely silent. A cool breeze crept through the house. Both men walked in different directions searching for the Davis family or anyone. But no one could be found.

Buddy yelled, "Davis, are you here!" His voice echoed throughout the mansion. Still, nothing.

Ivan ran quickly to Buddy, gasping for breath. "I think I know where they are."

"Let's go, boy. Ain't got no time to be wasting."

Ivan led Buddy to the large room that contained the secret entrance to hiding place for the slaves. He slowly crept toward the hidden panel. Slowly leaning his head against the panel, he listened for any sound or movement. Buddy stood back and stared. Ivan whispered, "Is anyone down there?" Still, no sound. He turned and stared at Buddy. Again, he leaned his head against the hidden panel and whispered, "I brought Mr. Buddy. The house is completely empty. No one is here. We brought wagons to transport the slaves." He stepped back and stood as erect as possible and gently knocked on the hidden panel.

Moments later, Mr. Davis slowly opened the hidden panel and peered out. Buddy stared and blurted out, "Come on out, Davis. Ain't no goddamn army troops around here."

Mr. Davis walked out as eloquently as one can who is just coming out of hiding. Mrs. Davis followed, and behind her the slaves slowly emerged. The slaves stood wide eyed and fearful. Mr. Davis walked directly to Buddy and shook his hand in a firm and confident manner.

Buddy stared into Mr. Davis's eyes and slowly asked, "What are we to do now?"

"We need to talk. Come follow me." He turned and headed directly toward the library.

"Excuse me, sir," Ivan gently replied.

"Return our guests to their rooms." He paused. "Thank you, Ivan."

Mr. Davis entered the library and sat behind his desk. Buddy stood and opened the cigar box on the desk. He took out the biggest and best of the cigars. "I always liked these damn things."

"They're from Cuba."

"Cuba. Hell, man, no wonder I never found none in town. So what's the plan?"

"I want to get the slaves up north as soon as possible. They're not safe here. You brought wagons?"

"Yeah, I brought wagons. I thought we'd be moving them to my place."

"No. We can use those wagons to transport them north."

"Those wagons weren't built for long-distance hauling."

"It doesn't make any difference. We're in a tight situation."

"I suppose we could take them up north."

"I can't go, Buddy. If Captain Burris ever saw me taking anything north, he'd surely stop me and search every wagon."

"You've got a point."

"Buddy, I'm asking you to take them north."

"Damn. I knew something like this was going to happen. OK, I'll do it. But I'm not hiding them in the wagons. We're going to put them in the wagons and ride by day and sleep by night. No one would ever suspect me of running niggers. Not even this Captain Burris. Hell, I'm one of the biggest slave owners around, even if it is just a front for the underground railroad."

"When can you go?"

"There's no place like the present. We'll leave today. I'll have a couple of boys ride back to my place and fill up on extra supplies."

"There's no need for that. I've got all the supplies you need and guns and extra wagons." Mr. Davis eased back into his chair. He stared intently into his friend's eyes and slowly extended his right hand. Davis stood and shook Buddy's hand with a firm grip.

Buddy knew that this mission had to be successful. He'd never personally taken slaves north. They both knew that if this was successful, many more could be taken to freedom the same way. Buddy slowly pulled the plush leather chair away from the desk and sat down. Davis hesitantly sat.

Buddy slowly replied, "We need the best goddamn plan known to man."

"You're right."

"We just can't load a wagon full of niggers and take them north."

"Why not?"

"We don't have any papers for them or anything."

"So what! All we have to do is get the ownership papers for the niggers you already own and use those papers for Mary Lou and the others. No one is ever going to question you."

"You're right. I'll ride home and get them. They're in my safe."

"I'll be getting the supplies and all you need while you're gone, and I'll explain to Mary Lou and the slaves that they are leaving."

"Good. I'll see you in a few hours." Buddy quickly got up and hurried out of the library to his horse.

Mr. Davis sat frozen in his seat. His mind raced. He slowly lowered his face onto his desk and whispered, "Lord, not our will be done but yours." Sweat immediately ran down his forehead. He leaned to the right and took a hanker out of his pocket and wiped his face. He slowly stood and headed directly to the guest rooms where the slaves were staying. He yelled, "Ivan, get the slaves. I need to talk to them."

Ivan quick walked in front of Mr. Davis and quickly knocked on each door, while Mr. Davis stood in the hall. Slowly, I and the others emerged from our quarters. He slowly began to explain. His hands trembled. He looked directly into each person's eyes. We looked intently into his eyes. I stood holding little Zeke. Zeke lay resting his head upon my breasts, fidgeting back and forth, hoping to find a nipple. I rocked him slowly in my arms, occasionally looking at him. I thought, *Zeke deserve to be free. We have a chance, and I'm gonna take it.* Bo stood patiently waiting for an opportunity to speak. Mr. Davis looked around the room, waiting for a response.

Finally, Bo said, "We didn't come this far to turn back. We ready as soon as you are."

"Well, then, it's settled. You all pack lightly. You will be leaving soon. If I don't ever see any of you again, remember I love each and every one of you. And you all will be free. Nothing in this world can stop the plans that God has for your lives. God didn't bring you out this far to bring you back again."

"That's right. He brought us out to bring us into the Promised Land, and he ain't never fooled. That's right. We serve a mighty God," replied Creasy.

Mr. Davis turned and left the hall. Ivan followed. They stopped in the adjacent room, and Mr. Davis explained, "Ivan, I want you to get them ready to leave. Buddy will return soon. Everything must be in order and kept completely secret."

"Yes, sir. I understand." Mr. Davis walked quickly into the forum and headed upstairs.

Ivan returned to the guest quarters. He knocked on each door, saying, "Bring only clothing, nothing else, and go into the forum right now."

We hurried and scurried around in our quarters, packing only warm clothes. One by one, we dragged our clothing into the main forum. Ivan waited. He seemed completely confident that everything was going to be just fine. Bo stood next to me, gently embracing me and little Zeke. The others stood staring at one another, looking for any sign of confidence. Barak, Jophkiel, and Raphael stood completely still. An aura of confidence surrounded them. Soon, everyone's eyes slowly rested upon them. Creasy slowly grasped Ben's left hand. She turned and glanced at him. He stared at the three as though he was hypnotized. She slowly returned her glance upon them.

Billy's eyes went frantically around the room. He became fidgety and finally said, "I'm ready to go. I knew all along we been here too long. I ain't never trusted staying in one spot. We gon' be just fine as soon as we get moving." No sooner had he finished talking than they heard the sound of horses and wagons pulling up to the front of the mansion.

Ivan opened the door and replied, "Mr. Buddy Smith has returned. You are to go with him. He will take you to safety."

Buddy sat wearing a heavy buffalo-skinned coat. He looked strong, proud, and confident. He barked, "Come on out of there. We headed north."

Slowly and cumbersome, Bo and I walked out and headed for the back of the wagon. Felix tied the reins unto the wagon and climbed over the wagon's seat and went to the back of the wagon. The wagon bed was full of hay and heavy wool blankets with food and water tied to the outer sides of the wagons. Felix extended his hand and helped Bo onto the wagon. Felix and Bo both grabbed on to my arms and lifted me and little Zeke onto the wagon. I carefully sat on a bale of hay and wrapped myself and Zeke in a wool blanket. Bo sat next to me and wrapped up as well. Barak quickly jumped into the wagon carrying me and, without saying a word, looked into both Bo's and my eyes and slowly sat next to Bo.

Raphael cautiously asked, "Is there room enough for me?"

"Sure, there's plenty of room. Come on up," Bo quickly replied. Creasy and Ben climbed onto the wagon behind theirs, and Jophkiel joined them.

No sooner had they sat down than Buddy screamed, "Come on, let's go! Get this wagon on down the road."

Felix grabbed both reins and yelled, "Come on! It's time to get going. We on our way north." The wagon jerked forward, and a cold wind blew upon the faces of all. In all, there was a total of four wagons, two carrying the slaves and two carrying provisions for the journey.

It was a beautiful winter's day. The sky was clear and sunny. They'd traveled two days, and they hadn't heard or seen any troop or bounty hunters. The wagons jerked and bounced back and forth in a rhythm that was so soothing that Little Zeke only woke up to eat.

Chapter Nineteen

The Road to Freedom

Bo kept an eye on Zeke and me and the other on the scenery. He'd fixed it upon his heart to watch every movement he could. He remembered the burning barn and the threats he'd heard against me, his wife. As he glanced around the wagon, he fixed his stare on Raphael and Barak. He looked into Raphael's eyes and politely said, "You two fellows helped us get out of that burning barn a while back." Bo was waiting for an answer.

Raphael looked in Barak's eyes and then mine. I smiled. Raphael slowly replied, "Yes, I was there. Jophkiel and Barak were there too. Didn't we explain already?"

"You didn't explain enough." Silence filled the air. Only the sound of the wagon and the horses' heavy breathing could be heard.

Barak replied in a compelling tone, "I will explain in detail. We are God's messengers. We were sent to help you. We stand in the presence of God and give him glory. Raphael has permission from Christ to heal. We have different gifts, which is why I'm explaining."

"Are you tell me that you, Joph, and Raph are angels?"

"I've told you from the beginning. You weren't able to understand. Now the veil has been removed from your eyes."

"Mary Lou, did you know?"

"I knew some things the Lord wants me to know and no one else. I'm sorry I didn't tell you, Bo. But I didn't think you'd have believed me anyhow."

"Woman, you should have said something."

"It wasn't your time yet."

"How long have you known?"

"I've known since the barn. They here to help us."

Bo lowered his head into his hands. Tears slowly ran down his cheeks. His mind raced back to all the instances they'd been helped. He tried to stop the tears. The more he tried, the faster they ran down his cheeks into his hands and down his arms. Finally, he said, "Good. My Mary Lou is going to be safe and free."

"God's plan will be carried out according to his will. All things work for good for those who love the Lord and who are called according to his purpose."

Bo raised his head and looked deeply into Barak's eyes. Barak's eyes, for an instant, revealed the glory of heaven. Bo's heart raced. He lost his breath and began to cough uncontrollably. He leaned over the side of the wagon and spit up huge portions of green spit. Doubt, despair, disbelief, worry, and hatred took on a physical form, and Bo spit them over the side of the wagon on the ground. Even though it was a cold winter's day, he sweated heavily. His hands shook. He began to get chills throughout his body.

Raphael crawled on his hands and knees over to the side of the wagon where Bo was seated. He placed one hand on his stomach and the other on the back of his neck. He leaned forward and whispered into Bo's ear, "Be healed in the name of Jesus. Let love fill your heart and mind. Replace doubt, despair, disbelief, worry, and hatred with love, for love conquers all things."

Bo slowly raised his head. He stared into Raphael's eyes. A warm sensation arose from the inside of being. It seemed to come from his stomach. The warmth filled him. He leaned forward and embraced Raphael. He cried. Raphael broke the embrace and peered into Bo's eyes. He held Bo at arm's length while peering into his eyes. In a loving and gentle voice, he said, "You are fine. Trust in Jesus. He loves you." Raphael crawled back to where he'd been sitting. Bo sat looking dazed. His heart burned with love.

He scurried over to me and Zeke. He placed his arms around us both and hugged us. I grabbed Bo's head and placed it over my heart.

Buddy turned and looked in the wagon bed and asked, "What's going on back there?"

"We just hugged up trying to keep warm," I replied.

"We're going to be making a rest stop soon. I know all this riding can take its toll on a person. Felix, when you get to that clearing over yonder, pull over. We're going to rest for a while and get warm."

Miles away on the Davises' plantation, Captain Burris and his men, with rifles drawn, were headed toward the big house. Mr. Davis sat at his desk in the library reading his favorite psalms. He heard the thunder of the horses coming. He thought, *Captain Burris must have unfinished business.* He closed his Bible and slowly walked to the parlor.

Mrs. Davis sat quietly knitting a sweater for little Zeke. She spoke in a very fragile and petite voice, saying, "It doesn't look like I'm going to give little Zeke this sweater. I wanted to surprise Mary Lou."

"We've done our job. We've lived long and fruitful lives." Mr. Davis slowly sat on the sofa next to his wife. She kept on knitting and politely smiled. He reached over and held her right hand. She stopped knitting and lovingly looked into his eyes.

The thunder of the horses became louder and louder. Mr. Davis called in a loud voice, "Ivan, please come here." Ivan immediately entered the room. "Ivan, I want you and your family to leave as soon as possible. We are going to have some unfriendly visitors soon."

Mr. Davis stood and walked over to the fireplace in the parlor. He reached up and took the oil painting down of his great-grandfather. Behind the painting, there was a hidden safe. He quickly opened the safe and handed Ivan a stack of papers and a large amount of cash including some precious family heirlooms. Ivan's wife and daughter stood at the parlor's entrance, cautiously waiting and hoping.

Mr. Davis handed the items to Ivan and said, "These are yours. You've served me faithfully. You'll know what to do with these." Ivan stood frozen, peering into his eyes. He'd never seen him so peaceful and calm. Mr. Davis pulled Ivan to him and hugged him. He whispered into his ear, "Leave as quickly as you can, and don't ever return. Go north." Ivan gasped to respond. Mr. Davis quickly replied, "Go quickly."

Without saying good-bye, Ivan turned and quickly left the room. His wife and daughter followed. Unknown to Mr. Davis, Ivan had packed a wagon with all his family's belongings and stationed it in the rear of the plantation out of anyone's sight. He and his wife and daughter went to the wagon as quickly as possible and left.

No sooner had he left than Captain Burris and his troops were riding down the soldiers course leading directly to the main entrance to the big house. Mr. Davis glanced out of the library's window, hoping that Captain Burris would pass. Mrs. Davis stood resting her head on Mr. Davis's shoulder. They embraced and waited. Captain Burris frantically dismounted and rushed into the mansion. His men followed with rifles drawn. The men ran throughout the mansion looking for hiding slaves.

Captain Burris went into the library with the subtleness of a snake. He stood glaring into Mr. Davis's eyes searching for any sign of fear. He found none. His eyes were blood red. He looked as though he were possessed by a demon. He cautiously milked behind the desk and sat down. He opened the cigar box on the desk and lit a cigar. After a long pull, he screamed, "You goddamn, nigger-lovin' son of a bitch! I almost fell for your bullshit. I'm going to find them niggers and kill every one of them."

No sooner had he finished speaking than a skinny redhead man entered the library. A heavy odor of musk filled the room. Mrs. Davis buried her face into her husband's chest to avoid the smell. He spoke with an Irish accent. "Captain, this entire house is empty. We looked from top to bottom."

"Search for hiding places and hidden room. Use the butt end of your rifles and hit the walls. I want you to find me something. You hear me, boy?"

"Yes, sir, Captain."

"Shawn, tell all the men to do the same."

"Yes, sir." He ran out of the library and screamed, "Tear this god-damn place apart! The captain knows something."

Invisible to everyone, the demons were stationed throughout the mansion inside and out. They darted to and fro in an uncontrolled frenzy, attaching themselves to the soldiers at will. Pakaaret stood next to Captain Burris, whispering to his conscience, "They're lying. They are nothing but some niggers. They don't deserve to live. They've lied from the beginning."

Captain Burris slowly walked from behind the desk. As he walked, Pakaaret lunged forward and pierced his heart and soul with his talons. Captain Burris yelled, "You hid niggers! I know you did. You hid that damn nigger Mary Lou."

Mr. Davis slowly stepped back. He pulled his wife's arm, and they both walked backward, unaware of Captain Burris's intent. Captain Burris slowly pulled his gun and pointed it at Mr. Davis's head. Mrs. Davis screamed, "No, he was against it! It was me. I talked him into it. I always believed the colored were the same as white."

"You both are no-good nigger lovers. The nigger is an animal." His face became pale. He choked on the cigar. Pakaaret had full control of him. He angrily grabbed a flask of brandy. Without hesitation, he forced it to his mouth and poured it down his throat. His eyes had become blood red. He looked at the Davises and screamed, "Spirits! I should kill you both right now. But I can make an example of you to my men. Let me think. What can I do with the two niggers sons of bitches?" He pointed his gun and fired. Within minutes, the entire room was filled with his soldiers. Shawn stood gaping and motionless. Captain Burris calmly shouted, "What shall we do with two nigger lovers?"

One of the soldiers replied, "We hang horse thieves where I'm from."

A loud roar came from the soldiers. "Yeah, yes, hang the nigger lovers!"

"Get me a rope," whispered Captain Burris.

A skinny, pale boy no older than fourteen ran outside to his horse and got a rope. He was trying to make a name for himself and win approval from the soldiers. He'd been treated badly since he joined. He believed if he could please them, they'd like him. He ran up to Captain Burris and respectfully said, "Here you are, sir."

Unknown to all, the demons began running to and fro, jumping and, making a hideous shrieking noise, which fueled the soldiers' longing for blood. The soldiers shouted again and again, "Hang them, Captain!" Soon, the shouting sounded like a chant.

The Davises stood fearless. They watched the soldiers in amazement. They'd never seen anything so disgusting. Shawn grabbed Mr. Davis's arm and jerked him away from his wife. He forcefully pulled him through the library and out of the mansion. The soldiers followed, screaming, "Hang 'em! Hang 'em!" Another soldier pulled Mr. Davis by the arm, following the men. They walked to the huge oak tree to the left of the mansion. Captain Burris followed the crowd with an evil grin on his face, approving every action.

Once under the oak tree, Captain Burris flung the rope over the strongest branch extending from the tree. He tied a noose and put it around Mr. Davis's neck. Everyone stood in a complete circle around the tree, watching and longing for death. Mr. Davis struggled and threw a few punches, striking Shawn in the nose and jaw. Only to be restrained by more men. He cried, "We die for freedom! We die a Christian death. You can't stop what's happening. God's victorious. Our God never lost a battle. You won't accomplish anything by killing me."

No sooner had he finished speaking than Shawn raised his rife and struck him in the face with the barrel. Blood poured down his face. His

249

entire face became immersed in blood. Mrs. Davis cried, "Stop it, you dev-ils. Stop it!"

Within a split second, Shawn had landed another blow to his head. Mr. Davis fell to his knees. The noose was still around his head. As he lay bent over, near unconsciousness, a number of soldiers grabbed the rope and yanked as hard as they could, forcing him to his feet and raising him off the ground. His feet dangled as he kicked in a vain attempt to kick one of the soldiers. His body jerked in uncontrollable convulsions.

Mrs. Davis buried her face in her hands and cried. She'd imagined her husband dying in a bed at a ripe old age. Never had she imagined such a terrible and cruel death. Her womanly heart broke as though it was pierced by a sword.

Shawn screamed, "You're next!" A loud scream came from her that shot chills through many of their evil hearts. Captain Burris flung another rope around the same branch and put the noose around her neck. With one violent pull of the rope, Mrs. Davis hung between heaven and earth. She jerked and convulsed for moments. Then it was over.

Shawn jumped back and yelled, "Oh, shit. Did you see that, Captain?" Body fluids of feces and urine ran down the legs of both onto the ground, making small mounds upon the ground. Many of the soldiers slowly walked away. Shawn laughed and joked, "I wonder which one of them is full of shit?"

'"Maybe they didn't hide the niggers."

"Well, if they didn't, they should have. They paid the price," one of the soldiers replied.

As soon as the soldier had finished speaking, Captain Burris released a backhand that struck the man in the mouth. Blood immediately gushed forth from his mouth. "Any sympathy for the nigger will be dealt with without hesitation. For chasing no goddamn niggers around this goddamn country to be friends with. I want that goddamn nigger dead. Do you sons of bitches hear me? Our only job is to kill us some monkey niggers. Do you hear me!" He turned and faced the soldiers and drew his revolver from the holster, pointing it at the head of each man.

"Now, you cocksuckers, is there any more sympathy for these nigger lovers?" Through the cold of the winter, sweat beaded upon many foreheads standing before the captain. There was no question—the captain was insane. Pointing his revolver and shouting treats, he yelled, "If any of you have suddenly developed some kind of sympathy for those who help niggers to freedom or the nigger, please step forward." The men stood froze. Their eyes were wide as silver dollars. They looked like deer staring at a bright light, unable to move. He finally lowered his revolver and walked through the crowd, pushing and shoving them aside. Once he reached the edge of the crowd, he fired his revolver and screamed, "Mount your horses! We're riding out."

At the campsite, Bo and Billy built a large fire. The horses were unhitched to trees. Creasy had unpacked her large stew pot and was preparing a pot with dried neck bones. I had quietly wandered off. I held close my bosoms. I had felt a burning desire to pray. I fell to my knees and prayed, "Dear Lord, you can do all things. I pray that your all knowing us as we continue our journey. Lord, it's not our will we want to do. It's your will we want to do. Bless us, Lord, and keep us safe. Thank you, Lord, for what you done." Tears slowly filled my dark-brown eyes. A single tear slowly flowed down my cheek.

Bo screamed, "Woman, what you doing out here?"

"I needed a bit of quiet time."

"It's too dangerous. You know what that man is after, and he ain't up to no good."

"I think something bad done happened to Mr. and Mrs. Davis. I think that man has said something to them."

"Well, we can't know what we don't know about. We'll focus on getting somewhere safe."

He threw himself into the air with full force and dug his talons into Captain Burris. The talons pierced the back of his head and spinal cord. He slowly drifted into unconsciousness.

Shawn yelled, "You all right, Captain?"

Captain Burris jerked quickly around and stared at Shawn. "I'm fine."

"You didn't seem yourself, Captain. I thought you were sleeping on your horse."

"Are you trying to insult me, boy?"

"No, Captain."

The whites of Captain Burris's eyes were dark red. Pakaaret's hunger for evil settled into Captain Burris's soul. They were one. Pakaaret's thoughts became unknown to him. His hunger for human blood grew. He hated everyone. Shawn slowed his horse down, allowing Captain Burris to ride ahead. He didn't know the captain anymore. Humanity had left him. Captain Burris was something he'd never met, nor would he ever want to.

As they rode on, a dark cloud appeared over them. The sun was setting, and the demons took shelter in the cloud. As soon as dusk began, the demons heard themselves in a frenzy. They fought frantically above the men, pulling and tearing, devouring one another until they were nothing but vapor. As the men continued to ride, the cloud lowered. The men rode through the cloud, breathing and digesting the demonic vapor. Their horse stopped and began to bolt and convulse. Many of the soldiers fell. The cloud slowly vanished. The soldiers had completely digested the vapor. Many of them began weeping and vomiting. The demons, even though they had taken another form, were still as deadly and evil even in vaporous form. They became one with the soldiers. Their outward appearance was making a transformation. Their hearts and souls were bleak, hardened, and black. The light had left them. Their eyes were black. The light of life had left.

Captain Burris screamed, "Get those damn beasts under control! We're camping a few miles down the road." As this demonic army went on, they passed a large white picket fence with a little girl to her home. A cattle ranch was stationed a quarter mile from the road. The sound of horses drew the child's mother from preparing dinner for the family.

Chapter Twenty

The Ranch House

The Fitspatricks, John, Sharon, and Little May, owned 250 head of cattle. John had met Sharon in Kansas City, Missouri. A few years back, John would occasionally visit Kansas City to purchase cattle. Sharon worked in the Old Time Saloon. This was more of a house of prostitution than anything else. She sold drinks and sexual favors unknown to John. She was one of the top girls. Yet she'd told John she never was a prostitute.

As Captain Burris rode by, he glanced at Little May running toward Sharon. Sharon' eyes caught his. He saw the sin in her heart. She hated the farm life and longed for the smell of whiskey and the passion of illicit sex. She and John were complete opposites. John loved the church, his family, and the cattle business. Sharon loathes it all, including Little May. Little May was only six years old and full of life. She had the smile of an angel. Sharon was jealous. She wondered how something so beautiful could come from her. She despised the child even more.

Captain Burris commanded, "Follow me.!" He rode directly to the cattle ranch.

Sharon eagerly looked as the horde of evil rode up. Little May stood clinging to her mother's apron, completely fear struck. Sharon replied, "Looks like we got us some Southern gentleman callers tonight." John was tending cattle in the north pasture alone. His hired hands had left for the day.

The soldiers, all sixty-six of them, stayed on their mount. Captain Burris patiently waited for Sharon to reach the ranch. Sharon was amazingly beautiful yet full of envy, hate, jealousy, and immorality. The riled as she strolled lit his way. She stopped and placed her left hand on her hip and sarcastically said, "You boys want something?"

"Yes, ma'am, we do," replied Captain Burris, slightly tilting his hat, the way Southern gentlemen do. He shouted, "Dismount, tie your horses, and pitch camp. We're staying here for tonight."

Sharon slowly strolled into the house, swaying from side to side, occasionally glancing back at Captain Burris. He dismounted his horse, handing the reins to Shawn, and followed her into the house. She yanked and jerked Little May by the arm, forcing her into the house. The ranch house was large and cozy with a huge fireplace. John was a hunter. He'd had deer heads mounted on the walls. His guns and rifles were neatly displayed in glass cabinets. Sharon loved to decorate. She'd placed pillows throughout the house, making it appear warm and homey. Cooking wasn't her strong suit. She hated it. Earlier, she'd cut potatoes, carrots, celery, and tomatoes, and placed them in a large kettle on the stove with chopped beef, her version of beef stew.

The captain immediately took a seat at the kitchen table, taking off his hat and placing it on the edge of the kitchen table. Sharon hurried around the kitchen, frantically thinking of ways to please the captain, forgetting her husband. He sat quietly, observing her every move. She asked, "Would you like a drink?"

He sternly replied, "Whiskey."

She smiled and hurried to the cabinet, grabbing the bottle she'd brought from Kansas City. She poured him a jarful and left the bottle on the table. He stared at her in disgust, watching her every move. Her mind raced not knowing what to expect. She loved the attention. His lustful eyes pierced her soul. She walked close to the kitchen table, attempting to provoke a reaction. He slowly and methodically pushed his hat off the table onto the floor directly in front of her. She stopped and glared into his eyes. She bent over, keeping constant eye contact, purposely revealing her cleavage. She picked up the hat and set it on the table. She walked by, brushing her bosom against the captain's shoulders. Their lustful desires grew.

Unknown to them, they were both under the influence of Desira, the demon of desire and lust. The captain quickly turned. He patted her on the butt without permission. She loved it. She loved being violated. She felt that only strong men knew how to treat a woman without saying a word. She turned her head, peering into his evil eyes, and smiled. The smell of whiskey, the pat of the butt—all brought back memories of Kansas City she missed so much.

Little May sat staring at the two of them, wondering who this man was and why her mother acted so strangely. She politely asked, "Mama, when's Daddy coming home?"

Sharon barked, "Don't you worry about him. I've got a gentleman caller." Sharon was drunk with lust. She swayed with each step, longing and hoping for the moment the captain could take her. She quickly went to Little May and snatched her by the arms, saying, "It's time for you to go to bed."

The captain finished the jar of whiskey with one deep gulp and poured another, never taking his eyes off of Sharon. She scurried from Little May's room and sat at the table across from the captain and poured her a drink.

"Where's your husband?"

"He's out tending cattle or something. He should be here soon." She watched his every movement, waiting, hoping. She didn't care if John came home or not. She leaned forward and took a huge gulp of whiskey. The captain reached out and grabbed her by her right wrist. He pulled her toward him. She smelled the heavy odor of musk and whiskey. Pressing her face toward his, she kissed him, teasing him, quickly jerking her lips away, tasting his bad breath, and pricking her soft skin against his whiskers. "A real man," she spitefully replied.

The captain unbuttoned her dress, exposing her firm breasts. She pulled away. He pulled her close to him, ripping her dress and exposing her undergarments. She pulled away and stood up. She slowly swayed back and forth as though listening to parlor music. None played. She smiled and swayed back and forth the way she used to in Kansas City to entice local drunks. Slowly, she undressed. She took her shoes off and threw them at the captain, toying and playing like a cat with a mouse. She pushed him back down onto the chair with her feet, smiling. She hadn't had this much fun since Kansas City. She considered John dry. She couldn't be herself around him. Now, finally, she could be Sharon.

The captain stood. He grabbed her by her right arm and swung her onto the table. Her face hit the hard wood. He raised up what remaining underwear she wore. Her breasts hung free. He quickly ripped open his trousers. They fell to his knees. He entered her, pushing her head onto the table with each thrust. She gritted her teeth and smiled. She raised her leg and lay her chest onto table until he finished.

Sweat poured down his face. A heavy aroma of sex filled the room. Sharon turned and gulped down her whiskey and wiped her mouth with her opposite hand. She looked at the captain with disregard. He noticed her disdain and quickly backhanded her. He knew she wasn't satisfied. He quickly dressed. She sat at the edge of the table, smiling. "You come back. I'll be waiting."

Her husband John finally and cautiously rode up. Upon seeing John, Captain Burris pulled his side revolver and shot him in the head as he attempted to dismount, killing him instantly. Sharon ran to the door. She saw John lying in gray brain matter and blood spread all over through the white snow. She placed both hands over her head and cried. She ran into the house and slammed the door behind her. She'd hated everything she'd done, herself mostly.

The captain barked orders, "Bury the body. This is part of war. Damn it."

Early the next morning, the men awoke to the smell of coffee. Sharon hadn't slept. She'd cried the night away, thinking of an excuse to tell the hired help. She'd brewed enough coffee for the entire regiment, hoping that no harm would come to Little May or her. They all lined and walked to the front door and filled their mugs with coffee. After they'd drank coffee and had breakfast, they rode north. Sharon stood in the doorway in her house-coat, completely broken and ashamed.

On leaving, Captain Burris tilted his hat, saying, "Thank you, ma'am, for your Southern hospitality."

Chapter Twenty-One

Michael

I the others were packed and ready for the long journey. Jophkiel, Raphael, and Barak had prepared breakfast of ham and eggs with coffee for everyone. The aroma had awoken the entire camp long before they'd finished cooking. After finishing his breakfast, Buddy yelled, "Let's move out! Make sure everything is tight and tucked." The wagons clicked and clacked down the old dirt road to freedom.

As the day drew on past noon, they saw a beautiful and odd-looking carriage on the side of the road. The carriage was drawn by two beautiful black horses and seemed to have smoke coming from a brass pipe protruding from the top rear. There were two distinguished-looking men standing on the side of the road with a young boy. The driver sat outside the carriage, screaming insult toward the horses. Their beautiful and odd-looking carriage was stuck. It started to lightly snow, and the ground was becoming extremely muddy.

As they rode up, Buddy slowed and asked, "Is there anything we can do to help?"

"Yes," replied the taller man. "We seem to be trapped by this confounded clay you call dirt."

"Good old Southern dirt. It will get you every time," Buddy barked. He tied the reins and jumped down from the wagon. "Come on, everybody. Let's push this here beast of carriage out of here."

The slaves all except Bo got behind the carriage and lifted, while the driver screamed, "Move it! Move it!" Within seconds, the carriage was free. "Thank you. I'm Michael. This is Elijah and his nephew Henry. We're on our way north. It looks like you are too."

"We are," Buddy replied cautiously.

"Are these your slaves? I don't want to offend you, but I'm against slavery. One day, this great nation of ours is going to be free to all men," Michael interjected.

Felix interrupted, "We're headed up north as well. Our business is personal."

"We're headed in the same direction," Elijah interjected. Michael and Elijah slowly walked toward the uncovered wagons, looking into them. They noticed me and Bo hugging, attempting to cover Zeke and keep him warm. "Oh, a baby. It's winter. Don't you know the further you travel north, the colder it gets?" Elijah burst forth.

"Yes. It's all we have. I have to make do, sir." I answered.

"I understand. It's fine. Buddy, can your slave girl share our coach? I have a wonderful invention. It's a heated coach. Come, come, let me show you."

The men quickly walked to the back of the coach. He pointed to a large brass tank. He opened the lid, and there were many red-hot coals in the base of it. On its sides were two brass pipes that ran from the upper portion into the cab. The lid had perforated holes to allow air in. The bottom of the brass container had a slot that allowed air to fuel the coal. He opened the cab doors and pointed to two large brass oval holes that were eloquently decorated and uncovered. There were brass covers hanging down from brass chains.

Elijah replied, "I invented this heated coach just for such an occasion. You see, I travel north every year. It's freezing cold. I grew tired of spending my days inside a freezing coach and my nights sitting outside in the cold. So a heated coach."

"That's a great idea. I've never even heard of such a thing," Felix replied.

"It's what I do."

Michael slowly strolled to the uncovered wagon. When Barak, Jophkiel, and Raphael saw Michael, they fell to the ground and bowed in front of Michael. Michael stood gleaming. His former appearance had changed in a twinkling of an eye. He was clothed like an ancient Hebrew warrior. Only his entire appearance glowed in unbelievable white. His hair was black. His eyes were blue as the sky. The belt around his waist was gold. He carried a sword seemingly made of crystal and diamonds. He radiated like a cool mist off a pond during the early rising of the sun. He spoke, saying, "The King of Kings is pleased with your work. You may continue." He drew his sword and gently touched the shoulder of each. They stood, bowed, and piled into the wagon.

Michael regained his human earthly form. He wore a black suit, black top hat, boots, spurs, was unshaven and strikingly handsome, with a white cotton shirt and a long black overcoat. He walked back to the wagon where I was sitting with little Zeke and Bo. He raised his hand, gesturing as the Southern gentlemen do, and asked, "Would you like to join us in our heated coach, lady?"

I blushed and looked confused but willing and replied, "Well, yes, for Zeke's sake, but my husband must come too."

"Yes, ma'am. We have plenty of room for your entire family."

"Thank you," I respectfully replied while attempting to climb off the wagon. No sooner had I stood than Bo and Michael helped me down.

Upon entering the coach, she sat holding Zeke, and Bo sat next to her. Michael, Elijah, and Henry sat staring next to her. Michael, Elijah, and Henry sat staring at the blessed family. Elijah replied, "This is the first of its kind."

"It's as warm as a summer's day," Bo cautiously interjected. He tossed and turned, looking for where the heat was coming from.

Elijah pointed to the left and right upper corners of the cab. "Here, here, my boy. Are you free?" Elijah asked.

"Yes, sir. We're headed north to freedom and to start a new life," Bo responded.

"There are plenty of opportunities for an ambitious young man like yourself. I don't believe in slavery. We're all created in God's image," Michael interjected in a respectfully calm manner. I stared at Michael, and for an instant, I saw his brilliance. My eyes watered. I lowered my head and prayed. Michael continued. "You're safe now. If you prefer, you can continue your journey with us. We would love to hear of your life struggles, and we have plenty of food and water."

"Thank you. We'd like that just fine," I replied and asked, "Michael, sir, did not God ordain slavery?"

"Yes, ma'am, he did, but not this. This is inhumane. Slavery, according to the Bible, was given in order that some may repay a debt, obligation, or disobedience of some kind. It was intended to enslave an entire race of people. But it was not intended that the owners should treat the slaves as animals but rather an extension of one's family. No, this is man's evil pride at its height. All men are created by God. Each man has his particular gifts to be used to glorify God."

"My god, Michael, you sound like a preacher," Elijah softly added. "Well, it's plain wrong. In Genesis, Noah cursed Ham's children, not the entire race, and the slaves here are Shemites, not Hamites. I don't believe God wanted one man to own another," Elijah continued.

"I think it's in the treatment and understanding of slavery, and the meaning of the word 'slave.' I think we are all slaves to one master or another. Don't you agree, Mary Lou?" Michael replied.

"Well, I believe that anything we present ourselves to be obedient to, we are slaves to that thing," I responded.

"Well spoken," Michael blurted. "So we can be slaves to wrongdoing or slaves to righteousness," Michael continued.

"It's God's choice to give mankind free will to choose, not mankind's choice to force men to do anything. That's how the Creator deals with humanity. He gives us freedom of choice," Elijah added.

"Yes, though some of us are created for his praise and glory only, and others, he gives a choice. So choose wisely," Michael replied.

"Are you saying that God has slaves, Michael?" Elijah asked.

"I'm saying that the Creator does what's good and just for man's benefit."

"So shall we continue to brutalize innocent people and force innocent people to live under the circumstance of slavery in America without any remedy of hope of freedom except from an owner?" Elijah replied forcefully, gesturing with his finger to Michael.

"I don't know. It's God's choice, They didn't keep the Law " Michael gently replied, looking away from Elijah out of the side window. Elijah did not know Michael was the Archangel Michael who looks upon the face of God. Michael, still looking out of the window, gazing at the beauty of the country, softly replied, "I think it's jealousy."

"Jealousy," Elijah quickly repeated.

"Yes. Jealousy. Look at Mary Lou and her family. Look at their skin color. They're beautiful. The sun has gave them a well-flavored tone, and whites can't achieve that. What else would you call it when one race of people is given technology and another race of people is given another gift? Yet the race who is given technology invents a weapon and forces the other race to do their work. It's jealousy. It's childish, simply put. Envy and jealousy has been a tool for evil and for generations. And because of it, generations upon generations will be enslaved in one form or another," Michael finished.

"That sounds insane. It's because the Negro is lacking in creativity," Elijah replied.

"We'll show them. They have gifts of spiritual worship, crafts, compassion that other races don't possess in the overall picture," Michael replied, still staring out the window, speaking, nonresponsive. "Stop the carriage!" Michael yelled. A farmer was crossing the road with a couple of hundred pigs. Michael jumped from the cab and immediately took up a conversation with the man. He scurried back into the coach, whispering, "It's deathly cold out there. I was inquiring about lodging for the night. That farmer has a ranch a few miles ahead. He'd just purchased those pigs from a friend, and he's willing to house us for the night."

"Sound wonderful," Elijah replied with a huge smile.

"What do you think?" Michael asked me and Bo.

"Good, real good. Just when I'm getting used to this heated buggy," Bo answered.

As they rode toward the ranch, an overweight woman with goldish-blond hair and dark-green eyes stood on the porch steps. She wore an apron and looked to be a housewife. She pulled a tiny scarf from her apron and waved it back and forth. She cried, "Hi, how are you? You must have seen my husband. Nobody ever finds our little road unless told." The carriage and wagons slowly stopped directly in front of her. She kept on talking, yet no one seemed to understand her.

Michael exited the coach and answered, "Yes, ma'am, we did see a gentleman down the road a ways back. He sent us to your beautiful home."

"That's my Frank. He's always bringing guests home so I can cook for them. I'm Betsy."

"I'm Michael. This is Elijah, Henry, Bo, Mary Lou, and Zeke. And those are our friends. We are looking for a place that we may spend the night. Looks like a winter storm is brewing."

"Sure, we have plenty of room. You can take your horses and Negroes into the barn. There's hay and water for the horses, and I'll make a stew for the Negroes."

"Well, thank you," Michael replied.

As they left the coach, Betsy screamed, "Oh, a baby! Can I see?"

"Yes, ma'am. His name is Zechariah. We call him Zeke for short. Zechariah is a mouthful."

"Oh, look at those little hands. He's so sweet. I love babies. Frank and I haven't been able to have children. Come into the house. It's warm."

"I could do that. I would be leaving my husband."

"Well, I suppose. Bring him too." Everyone in the carriage went into the ranch house. The coach driver along with everyone else went into the barn. The house was large with polished wooden floors and mounted deer heads on the walls. All in all, quite roomy.

Betsy ushered the men into the parlor, including Bo, and offered them brandy, Elijah's favorite winter's eve drink. He, with a huge smile, said a shallow "Yes, thank you. It's the perfect drink on a cold winter evening" Michael declined. Bo stood silent, observing and wondering the point of drinking on a cold night. Henry stood clinging to Elijah like an extra limb.

Betsy asked, "Is that your son?"

"No, he's my nephew from up north. Henry Fordham is his name. He's shy. He's only ten years old. When his father goes to Europe on business trips, he sometimes stays with me. He likes my tinkering and inventions."

Betsy poured Elijah a drink and ordered, "Make yourself at home. The fire is just starting to warm this old place, and there are plenty of books. I'm going to get your friends something to eat. Would you care to help me, dear?"

"Yes, ma'am," I replied. Betsy exited the room. I followed close behind, carrying Zeke, and Bo followed.

Seconds later Frank, entered the side door, brushing snow from his brown-and-tan flannel coat, taking off his boots, scarf, coat, hat, and slipped on his favorite house shoes. He went directly into the parlor without greeting Betsy. "It's really starting to come down. Snowflakes as big as silver dollars. I see you found the place just fine," making eye contact with everyone.

"We're enjoying your Southern hospitality," Michael replied.

"Those damn pigs. I finally got those blasted animals in the pen. Nasty creatures. Did your Negroes go on?"

"No, they're in the barn. Your lovely wife is preparing food for them as we speak," Elijah answered.

"Did your friends find you?" Frank asked.

"No. What friends?" Elijah asked.

"The soldiers? Your buddies from down south. They asked if I'd seen your wagons full of Negroes. I told them you'd probably be at my ranch. His name is Captain Burris."

"Captain Burris is here," Michael excitedly responded. Michael quickly left the room. He rushed into the kitchen and grabbed me by the arm, shouting, "Go into the parlor! Take everyone. No questions. We're all in serious danger. Captain Burris is here."

Chapter Twenty-Two

Angels, Angels, Angels

Betsy, Bo, and I and everyone were standing in the parlor. Michael told everyone, "Join hands and make a circle. Pray."

"What's going on?" Betsy asked.

"We have some trouble. Soldiers from the south," Frank answered.

I burst forth, "Father of heaven and earth, send forth your angels. Send forth your heavenly army, Lord of Hosts. Protect us, your children, from evil."

"Angels? Can I see?" Henry asked.

"Henry, it's not the time," Elijah forcefully replied.

"But I love angels, Uncle. I always wanted to see real angels."

As they all joined in prayer in one accord, the Holy Spirit filled the room. Henry closed his eyes. He bowed his head. He prayed, "Dear Lord, can I see your angels who protects us from bad people?"

Michael left the room and went onto the porch. He lifted his black-and-silver cane into the air. In a twinkling of an eye, he became the grace of God's Archangel Michael. His wings spread from his back as if searching for air. They spread ten feet in each direction, pure white. Twinkling snowflakes lightly sprinkled his wings. His body radiated light. As he stepped from the porch, Barak, Jophkiel, and Raphael emerged from the barn in brilliance. They were arrayed in every color of the rainbow, colors unknown and never seen by the human eye. They glowed. Their wings were fully spread with swords drawn, ready for battle.

In the house, Mary Lou prayed, "The Lord is my light and my salvation. Whom do I fear? The Lord is my life refuge, of whom am I afraid?

267

When evildoers come at me to devour my flesh, these, my enemies and foes themselves, stumble and fall. Though an army encamp against me, my heart does not fear. Though war be waged against me, even then do I trust."

As she continued, snow filled the sky, seemingly a whiteout. Snowflakes as big as silver dollars began to grow. A transformation began. Wings began to sprout from each flake. Then legs, arms, faces appeared— human faces in brilliant colors of every tribe of the children of Israel. Every culture, race, and nationality where the lost sheep were scattered was represented. Angels appeared everywhere—on the rood, in the trees, on the fence posts—all with their swords drawn, ready for war. In an instant, the snowstorm ended. An army stood before Michael—Michael in unimaginable beauty, power, and glory. All waited for a word, a word from God. Silence filled the air. The wind stopped. No bird sang. The tress didn't sway. I and the others continued in prayer with our heads bowed, eyes closed, completely unaware of the multitude of angels.

His face became completely flushed. Fear seized him. His hands, legs, and feet began to shake uncontrollably. His eyes grew in excitement. Joy, love, and peace filled his heart. He felt safe. A warm feeling welled up inside of him. He pulled his uncle's arm, attempting to get his attention to no avail. "Uncle, Uncle, look." His voice trembled. "Uncle," pulling his arm harder. "Uncle, look."

Elijah, still in meditative pray, peered into Henry's eyes. Henry's eyes told Elijah something was happening, something was going on, but where? Who? Elijah followed Henry's eyes out of the window of the house. He screamed, "Oh my god!" Every eye focused on Elijah's burst of excitement. They peered outside seeing the army of heavenly hosts. Elijah fell to his knees, whispering, "This can't be real."

Everyone slowly fell to their knees. Tears filled every eye. "What's going on? Who . . . what are those . . . Angels," Frank blurted.

"They are God's messengers," I whispered.

Angels were flying in the air, sitting in the trees, standing on top of the barn, sitting on the fences, standing along the road that leads up to the ranch house. They completely surrounded the house and its landscape. Wherever a snowflake landed, an angel appeared. More than the eye could count. It's an army. "My god. It's an army of heavenly hosts," Elijah whispered.

"Who? What the hell's going on?" Frank cried.

Michael spoke, "It's good to see you, my friends. We have a very special mission. Some of you will go to the north, south, east, and western parts of this country. We are the answer to three hundred years of prayer. The south is our main focus. Our mission is to heal this nation. Slavery is ending, and we are to aid the scattered sheep. Prayer is our calling card. Faith is our power to heal."

The glow of the moon radiated off their divine bodies. Everyone was amazingly beautiful. Barak, Jophkiel, and Raphael stood just in front of Michael, ready and waiting for orders. Obedience was their joy. Serving the King of Kings was beyond what human life experience allowed.

Michael's eyes twinkled in a brilliance of azure, crystallites, topaz, and amber. Love flowed and radiated from his being. Lovingly, he softly spoke. "God has chosen you three to remain in human form. You will have your heavenly strengths on earth. Nothing on earth, under the earth, shall be stronger than you. No depth of water too deep for you. No height beyond your reach. Nothing man has made, nor will he ever make, shall prevail against you."

Michael peered deeply into each of their eyes looking, searching for any sight of regret. "You will remain in your human form protecting the human race from all harm, visible and invisible. You shall feel what they feel, hear what they hear, taste what they taste. In every appearance, you shall be human, yet much, much more."

With those last words spoken, Barak felt a twitch of human emotion. He leaped with excitement. Every angel gazed heavenly for he was thousands of feet into the air. Their gaze immediately shifted back to Michael. Barak looked down and saw the ranch house slowly getting smaller and smaller. He thought, *Must stop.* Immediately, he stopped. He felt the ice-cold wind blowing against his face. Reaching out, he grasped what seemed to be a cloud in his hands. He watched as it slowly slipped through his fingers. *What have I done? I must return.* Immediately, he headed earthward. His thoughts controlled his movements, unlike being completely angelic, where he was willed to an action by a heartfelt desire. Coming closer to earth, he thought, *I must land very slowly not to alarm anyone.* Realizing that time had elapsed, he felt embarrassed, a feeling he'd never felt before. Slowly, he returned to the exact same point of origin.

Michael glanced his way with sign of emotion, saying, "Now, heavenly hosts, go to your assignments."

Without any sound, in complete and utter beauty, the angels flew. Their wings grasped the air, seemingly beyond time and space, almost transparent. Their bodies deemed in a mystical glow of burst of illumination, utterly beautiful, like a flock of swan, yet one thousand times more graceful, in complete disarray. Airborne, they surrounded the ranch house and sang, "Great and wonderful are your works, Lord God Almighty. Just and true are your ways, O King of the Israel. Who will not fear you, Lord, or glorify your name? For you alone are holy. All nations will come and worship before you, for your righteous acts have been revealed."

Bo whispered, "Do you hear that they're singing? They're singing of victory to Jesus." He looked into his wife's eyes. Tears were streaming down my cheeks. Beauty, love, and compassion radiated from my soul. We had just witnessed what had only been seen two thousand years before, announcing the birth of a baby to shepherds in the field. As quickly as they appeared, they vanished.

No sooner had the heavenly hosts departed than the loud thunder of horses was heard. Michael turned and whispered sternly to everyone in the ranch house, "Close the curtains. Whatever happens, don't look out of any windows. Instead, cover your faces and ears and pray silently." No sooner had he finished speaking than Captain Burris and his demonic army headed directly toward the ranch. "Lock all the doors quickly. You will be safe!" he shouted.

The road was narrow. It was only wide enough for two horses side by side. It was covered in about six inches of snow with trees overlaying the road. Michael, Jophkiel, Raphael, and Barak stood at the edge of the clearing leading to the ranch house with their swords drawn and poised for battle. "Destroy them! Leave nothing of remembrance!" Michael shouted.

The soldiers rode hard and fast directly toward the four. Their human features had changed. Instead of men, the soldiers looked like they were dead and hopeless. Any form of human characteristics was mutating into demonic being not fit for this world. Their arms and legs were shorter. Their heads and torso were larger, including the feet, eyes, ears, and nose. A hideous sight form the pits of hell.

Michael swung his sword upward, cutting off one of the demon's arms. The demon rode on, ignoring the missing arm. The arm lay in the snow, gushing blood and still moving as if still attached. The blood was black and smelled of putrid flesh.

Jophkiel took flight with amazing speed. A blur with sword drawn, he beheaded three of the demonic brigade within a fraction of a second. The oversized heads fell to the ground with their mouths open and eyes moving. Their bodies were still trying to control the beasts they were riding.

Standing his ground, Raphael flung his sword with superhuman strength. The sword heralded end over end, slicing into the beast and demon alike. Beast and demon completely cut in half. They both fell one-half to the right the other to the left. In a twinkle of an eye, he'd run to the sword's point of destination and caught it. The silver, gold, and diamond-studded blade fining in his hand from the force of his throw and catch.

Barak ran directly toward the charging army, waving his sword in an amazing, extraordinary display of swordsmanship, slicing, carving, and beheading limbs from beast and demon alike. Within seconds, the entire army was cut into pieces.

Captain Burris alone had escaped the massacre, eluding the destruction, clever as a snake. The angelic force slowed to human time and speed. The entire defeat of the demons took less than thirty seconds in human time. Michael stood looking at the destruction, poised and calm, a battle he deemed nothing in comparison to the vast victories he fought throughout the centuries.

In the ranch house, we continued to pray with heads bowed, eyes closed, completely focused on Jesus, completely unaware of the devastation only yards away. Michael took flight in divine angelic form with sword drawn. He pointed his sword toward a clearing, signaling the heavenly three. His sword glowed and radiated in his hands as bright as the sun. The battle was over and just beginning.

The midday sun was illuminating the entire area and still growing brighter. He pointed the sword earthward. A beam of light emerged from the sword, devastating the ground below. Within seconds, a huge crater had been dug into the clearing over thirty feet deep. Michael directed Barak, Jophkiel, and Raphael to dispose of all the remains of the demonic army into the crater. Unseen by the human eyes, the angels moved as quickly as lightning striking the ground, removing every piece of evidence of the battle. Michael redirected the energy emerging from the sword and completely covered the land with earth and snow. No shred of evidence remained of the battle.

Buddy, Felix, and the slaves in the barn all exited the barn one by one, seemingly sneaking from their secure hiding place, completely unaware of what had just occurred moments ago. They headed toward the ranch house carrying bowls and eating utensils. Inside, not a sound was heard; nothing was noticed. Yet an amazing bloodbath had taken place, a complete and utter massacre of evil unknown to any human. Prayers continued by me and the others. Victory was Michael's and the heavenly hosts in the name of Jesus Christ.

The only survivor was Captain Burris. He hid, watching and leering in a fit of rage and hatred in the surrounding forest. Slowly and methodically, he forced himself to abandon his mission to go north.

Michael regained human form and stood eloquent and dignified in front of the ranch, unfazed by the battle. Buddy and Felix slowly approached Michael, peering into his eyes, seeming confused. "I don't think it has anything to do with color, sir. Please, sir, you and your friends come inside." Buddy turned and said, "You all go on back into the barn. Build a fire, keep warm, and don't burn the damn barn down." They quietly and slowly turned toward the barn. Buddy shouted, "I'll send Felix with some hot food just as soon as it's ready!"

They entered the house and quickly went into the parlor. Tears were gently flowing down my cheeks. A gentle and eloquent ambience filled the room. Everyone stood in a circle, silently praying.

"You are having a prayer service, for God's sake!" Buddy shouted.

"It's prayer for all our burdens and trouble," Bo replied.

"It's good to pray. I've never known anyone to be disappointed from prayer," "Michael interjected.

"We've been praying awhile. I guess it's OK to stop now," I replied.

"Yes, you can. The danger has been averted," Michael said.

"What danger?" Buddy asked.

"Captain Burris and his men were coming. They didn't make it," Michael answered.

"I didn't hear any horses. I didn't see any soldiers," Buddy replied.

"No, sir, you did not. That is a gift. God's grace has saved us all from that inhuman tyrant and his evil plans. We shall continue on our journey safe and sound," Michael answered.

Everyone in the parlor took a seat, including Buddy. The room became deafly silent as they peered into each other's eyes. An air of bewilderment filled the room. The fire kissed the edges of the fireplace, giving the room a beautiful allure of tranquility and peace.

"This can't be real." Everyone slowly fell to their knees. Tears filled every eye. "Whats going on. Who.

What are those, Angels?" Frank blurted. "They are GOD's messengers." Mary Lou whispered. Angels were flying in the air. Sitting in the trees. Standing on the top of the barn. Sitting on the fences.

Standing along the road that lead u p to the Ranch House. They completely surrounded the house and its landsca pe. Where ever a snow flake landed, an Angel appea red. More than the eye could count. It's an army. My GOD. It's an army of heavenly hosts." Elijah whispered. "Who. What the hell's goingon?" Frank cried.

Michael spoke "It's good to see you my friends. We have a very special mission. Some of you will go to the North, South, East and Western parts of this country. We are the answer to 300 years of prayer. The South is our main focus. Our mission is to heal this Nation. Slavery is ending, and we are to aid everyone who's ailing. Prayer is our calling card. Faith is our power to heal." The glow of the moon radiated off their divine bodies. Everyone was amazingly beautiful. Barak, Jophkiel and Raphael stood just in front of Michael ready and waiting for orders. Obedience was their joy. Serving the King of Kings was beyond what human life experience allowed. Michael's eye's twinkled in a brilliance of azure, crystallites, topaz's and amber. love flowed and radiated from his being. Lovingly he softly spoke. "GOD has chosen you three to remain in human form. You will have your heavenly strengths on earth. Nothing on earth, under the earth shall be stronger than you. No depth of water to deep for you. No height beyond your reach. Nothing man has ma de nor will he ever make shall prevail against you.

Michael peered deeply into each of their eyes looking, searching for any sigh of regret. "You will remain in your human form protecting the human race from all harm, visible and invisible. You shall feel what they feel. Hear what they hear. Taste what they taste. In every appearance you shall be human, yet much, much more. With those last words spoken Bara k felt a twitch of human emotion. He leaped with excitement. Every angel gazed heavenly for he was thousands of feet into the air. Their gaze immediately shifted back to Michael. Barak looked down and saw the Ranch House slowly getting smaller and smaller. He thought. "must stop." Immediately he stopped. He felt the ice cold wind blowing against his face. Reaching out he grasped what seemed to be a cloud in his hands. He watched as it slowly slipped through his fingers. "What have I done?" I must return." Immediately he headed earthward. His thoughts controlled his movements. Unlike being completely angelic, where he was willed to a n action by a heartfelt desire. Coming closer to earth he thought, I must land very slowly not to alarm any one." Realizing that time had elapsed, he felt embarrassed. A Feeling he'd never felt before. Slowly he returned to the exact same point of origin. Michael glanced his way with" rfv sign of emotion, saying. "Now heavenly hosts go to your assignments." Without any sound in complete and utter beauty the angels flew. Their wings grasped the air seeming beyond time and space almost transparent. Their bodies deemed in a mystical glow of burst of illumination utterly beautify. like a flock of swan, yet 1000 times more graceful, incompleted isarrayef . Air born. They surrounded the Ranch House and sang. "Great afld wonderful are your works Lord GOD almighty. Just and true are your ways O King of the Nations. Who will not fear you? lord or glorify your name? For you alone are holy. All nations will come and worship before you, for your righteous acts have been revealed." Bo whispered. "Do you hear that? They're singing. They're singing of victory to Jesus." He looked into his wife's eyes. Tears were streaming down her cheeks. Beauty, Love and compassion radiated from Her soul. They had just witnessed what had only been seen two thousand years before. Announcing the birth of a baby to Sheppard's in the field. As quickly as they appeared, they vanished.

The Battle was over, and just beginning.

ABOUT THE BOOK

She is dead and buried. By the grace of God, she was allowed to see how her life affected others before entering heaven, recalling details of the events that led to her amazing life, which began in slavery and ended in freedom.

Mary Lou was born into a highly religious Christian family, and she was born into slavery, experiencing all the horrors of slavery. Yet she retains her innocence, handling her problems by prayer. During a spring thunderstorm, Mary Lou was struck by lightning, and after her incredible survival, she was removed from her family and placed in the big house to be trained as a domestic house slave.

It was there that Mary Lou realized the supernatural gifts given to her from the lightning strike. When her abilities became widely known, it became clear that she was a threat to slavery and their way of life. Forced on the run in hopes of finding safety, Mary Lou, instead, discovered a demonic plot to kill her and everyone she had come in contact with.

ABOUT THE AUTHOR

Mr. Fowler grew up on the south side of Chicago. He graduated from St.Rita H.S. attended Chicago State University, and received a B.A. from Lewis University,. After graduating from college, he taught school and coached basketball. He is married and has four children. Mr. Fowler loves to play chess write, paint, and spend time with family and friends.

Made in the USA
Monee, IL
08 April 2024

56139774R00157